Undead Reb Down Under Tales

I0653048

Author
Rod Marsden

Publisher
Night to Dawn

Publisher Night to Dawn
www.bloodredshadows.com
ISBN: 978-0-615-26303-8

Copyright by Rod Marsden
First edition 2008

*http://www.bloodredshadows.com Printed by
Lulu.com in the United States item #*

Editor: Barbara Custer

Cover Art by Marge Simon

To Irene May Marsden...

May; that special time of year between summer and the onset of winter. It was and is a time to stop, look and listen to the environment. It was and is a time to reflect upon the past and to contemplate a better, shinier future. It was and is a time when mother-nature reveals herself as a loving and caring force to be reckoned with. But what does this have to do with Irene May Marsden you ask? In a word: everything.

Acknowledgements:

I wish to acknowledge the help and inspiration of Barbara Custer and the fine writers and artists at Night to Dawn magazine. I wish to thank the cover artist for a grand effort and also Don Boyd for his input into colonial history. Then there's New Zealand novelist Lyn McConchie whose friendship and knowledge of the world of the modern professional writer have proven to be invaluable. I also wish to thank my parents, Charles and May Marsden, for looking out for me for the better part of five decades and my sister, Debra, who despite having a difficult brother, still hasn't given up on me.

TABLE OF CONTENTS

Introduction

Concerning Undead Reb Down Under and other Vampire Stories…

The menace of the vampire has been with us for a very long time. Over the centuries people in various societies have developed their own methods in dealing with it. The Japanese in the 17th Century, for example, created the *Rising Sun Group* of specialist ninjas and samurai. In the West the *Invisible Compass*, an offshoot of Freemasonry, came to the fore. In the USA there was the *Pinkerton Detective Agency* out of Chicago. Over time such organizations have come to share information, resources and even personnel in the continuing fight ("The Thirsty Blade" and "The Life, Death and Unlife of Sue Ling").

In this collection not all vampires are completely evil ("A Conversation on Saint Patrick's Night" and "Killing the Jocks") and some actually do battle their demonic side ("Five O'clock" and "The Goodbye Demon"). Also not all humans are innocent and there are some who wish to take from the vampire either its strength to use for diabolical purposes ("The Trials and Tribulations of Kara") or its longevity for personal use ("A Treasure beyond Price").

A number of tales are linked by returning characters but all stand alone as complete. For the reader there are scrumptious moments of high *adventure* ("The Inquisitor" and "Warriors of the Rising Sun"), saucy *surprises* liberally added ("Ring the Bells" and "The Big Aunty Curse") a seasoning here and there of humor ("Undead Reb Down Under," "The Perils of Sheila Grahams," "Cold Comfort," and "A Candle to Light the Way") together with a slice or two of *horror* on the side with social comment ("A Demon's Heart," "The Panhandler," and "Saving the Night"). Bon Appétit.

Undead Reb Down Under

On January 25th, 1865, Captain James Waddell of North Carolina sailed CSS Shenandoah, an iron-framed, fully-rigged vessel with auxiliary steam power, into Melbourne harbor, Victoria. Since leaving Britain, where she was purchased, they had had tremendous good fortune. They had destroyed at least six enemy ships without sustaining permanent damage and, though they were low on supplies, there was every chance that their good fortune would continue.

The only real problem was two madmen they had on board who insisted that they required human blood in order to remain among the living. They were chained up in the most distant, darkest part of the hold. If the Victorian press saw them they might think the captain and crew were in the white slave trade which wasn't true. Either that or they were exceptionally cruel to sailors who disobeyed orders.

Jeb Klem and Walt Page, the madmen, had been sane enough when they joined the crew at Funchal, Madeira off the coast of Africa. Both were adventurers in their late twenties who were born in Texas and who felt the southern cause very much their own. They had been hard workers and as dedicated to their ship as any sailor could be. Then something went wrong.

Captain Waddell thought it might have something to do with the Spanish lady aboard the last craft they'd sent to a watery grave. She and the others had been on the Shenandoah for some weeks before they could be put off at a neutral port. During this period she had managed to somehow get out of lock-up a half dozen times and was once seen in the steward's cabin with blood on her lips. She had a dark beauty the secrets of which were only known to the Spanish and perhaps certain Mexican women. She was too enchanting even for the captain. It was all he could do to remember his role and to keep his distance. Others he suspected struggled with her soft voice, jasmine scent and wherewithal and failed. It wasn't any wonder then that the captain saw it as a blessing when he was rid of her. Most of his crew, who knew they could not have her and had become sick at heart due to such an overpowering want, felt the same way. Those that didn't were, according to the captain, burning inside the way men tend to burn for women and were raging too hotly to possibly see reason.

First it was able seaman Todd Henry attacking new recruit John MacLean for his blood. Somehow they got him off MacLean and up top from the crewman's quarters. From there such a struggle ensued that he was accidentally pushed overboard. There he was swimming to catch up with his vessel and his shipmates, who were convinced he'd become a danger to them, firing on him to prevent him from doing so. He drowned or so went the report.

After that new recruits Jeb Klem and Walt Page went missing, presumed dead – victims of able seaman Henry. They were not found for three nights. When they did turn up, blackness circled their eyes and their fingernails were longer. They were caught in the scullery sucking the red juice out of a dead rat. They became wild when approached by the scully and avoided capture with strength which seemed more than human. Captain Waddell gave orders to chain them rather than throw them over the side. He felt a need to get to the bottom of what was happening to his men and he thought he could get some answers from those affected by whatever was going on. Was it a new disease? If it was, then the afflicted needed to be isolated from the rest of his crew. Was it hypnosis of some kind that lingered from that haunting Spanish woman? If so could the men affected be cured with care and patience? One thing was certain. He could not afford to go into battle again with insanity creeping up on them all.

It took a number of black eyes and bloody noses given out to at least two dozen men, but the miscreants were placed in sufficient irons and forced deep into the hold where leg restraints were applied to add to their difficulties in escape. Guards were posted and the officers told to carry firearms at all times, even to bed. Even so no one felt safe.

At the end of this drama the crew experienced some relief, but it was short lived. Men looked toward other men for signs of the madness. Giving them extra rations of rum helped and getting them to sing their troubles away turned out to be a good idea. In the back of their heads,

3

however, remained the fear of turning into the men in the deepest part of the hold. Either turning into them or becoming their victims.

Captain Waddell kept the men too busy to be thinking black thoughts. He drilled them on cannon, reminding them they were a fighting ship in the proud service of the Confederacy and not a pleasure cruiser. He drilled on sail and had his officers, including the somewhat belligerent Lieutenant Grimball, put to memory the various flags of friendly, hostile and neutral nations.

"We must stay alert," the captain told them. "We must be ready for anything and the men too must be ready."

The captain was almost grateful when coal reserves for the boiler ran low and it became obvious further repairs to the infrastructure of the Shenandoah would be needed and soon if they were to continue their mission of harassing the enemy. They set sail for Australia, a neutral series of British colonies, and on the way met up with storms and high seas enough to test them as seamen. This testing was also, in its way, a blessing, the men kept from dwelling on those in chains.

Under orders of the captain only the ship's doctor and ship's scully, armed with a pistol, were allowed to visit Klem and Page. The ship's doctor, a compassionate man in his late forties, tried laudanum to calm the nerves of his crazed charges. It didn't work. In the end he found he needed the laudanum for himself simply to face them. He tried bleeding them but that agitated them further. They were given the usual ship's rations but seemed to survive on the blood of insects and spiders.

One day the ship's cat went missing and turned up, beside Klem and Page, dead and drained of blood. The crew, when they learned of this, found it to be intolerable and wanted the feline killers executed and thrown overboard but it was by then too late. They were nearing land and the people who were to greet them would not understand such actions without a full history of their voyage. With such a history they might face quarantine and none of them wanted that. So Klem and Page would have to remain with them, hidden away, to possibly be disposed of later.

They eased their way into Sandridge now Port Melbourne. Word was sent to Governor Sir Charles Darling of their arrival and of their intentions. The international laws of neutrality meant that the governor could allow for repairs and re-supply of the Shenandoah which he did. The US consul, William Blanchard, protested strongly saying the ship in question was a privateer and not a war vessel from a recognized nation but he was ignored.

"We must do what we can," the governor told the newspaper men who'd gathered to discover his views concerning the Confederates. "I repeat: we must do what we can for the poor souls in need of our aid. Otherwise their fellow sailors plying our waters and you journalists here and abroad would see us as unnecessarily inhumane."

John MacLean, seeing his chance, eased himself into the waters of the port and thus removed himself from the Confederacy. He had joined the crew of the Shenandoah with the spoils of conquest in mind and had deserted the ship for a number of reasons including the presence of those brutish, unspeakable men deep in its hold. He spoke of these men to the Melbourne press but they would not print a word of it. They would, however, carry what he said about the savagery of one Lieutenant Grimball who was as much in a state of fear as the others on board but who could take his fear out on the men he was in charge of. Brutality had a flow on effect, the same as insanity.

"Such cruelty must not continue," MacLean told reporters showing them the markings from a leather strap he had on his back. "People such as Grimball must not be allowed to continue to serve on any ship."

The people of Melbourne were divided over the issue of the American Civil War. Those against slavery saw the freeing of the slaves as the only possible good thing to come out of the conflict. They favored the Lincoln men. On the other hand, there were those who saw the war as a battle for state's rights and saw the Lincoln men as invading bully boys. They favored the Confederacy.

In 1852, in the gold fields of Ballarat not far from Melbourne, the Eureka Stockade gold miners had staged a revolt against unfair tax being imposed upon them by local authority. They had pressed for self-government and, though defeated in battle, they would win certain concessions in court. There were those in Melbourne in 1865 that saw the struggle of the South in America against the North as a similar fight. The Eureka flag and the Confederate flag share certain similarities. Both feature crosses emblazoned with stars. Some American gold miners fought along with the Australian rebels at Ballarat thus cementing the notion that both causes, the one in Australia and the one in America, had to do with the freedom of the individual against those wishing to impose their will upon others. Thus it was by the mining community that the sailors of the CSS Shenandoah were most handsomely greeted and shouted drinks.

"We must not be slack with our brethren from over the waters," said one miner. "No doubt they would not be slack with us were the situation reversed."

Officers from the Confederate ship went to Ballarat for a visit where they were met by a cheering crowd. There were shouts of hurray for Jefferson Davis and Robert E. Lee and the stars and bars forever. Also down with the Blue Bellies and down with Lincoln's Yankee hirelings. A band played tunes like Dixie and The Yellow Rose of Texas and The Single Star. They were then wined and dined by Brayton, a New Yorker who had made his money in Victoria. All up they had a grand old time, but rumors were stirred up about what the Confederates had deep in their hold. The supporters of Lincoln would have it that men were being held against their will, even tortured on a regular basis and this, in the land of Victoria, could not be tolerated.

Police were sent with a warrant to look over the Shenandoah. Captain Waddell, knowing what would be made of Klem and Page, refused them entry. Then Governor Darling was pressured by his underlings and by the press to react to this blatant defiance of his authority by canceling repairs and the re-supply to the Confederate ship. He went as far as aiming land cannon at the vessel which, at the time, was still in dry dock and not likely to go anywhere until she had lots of sea water tickling her hull. Smooth talk prevailed. The governor backed off and the ship was not searched. There were rumors that Captain Waddell was recruiting men from Melbourne which was against international law. These rumors were true. It was a case of anything that could be done, legal or not, would be done for the Confederacy and the mission they would soon resume.

On the night before the CSS Shenandoah was to set sail, Klem and Page snapped their chains, slugged their guards and two deck hands and dove into the water. Before Captain Waddell, Lieutenant Grimball or anyone else could do anything; they were ashore and ready to cause havoc. Captain Waddell could see nothing for it but to let them go and let the local police handle them. They had to be away. Already they had worn out their welcome. If the fugitives were apprehended before they sailed then they would disavow knowledge of them and hope for the best. All up it was essential they got underway and, without those two on board, their voyage might be much more pleasant and more profitable for the South.

And so CSS Shenandoah left Port Melbourne at half speed. The sea beckoned and so did future successful battles. They would spend months harassing and looting Lincoln shipping well after the actual war they were fighting was over. It would take the British to inform them that the war had reached its conclusion thus ending their reign of terror. They would go down in history as the most successful ship's crew ever to fight for the South and this would allow Captain Waddell and his men some hero status when they did return to their precious former Confederacy.

On the night they'd jumped ship, Klem and Page had gone their separate ways. Lured to the bright lights of a revivalist tent, Klem entered in time to hear some preacher finish belting out a sermon about demon liquor and how it ruins families. Then came the healing of the afflicted. There were a dozen actors pretending to be blind, deaf, wheelchair bound and so forth. Klem got on the end of this line and was taken by the preacher to be one of them. He was in rags and looked crazed so it was obvious he needed God's good grace.

The preacher used words from the Bible and a bottle of holy water to exact the cures he was supposedly exacting. Each so-called cure got the congregation excited. Then it came Klem's turn. The words had no effect because the preacher didn't believe in them. The holy water however was from France and it was genuine. For the preacher it was the case of having a fancy looking bottle that could draw attention. For Klem and the congregation it turned out to be something else. When the water hit the Confederate's skin it burned terribly and he ran out of the tent screaming and smoking. This broke up the revivalist meeting. No one wanted to get near that water or that preacher. Was he crazy to try a stunt like that? Was he using acid on people? No one hung around to find out. No one suspected, not even the preacher, that it was an undead reaction to something pure.

Klem came to wash his face in a nearby horse trough. The holy water still hurt and he knew he was burned something awful but the dirty water of the trough helped. A Salvation Army woman saw him and, taking pity on him, gave him a pamphlet to read and a donut to eat. The donut was harmless enough but the pamphlet, being in a very real sense holy, burned his hand. He yelped, threw down the offending paper as well as the donut and ran. He was hungry for blood, but the locals were turning out to be dangerous. What was he to do?

He made his way into a pub where a conversation about the American Civil War had turned nasty. There was busted up furniture and, when he entered, someone inadvertently pushed him onto a broken off table leg. The table leg had a sharp end which pierced his heart. He hissed and struggled but, whatever he did, it was the end for him. At least his dying broke up the fight. It was a battler for the cause of the Confederacy who had broken up the table in the first place by bashing it over the heads of a couple of Lincoln supporters. Thus was the fate of one true Johnny Reb Down Under.

After stealing clothes off a clothes line and putting them on, Page climbed aboard a train. There were a couple of hobos already there in this livestock car together with a couple of horses and a half dozen sheep.

"Free eats," he said out loud with glee.

"Where?" asked one of the hobos wondering what the newcomer was on about.

"You got some grub on ya?" asked the second hobo.

"Never mind," said Page, a gleam in his eye and an enigmatic smile on his lips. His smile widened.

For once Page had his fill of rich red and, as morning broke, felt quite stuffed. If someone had, on that day, offered him the most succulent looking woman with the most perfect neck he couldn't have managed.

Now when the Spanish vampire had sired able seaman Todd Henry it was as a trick to be played upon the crew of the Shenandoah. She had made him over without telling him anything about vampirism or what he should be aware of except how to turn people. After making over Klem and Page, Henry told them nothing about their new situation because he had been thrown overboard before they had awoken and, even if he could have said something, it would have been of very little value. It was thus, as unprepared for the consequences as the rawest of raw recruits to the darkness that Page jumped off the train car when it stopped outside a small town. The heat smacked into him like a great fist of heavenly righteousness and before he knew it he was roasting like Sunday's leg of lamb without the baked potatoes. He burned up before the startled early risers of the town and it was put down by the local doctor to the phenomenon known as instantaneous combustion. It made the papers. No one knew who the victim had been. All they knew was that he had been riding in a train car full of the dead. Thus the second and presumably the last of the undead rebs met his end as a flaming mystery not likely to be solved.

The ashes were collected, examined and then dumped in the local river. As the ashes turned from reb gray to black in the water, prayers were said and words of comfort intoned. The ashes would one day make their way out to sea and perhaps, in some century to come, back to the waters of the Mississippi or perhaps to the Florida quays. Someone wished him a happy journey. It only made sense, in the scheme of things, to do so.

Six months after the CSS Shenandoah sailed away from Port Melbourne, Victoria, able seaman Todd Henry washed up late at night on the shores of Port Moresby, New Guinea. He was malnourished, in gray tatters and in desperate need of blood, any blood. Land crabs were first up on the menu. They provided the only nourishment, aside from the occasional blood from a stingray or a shark; he'd had in a very long time. After filling himself a little on the sickly taste of crab (shark was somewhat better), he moved inland where he spotted two natives playing hide and seek. One was a young woman and the other a young man. The young man had a cross on a string around his neck which Henry, for some reason, found off putting. The young woman's neck was bare and very tempting. He went for her without any thought as to what the young man had in his hands. This was a mistake. It was a wooden spear with barbs for fishing and it went into action as soon as he barred his fangs and showed his intent. Henry got it in the heart and went down onto his knees. The native pulled out his spear which being barbed created a bigger hole.

"What have you done?" cried an old Catholic priest as he approached the native couple. He was coming from the town which was not far away.

"Slaying a demon," said the native lad.

"Killing a man you mean," stated the priest, crossing himself. "Thou shalt not kill!"

It was then the native reached out and took the priest further by surprise by snatching his crucifix from around his neck.

"Watch!" cried the native lad, placing the crucifix on the dying Henry. "If he good cross no hurt but if he bad…"

The crucifix sizzled and made a burn mark on the vampire's chest not far from where the spear had gone into him. The lad then gave the symbol of Christianity back to its rightful owner.

"Tried to eat me!" said the young woman. "Teeth really sharp, really scary. I afraid!"

"I was wrong," said the priest to the lad. "You have done God's work."

"Done God's work," echoed the lad proudly. "I have demon's blood on spear."

"Demon's blood," echoed the young woman proud to be with such a warrior.

"Yes," agreed the priest, feeling quite out of his own depth on such matters. "And now I must pray for this poor, deluded soul."

And so able seaman Todd Henry approached death a second time unaware of where he was, but well aware that his impatience had been the end of him. If only he had seen the spear and done something about it before letting his hunger get the better of him. Surely if he could slay stingrays and sharks underwater he could take care of two puny dark youngsters and a pathetic priest. Who was this priest and what was he saying? It was something in Latin. He wasn't helping; that was for sure. He wasn't helping at all. Some bandages might be in order as well as blood to drink. Why wasn't he helping?

With a last wheeze Henry fell on his side and, apart from an empty shell that was also on the way out, was no more. The priest and the natives looked on with amazement as nature caught up with what was once a supernatural being. He deteriorated to a skeleton within minutes of his second demise adding more proof to his status as demon and to the native lad's new status as demon slayer.

Five O'clock

Robert Paisley waited until the precious hour. He waited for the time he usually rang before upending the bottle and gulping down the contents. This night the red was human, not animal. It had to be to help him to remember, to help him to remain relatively sane in the face of such tragedy.

The redness warmed him going down like a smooth Scotch might do for someone else. But there was something that remained cold and aloof. It was his heart. Just because it hadn't beat once in five decades meant little to him anymore. He was used to that. Still it usually defrosted with the red giving him the feeling that he hadn't really changed in all that time. What it was doing was responding to the absence of another richer, kinder heart that had stopped but for good and could never, ever be revived.

He wiped his lips and threw the empty bottle against the wall, shattering it. No one came running to help clear away the debris. No one cared. There was a police siren wailing in the distance and also the sound of a speeding freight train. His alarm clock indicated the hour of hours on the night of nights was slow but it was passing. He wished he could stop time and then reverse it to but a week ago. If he could do so then he would keep that week and treasure it forever.

Sunday night at five o'clock. The sun had barely set and in summer had not set at all. Even so it had been the designated time to talk with the most wonderful woman in the world. She was always by her phone awaiting his call. She knew of his predicament and of how to keep his inner demon at bay. Now he would have to continue the taming of that inner demon on his own. It had not been easy. Now it would be infinitely harder. No more gentle humor. No more coaxing or well meant advice. No more love.

Outside the door to Robert's unit in the suburb of Hurstville the wind blew hard against nearby homes. An antenna snapped its moorings and crashed against a roof. Tiles smashed. Rain came in freezing sheets. There was the sound of thunder followed by the blasting to a stump of an old ghost gum. Somewhere a dog the size of a wolf howled Robert's feeling of abandonment.

"Gone," Robert said out loud. He had not felt so helpless in at least a decade and he didn't like it.

He'd been turned back in '57. A barmaid at The Bat and Ball did the trick. She had wanted him to follow her into an unlife of murder and mayhem. He was glad he didn't. Some six months later she came to a sticky end on the lance of a Secret Compass vampire hunter. A voice on the phone had saved him from taking her path. Now there was no longer a voice and murder and mayhem had their appeals.

Robert made the phone call. He knew it wouldn't be answered. It was already a quarter past the hour but he made it anyway. There was a thin line of hope that a godly force would intervene in the normal fabric of reality and give him the voice. This hope was based on the certain knowledge everyone of his ilk who'd been around long enough had that there was indeed a hell. If one existed, then why not the other? Why not heaven? And if there was a heaven, why shouldn't it have telephone lines and switchboards?

No reply. He tried again and again. Still no reply. Maybe it was a wee bit early in a death for the deceased party to have her own number and the wherewithal to be able to contact the unliving. Maybe next Sunday or the Sunday after...

It had been a heart attack. The open heart surgery had gone well, but the patient had not survived because her lungs were not up to it. During such an operation the lungs are collapsed and then re-inflated. This puts stress upon them and, if they can't take it, the patient can linger thanks to modern medicine but the show is over. Her lungs were like tissue paper. She was too old.

The first night Robert was tempted to go on the hunt he'd phoned her instead and was told of the alternatives. He knew of them but it helped hearing about them from someone else. He felt stronger than he had ever felt before and his senses were a lot sharper. "Why not prey upon humans?" he asked her. "I was picked on when I was human."

"I'm human," the voice had replied and that's all she needed to say. She went on though reminding him of the good times they'd had together and of the good people still in the world. It was a big ask to have him slack his thirst on anything save an open vein he'd opened himself. Yet she did ask and he knew, while she was around, he'd try to keep away from temptation.

He had a night janitor's job. It didn't pay well but that didn't worry him. So long as he could buy his bottled blood he was fine. In his unlife he'd been a newspaper reporter, a police officer and a hospital orderly. Every fifteen years he had to change careers because he didn't age and not aging tended to make people nervous. Dying one's hair grey could only do so much to dispel their fears and then it was a case of too many questions being asked. With the coming of the computer age, there was the possibility of a permanent position. If he was to work from home on his own P.C. who would know how young he looked or how young he remained?

When Robert was reborn his rebirth came with all the instincts, desires and needs of every vampire that had ever walked the earth. Even when full all he had to do was run his tongue over his teeth as a reminder of what he was and where that could take him.

Fighting instincts, desires and even needs hadn't been easy. Years gone by, he was able to take from a victim enough blood to preserve his existence but not kill. Now he wondered if that was possible. He was better off buying what he needed from butcher shops specializing in the animal varieties and disreputable dealers selling the human varieties. Sometimes he was reduced to stealing it from clinics and hospitals.

One time, in the country near Orange, he went through an entire herd of cattle without anyone noticing. Each night he'd only take enough to satisfy his needs while keeping the respective cow alive and relatively healthy. Still, living in the country was not for him. You got too close to people when you are in a small community and then out would come the inevitable questions about one's past that were difficult to answer to anyone's satisfaction.

Television had been a distraction but now it was waning. Very few good shows were being made and too often the good ones were cancelled within a year of creation due to penny pinching studio heads and television station executives. "Candid Camera" had been but a minor upset in the 1950s and '60s. Now, under many names, it was a regular torment. Meanwhile some crazy European experiment in the '90s concerning the filming of ordinary people in an ordinary house doing ordinary things was continuing prime time. Humans had the technology to do much, much more with the so-called 'idiot box' but no longer had the will to even try. Roddenberry's widow, one of the last pioneer producers of good television, was barely holding her own. It was enough to make one weep. It was enough to tempt one to go out and kill a few

13

of the more stupid humans simply on principle. When all was considered, they shouldn't mind. They were not truly living any more than he was.

Novels did a little better. He had a most impressive Star Trek collection and was half way through Terry Pratchett's Discworld series. Local novelists were a letdown. They were finding their place in the world of literature and relying too much on the snob factor produced by some universities and colleges to sell their wares. Writers such as Richard Harland *(The Vicar of Morbing Vyle)* and Peter Corris (the *Browning Series*) were lively exceptions to the rule. He was happy to read American and British novels and to wait until Australian writers caught up to them. New Zealand writers such as Lyn McConchie had already done so.

Now, with that special woman out of his existence, all he had done to quell his hunger and his less admirable desires seemed somewhat pointless. What did it matter what work he did or what he watched or read to make himself feel human if she was no longer capable of guiding him?

Maybe he should visit the new casino in Sydney and gamble for a while. Not only would he be gambling with his money but, by being in close proximity to people for an extended period, be gambling with his fellow gamblers' lives. They'd be there and he'd smell their sweat and their blood and maybe at last become the menace he always suspected he would become.

With trembling hands, Robert opened a window to the night's fury. Anger enveloped him. How dare she die and leave him all alone? How dare the fates allow someone so wondrous to go the way of all things? It wasn't fair.

With the ease and grace of long practice he morphed into a bat and flew outside where the rain pelted him and the sound of thunder fuelled his gathering rage. He plotted a course that set him against the wind and thus tried his strength. Working his muscles and leathery wings helped calm his mind a little but only a little. It had to compete against his super heated thoughts and the overall vileness of the weather.

Over Bexley North he spotted a stray dog wandering the streets and zeroed in for a closer look. He landed beside it and was not surprised to find the wettest and most miserable mongrel he'd come across in ages. If he drank its blood no one would miss it. After all he'd been through, he was entitled. Then he saw a middle aged man running in the direction of the mongrel and realized it was, despite appearances, someone's pet and that it would indeed be missed. He took off before master and dog could meet up, before the man could ask him who or what he was.

Wheeling past Arncliffe, Robert saw a young woman fighting the elements to keep her umbrella. She looked rather comical and quite vulnerable. No one else was around. He could swoop in, destroy her and her umbrella, and it wouldn't be until the morning that others would come to know of what had occurred. He'd be safe and she'd be dead. But he couldn't, not on a Sunday, not even on this Sunday. He flew on toward Central and toward a certain truth concerning what is and what might be.

Central Station, as per usual, was aglow with nightly lights only gifted humans, the undead and the deceased were and are capable of seeing. The lights emanated blue from souls marking where their graves used to be before they were moved. Why so many had not crossed over was a mystery. Occasionally they made their presence felt to the living but this was rare. They were content to moan and move about in circles around where they were once expected to rest in peace.

Robert swooped in for a closer look and a talk with a couple of these less than happy entities. Once he was satisfied that the particular 'she' he was after was not among their number he took off and then headed back to his abode. *Of course she's not there,* he told himself on the flight back. *She's too good for the likes of them and surely she would have crossed over and not be stuck in any God awful situation such as they were in.*

Heaven was where she belonged and no doubt where he would find her if there ever was a chance of him, in his condition, going to such a place. Being damned because of what had happened to you was not much fun. In fact it was downright unfair.

The flight back had the wind on his side and so the journey was made without incident. The weather was improving. The rain was now a mild drizzle.

What was I thinking? He wondered after morphing back to human in the comfort of his home. *Why would she be conversing with the long forgotten at a long forgotten cemetery that was now part of Sydney's railway system?*

He then realized that he missed her so much he was even willing to put the absurd to some kind of test. Anything to hear her voice or, in the hope of hopes, to see her face once more.

Bone weary, he shut the window and drew the curtains closed against the rising of the morning sun. He made his way to his bedroom and dropped onto his bed with the intention of getting a little rest. He didn't think he would sleep but the exertions of the night did catch up with him and so he began to drift.

Sometime between noon and three in the afternoon the smell of homemade biscuits and roast leg of lamb came to him. Such smells did not relate at all to his present way of being but harkened back to an earlier more promising time. When he opened his eyes, he saw, against the back-drop of his wardrobe, a certain someone outlined and as warm and fragrant as cinnamon atop freshly baked apple pie. "You!" he called. "Here?"

She did not answer. Perhaps she couldn't as yet. Maybe it was too soon for that. She tried to take his hand but that was not quite possible either. Her smile, however, was there and it was as radiant as he remembered it from long ago. How indeed could it be otherwise? She knew how he had suffered and how he had sought redemption over the years for something that was not even his fault. Now he could feel her urging him on in spirit because that's all she was anymore.

"Is this our new five o'clock?" he asked but she did not, could not answer.

It was then, through a kind of sixth sense, he knew she would always be with him and that she would fight for him past the pearly gates and beyond. All he had to do was to keep to the covenant he had made with her so long ago. It was that or never, ever be with her again.

Soon after he had been made they had turned to phone conversations and the occasional letter and photograph in the mail. It was too dangerous to continue meeting in person. She trusted him not to turn on her but he was loath to trust himself. Now communication was down to this but, at least, it continued. And he could draw strength from its continuation no matter how tenuous that continuation might be.

As she faded out he said: "Next Sunday?" She nodded and then was gone. It wouldn't be five o'clock in the afternoon ever again because it couldn't be but it could be Sunday. It was something he could take to heart in his continuing struggle to not betray the human he once was and to somehow move beyond the pain created by his present state.

The next night he rummaged through his old boxes and photo albums to revisit that place in existence when he was a young man meeting young women for the first time and expecting, somewhere down the track, a family all his own. Among the snapshots were those of that special woman who would forever want that better eternity for him. Among the other trappings were details of that special someone who had nursed him through the usual childhood ills and had stuck with him even when vampirism promised to tear their feelings for each other asunder. She was, all up, that someone everyone had but he had in spades. She was, cherished being that she was in any plain of being, his mother.

Lilies for Rose

On the outer suburbs of Sydney there's a cemetery dating back to colonial times, before Australia became a federation. Most of the tombstones are old and cracked. Some have been knocked over by vandals while others have been graffitied upon. A quarter of the graves are at a crossroads. It is a dangerous thing having graves at a crossroads, a deadly happenstance for those who meddle in what should not be meddled in, even more so on an occasion charged with arcane energy.

About a year ago some punk kids in their late teens strode into this cemetery. Gary, the male of the group, was tall and grubby. He was grubby from spending every spare moment he had under the hood of the fixer-upper he was going to someday drive. It was an old Morris Minor and what it lacked in glamour it made up for in the need for more maintenance. His girlfriend Starlight was a Goth with black clothes, black make-up, black attitude – the works. Nobody would have guessed she was the love child of two spaced out hippies. Bringing up the rear was Starlight's sister, Sunshine who was a year younger than the other two but managed to look even younger with her pink fairy floss hair and pink Ninja Kitty top. She was the one with the tape recorder.

It was almost midnight and they were looking for the right spot.

"How about that one?" asked Gary, shinning his torch on a broken marble angel that used to point to heaven. Now she made a fist. He thought it ironic and hoped the others would come to the same conclusion. Surely ironic would be good enough.

"I don't think so," Starlight said. "According to my occult book, it should be unconsecrated."

"Well let's not get too fussy," he replied, "or we'll miss the hour. If we do, we'll have to come back next year."

"What are we doing this for anyway?" Sunshine asked.

"Just curious." To Starlight, the words "Keep Out" or "Danger – Do Not Enter" had always piqued her curiosity into doing something stupid. How then could she resist a warning in red ink in an occult text a half century old? If she had been in London during the blitz, her reading the words "Danger – Unexploded Bomb" on a hastily put up sign marking off a street would have seen her blown to bits. What's more, the others would have followed her in and have ended up in as many pieces.

"It's not as if anything for real is going to happen," put in Gary to Sunshine. "But we'll do it right to make your sister happy and so she can't say we mucked it up on her."

"Here!" Sunshine flashed her light on a raised clump of earth. "There's no headstone, nothing. If there's a body underneath, it could be unconsecrated."

"Good thinking." Starlight patted her sister on the shoulder. "We'd better get to it."

And so, five minutes before the witching hour on All Hollow's Eve, Sunshine placed her tape recorder on the clump of earth she rightly took to be an unmarked grave of a less than godly fellow and switched it on. At one in the morning she switched it off. In the interim, thanks to the crossroads, the date and the skeleton untouched for many decades by holy word or holy water, direct communication was entered into with the dark realm eternal. A direct link had been established with the most erstwhile followers of the fallen one. What Sunshine carried back to the home she shared with her family was nothing short of their damnation.

It was Starlight who was most anxious to play back the recording. It was a game to her as it was to the others. Maybe there would be an eerie whisper. Maybe something from beyond was going to say obscene things to them they could laugh and joke about. At worst they figured there wouldn't be anything on the retched thing at all.

In Sunshine's room Gary lit a dozen black candles that would throw shadows. Starlight drew the pink curtains for further atmosphere and, after rewinding all the way, Sunshine pressed the play button.

At first nothing happened. As might be expected, not a sound came out because, nothing had been recorded. Then there was the noise of a car roaring past the cemetery and then more nothing. For a second the car sound had made the back of Starlight's neck tingle and Sunshine's hair became electrified. Gary yawned. He'd humored Starlight long enough and now he was bored.

"That was a bust," he said, his finger on the stop.

"Don't!" Starlight cried. "Leave it run. You never know."

"Yeah." Sunshine winked at Gary. "You never know."

Gary looked toward the ceiling in exasperation and Sunshine got out a pack of cards. They played poker as the tape continued from one spiel to the other. Before it ran out, the lights went out. Not only the electric lights for three blocks but also the lit candles. The total blackness was frightening in ways not easy to imagine. It brought up primeval feelings of unease most people have but few ever fully experience.

"That's something," Gary said, relighting the candles. His voice sounded nervous despite his best effort to keep calm.

"A power failure I can understand," Sunshine said. "But what put out the candles?"

There was a cold breeze but where it came from could not be determined. It seemed to circle them. The windows were closed with the curtains drawn and the only door was locked tight. Two layers of solid brick separated the room from the immediate outside world. If it had been a room in an old, beaten up weatherboard place there might have been an explanation. As it was, on a warm spring morning, Sunshine put on a jumper without knowing why one was required. Gary took Starlight's hand into his and Starlight, when she was able, grabbed hold of Sunshine's. Then with a whoosh the candles went out a second time.

Later that morning the lights came back on. Sunshine found herself curled up on her own bed. She took off her jumper and went into the bathroom across the hallway to wash the sleep out of her eyes. What she saw when she looked in the mirror shocked and horrified her. There were black greasy smudges on her nose and cheeks. She had seen these smudges on her sister's face after she had spent some quiet time with Gary. How then had they come to appear on her face?

She went back to her room and looked around but neither Starlight nor Gary was there. Next she stormed into her sister's abode to demand an explanation. Maybe they were fooling with her to get a reaction. Maybe nothing more had happened than Gary had taken car maintenance muck from his face and hands and put it on her. Or it could have been worse. Maybe he snuggled up to her while she was out of it. She felt violated and very angry.

Sunshine came upon Gary and Starlight still in their street clothes. They were outstretched on Starlight's bed in two different places and in a strange way for sleeping. She shook them, first Gary and then Starlight. She shook Gary first because he was closest. They moved like rag dolls. She yelled at them to get up but they wouldn't. Then she turned her sister over and saw the staring eyes and the stark white face. She turned over Gary and found him the same way. At first she thought it might be an elaborate prank. She touched Starlight's face to see if stage paint would come off onto her hand. Nothing came off. It was when her tongue found blood on the corner of her own lips that she began to scream and scream and scream.

A day later, Sunshine's parents, Matt and Silvia, were still trying to come to grips with the bizarre and sudden death of her sister and the boyfriend. The police had probed her with questions but all she could tell them was that it must have happened during the blackout. She was even hypnotized to remember more but it was no use. It was as if time for her, from the second going out of the candles until she awoke, did not exist.

Even the corpses were unusual. How could they be so empty of blood? How could it happen without Matt, Silvia or Sunshine knowing about it and at least making the attempt to stop it? If Starlight and Gary had perished where they were found then Sunshine, who was next door in her room, should have heard something. Matt and Silvia, who were down the hall in their room, shouldn't have been deaf to what was going on even if Sunshine, for some reason, had been. It didn't make sense.

Carl Compass, one of the investigating detectives, a red-faced street brawler of a cop, took away all of Starlight's books on the occult and her diary. He made off with Sunshine's tape recorder. He had to make up the excuse that he found traces of blood on the machine before taking it but the truth was he got bad vibes from it. Despite appearances, he was a trained sensitive. What he collected ended up in a secret lab deep in the bowels of Mitchell Library in Sydney. It was a place unknown to all visitors to the library except those who needed to know and was the headquarters in Australia of a secret order of Freemasonry most Freemasons had no idea existed. It was Freemasonry dedicated to the eradication of vampirism, lycanthropy, demons and other associated evil. Detective Carl Compass was a member in good standing.

A week later, as the sun went down, Sunshine collapsed onto her bed. Moments passed and, when she got to her feet again, she was no longer Sunshine. Her canines had lengthened into proper fangs and there was a mocking sneer to her lips and crinkling nose.

She was now Rose Tythe, the daughter of a 19th Century Freemason. She had succumbed to vampirism in 1901 on a lonely stretch of beach near Wollongong in southern New South Wales, and had had her original body destroyed by Freemason vampire hunters in 1925. She still had vivid memories of gin joints, taverns, cool jazz, body hugging dresses, vamps pretending to be vampires and oh so willing victims of either sex. She could remember the hunters who had slain her and of what they or their descendants were no doubt still guarding.

She opened a window, transformed into a bat, and on leathery wings, made her journey to Sydney proper. It was not by accident that a cop in an unmarked car a short distance away observed the bat leaving and transferred his observations, including the direction the night creature had taken, via mobile phone to Detective Compass.

There in Sydney proper, not far from the Woolworth's building in Pitt Street; Rose took on once more the semblance of a human. She looked at her reflection in a shop window and made a face. Why, oh why, did she have to look so disgustingly pink? Still she appreciated the warmth of the body and its youth. Did the pink really matter when she was free once more to move?

She was heading with slow determination toward the harbor and toward her goal in Macquarie Street. She marveled at the changes to Sydney and at the fact certain places had remained almost exactly as they had been last time she had been around. Humanity was contradictory. The more it seemed to change the more it remained the same. People went to drinking holes to either drown their sorrows or to try to pick up company; people danced and, though roadsters may have changed in appearance, there remained something about a fast, shiny red car that still excited comment. And, amidst all this, she had to look like an animated stick of cotton candy!

Rose's goal was to free the most infamous blood sucker of them all. She'd been interrupted in doing so once and vowed not to be interrupted, even by a third death, a second time. All it would take would be a few drops of blood—her own would do—and the right words. She wanted to see Sydney, if not the whole of New South Wales, terrorized by vampires. She knew she couldn't do it on her own but the king of all the undead would have some useful ideas.

Count Vlad Dracul, whom the novelist Bram Stoker had fashioned into Dracula for his semi-fictionalized work, had been incarcerated as a pile of ashes in an oak container, no bigger than two shoe boxes put together, since the late 19th Century. Sometime after his defeat, he had been transported, via steamer, to what was then considered to be the farther most reaches of the British Empire from London, barring New Zealand and the South Pole, for safekeeping. With him went a band of special Freemasons whose sacred duty unto God and humankind was to see that the monster of monsters never escaped. To this end they married and their children continued on after them. Generations passed and, even amongst the special Freemason, Count Dracul was drifting further and further into legend. The occasional vampire found and slain renewed their faith and so the guardianship continued.

Apart from the special Freemasons, only Heaven and Hell knew where Dracul could be found. Since Rose had come fresh from Hell she too knew. What's more, she had a plan. It belonged to her and she hoped it would prove worthy of the dark faith that had been placed upon her.

Very few creatures of evil could pass through the ancient mystic barriers created every morning and evening around such edifices as News Limited near Central, the Defense Plaza near Town Hall, the town hall building itself, and the grounds as well as the entrance to Mitchell Library. What Rose needed was the perfect dupe. She needed someone who would not be harmed by such barriers because they were human but who would act on her behalf. Sunshine came to mind.

Just as she was approaching the swinging doors to the night entrance to the library, Rose fell down. When she got up again she was Sunshine. Though the mystic barrier gave her a headache it didn't stop her. She was disorientated not knowing how she got where she was or what her apparent blackout might mean. She had been in her room and now, she was in the heart of Sydney, many miles from her home. A voice inside her head urged her to seek a pay phone to call her parents to come get her and directed her toward an antique elevator in an alcove a few yards from the lobby. Fear made her tremble but it made her obey the insistent voice.

The elevator had been in common use since its creation some-time in the 1920s. Most people thought it had five buttons for five lower levels. The other five were there but cloaked by a powerful glamour. Rose allowed Sunshine to see lower level button number ten and urged here to press it. A shaky finger did the work.

It seemed weird to Sunshine to imagine that the phone she wanted was on such a low level. If she were thinking straight, she would have realized that the nearest phone, which could have been on ground level, would have done as well and, also, that she didn't have any money on her for it anyway. Common sense dictated that the nearest police station was her best bet. But the voice insisted and the voice seemed to know what she was on about.

Visions of crucifixes and of priests forming the sign of the cross came unbidden into her head making the voice groan. Somewhere on the lowest level there was a box kept in a safe and the only way to get to this safe was to pass through a room being sprayed with a light mist of holy water. There were other traps. A misstep meant falling into a pit with stakes as sharp as knives to greet you or an arrow flying from the wall aimed at your heart. The only way forward was not to be concerned with things holy and to know where to put your feet. The combination to the safe was known to a handful of living humans and, of course, to Heaven and Hell. Vampires, being undead and therefore not having journeyed fully to either Heaven or Hell, though they had a ticket for Hell, didn't know a thing. Rose was a dangerous exception.

The elevator stopped and Sunshine got out. She took two steps toward the door of doors, where Dracul resided in his powdery state, before being grabbed under the arms by two large men in black suits.

"Just want to use a phone…," she began and a smelly cloth went over her face. It made her feel sick and dizzy. After a minute of intense struggle with two living, breathing brick walls, she collapsed into unconsciousness.

It wasn't Sunshine who came to choking from the chloroform that had threatened to make her throw up but Rose. She was tied via thick steel cords to a steel chair which was clamped to the floor. One of the black suits fastened two electrode wires above her heart and left. In the semi-darkness she noticed a still female figure staring at her with unblinking eyes. A guard, perhaps?

"What's your name?" a voice came over an intercom system. It was a male, possibly in his mid-fifties and no doubt the superior of the two thugs she'd already met. It was reminiscent of the voice of one of the Freemasons she had done battle with when she was still in her own body. That particular man was likely to be dead and the person she was now conversing with a relative, maybe the man's son or grandson.

"Why am I still alive?" Rose asked, pouting.

"We're curious," the voice said. "You're the first of your kind to make it as far as you have in, oh, twenty years or so."

"Good for me."

"Are you going to answer my questions?"

"No."

"I take it you're not Sunshine?"

"Believe what you like."

"I think I will."

"Wait!"

A switch was flipped and the body Rose was dominating rocked on its pins with sharp pain. She could not help but scream. They zapped her three more times and each time it was longer. The thought came to her that, if she remained, she was going to be zapped to death along with Sunshine. No way could she allow that to happen!

In a panic, Rose fled the body she was in, allowing it to collapse and be supported by the cords. She fled the body for the other female in the room. With any luck, her assailants would kill Sunshine and call it a night. Then, in this other woman's form, she might stand a chance of freeing the Count and changing the odds. With the help of the Count, she might even have revenge on her present day tormentors.

This other body she entered wasn't quite right. For a start, there wasn't a brain, nothing up top but some chalky resin substance. She had been attracted to it by the smell of blood, but apart from a few quarts of the precious red liquid in its stomach, there was either emptiness or solidity most profound. It was nothing more than a storeroom dummy with a couple of bottles of AB negative in a hollow in its center. By the time she realized this, it was way too late. A rope wall with garlic bulbs attached descended, cutting her off from returning to her previous host.

Rose cursed the fates. If she had been in her original vampire body, her vampire eyesight would have prevented her from being tricked by use of a dummy in a semi-dark chamber. She may have been able to give Sunshine's body superhuman strength and the ability to transform into a bat when she was fully in charge of it but not extra keen vision. Or she wasn't able to do so this early in her relationship with it and the mind of Sunshine. Given time, the trick might not have worked on her but; of course, Rose had to be in a hurry. She cursed again.

She tried to move out of the dummy but the odor from the garlic prevented her from doing that. Then the black suits came in with a coffin lined with crucifixes and lowered the dummy she was occupying into it.

"I'll get you!" she cried from the coffin, though how she managed through dummy teeth is a wonder, as the lid was lowered and nailed shut. It was then she realized that, beside the dummy was the tape recorder that had taken her from Hell and back to earth. Apparently they wanted nothing more to do with it or her.

"I'll get you!" she cried again as they carried the coffin she was in away.

Sunshine was beginning to revive. Before she could fully come to, a small man in half-moon glasses carrying a needle put her back out to it.

"What will happen to her?" asked the small man with a touch of genuine concern.

"Detective Compass will sneak her back into her room in her parent's house," said the voice on the intercom. "With luck she'll come to believe that tonight's adventure is nothing but some wild dream."

"She's an innocent," Detective Compass added as he entered the room. "We don't kill innocents. I'm sorry we couldn't have saved her foolish sister or that young man they were with."

A week later, in the middle of the Indian Ocean, a steel coffin containing a wooden coffin containing a dummy, an evil spirit and an equally evil tape recorder was dropped into the water. It was a nice, sunny day, the kind vampires hate most.

A priest said prayers and Detective Compass, who insisted on seeing it through to the end, threw lilies onto the bubbling surface. Lilies are flowers for the dead best known for both their beauty and lack of ornamental scent. It is believed by the Balinese that the dead feed off the odor of certain foods including certain flowers. By offering lilies then, flowers without strong scent, Detective Compass was attempting to offer an unclean specter the hope of eternal rest. The flowers followed the coffin down into the inky depths.

"Do you think she'll get out of that?" Compass asked the priest.

"Eventually," the priest told him. "With the ravages of time and water pressure, the metal will fail and the wood will rot. The crucifixes holding her in place by God's good grace, because she is only a spirit looking for a body to inhabit, will also disintegrate. All of this will take decades, even centuries, unless the water pressure becomes too much and the coffins, one within the other, are crushed, but she will be free. More time will pass as she finds her way out of the darkness down there, which is absolute, to the light and back to being a thorn in the side of humanity. All we can say is that we've done our best with her and hope it will be enough for the future."

"She may be insane when she does emerge into the light."

"Most probably."

"I wonder who she was. I wonder who she is."

"Rose Tythe, perhaps?"

"Rose Tythe? I remember reading about her a long, long time ago. Why Rose Tythe? Just because her father was a Freemason?"

"Yes, my son."

"I don't get it."

"It is a little known but important fact that the devil does, indeed, have a sense of humor."

"And using the daughter of a past member against us in this way would tickle his fancy?"

"That is correct, my son."

Ring the Bells

It had been fifty years to the night that Paula Yarley had walked the streets of her native town of Trench near Dubbo in the middle of New South Wales, Australia. The streets were wide and dusty like every other country street in every other country town. There were three pubs for a population of about a thousand people. There was a post office, a church with an old Kirk yard, a school, a doctor's surgery, a second cemetery on a hill and not much else. Oh, and in summertime about a trillion tiny black flies. Trench was dying and had been doing so for a long time. It was hard to believe it was ever not dying. Paula hated the place.

One hundred and fifty years ago she'd been an ordinary woman with an ordinary future. She had been a milkmaid engaged to be married to some landowner's son. Back then there were a few Aboriginal families. They came to an end in the 1920s when diphtheria attacked them a lot harder than it did the white people. Paula wasn't there to see them go but she did pick up a Sydney newspaper that told the tragic story. Few there were who mourned the passing of the Trench Aborigines. Few there were who mourned the passing of the white roustabouts, jackaroos and layabouts that followed them to the grave.

During the first couple of decades of her transformation Paula traveled. She went all over New South Wales then Victoria and finally Tasmania. Europe called and she responded. Since those heady early days she had trekked the globe and had done everything it was possible for her to imagine a vampire could do. Now she was weary with it all and some strange power, some mysterious instinct had dragged her back to where her journey had begun. It had done so fifty years ago and was doing so again.

It made little sense. She no longer had a true Australian accent and it had been so long since she cared about her own people she wondered why some force would want her to now. "Let them all die!" she cried out to the black, starless sky. She kicked a stone into a fast moving stream and watched with her excellent night vision the swirls in the water made by her action. No human could have seen the swirls but then again she wasn't human.

"That's gloomy," an amused voice came from a nearby stone bench. She turned in the direction of the sound and came upon a gaunt male figure in black. Paula was in Trench's War Memorial Park late at night. She wasn't expecting company.

"Let me guess," she said, eyeing the fellow's long, sharp claws and teeth. "Lycanthrope, right?"

"No. Sorry," he toothed. "Good guess, but I'm not hairy enough. I'm the undead. I just like to keep my sharp bits long, especially when I am out and about."

"Who are you?" asked Paula with a touch of annoyance. She wanted to be alone.

"The name's Dracula," he said with a slight Eastern European accent. "Count Dracula at your service."

"Right!" she said. "And I am Queen Elisabeth the First! I suppose you have come to drink my blood! Or something, right? Wrong! And Dracula, if he was still around, wouldn't be in the middle of New South Wales talking to me as if he were straight out of some 1930s flick."

"Alright!" he said bowing and smiling with all his whites in a rather cheeky fashion. "You caught me out! No, I am not quite that famous or infamous. I did originally come from Eastern Europe but my name is Victor Vargas, the son of a blacksmith. Somewhat down the social ladder to a count I am afraid but there you have it. Still it is fun to put on heirs sometimes, isn't it?"

"I don't know," she pouted. "I wouldn't think of trying. What do I care what my food thinks of me anyway? And as for my fellow vampires…too many of them put on asinine heirs before they die. Silly, really, if you take my meaning."

Paula looked at the scruffy jeans she wore and at her old, battered Saint George T-shirt. She was dressed to blend in with the locals and to get her nightly feed with as little to-do as possible. She could of course have dressed in tight leather and put on a black cape with red trimmings like that Vampira character out of that old 1970s comic she came across one night in the hands of one of her younger victims but that would only have led to a thousand and one little annoyances.

"I'm just passing through," said Victor. "Thought I'd say hi. You from around here?"

"Not anymore." She picked up another stone and threw it into the stream. They both watched the water ripple. She imagined the stone tearing away the fabric of the last five decades. The stream seemed consistent with the way she had seen it low those decades ago. If it had changed, it hadn't changed by much.

"It gets that way, doesn't it?" he commiserated. "Always on the move. You had a meal?"

"Some twerp at the station anxious to catch the next train. She smelled of sheep dip. I probably smell of sheep dip. And you?"

"Some old drunk fresh out of the pub," toothed Victor.

"How did you manage that?" she had to ask.

"Looking the way I do?"

Victor passed his hand over his body and he was transformed into an overweight man in his forties. He looked like a regular at one of the pubs.

"A glamour," he told her and then transformed himself back to his original shape. "If I wanted to, I could look handsome to a potential snack. I learned the art in the old country. Around vampires, of course, I prefer to look the way I really do if you catch my drift. Come sit beside me. I want to have a proper conversation with you. And I am happy to take my chances on the smell of sheep dip."

Victor passed his hand over his body once more and became once again a more congenial looking member of the undead community. Paula had lost her annoyance with him and was now warming to his nonchalance if indeed she was capable of warming to anything. She sat down beside Victor. If she had been human, the bench would have been cold, even icy through the jeans but she wasn't human and neither was her companion. Up close he was taller and skinnier. He had thinning black hair, deep set hazel eyes and, despite not being an aristocrat, an aristocrat's long, pointy nose. His sharp parts gleamed with elegance.

"You ever feel like giving it all up?" she asked him. "You know the old stake, or holy wafer or sunlight trick? I think munching on a wafer would be the least painful, but who knows for sure?"

"None of that for me." Victor shook his head. "I like my unlife. The things I've seen, the things I've done in four hundred years…And I'm still young. By human standards I am in my early thirties."

"Don't you ever get tired of the hunt?"

Victor sighed and shrugged his shoulders. Somewhere in the distance a cat could be heard yowling at something. Perhaps there was a catfight in the offering, a territorial battle between two Toms. At one stage in Trench's history it might have been the guttural love call of a possum for his mate, but that would have been a long time ago.

"Well," Victor ventured after a minute of creeping silence, "I did feel that way back in the 1960s. I had a nice apartment in New York and ordered out."

"Ordered out?"

"For a hefty price, an orderly at the local hospital was happy to supply me with fresh blood. I was well off so it worked out fine. I got my rest from the hunt and I caught up with television and radio. I visited the theatre, something I hadn't done in more than a century, and went to the cinema to find out what the fuss was all about. It was fun for a while. Then the old urge to hunt came back and that was that. Besides, my supplier had figured out that it was cheaper and safer to supply me with pig's blood instead of human so I had to put the bite on him just to make sure he understood the difference. After that he became even more unreliable."

Victor scraped his fingernails against the stone bench, sharpening them. There were sparks. Paula couldn't help but be a little impressed.

"Don't you ever get tired of being hunted?" she asked in a deceptively bland voice.

"Sure I do," he acknowledged with a slight nod of agreement. "Back in 1864 I killed a Pinkerton agent outside windy city. He tried to drive a stake through my heart so I put a fist through his instead. Back then I didn't have very long or sharp nails. Fair enough a present day Aussie might say but those Pinkertons...They picked up my trail in New Jersey. From there I headed south. I was in New Carolina before I lost them. It took me the better part of four years and about a dozen close calls. I still look over my shoulder just thinking about them."

A rat crossed their path and Victor skewered it with a fingernail. It gave a high pitched squeal. He then tossed it into the stream. Paula was taken with how fast he had moved.

"The Freemasons are a pain," she warned. "One time they were all over the world. What's more, there's an order of Freemasonry, called the Secret Compass, with a special interest in disposing of our kind. They have their headquarters in the vaults of some old library in Sydney. You never know when they'll turn up in a town like Trench. Be sure to dump your catches in the local river so they'll be taken for drowning victims. It's the best way."

Victor leaned back and smirked. "You don't sound quite as suicidal now."

"I can still be thinking of doing myself in," she corrected with a sigh. "I just don't want to give anyone the satisfaction of doing it for me, especially the Freemasons. They were once accused of having misogynistic leanings."

"How long ago was that?"

"About three decades. Nothing to one of us."

"I suppose not. You staying long or will you be doing yourself in soon?"

"What's it to you?"

She wasn't sure why Victor was asking. Did he want to save her or was he bucking for a front row seat?

"I lied to you when I said I was just passing through," owned Victor, covering his face for a moment with his hands in mock humility. "Mind you, a year seems like such a pitifully short period but, as the locals say, this has become my patch."

"I'll most likely clear off tomorrow," she said. "I don't know why I am here. It's just that, when I am really depressed, I tend to head in this direction."

"I think I know."

"Know what?"

"Why you are here. Legend has it that a vampire may find eternal rest once every living member of his or her own original community is no more and she has rung the church bells three times."

Paula looked at Victor, blinked and smiled. She cocked her head to one side to see if he was serious.

"That's absurd!" she snapped. "That is utterly ridiculous! So what you are saying is that if I kill everyone in Trench then ring the church bells three times I'm gone?"

"If you believe the legend."

"What about the ones who packed up and left?"

"They don't count. Only the ones here count."

"This is sounding better and better. There are about a thousand of them now. In fifty years there might only be five hundred. In fifty years after that I might have numbers I can work with."

"That's true."

"Destroying the town along with myself does have its charms."

"And damning it for all time. Don't forget that. No one will be able to live in the town ever again once those bells are rung. No newcomers, no one at all."

Paula looked into Victor's eyes. She wanted to believe him, she really did. But the idea of damning something, anything forever, even a vampire who was said to be damned simply by being vampiric, seemed too fantastic.

"And this legend is true?" she ventured.

"Only one way to find out. I don't know of anyone who has tried it. Me? I still have plenty of unliving to do. I'll catch up with you later."

With that having been said, Victor spread his arms which became leathery. The sun was beginning to rise and he had to be off. In the next instant Paula too took on bat form. They flew off in opposite directions to sleep away the day.

Paula now had plenty to think about and dream about. Perhaps what she had been told was a comforting untruth. But to damn and blast a miserable, boring and, to most people, insignificant place like Trench forever? That certainly had its appeal. She wanted to believe her new acquaintance. Something about him made her feel less despondent and that in itself was good if indeed good was a word a vampire should use. Also there was his glamour trick. Perhaps he would teach it to her though she did wonder why he didn't use it when the Pinkertons were chasing him. Perhaps it had its limitations. Perhaps it required concentration and could not be used all the time.

And there was the notion of taking a break from feasting on victims, of finding someone to get the blood for her. Due to the need to hunt she hadn't had time to study art or music or anything. What would it be like to read a novel, learn to play a musical instrument or stroll along a beach at night at Coffs Harbor or somewhere on the Gold Coast for no other reason than the stroll itself? So many questions. So many new possibilities. Yes, she would see him again, her toothy friend, and perhaps get the answers she craved. Unlife was suddenly exciting. For the first time in ages she was looking forward to yet another night.

The Big Aunty Curse

Tommy Tyler was not your average television personality. He was neither a singer nor an actor. What he knew about politics or human rights would fit onto most postage stamps. He was dumpy and smelly rather than handsome and neat. Yet he was able to name a fee in the thousands of dollars for a single public appearance and all he had to do to gain applause was to slap some woman's – any woman's – behind.

He made his debut on the screen in a reality based contestant style show called *Big Aunty Twice Removed*. For fame and fortune he spent six weeks in an expensive home somewhere in Rose Bay, Sydney watching the idiot box, talking down to the other five contestants and, every chance he got, slapping the backsides of the two females who were on the show. They didn't seem to mind. What's more, not only did the general public go along with such behavior, but they constantly voted for him to remain on the air.

The only person to raise objections to Tommy was Paula Yarley. She had just moved from the country to the city when the first episode of *Big Aunty Twice Removed* was aired. She was appalled at how many otherwise level-headed, sane men and women not only watched the show but were charmed by Tommy's antics. When *Big Aunty Twice Removed* ended its run and Tommy collected fifty thousand dollars prize money, his fame and popularity didn't end there. He was seen at all sorts of clubs and events. Talk back shows wanted him. The public couldn't seem to get enough of him. The whole thing was pathetic even for humans. What the hell did they see in him?

Despite the fact that Paula was trying to keep a low profile, she was so incensed by Tommy's fame that when she saw women lining up to have their bums whacked by the low life, she felt she had to do something about it. And so, in a fit of anger, she snatched a waiting teenage girl, dragged her to a dark corner of a nearby building and sank her teeth into the little fool's pulsating neck. The richness of the nectar brought her back to sanity but not before she drained the stupid young creature. She then managed to transform into a bat and fly off before anyone was aware of the lifeless husk she had left behind.

Having sated her thirst, and having realized just how careless and ridiculous she had been when she had a nice supply of bottled blood, Paula headed home. Someone would find the dead girl and raise the alarm. The hunters would be on the alert and a new search for her would begin. She sighed at the thought of becoming hunter and hunted again. It was almost too much. Before she knew it, her little holiday would be over. And she'd be back to the same old unlife she was trying to get away from for a while.

Back in her apartment, before slipping under the covers, she made sure there was native earth under her bed. It wasn't as if she needed the warmth of blankets on a chilly day. But they felt good against her skin. It was like being touched all over by a gentle lover and so beat a restrictive, impersonal coffin any time. It's funny but it had taken her a century and a half to realize that the earth under her while she slept was essential to her continued healthy existence but not the wooden structure she was buried in.

As she dozed, thoughts about Tommy and Big Aunty came to her. At first it was simply the nightmare of a sick mind being indulged, even rewarded, by so many people. She could even imagine herself being part of the bandwagon for the creep. Then the other contestants turned up as lost souls pleading for her help. Their hands went out to her. Their eyes brimmed with tears. Their mouths formed words but nothing was said. Their faces were pale, anemic...*Anemic?!* She woke with a start. Was that the answer? Could that be what was really going on?

The following night Paula rented the DVDs to the Big Aunty series. Prior to this she had caught snippets in commercials of the show and they were enough to drive her to distraction and a desire for revenge. She found the episodes incredibly boring. There was a dullness that tried to seep into every cell of her brain. It didn't succeed, and she came away with some intriguing clues. Her desire to get even was further fueled.

The five people Tommy competed against for the money seemed to be superior to him to the point where he must have been allowed in as some kind of joke. There was Susan Wright, better known as Madam Rattan. She was a tall, cool dominatrix trained in the orient with a dozen years worth of experience in her dubious trade. Yet within a week Tommy had her apologizing to the men she'd mistreated and admitting that her lifestyle was wrong. She spent the first week in skin tight leather and the last week in a baggy floral dress.

There was Shane Manning, a well-built athlete getting ready to enter the Olympics as a long distance runner. The producers promised him he could continue his training during production. Time and time again, Tommy broke his concentration to where he could no longer do it.

Rose and Edward Hillman were newlyweds who saw the show as a way of getting a substantial down payment on a house. By the time Tommy was through with them, they were both eager for a divorce. During the first week they were inseparable. On the final day they were ignoring one another and looking to Tommy for advice.

Number five was a small, beetle-eyed computer expert named Rodney Winters. He was a programmer on the cutting edge needing only a little funding to start his own software business. He tried to be a good conversationalist and to win the support of the home audience but it was no use. In grubby innuendos and seedy remarks Tommy ran rings around him and that's what seemed to count. Or was it all so straight forward?

Paula noticed that Tommy's five competitors had entered the Big Aunty house fit and healthy. By the time they left, however, they were as white as so many sheets. Their eyes were sunken and lacked energy. The others were often filmed eating and drinking but not Tommy. It was as if he didn't need to eat or drink. Was it a coincidence that all of what he said and did was shot at night?

Also there were rare moments where Tommy's eyes glowed red. No doubt most viewers put this down to a trick of the light. Paula might have done the same thing only there was another so called trick of the light which brought the first into question. Tommy wore a ring that had a large, white crystal that brightened to crimson at the same moment his eyes brightened. Was this a coincidence or something more sinister?

Tommy had completed a personal appearance at a tavern in Newtown when he was approached by a medium sized willowy woman with long, black hair. She was dressed in black stylish jeans and a frilly black blouse. He was in his dressing room and there was a do not disturb sign on his door. She had turned the knob and walked in.

"Go away!" he grumbled. "The performance is over."

"I'd say it's just beginning," she told him.

Tommy grunted, shifted his bulk in her direction and eyed her. Where had she come from? Surely the bouncers belonging to the tavern would have seen her on her way. Well, if they weren't earning their keep, he'd have to deal with them. There was plenty more muscle out there looking for work.

"You need to go away now," he informed her. He tried to sound threatening but didn't succeed.

She didn't leave; she came closer. There was something about her he found disturbing. She wasn't just another brain dead fan. She had a scary kind of intelligence.

"And miss out on your colorful insights?" she cooed.

Anger radiated from him. He didn't like being spooked and he hated being mocked. His eyes took on an unnatural light and so did the adornment he wore on his finger.

"Go!" he ordered, pointing to the door. "While you're at it, do something about ending your miserable existence. There's a good girl."

"No."

"What…What did you say?"

"I said no. I'm not feeling the least bit suicidal though I was some time ago. Besides, we have matters to discuss."

Tommy's jaw dropped. He looked at his ring. Yes, as far as he was concerned it was operating. Maybe she's a bit deaf.

"Go!" he yelled.

In response she crossed her arms, smiled and said: "Give it up. I've done my research. It took going through a dozen places, but I found an informative volume on the supernatural in an all night bookshop in Darlinghurst. It had a chapter on rings such as the one you're wearing. Apparently they boost a vampire's ability to mesmerize humans, but they have no effect whatsoever on the undead."

"And you're…"

"That's right."

Tommy was taken aback. He nursed his ring finger as if it had been injured.

"What do you want?" Even when he was alive it had been his philosophy that everyone could be bought at the right price. Besides, what did he need to fear from another vampire?

"I want you to leave Sydney forever," she stated in no uncertain terms. "Even though I am no longer one of them, I find what you do with human females far too demeaning for me to allow it to continue."

"And if I refuse?"

"What if you were to meet up with vampire versions of Shane, Rose, Edward and Rodney? How about Madame Rattan? Considering the longevity of our kind, you two could be together for a very long time. Whips, canes and so forth…And you have been a naughty boy, haven't you? Does that appeal to you?"

"You haven't! You – you wouldn't!"

"Not if you leave tonight and never come back. I hear Bathurst is nice this time of year. It's in the country."

"Look! I have a good thing going here. Plenty of blood. Plenty of money. I could cut you in."

"Be out of here by midnight or suffer the consequences."

There was a midnight train to Bathurst. Tommy was on it. He didn't want to be but he figured he was dealing with a mad, supernatural being who didn't understand the value of blood or cold, hard cash. Courage was not his middle name.

Once the train was out of Central, he opened up his laptop to check on his earnings only to discover his entire bank account had been wiped clean. "Damn!" he said under his breath, realizing it was probably Rodney Winters' doing. *I'll get even with that hacker some day.*

An hour before dawn, when Tommy was anxious to change into bat form and leave the train for a prearranged hotel room containing a bag with his native earth in it, he got visitors. Madame Rattan entered his cabin sporting a fancy silver crucifix in her hand. She was followed by Rose and Edward Hillman and Shane Manning.

"What is this?" Tommy tried to look Madame Rattan in the eye but his gaze was deflected by the crucifix. Meanwhile Edward and Shane were stringing cloves of garlic around the tiny windows and the small sliding door. Rose kept busy with a can of vanilla scented perfume she sprayed him with to mask his rising personal stench. It made him smell better. It also made him sneeze.

"Retribution," Madame Rattan said. "Our friend Rodney has diverted your funds to various other accounts. All will get a share, including the mysterious woman who put us on to you and what you've done. Shane will be compensated for what you did to his training. Rose and Edward are back together but need counseling. You are paying for that. I will be able to restart my career in another country and Rodney will have his software company."

"Yeah! And what about me?" Tommy grumbled. "You got off light as far as I'm concerned. I could have done far worse to the lot of you. Ha! I might still do far worse!"

"Here's something for your troubles." Madame Rattan flipped a coin from the pocket of her black slacks in Tommy's direction. Without a second thought he snatched it out of the air and paid the price.

"It burns! It burns!" he screamed in pain, smoke coming from his closed hand. He tried to drop the metal disc but he couldn't. It wouldn't let go. It had fused itself to his flesh and it was smoldering. With tears in his piggy little eyes and with some difficulty, he peeled it off his damaged palm and hurled it to the floor.

"Wow! What was that?" Rose asked.

"My Saint Christopher medallion," Madame Rattan replied. "I thought he might want it."

Tommy made a lunge for Madame Rattan's throat but was driven back by a wave of the crucifix.

"What do we do now?" Shane asked. "Bring in the police?"

"No," Madame Rattan said. "According to our contact from his world, we wait."

"Wait?"

"That's right."

Tommy made several more lunges at Madame Rattan but the crucifix remained effective. He tried to attack the others but their close proximity to the garlic weakened him too much for such actions to work. Not being able to make eye contact with them for any length of time meant the ring could not be brought into use.

"Let me go!" Tommy cried as the sun began to peak over the mountains to light the day. "I have money! Yes! Money! It is yours if you find me a safe haven. Oh, and gold! Lots of gold!"

"And jewels I suppose," put in Edward who had been silent up to this time. He had been in a daze over what they were doing and why they were doing it. He still felt as if he was in a daze. Dealing with the supernatural was too unreal.

"Yes! Yes! Anything!" Tommy pleaded as his clothes were shriveled up by the morning rays. Then his overly generous flesh quivered and scorched. Slowly, agonizingly his flesh was stripped away from his bones to become ash. His bones broke down and crumbled. Within twenty minutes all that was left of him was ash and a small burn mark on one of the floor boards plus one final item.

"Wow!" Rose cried.

"Indeed," Madame Rattan agreed.

Among the ashes was the ring. The clothes Tommy had worn, including his shoes and belt, had disintegrated with him but the ring remained. Madame Rattan picked it up and put it on. She thought about giving it to the woman who had orchestrated their attack upon its former owner but came to the conclusion that it might not be such a great idea. Why give another vampire such power? On the Madame, of course, it would only have sentimental value.

The following night Paula received a phone call from Rodney telling her of Tommy's fate and informing her where she could pick up her share of the loot. They'd given her a bank account on the internet. She was glad that they weren't going to try to cheat her or bring her down. She was made less happy, however, by the latest issue of TV Week. A new reality program would soon be replacing *Big Aunty Twice Removed*. It was quite a blow to her viewing pleasure. It was no doubt going to be promoted and commercials that would send her around the bend would be aired during breaks in such wonderful shows as *Stargate*, *Enterprise*, and *Smallville*.

"Humans!" she said under her breath. "Won't you ever learn? Does dullness become you?"

Well, even if television had proved less than an admirable form of modern entertainment thanks to cost cutting, viewer stupidity and promoters seeing a way to make a fast buck, there was always live theatre and the movies. Paula had just seen the complete version of the old 1930s film, Dracula, and was surprised to find that it was better put together than she had thought. Last time she saw it was in the 1940s in a small complex at Dubbo. There she was so busy sinking her teeth into a young man to get her nightly nourishment that she missed most of the plot and only caught some of the highlights. Not having to put the bite on someone – anyone – was such a relief.

The community hall art class she attended Thursday nights was proving to be promising and so was the university course she was taking in economics of a Friday. All things considered, she was still on holidays from her old life of hunter and hunted and would be for quite some time. There was much to enjoy and no real reason to hurry back.

The Perils of Sheila Grahams

Bankstown, NSW, Australia, spring, 1975:

Sheila Grahams was a freckle faced redhead in her early twenties. It had taken a while but she'd grown out of that gawky, awkward stage of development where she was all arms and legs and not much in between. Her dad had called it her Olive Oil phase. When she complained about his comparing her with a cartoon character with a horribly squeaky voice and a big head, he just told her that at least Popeye would be interested in her. He then told her to eat her spinach and to cheer up.

Once she'd gained a bit in the right places and got herself a boyfriend, Sheila thought her life was beginning to make sense. His name was Marty Sexton. At first, when they were going out, she couldn't understand why he hung around with such a goon squad of losers as Al, Benny, Chris and Denny. Surely he was too good for that lot. Then she got the picture in full cinemascope and wanted out. Getting out, though, was not going to be easy.

She was hanging around the local fish and chip shop when she overheard Chris and Benny whispering about how they were going to knock over a bank. She knew they'd seen her listening in but she thought nothing of it. No one would have given them credit for having brains enough to pull such a stunt. It was like two kindergarten kids planning to blow up their school with accumulated gunpowder from firecrackers. It wasn't going to happen. *God they're dumb,* she'd reasoned at the time and had let it go at that.

Later that week, when she read about five men wearing masks threatening the tellers of the local bank with lumps of wood and

39

plumber's pipes if they didn't fork over all the money, the penny still didn't drop. Not even with Marty's help could the goon squad of losers do something so melodramatic and daring. It was almost stupid in its simplicity. Stupid? Now that should have been a clue. She should have figured out that it doesn't take a whole lot of gray matter between the ears to threaten people with bodily harm. It takes nerve. It was something the others didn't have much of but Marty had plenty to spare. He could sit on the edge of a cliff and not give a damn. He could swim in shark infested water and dare the sharks to make their move. Maybe he could even rob a bank?

It was the week after the robbery that Sheila decided to break it off with Marty. When she told him they were through over milkshakes, he seemed more sad than angry which should have been clue number two. He suggested they go to the drive-in at Greenacre one last time. Like a born again dummy, she agreed. *It's the fair thing to do*, she told herself.

"You'll like what's on," he told her. Usually, he was right.

Marty had an old rust bucket panel van. In the back he stored all sorts of useless things. On the last night he'd take Sheila out, the useless things included the goons. He met her with the van outside her parent's home and he took her straight to the drive-in. He was in a strange mood as if making up his mind about something. She thought he didn't want the break-up and would try to talk or smooch his way out of it. She didn't mind if he tried, but they were through and that was that. *I've got to move on*, she told herself.

There was going to be a double feature of '50s Science Fiction on the big screen. As they were pulling up to their speaker, there was an ad showing people eating popcorn and peanuts. She told Marty she was going to get food out at the drive-in tuck shop before the first movie started. This was all right with him. So there she was buying popcorn and peanuts when she looked back at the van and noticed Marty talking to the goons. Those idiots were in the back and had no doubt been there since before Marty picked her up. This was clue number three. It was followed by clue number four when she saw that fool Benny sniggering over something in Marty's hand that looked like a real gun. *God, what are they up to?* She wondered.

Well, that was it. No way was she going back to the van. Whatever they were planning, she wanted no part of. The last thing she needed was a criminal record. So she sneaked on past the van and began a long walk home. She had the peanuts and popcorn to eat on the journey and there was a big full moon to light her way. She was feeling pretty good about giving Marty and his pals the slip when, about half an hour later, she caught sight of the van's headlights coming up behind her. *What the hell is he playing at?* She wondered. *Is he trying to scare me or what?*

She didn't think he'd run her down but he did. The impact was a real stunner. It didn't hurt much at all, but trying to move afterwards was bad news. So there she was in the road dying, bones with names she couldn't remember broken and those responsible were driving off. One might even have been snickering at getting away with it. God knows what was running through Marty's head. She was too out of it to have anything going through her own except how much everything hurt when she tried to do this or that. Even breathing brought with it a wave of tremulous agony.

Sheila felt herself coming to the end of her own trail and was glad when a blue Toyota Corolla pulled up near her wrecked body. A tall man in black with white hair got out. He approached her and asked her if she wanted to go on living. She must have said yes, that part she couldn't remember because she was in so much pain at the time, but he looked pleased afterwards and that's what counted. He cut himself with a penknife and put his wounded finger into her mouth. She tasted something warm, vital and rather salty. Then he was sucking on the ruptured vein in her leg and she was wondering why. She didn't think she'd been bitten by a snake and why should a snake bite matter so much when there was a lot more besides wrong with her? Wasn't that treatment no longer recommended for snake bite? Her mind was rambling on like an old time piece running down for the last time and then, she was dead.

Death was no big deal but coming back to life after being deceased three nights was scary. People weren't supposed to do that. She wasn't supposed to do that. What's more, apart from being naked on a slab, she was as good as new. She could now move whatever she damned well wanted to move without suffering for having done so. The tall white haired guy was there to welcome her into the ways of the undead. He even had a change of clothes for her and a cup of warm blood. *What a gentleman!* She thought. He was an improvement over Marty even if he was too old for her. He was too old for her by a hundred and fifty years or at least that's what he told her. *Is he part of some dream? If I wanted a father figure but not my real dad would I have created someone like him?*

He was happy to treat her like a child and she was happy to let him. He asked her if she wanted to avenge her death and, after a few moments of thought, she said yes. He then told her what she could do. He left her with some sage advice telling her it was unlikely she'd ever see him again.

A few nights after Sheila's body had vanished from the morgue Al, big and dumb as they come, was about to go into his favorite pub when he thought he caught sight of Marty's ex-girlfriend. She had slipped into a fried chicken shop. He slipped into the place after her expecting not to find what he indeed did find.

"You're dead," he told Sheila.

"Yes," she agreed. "That was Marty's doing."

"But you're dead."

"So you keep telling me. Want to step outside and talk about it?"

She stepped outside with him and he dragged her around the corner to a dingy dead end street. He pulled a knife out of his belt and stabbed her fifty times. It hurt but not as bad as moving after the car had slammed into her. She fell and he watched her do so. There was blood everywhere but that was to be expected. He tossed his knife into the gutter and, without looking back, walked away.

He didn't see her blink and then smile. "That's no way to really kill a vampire," she told herself. "My but you boys have a lot to learn."

The following night Al, after telling Marty and the rest of the gang about his weird experience of the night before, and how they were now all safe from Sheila blabbing to the cops, went into a Chinese restaurant to pick up take away. He was in there for no more than five minutes when he saw Sheila waiting in line to be served and smiling in his direction.

"But you really are dead," he told her.

"Yes," she agreed. "I've been killed twice, once by Marty and once by you."

"This doesn't make any sense."

"Want to try for best out of three?"

"Okay."

She stepped outside with him and he dragged her around the corner to a dingy parking lot. He pulled a brand new knife out of his belt and was about to stab her with it when she broke the blade in two with her fingers.

"You don't get to do that twice," she told him. "Want to kiss me instead? I want to kiss you."

She propped him up against the wall and, slowly so he felt it, leached the very life out of him. The police found his body the next day and were baffled by the way he perished. He was as white as God's tennis shoes and, apart from two little wounds on his neck that didn't appear to amount to much, he was fine. Why then was he not among the living?

Benny, Chris and Denny were real shook up about what had happened to Al. It wasn't as if they had liked the bloke that much, but they figured that what got Al could get them too. Marty thought that kind of thinking was going to get them nowhere fast. He told them to cool it and let the police handle it. Besides, now they didn't have to split the bank money with Al, everyone was going to get a bigger share. Surely that was cause for celebration.

"Look, he was slow in the head," said Marty. "Because he was slow he got into trouble he couldn't get out of. We're smarter than him so let's not worry about it. He probably saw some girl who looked like Sheila, done something stupid with her and this other dame's boyfriend done him in. Doesn't that make sense?"

They nodded in agreement because it made the kind of sense they liked. Now they could forget all about Al and have a good time.

Denny was a pot smoker from way back. Every spring he'd go to Bathurst or Orange in the country to build up his own personal stash. It wasn't surprising then that, the night after Al's demise, Sheila found him puffing away on a bench in the local park. He looked thin and scruffy but then, he always looked that way. It was his eyes that said something new. Despite the dope, they were haunted.

Sheila decided not to play games with him. She walked up to him and twisted his neck until she heard a satisfying crunch. With her vampire strength it took five seconds. She didn't bother drinking his blood. She figured it wouldn't be nourishing. Besides, he had a dirty neck.

The death of Denny put Chris and Benny into a tailspin of panic. Marty tried to calm them; but in the end he had to wash his hands of them. If they didn't meet up for a while maybe whatever was happening would stop. Surely it couldn't be Sheila's doing. The coroner said she was dead. He couldn't have been wrong, could he?

"Coroners don't lie," he told Chris and Benny. "Sheila's dead, gone, kaput. The sooner you guys accept that the better. Denny couldn't, so that's why he's dead, too. He was probably in a daze trying to forget her when some doper like himself saw his stash and killed him for it. If you two can't manage to understand that, then you're on your own because I refuse to get caught up in these useless, God awful fantasies started by Al of all people."

What Marty had said sounded reasonable to the others, but they were still scared. It was becoming obvious he was more likely to punch their lights out than hold their hands to get them through this crisis made perhaps of fear if nothing else. *Maybe we're better off without Marty for a while,* thought Chris and Benny. They agreed with Marty not to meet with him unless it was real urgent that they do so.

Chris was the one with the muscles who worked out at the gym. He was there every Friday evening without fail so he was easy to find. Sheila met him there on the second Friday after her original death. He was not surprised to see her since Al's declaration that she was still around, but he was taken by the fact she didn't appear to have any injuries. He was expecting to see a twisted and bruised woman, but if anything, she looked healthy and in charge. She was with him in the change room while he was getting dressed. She was wearing jeans and a tight fitting red T-shirt. He had finished his workout and shower and wouldn't have minded some sensual action but not from her. She should have been dead and those close to him were dropping like flies. Something was very wrong.

"Stay away from me, bitch," he said, putting his shirt on as fast as he could. He grabbed his bag to leave. She blocked his way.

"You're not afraid of me, are you Chris?" she pouted ever so sweetly.

In response he shoved his way past her and out into the main area of the gym where all the machines and weights were kept and used. The gym was on the fourth floor overlooking an office building under construction. She followed him.

"You could have stopped Marty from killing me," Sheila told him. "Now I suppose I'll have to tell the police all I do know."

"That wasn't a smart thing to say," Chris told her. He picked up some heavy looking dumbbells and advanced toward her. She backed away toward the windows. He tossed the dumbbells at her and they landed square on her chest. This made her overbalance and, despite her vampire strength, fall. There was the sound of breaking glass and in seconds there was Sheila looking smashed up on the new concrete floor down below. Her legs were bent at odd angles and her neck didn't look at all right. She was gone for good now. Nobody could have survived.

Chris left the gym and phoned Benny via the pay phone at the nearby Chemist to tell him the good news. The comings and goings of Sheila were hard to take. Benny snickered like he usually did but it meant nothing. It was his nervous twitch. He didn't know what to believe. First she's dead, and then she isn't; and then she's dead once more. That was crazy talk and he didn't want to go there. He told Chris as much and hung up.

Others heard the crash of Sheila hitting concrete and an ambulance was sent to collect the body. Once more, she ended up on a slab. She wasn't dead in the conventional sense, but without a heartbeat she could fake the real thing quite well.

If she had stood correctly to have received the weights, she realized, she could have brought her vampire strength to the fore and she wouldn't have fallen. It was now a case of unlive and learn.

She was there for the rest of the night, one whole night besides, and then she scarpered. The coroner didn't know what to put in his report. Corpses stayed where you placed them and didn't make return visits only to run off a second time. The only explanation that he could come up with was that someone was playing games with him and his office. The police were informed and, once more, they took up a search for the missing corpse. The fact that it had gone walkabout for a second time ended up in the papers.

Chris was shaken by Sheila's disappearance. Who could have taken her? Maybe Marty was fooling around but why would he do that? Maybe he wanted to keep all the money so he was sending his old mates mad. That was it. What other explanation could there be? *Damn you Marty,* he thought sourly. *And I figured you for a friend!*

Four nights after her second trip to the slab, Sheila paid a social call on Chris who lived in an apartment three stories up in a new residential building. She rang the doorbell and he opened the door. He tried to stop her from gaining entry, but she pushed her way in. Before he knew it, she had him on the couch and was sucking the life out of him. She had presence of mind to stop three quarters of the way through, pick him up off the couch as if he weighed nothing and toss him out his open window. He managed to scream before he hit the pavement. He made an awful sound on the way down and during his unfortunate landing. It was music to Sheila's ears.

The next day Benny snickered and giggled when he read about Chris' apparent suicide. Now the money could be split two ways. But who would be the next corpse and how did Sheila fit into all this? For once he wanted to go straight but he figured it was too late. Even if he turned himself in, would that really prevent Sheila from getting to him? He smoked. He drank. It was getting dark and he was out of hard liquor and smokes, so he left his granny flat, jumped into his old blue Mini Minor and drove to the nearest bottle shop. There he saw Sheila. She was hanging around as if waiting for someone. It was him she expected. He grabbed his tire iron from the passenger's seat, sneaked up behind her and hit her over the head. She went down a treat. He then took her into his car and drove off.

Along George's River near the airport he stopped, tied her up, weighed her down with a rock and threw her in the river. Before long she disappeared into the murky brown water.

"Try getting out of this one, bitch!" he cried with maniacal glee in his voice as he witnessed the last of the bubbles break the top of the water where she had entered. Then he sniggered and giggled all the way on the drive back to his makeshift home.

Sheila hadn't expected to be hit from behind and when she did regain consciousness she found her lungs full of water. This was an uncomfortable state to be in but not unlife threatening. Drowning was no way to destroy a vampire unless it was with holy water. With her power, the ropes were dealt with. As she made her way out of the river she coughed up a lot of it and thought to herself that there was definitely a lad in need of a hard lesson only she could give.

Anxious, excited and relieved at the same time, Benny phoned Marty. He told his old friend who he supposedly was avoiding how he was the one to put that nuisance of a redhead to rest. Marty told him to sober up and hung up. Benny snickered and smirked at this rejection, figuring he'd get back in Marty's good graces later on. It hurt not being believed, but there was the money to consider. He was determined to move out of the granny flat and live a better life. Marty would understand and he'd get his share. That's all that mattered.

The following night Benny got a knock on his door. He opened it and there was Sheila, forcing her way in.

"You're dead! Ha! Ha! Dead!" cried Benny in shock and horror.

"So people keep telling me," Sheila said. "It took me a little while to snap your ropes. Lucky for me I don't need to breathe nowadays."

"Not breathe? Ha! Dead! Ha! Dead! Dead! *Dead!*"

"That's right. Dead."

Benny was in hysterics and could not control his laughter. Sheila couldn't have cared less. After taking a small sample of his blood, she forced him into his own car and drove him back to George's River. There she tied him up the way he must have tied her and dumped him in the water. The only difference this time was the fact that the victim wasn't unconscious but well aware of what was going on. Benny did struggle but there was nothing he could do to save himself. He no doubt laughed and giggled and snickered in his head as he drowned. Two weeks later some people were skiing on the river when one of the boat's rotor blades got stuck on something. The engine was turned off and what remained of Benny was found. It made headline news.

Marty was getting spooked. He was beginning to think the money might be cursed. He was wondering if he should leave the country for a while until whatever needed to blow over blew over. During the robbery, he had acquired a gun. All he did was threaten the old guard with his lump of wood and the fellow handed it over. The gun made him feel secure. No one was going to get at him with a gun in his hand. He had to make sure he had it on him at all times.

It was the beginning of summer and the little house in Revesby with the tin roof Marty had rented was heating up something fierce. He took a drive in his van to Cronulla and hit all the beaches including Wanda. Swimming with a gun on him wasn't something he could do and still rely on it when he needed to so he paddled his feet in the water. He had lunch at a fish and chip shop and spent the afternoon at one of the local pubs. He was beginning to unwind and it felt good. He hadn't felt this good in a long time. *Must get here more often*, he thought. *No sense having money if I don't enjoy it.*

The sun went down and he was still there. He had dinner at a trendy restaurant that sold paintings of surf and sun on the side. Before heading back to Revesby, he decided on one last visit to Wanda. He hadn't felt this relaxed in ages. Then it dawned on him that this was where he had taken all his girlfriends at one time or another, including Sheila.

There was the leathery flap of wings not far away and Marty was facing the woman he'd run down. She was smiling a smile that wasn't very pretty because her eyes were blazing red, setting off the natural color in her hair and giving him the jitters. Marty responded by getting the gun out of his belt. He had it half-hidden in his underpants so it took some effort but he was desperate for its protection. Sheila waited.

"Stay back!" he cried, waving the gun at her.

"You're not going to kill me again, are you?" she pouted.

"What do you want from me?!" he cried. *This isn't fair*, he wanted to shout but that, under the circumstances, would have sounded absurd.

"Just the money. Where is it?" she asked.

"In the van. In the back stuffed in Woollies bags. Take it and go," he said in a shaky voice. *I might as well order her around. It's not as if I can make her any madder at me than she is already.*

"Oh, I lied. I also want you."

She advanced on him and he pulled the trigger. The first bullet slammed into her chest, but she kept on going. He pulled the trigger again and again. The bullets smacked into her arms but did not stop her. The other shots fired hit her in the stomach and legs. By his seventh shot, she was breathing in his face. There was blood on her mouth and blood on her once white blouse, but he'd never seen her more alive. She breathed on him and what she breathed was the closed grave in all its accumulative horror.

"No," he screamed. "Don't!"

"But I want to," she cooed. "You're so handsome and I'm so dead. Can't you see that I love you? Can't you see we were meant to be together?"

She kissed him on the lips then went for the neck. In less than twenty minutes he slumped to the sand, dead as dead can be. She looked down feeling a little disappointed. She should have played with him longer. Those bullets did hurt going in, but the look on his face when they didn't put an end to her was priceless.

Sheila took Marty's keys from his pocket, his wallet, and looked to where he had parked the van. It was where he always parked at Cronulla. The money was where he said it would be. All up, her now very X boyfriend was no great thinker. She was so glad now this was, in fact, the case.

After being dead so much of late, even pretend dead, she felt happy to be alive or at least alive in her own way. She drove back to her new digs at Padstow, slept away the day and, when the sun set, took off in the van for Queensland. The thought of giving the money back to the bank had occurred to her, but the demonic side of her that had emerged since she'd become undead thought it a very bad idea. Besides, she felt she deserved something after all she'd been through. It wasn't as if she could go back to her parents. They would not understand having a daughter that only comes out at night and who might one day take their blood. No, it was best to move on.

Among the rubbish in the back of the van was a Beatles tape. She shoved it into the cassette player and listened to it on her way to her new unlife. Things could not have been better. Marty, who was a real prince of scumbags, had at last done right by her.

A Conversation on Saint Patrick's Night

There's an Irish pub near Centennial Park in Sydney, Australia famous for its verdant ambiance on one particular day and night of the year. It's not difficult to get to, the barmaids are pretty, and the barmen are quick with a joke. Kissing the blarney stone, metaphorically speaking, before you enter is the tradition and it's a good one. There are plush chairs in various places. Real leather covers the barstools; the suds are rich, creamy and oh, so black. The whisky's fine if you've a taste for it.

One year Bill Lake, a robust man in a brown suit, wandered in on that particular night. He had green socks on so he could blend in with the occasion. He wasn't sure what he was looking for but perhaps that was just as well. Adventure would have been the word he would have chosen, but adventure means many things to many people and the meaning changes over time. He got himself a schooner of Guinness from a barmaid and settled down on a form-hugging chair to listen to a man and his cat (yes, the cat does contribute) read from Ulysses. Since that kind of listening is thirsty work, he soon needed another schooner. He went back to the bar for a refill. There he met a tall man in black nursing a whisky. He had the mood of a poet about him and Bill suspected there was a tale or two to be had from the fellow. Perhaps it was a tale or two he was after.

"My name's Felix Peach," the man said. "If you've a mind, I have some stories, real life stories, to share with you."

"Sure," Bill said. "Why not? It is a green enough occasion and I've heard bits and pieces from Ulysses before."

"You'll not regret this." Felix took his drink and Bill into an area of plush chairs not far from where he'd been before but, in terms of storytelling, a universe away.

"There was a young man once," Felix began, "who was born with a lucky charm. No one had been born this way in generations and it was probable that no one in his bloodline would be in such a way for generations to come. You see, from the outset, women adored him and couldn't do enough for him. It wasn't just his mother; there were aunts and neighbors too. There were even strangers. Everyone of the more charming sex said what a little darling he was. Some said he'd break hearts some day. Others said he'd do well in movies or on television. In their eyes he was really something. Straight off, he had that gift other males could only envy.

"Usually this state of affairs ends when the child is bike riding age. Acne comes in, along with disconcerting growth spurts. For this lad, I think his name was Peter Smart, this was not the case. Sure, he grew but in a well balanced, well proportioned way. Acne never visited him and it never would. Throughout his teens he was sought after by the opposite sex who couldn't do enough for him. He took it all in his stride. He wasn't big headed about it. He had a magnet he couldn't explain and that was that."

"Sounds like quite a life," Bill said.

"It indeed was. Peter romanced 'em a treat going from his teens into his twenties. People thought there wasn't anything he didn't know about them because he was so good at it. He got a job easy enough in a glass factory and worked hard there. But weekends were his and he made the most of 'em."

"An envious life," murmured Bill. Felix nodded.

Bill was getting restless. So far this story wasn't making him feel all that good. Not many men, you see, have envious lives like that. He knew that drink could make him morose and he didn't want to go there. He wanted, above all, to be uplifted. He was now thinking about leaving Felix and drifting back to Ulysses. At least there none of the characters were pictures of perfection.

"Not too envious," Felix replied after a pause. "He was fine on one-night stands and with the girl over a weekend or maybe for a couple of weeks. Then relations either evaporated or changed. Usually they evaporated. Women weren't disposed to taking him seriously. He was an adventure for them and when the adventure was over that was that. If he heard from them again, it was as a friend. The lover part was short lived. He couldn't understand this, but learned to accept it."

"Still sounds pretty good." Bill tasted his Guinness. What man had never dreamed of being the king of one-night stands? Sure, he could sometimes think of better things to be but not, then and there, in that pub.

"Oh, it was, it was," Felix agreed in good humor. "Right up till Peter made his one big mistake. There came the day he met Kate. She was everything he could want in a woman. She was as beautiful as he was handsome. People thought they were a lovely couple. And, as the weeks of them being together turned into months, he figured he'd hit the jackpot. They became engaged and, before long, they were married."

"Still sounds pretty good." Bill swallowed more Guinness. Going from one-night stands glamour to a beautiful woman, who could argue with that kind of fate?

"And what a lovely wedding!" Felix enthused. "Every one of their friends was there including a few ex-lovers. No one knew, as they toasted the happy couple, what was beginning to stir under the surface."

There was a pause in which Felix allowed Bill to imagine this glorious event and wonder what indeed could have been stirring. In his mind's eye Bill could only envision the wedding with the happy faces and good cheer.

"Within three months there were all sorts of arguments and Peter was spending more and more time with his mates at the pub," Felix said. "Then when he got the sack from his job, he was spending at the pub like a hopeless alcoholic. Can you guess what went wrong?"

Bill thought about it a moment but had to shake his head. Perfect life before marriage, perfect marriage, what could go wrong?

"Well when it came to women," Felix intoned, "Peter had never been to the school of hard knocks. He never had to spend any time searching out what pleased them. He just took the sweet delicacies they offered him and came to think he had a natural right to them. But there's a world of difference between a one-night stand, a two week love fest, and a permanent arrangement. The thing was, no one had told him. Sure, the preacher did say words like partnership and cherish, but for Peter the concepts were alien or, if at all understood, they somehow favored him. Oh, even the first month of marriage, when the wife was expecting a real husband and not just a romping sex partner, he was in trouble. He stayed in trouble without a clue as to why. It was awful. He loved her in his own way and wanted no other, but that wasn't enough. She wanted understanding, devotion and a whole lot of other things. Do you want to know what happened?"

"Sure," Bill said, now caught up in what was being told. He was so caught up he hadn't noticed that Felix hadn't touched his whisky.

"Well, since you asked so nicely I'll tell you. Two years later they were divorced and Peter was still drinking. What's more, through drink he was beginning to lose his looks and all prospect of again getting permanent work.

"His whole life would have gone down the gurgler if he hadn't met this stunning blonde. They had met at his favorite drinking hole and she was the death of him. She was a vampire and she sired him."

"A vampire?" questioned Bill.

"Yes. A vampire. Three nights after his death his new life began. His ex-wife, Kate, he murdered. He sucked her dry of blood and there was no coming back for her nor did he want her back. There were lots of other women. Every night there was a woman. It must have felt like old times. One-night stands with a difference you might say.

"One night, however, he met up with a bunch of Freemason hunters calling themselves The Invisible Compass. He was lured into their trap by a pretty face belonging to the sister of one of his victims, not that he was able to see his blood feasts as actually producing victims. You see, he was rather self-centered.

"Anyway, The Invisible Compass had crosses and wooden knives and special guns with special bullets. This meant he was dead that second time before he knew it and there was no coming back this time. It was the finish of Peter Smart."

"That's…some story," Bill said, and meant it. Then, out of the corner of his eye, he caught movement at the bar. A young lady was leaving. She was short, blond but with that sort of pretty face that might have doomed someone like Peter Smart.

"Must dash," Felix said. "There's someone I must say a few words to. I'll be back in twenty minutes."

"I'll get another schooner," Bill replied. He finished his drink and went to the bar to get another. He could not help noticing how fast Felix left the pub to catch up with his friend. *She must be some friend*, he thought.

Felix was as good as his word. He returned twenty minutes later to his seat ready to spin another yarn. It was strange but, for a moment, Bill thought he caught a whiff of the slaughter house coming from his companion. Also Felix looked younger. His silver hair was a darker shade and his face had lost some of its paleness. Bill wondered if it was the alcoholic content of the Guinness catching up with him or if it were possible for Felix, or for that matter anyone, to change even in such subtle ways in such a short period of time.

"Ready for another?" Felix lifted his whisky glass as if he were about to drink but put it down again. He seemed reluctant to spoil its visually pure mountain water depths by consuming it. He was not a real drinker.

"Sure," Bill replied. He wondered what this one was going to be about.

"Just let me get into character; find the right voice for this one. It's a bit tricky…Been a while since I was around them there parts…Ah! Got it. It began some time ago in South Dakota in the USA," Felix began with enthusiasm, "back in the days when Dakota was still a territory and a chunk of it belonged by treaty to the Indians. There had been some rustling of cattle whose beef was earmarked for the local fort. Ranchers thought the Indians responsible. Thus tensions between ranchers and Indians rose. It seemed that war between white man and red was inevitable."

Felix paused and Bill pressed him to continue.

"One night a horse like no other galloped into Corkscrew. It was all black except for the eyes which were a blacksmith's kinda red. He might have gone unnoticed being black and all but he kicked up such a ruckus folk couldn't help but know he was there.

"He kicked his way into the livery, disturbin' the horses, and kicked his way out the other end. He harassed the ladies of the bordello by bustin' in on 'em and bustin' out. One thing was certain. He was searching for something or someone. With great gusto, he broke into several other places including the gun shop, but it was when he made his way into the saloon that he got to eat lead. A dozen cowpokes were not happy with having a horse of all things upset their drinking time, so they opened up and let him have it. Pistols blazed. A couple o' shotguns chugged. Being as there was that much artillery hammering away, there was a hell of a lot of smoke. People expected to see a stallion in pieces when it cleared. They were surprised to see not only the animal alive but in a temper.

"Well that critter busted up that saloon something awful and, as he made his way out, there was a call for him. Someone shouted out Thunder not far from where the bordello was, or perhaps I should say had been on account of how broken up the entrance way and the ground floor furnishings happened to be. Anyway, townsfolk were flabbergasted when the beast bolted to that voice so lickety-split there was a long trail of dust mixed in with silvery sparks shooting from the animal's shoes; following close behind. They were also amazed when they saw this man all in black glide onto – not jump onto mind but glide onto – the feisty creature's back and ride out with it to the prairie wilderness beyond.

"'There are caves in that direction,' said an old mule skinner to the sheriff of Corkscrew. 'I betcha a week's pay an' no mistake that's where we'll find 'em.'

"A pose was formed and they rode out in the direction of the caves. There was about twenty of 'em. Included was the preacher who was said to be a learned man from some place in Eastern Europe. Of note there was the sawbones and a couple of sharp shooters from the fort along with the usual bar flies and cowboys.

"When they got to the caves, daylight was breaking over the plains. It was a beautiful sight, all full of glorious colors you never get to see in the city, and the men took it to be an omen that everything was going to be all right.

"In the third cave, they found the horse and it appeared to be dead standing up. There were all the missing cattle also dead and a coffin in which a dead man lay. Someone swore. The preacher gave a prayer.

"Now cowpoke and general riff-raff aren't normally a superstitious lot, but the sight of all this fresh 'passing away' made the hairs on the back of their necks stand on end. It put the fear of God into the sharp shooters and the sheriff. Everyone turned to the preacher. All he had with him was a little silver cross and the good book. He was determined, however, to make the most of being there. It isn't every day a man of the cloth faces what he considered to be evil of this caliber.

"Someone had brought along a few sticks of dynamite. The preacher had the man put them at the entrance to the cave and to light the fuse. It was a one minute fuse which gave everyone plenty of time to skedaddle. The preacher was the last to leave. He hung back waiting for the others to go then flung his cross and book into the coffin.

"The sheriff thought he heard a cry of outrage and of pain coming from the cave that didn't belong to the preacher but he couldn't be certain. In any event, the entrance was blown up and everyone went back to town.

"They say that an hour or so later the preacher returned to the cave to plant wooden crosses he'd gotten from Boot Hill near the destroyed entrance. He also said prayers and tossed about some water. People wondered if he'd gone loco. The heat of the day does that to some and the sun did come on strong. Minds can come unhinged when faced with the bizarre and, let's face it; those animal remains and that coffin with its, no doubt, human corpse were a pretty bizarre find in those parts. One thing for sure, though, they never did see that horse or his rider ever again. What's more, the poaching of cattle stopped for good and relations between white man and red could get back to normal. At that stage neither Indian nor white man really wanted a dust up."

Felix lifted his drink, sniffed the heady contents and put it down. Bill took this to be the sign that the tale had ended. It was a pity because he was finding it quite enjoyable. He had hated Westerns growing up, but this was something different.

"Very entertaining," Bill said. "I'm going to get another refill."

"Just as well," Felix replied. "I see a friend leaving. I should say hello to her."

"You mean the blond girl with the sea green ribbon in her hair? You will be coming back then?"

"I have a beauty set in Berkley, California in the '70s," Felix said, anxious to be on his way but, at the same time, set the scene for his next masterpiece. "A sightseeing bus full of kids and teachers breaks down on the way to the college. It grows dark and they're set upon by vampires and become vampires themselves. Decades later they are still in school. It's their cover against the outside world getting wise. Imagine ice blocks on a stick made with frozen blood. Imagine a school where the students look like they are eleven and twelve but are over forty. Pretty good, eh? More later. Must dash."

Bill did get a refill. He decided to venture outside. He felt his head needed clearing from what he'd been drinking, and fresh air would do the trick. He also felt there was something going on, and he wondered what it was. Could Felix have two young lady friends he needed to chase after to talk to in the last minute way he'd been chasing after them?

At the entrance to the pub, as lucidity returned to his brain, Bill thought he heard a muffled cry coming from around the corner. With much trepidation he ventured forth only to be hissed at by his friend, Felix. It was a hiss that came from surprise, outrage and of having too many large teeth in an otherwise ordinary mouth. The large teeth in question were bloody and there were puncture marks on the young woman's neck. The young woman was in a daze looking paler than she had before.

"Go home," Felix said to the woman. "All is well. You had a great time tonight. Remember that. Drink plenty of fruit juice before you go to bed. There's a good girl."

The young woman, with a smile on her pretty face, dutifully walked away. She was under a spell – Felix's spell – that much was obvious. *Am I under his spell, too?* Bill shivered at the very idea.

"Now you know my secret," Felix said to a confused and frightened Bill.

Just then the barman, who had been at the bar when Bill followed Felix out, came around the corner and said: "Is everything all right Mr. Peach? This young fellow isn't causing you trouble, is he?"

"No, No," Felix said, smiling. "I just spooked him. He'll be fine. That's true, isn't it Bill?"

"Sure, sure," Bill mumbled, wondering if indeed he would be fine. He was still coming to grips with what he'd seen. Was it the alcohol talking or did what happen really happen? No one could possibly get that drunk on the number of schooners he'd had.

"Then I'll be off," Felix said. "I think our friend Bill here has had enough of my stories for one night and I have drunk my fill. I'll be back same time next year. And do be a good fellow and explain to Bill our arrangement. I wouldn't want any unexpected difficulties to occur next I appear here if you understand my meaning."

"I'll do that," agreed the barman.

"Cheerio then," Felix piped before transforming into a bat and flying away.

Seeing a man become a bat was almost too much for Bill. He looked to the barman for help in this matter. Maybe he was losing it.

"Well now you know most of it," the barman said to a still rather spooked Bill. "Felix Peach has been coming here every Saint Patrick's night since the place was first built. His story telling is pretty good and he always sends a couple of ladies home with such fond memories they become regulars in the hope of meeting him again. As far as I know, he hasn't killed anyone. He takes a little blood here and there. We like him and look forward to his visits even if he does have a habit of nursing his one glass of whisky till closing time. Are you going to keep our secret?"

"Sure," Bill agreed, still feeling thunderstruck. "Who'd believe me anyway?"

"That's the spirit," the barman said jovially. "Come inside and I'll shout you a schooner of black amber to celebrate in grand style our glorious saint."

"Why not?" Bill shrugged. "After all that's happened, I could do with a drink."

A Demon's Heart

Lucy watched over the city from her perch atop a plaster gargoyle. It was something she took pleasure in doing; that, and taking to the night wind. In bat form she felt she had complete control of the goings on below her. From above, she could perform the duties of judge, jury and, if taken by the mood, executioner.

Near a department store on 42nd Street a middle aged woman and her teenaged daughter were about to catch a bus home when two scruffy looking teenage boys with knives decided to change their plans. The bus driver might have played hero, but he took off with the bus instead. Possibly, a few hundred yards down, he radioed into his depot for the police but by the time they arrived, it would be too late.

Lucy decided to intervene. She swooped down and, as the boys were going through the middle aged woman's purse and bags for valuables, transformed herself into a tall, regal woman with violet eyes like a twenty-something Elizabeth Taylor but with an impish smile that was all her own. She was prepared to enjoy this little venture of hers into the world of street crime and inadequate street criminals.

"I see I am not the only predator out tonight," she told the thieves in a conversational tone. "Get much?"

"Back off, lady. Back off or get cut," said the taller of the young thugs, trying to act tougher than he felt. She could smell the fear on him. It reached out to her like an old friend.

"Oh, God!" the middle aged woman cried, grabbing her daughter by the hand.

The smell of fear was in the potential victims too and it was as rich a mix. *Who are the potential victims more afraid of? Me or the criminals?* She was taken aback when her rather sensitive nose said it was the criminals.

57

"I take it no one watched me arrive?" Lucy reasoned in mild disgust. "I suppose you were all too busy."

Humans could be the most unobservant of creatures. They were so obsessed with their own day to day or night to night trivialities they missed out on seeing a lot. They even missed out on witnessing the fantastic when it rubbed itself up against them and shouted: "I'm here! Look at me!"

"Cut you, bitch!" the smaller of the two robbers cried as his knife came close to making contact with Lucy's shoulder. He was using his words to get his courage up and to produce the rage necessary to make a strike. Of course he didn't have much of a chance of getting anywhere near her unless she wanted him. His first strike, which hit empty air, was proof. Her senses were so acute it was like he was moving in slow motion. But part of her fun was letting him believe he might succeed. With this in mind, she let him get closer with each pass until he was only a gnat wing's distance from his goal. Then, like a Venus flytrap, she snapped and so, for that matter, did his arm. He shrieked in a mix of extreme pain, horror and surprise.

"No!" cried the wounded robber's accomplice and tried to run. He didn't get far. Before he knew it, she was on him, using his own blade to slit his throat. Of course she had no need to play with his weapon at all. Her fangs were capable of rending flesh, but she was enjoying the irony of dealing the death blow with his own tool. She sampled the blood pouring forth from the great cut she'd made. It was lovely and warm but too much was springing forth at once. She sighed when she realized great amounts of it were going to go to waste. She hated waste and was saddened that she'd broken the hunter's code of making the most of a kill. She took as much as she could in before his well ran dry and that had to count for something; but the well drying up happened too quickly to satisfy her needs.

"Stay away!" the robber with the arm break shouted as she turned her attention to him. Covered in his friend's blood the way she was, she must have looked wild, even bestial. She noted he had tears streaming down his face from hurt and peaking fear. He was trembling and she could smell the sweat heavy upon his skin like salt upon potato crisps.

"We done killed no one, we done stabbed no one," he told her in an attempt to evoke her sympathy and understanding. "It's an act, a way to get money for food an' the bills."

"I am for real," she assured him as she went for his neck. This time she didn't bother with the knife. It was clumsy for her requirements and she respected the nature of the kill too much to ever use it again.

Besides, she wished to shut him up. His misuse of English was so abysmal she almost considered it a mercy slaying.

After she had feasted, Lucy turned around to converse with the mother and daughter only to discover they had gone. She was taken aback by this.

"How ungrateful," she said to herself and transformed back into bat form. She flew off peeved that the female humans hadn't stuck around to thank her. *How very rude of them,* she thought as she winged her way back to her wine cellar base. She could no longer put herself in their shoes in order to understand why. All she knew was that her sense of what was right had been violated and, because it had been violated, there would be consequences for the couple.

That night, curled up in her coffin with the pretty rose design lid and the silver (not brass) handles, she dreamed of her life in Kent, England where she had been an English teacher at a boarding school for young ladies. It had been the winter of 1895, and she was looking forward to her annual Christmas leave, when a horrid creature with red curls and freckles put the bite on her. There was no "by your leave" or "my apologies, Miss;" just breath smelling like rotten meat, a snake's hiss and her skin broken into by white ivory glistening under a street lamp.

She had gone for her usual evening constitutional around the school grounds and, three nights later, was in a confined space being stared down at by all and sundry. "This will never do," she told a priest who promptly fainted. Some nasty little girl with braces in her teeth screamed. Another girl, with straight blond hair and showing some decorum, tugged on a living teacher's dress and whispered that there appeared to be something amiss with the contents of the coffin.

A great fuss was made when Lucy Trubridge, deceased, climbed out of her supposedly eternal accommodation (a tacky pine construct with linen not silk lining and no pillow) and walked away. The service for her, she decided, had been abysmal and she told the quaking governess so on her way out of the church. The eulogy didn't even mention her founding the school magazine or how she had organized the school chess club. In all, it had been quite a shower. Perhaps it would have been best if she'd missed out on being there entirely.

The following night, she met up with the teenager who had sired her and she gave the naughty little minx such a scolding steam must have been coming out of her ears. Before long, the brat had tears running down those freckled cheeks of hers and down her gleaming fangs. "I didn't mean to offend, Miss," the red haired wretch blubbered. "I thought you'd have more fun as a vampire."

More fun? Since when had she mentioned fun as a concept to this little scruff?

Not wishing to be too mean, Lucy wiped away the tears from the girl's face with a handkerchief and said, "There, there. I take it the damage has already been done and there is no turning back. Best you cheer up and tell me all you know about vampirism like a good girl."

"Yes, Miss."

Lucy learned enough from the child to stay out of trouble and more besides from other vampires. She went to London to make an unliving there but certain belligerent men with stakes and crosses made her feel most unwelcome.

Tom Pool, an East-ender with large ears and a ruddy face, was the most belligerent. He and his team of Freemasons made unlife less pleasant for her than it should have been. He seemed to be able to sense where she'd turn up and act accordingly.

Once he'd cornered her outside a theatre showing an excellent English version of the French play Cyrano de Bergerac. She had been supping on a theatre attendant while enjoying the action and the dialogue and was not in the mood for Pool's brutal use of language. On this occasion, crosses were shown, forcing her to turn away. Four of Pool's strongest aides rushed forward to hold her while he shoved in the stake.

"Got you now, Miss La-de-da," Pool had crowed. By this stage she had murdered two of his men and sired three others so he, no doubt, had a right to feel peeved by her. The ones she'd sired had to be staked by Pool adding, no doubt, to his dislike of her and his desire to see her removed from his turf.

Having the men rush forward was a great mistake. They came between her and the four with the crosses thus negating them. She broke jaws and twisted limbs. There was self-righteous fury in her blows that spoke of a wonderful night spoiled by people she considered to be society's underclass. She could smell the repugnant odor of boiled cabbage on their flesh, no doubt expelled from their pores, reminding her of her days of boiled cabbage before she made something of herself. Reminding her of growing up as a commoner and how she fought hard to become a teacher in a well respected school for young ladies. Then, when she was settled and happy, she had to die and lose it all. Remembering all this, including the loss, added to her outrage.

She only stayed three or four decades in London before choosing to move on. By then Pool was dead, having died of a heart attack, and most of his men, thanks to her efforts, were gone as well. A new breed of vampire hunter was emerging onto the scene with new, scientific methodology she felt uncertain about. This feeling of uncertainty told her it was time to go.

She suffered a similar lack of hospitality in Manchester, Oxford, Leeds and Dover. Some old vampire suggested America was the place for her and so here she was in New York, in the summer of 1972, trying to acclimatize herself to, not only the way the English language was being tortured by common grammatical misuse, but the total lack of good manners by the locals. It was the land of the barbarian.

Of course, to be fair, London, Manchester, Leeds and Dover hadn't been much better. London had its great art museums with the marvelous lighting effect works of Henry Wallis, Dante Gabriel Rossetti's romantic paintings of times past and Sir John Everett Millais' moments of grand rural life. Manchester and Leeds had industry and movement while Dover had a great view of France across the channel.

Dover had pelicans. In late evening or at night they could be seen taking off from the water or the beach, circling and landing. Lucy thought, no matter how many times she saw it happen, she couldn't help but believe it to be a wonder a creature of such bulk could fly at all. Yet once airborne they were majestic and, in their own peculiar way, quite beautiful. Take offs and landings, however, were always clumsy, abysmal affairs. Seagulls, which Lucy came to despise, tended to laugh at them but stopped when the conquest of the air was achieved. In this way pelicans were never meant to be land bound but to soar like the best and to show the luckless gravity trapped mortals below how it could be done. Yes, showing how it could be done had, in many ways, been Lucy's crusade. It had been her very existence, her lot in life.

Lucy saw her struggles against personal poverty of both body and spirit as a pelican talking to the air. She had been pitiful once, even comical and she knew it. Dressed in hand-me-downs as a child she shouldn't have had much of a future. Yet, like the pelican, she had left the ground and in leaving it she had become her true self.

For her music, art, novels, theatre and self-discipline provided the propulsion she needed to break with the earth. Her job in the country dealing with the children of the well off and the well-to-do had kept her in the metaphoric sky. The clumsy landing, of course, came with the transformation. Life deserted her and unlife could only, in a physical sense, see her into the heavens. Yet she clung to the beauty she had known even if the beauty no longer belonged to her. She would never, ever accept herself as being a grounded soul. *My wings nowadays may be leathery rather than feathery*, she told herself as she thought of Dover and its pelicans, *but they're still wings*.

61

Oxford had been barely more acceptable than the other places in England where she had, for a time, made her unliving. There, she had almost had her head removed from the rest of her body by a ghastly Shakespearian actor wielding a real medieval broad sword as Bottom in a production of A Midsummer Night's Dream. What he was doing with a broad sword showed how little he knew about Shakespeare, the play, the role of Bottom, and Elizabethan England. She enjoyed taking his life. She saw it as a mercy to a poor player upon the stage and as a necessary protection to a great theatrical work. It was in Oxford she came to terms with certain abbreviations in speech that had crept into the language and began to even use them on occasions. *I must keep up with the times*, she had told herself and she meant it.

Now she was in New York and the sun was setting. With a yawn and a stretch she got out of the coffin she had imported from Italy (the dirt in the bottom of course was from England), washed up in the basin of water her man-servant provided for her use, toweled herself and set off into the city proper.

She flew around 42nd Street hoping to catch up with the mother and daughter who had snubbed her so she could punish them. When it was obvious they were elsewhere, she took to the direction of the zoo. At the zoo, she came across two louts in their early twenties trying to poke caged grizzly bears with the nasty ends of broken wine bottles. This she considered to be the height of poor sportsmanship. What chance did the grizzly bears have? As she descended to join the bear baiters, something that should have gone out of fashion in Shakespeare's day, she once more took on her humanoid form.

"Desist and go," she told the cruel ones in a cold voice, "and I may allow you to live."

They decided to use less than proper words when addressing someone of her sex so she concluded that any further discussion would prove pointless. What's more, they were not afraid of her as they should have been. This was made clear to her by their smell.

Didn't they see my entrance? It was magnificent but apparently wasted on them. Why are humans so self absorbed?

The first one to strike out at her with his broken bottle was knocked flat by a blow to his proverbial glass jaw. She took little pleasure in seeing him go down so quickly but it was so hard to hold back in order to draw things out.

For the second one she had something more special in mind. To his astonishment, she took on her bat form, wrested the glass out of his hand with her claws and flew him to the top of a lion's cage. There he gawped as she became humanoid and began to bend some of the bars. He didn't understand what she was doing at first but, when she had made a hole big enough to fit a man through, he knew.

He pleaded with her not to do it but she dropped him into the cage. He landed relatively unhurt. He might have been all right just keeping out of the way of the big cats if not for one thing. His fall had been softened by his landing on the lioness' head. The lioness was perturbed at having her sleep interrupted. Her male companions, three adult brutes also used to being left alone when the zoo was closed to the public, seemed equally upset. The nasty human who had given the lioness a headache did not last long. Come the morning, the lions and lioness were not very hungry for their usual steak breakfast.

While this was going on, the first bear baiter was coming to. He was trying to shake off the effects of Lucy's punch so that he could run. As he was getting to his feet after numerous attempts to do so, the vampire was there to grab him by the shirt collar and draw him to her teeth.

"Please! Don't! No!" he cried. She stopped long enough in her drinking to say: "I wonder what those words would be in bear talk and whether we heard them here earlier." She then resumed her drinking until he was nothing more than a husk.

A week later, Lucy did catch up with the mother and daughter she had a problem with. They were near the old fish market. With an effort, she managed to pick them both up with her bat claws and drop them in the middle of the harbor. The daughter could swim quite well but not so the mother. One lived and the other drowned.

Around about this time there was an open air production of Hamlet being staged in Central Park. Lucy went along to one of the night performances. The staging was quite basic, which was reasonable for a tragedy in the epic tradition, and the acting superb. Her only complaint was a spear carrier in the second act that fidgeted too much and thus was distracting to the audience. In her usual style, she made sure he'd never fidget during a performance again. She figured he could be replaced.

A month passed in which Lucy did little beside take down the occasional drunk or panhandler. A young vampire had told her the heat was on and that she had better lie low. After getting what was said translated into more digestible English by yet another, older creature of darkness, she at last saw the point being made. Bodies had been turning up too regularly and, if she wasn't careful, the hunters were sure to find her. Since she was beginning to like New York, especially the Battery Park area where there were lots of lovely shadows, she was loath to move on. She considered being careful to avoid certain unpleasantness but a small price to pay to be able to unlive where she wanted to unlive. *I can be practical,* she told herself.

Culture had been a big part of Lucy's life and she tried, as much as possible, to make it a part of her unlife. When an art exhibition, with paintings celebrating things gothic, opened in the Bronx, she couldn't wait to attend. Since it was on at night, she could go; it was just a matter of deciding whether to feed before or after. She chose after because she might find someone there she might want to sire. It was something she hadn't done in recent decades but something that had crossed her mind of late more than once.

Unlife could be lonely without proper companionship. What she needed was a gentleman of the old school. He had to be strong and passionate with more than a passing knowledge of fine swordsmanship but with a poet or a painter's whimsy. She hoped they were still being bred somewhere and that at least one was willing to take the dare of coming to America. If so, then an art exhibit seemed the perfect place to find him.

It was strange being among humans and not concerning herself directly with the hunt. She was, after all, looking for a mate rather than a meal which was a somewhat different proposition. The demonic side of her vampire nature she had set on simmer and the more human side she had turned up as high as it would go which, these days, wasn't high at all. She remained aware that she was different from the humans gathered to view the art and did what she could to blend in. She could handle small talk even if she felt it was a complete waste of her time.

The painter's name was Carl Schuler and he was of German ancestry. He stood tall and aristocratic in his gray suit. He did not slouch like many men and women in the modern age did and his diction was beautiful. He even clicked his heels together and bowed in the best Prussian tradition when introducing himself. It was an affectation, since he did have an American accent and no trace of German, but it was quite charming. He had the heart of a poet and, if this meant he liked to pretend at times, that was fine with her. She found herself taken with him. Was he also good with a sword? Only time would tell.

"What do you think of my little display?" he asked her. She knew by his eyes that he really did want to know.

"I take it that your earlier efforts were neo-primitive such as the work of Paul Klee," she began. "You could bring moldering skulls and wandering plague victims to life with great panache. Then you turned to a more realistic style. I find your ruined castles and churches fascinating."

"Is there anything you don't like?"

"Your women."

"My women?"

"They are too docile. Not all 19th Century women were like that. Mary Shelley, for example, wasn't docile and nor were the Bronte sisters."

"No. I suppose you are right. Is there any particular painting that takes your fancy?"

Lucy didn't answer him at first. She took her time perusing some of her favorites. In terms of color they were blues and grays and blacks with the occasional splash of red, but one was a little different. It was of a modern hippy girl staring up in delight at a pyrotechnic sky. The lightning was bruising the heavens and the girl was in raptures over it. She was about to get wet from the oncoming storm but she didn't care. She was far from dominant but she wasn't as passive as his other women.

"This one," she said, pointing at the happy hippy that was as one with the violence of nature.

"You are a true romantic," he told her and took the painting from the wall. "Here. It is yours and with my compliments."

"I couldn't."

"You must. I insist. Will you have dinner with me tomorrow night? We can meet here an hour before the exhibition opens."

"Yes. I would be delighted."

"For now please take the painting. You understand art much better than most people here. I regret I have to leave you but my sponsor would not forgive me if I did not mingle with my other guests."

"Farewell until tomorrow."

"Farewell."

He kissed her hand before taking his leave. It was a proper as well as, no doubt, sincere gesture. *You are impressive*, she thought.

Lucy took the painting. She didn't realize how much she wanted it until it was in her hands. On her way back to her digs, she came across a street bum to snack on. The poor creature was swept off his feet and drained before he knew what was happening. It was only a small effort to keep the painting safe in one hand while she used the other plus her fangs to feed. The bum didn't seem to notice. The smell from such a putrid creature didn't bother her. She had other things on her mind.

Back in her coffin, with his painting up against the wall near the racks of fine wine, cognac and whisky, she settled down to dream the day away. Yes, Carl Schuler was going to make an excellent vampire and companion. She could hardly wait to sink her teeth into him. It was different to her usual hunger but it was hunger.

Three hours before nightfall something happened. There was a loud crunching sound as a modern battering ram smashed in the door to her cellar. She woke with a start, threw the lid off her coffin to go deal with the disturbance and reprimand her man-servant for allowing her rest to be disturbed. Bullets fired from above smashed the older wine, whisky and cognac bottles. Next, two lit torches were tossed down to where the contents of the destroyed bottles lay spilled. The result was spectacular. There were flames and, when other bottles got overheated, explosions.

In fear of being burnt alive, Lucy grabbed her painting and ran up the stairs. Blinded by smoke and the horrid sun, she didn't notice the bamboo spear in her way until it was too late She ran straight into it, impaling herself upon it. The sharp end went into her heart piercing it most savagely. The person holding the weapon held it firm. She was a young twenty-something woman with long red hair and freckles.

With the shock of what was happening to her, the painting left Lucy's hand and fell back into the cellar to be engulfed in the raging inferno. She let out a moan of despair but could do nothing about it. In the distance she could hear sirens. The fire would be put out but neither she nor the painting could be saved. The sun was doing its work upon her and so was the bamboo. Pain engulfed her informing her that her time would soon be at an end.

"Die!" cried her freckle-faced executioner. "For my brother who wanted to be an actor."

Brother? Actor? Thought Lucy as her breathing became more labored and horrendous. Then, in a flash of insight common to people who are dying, she realized her killer was the sister of that poor player who could not stand still during the outdoor performance of Hamlet. Despite it meaning now her finish, she could not regret removing that particular incompetent from life. She did admire the sister's loyalty to her sibling and her determination to avenge him.

As her vision began to blur, the two men in plain black suits standing next to the vengeful one began to talk to her. One was bleeding from a shoulder wound. Perhaps her man-servant had tried to defend her with his revolver but was outnumbered and outclassed.

"We're CIA," the larger of the two informed Lucy. "Both INTERPOL and the English Freemasons told us a vampire of your description was likely to turn up in the Big Apple and here you are."

"We caught up with your movements at that Hamlet highbrow gig," said the other one, putting an already bloody handkerchief to his shoulder. "The sister of the man you murdered thought it would be apropos if you went out on the end of a spear."

"The English Freemasons told us what a culture vulture you are," added the redhead, twisting the spear as she spoke. "They suggested drawing you out with an art exhibition. Carl cooperated. He's a friend of mine. We thought if you took one of his paintings it would slow you down and we would be able to follow you back to your lair. As it turned out, we were right. You didn't risk turning into a bat for fear of scratching the paint with your claws."

"We ran into a little difficulty with your bodyguard," said the wounded man. "But it was nothing we couldn't handle. He's up the road with a bullet in his head."

"I...will...have...my...revenge!" Lucy gasped, her eyes going milky and her skin and hair peeling away from her body.

"Just die!" cried the redhead, twisting the spear in her hands.

"No!" Lucy shouted and made a lunge with both hands for her tormentor's throat. The combined weight of the two women as they fell onto the pavement snapped the spear in two. Lucy grabbed one of the pieces and shoved it, with all her remaining might, into her enemy's chest. She then sighed, there was a death rattle and she was gone. She would deteriorate to a skeleton and then dust but, in terms of spirit, she was already gone. Minutes later, the woman who would destroy a vampire also perished.

The men threw both bodies, with the battering ram they had used, into the holocaust below. Then the firemen arrived and they blended into the gathering crowd. They were nowhere around when the police got there and started asking questions. The firemen managed to put out the fire before other buildings could be consumed. Reporters tried to find out what had happened but no one mentioned vampires and man-servants and no one ever would. The CIA, INTERPOL and a special Freemason group in London all added to their secret files and then locked them away. The case was closed.

Over the phone, Carl was informed of what had happened. In his studio he poured himself a glass of port and drank a toast to a most splendid creature of the night that was no more. He then toasted her executioner and the war between light and darkness that continued and would continue forever. He became determined after that to get drunk by making further toasts.

The Panhandler

Sydney, NSW, Australia, winter, 1978

Carl Turner was cold and he was going to get colder. There was a wind whipping up Elizabeth Street from the waters at Circular Quay that was ghastly. He had on a few tattered old jumpers and a pair of patched up pants. His socks and shoes had matching holes. He had a shopping bag containing one moth eaten blanket half his size and a bottle holding no more than a few mouthfuls of the roughest rough red. Still he couldn't complain. It hadn't been a bad day.

He'd managed to scrounge enough money off passersby outside the big cinema complex in George Street to buy lunch which consisted of one hot dog and a can of Pepsi. For dinner he got bangers and mash washed down with orange juice and coffee at the shelter. He would have liked to have stayed the night there but they didn't have the room. So now he was looking at the park benches near Central, deciding which one faced away from the bitter breeze enough to offer some shut-eye for weary bones.

There was a time when the local coppers would come around the parks at night and pick bums up as vagrants. It wasn't a bad deal. If you couldn't be fixed up at the shelter then you'd make yourself available to be run in by the law. For your trouble, they'd give you a place to wash up, decent food and a warm spot with plenty of blankets to help you sack out. Hell, most of the time they didn't bother locking the cells. They figured why should a bum run away when he had all the comforts and somebody looking out for him?

Yeah, it was a sweet deal that came to a close when the vagrancy act ended. It no longer mattered if you didn't have a cent on you. The police didn't have the power to arrest you. Some wanted to, especially in the middle of winter. So-called vagrants were taken into custody on suspicion of this and that on so called mercy raids. Such raids couldn't be kept up forever and too quickly vagabonds found they couldn't get the help they once got from the cops.

The first winter without the vagrancy act took its toll. The shelters that couldn't cope before still couldn't. There were deaths from pneumonia and tuberculosis that, if the cops had been allowed to do their jobs, might have been prevented. A bum in police custody got food, warmth and medical treatment. A bum on a park bench got nothing.

It was difficult for Carl to remember back to when he wasn't down on his luck. His dad had been all right up until his mother died of cancer. Then he remarried and things went wrong. Carl came to feel like an outsider in his own home. Then, at fourteen, he no longer had a home and was forced to take to the streets.

There wasn't much a fourteen-year-old kid could do to make a crust. He did manage to get a paper route and that left finding a place to shelter for the night. At first he used the public school grounds until the principal got wise to what he was doing and security chased him out. Then it was the beach areas in summer and park benches, bus stop shelters, and telephone booths in winter.

"Hey! I'm Doctor Who," he told himself on occasions when he did find a cozy telephone booth to settle in. This was on account of Australian telephone booths, apart from being red instead of blue, looked like British Police Call boxes. This was a few years after he'd taken to the streets. He knew the British science fiction show from old newspapers and magazines people had discarded.

The paper route lasted a year. The newsagent said he had to let him go because of his unkempt appearance. He was beginning to smell and customers complained about that as well.

"Look, kid," the newsagent had said, not wanting to be too big a bastard, "when you straighten yourself out, I'll be glad to have you back."

"Sure," Carl had replied, gulping down his anger. He felt there was nothing else for him to say and where there was once a bit of help and pride in work well done there was now nothing. He cried that night, but it was the last time he'd do so for a long time. Tears didn't buy much in the real world or so he thought at that particular juncture in his life.

He wandered from town to town hoping to find work and a place to call his own. Sometimes he did all right as a fruit picker. The wages weren't terrific but they came with bed and board. He ate well, showered every day and could put aside money for clothes. But fruit picking was and still is seasonal and, when the season for it was over, he was once more unemployed.

At eighteen he tried to get into the army but they wouldn't have him. He had flat feet and he could barely read and write. Also, he had a bad attitude toward taking orders as revealed in the psyche test they gave him. Then there was the matter of his birth certificate and other items to prove his identity. The fact was he didn't possess any evidence that he was born, that he had any schooling at all or that he could call himself an Australian citizen.

"I didn't drop out of the sky, you know," he had told a recruitment officer.

"I know son," came back the reply. "But we still need proof."

Decades rolled by and he was no longer fit for fruit picking or other manual labor. The years on the streets had taken a lot from him and he could no longer pretend he was capable of lifting and carrying all day for someone else. There was nothing left to do but panhandle. He had done it over the years between jobs but now it was all he could do.

"A couple of bob please, guv," he knew to say and to give them the sad eyes that reflected best the trouble about himself and his situation. He knew to thank them kindly for anything given in case he came across them again.

He figured Sydney was the best place for him to be. Panhandling, after all, was best done in major cities where the crowds gathered and there were lots of people with spare change. He thought he'd see out his life begging outside movie theatres and cafés. What else could he do? What else could this world offer him?

On a wind blasted night, when he couldn't get into a shelter and he had settled as best he could on a bench to endure his lot, something unforeseen happened. A lady adorned in a fine black silk dress walked by. She was tall, majestic and rather beautiful in a severe, angular sort of way. Someone could have cut bread with her chin and cheek bones. How she could wander around like that when his lips had turned blue and he'd only just stopped shaking was a question he didn't bother contemplating. He accepted the fact that he was cracking up and she wasn't real. Either that or he had left his mortal coil.

Her eyes were opals like the expensive ones he'd seen in a shop in Town Hall that had come from Broken Ridge. They were black, sure, but within the blackness, you could see an amazing amount of color and life. This color and life drew people to the stones just as the deeply set color and life in her orbs compelled him to go with her. She didn't have to say anything. She stood still for a moment and waved her hand indicating that he should follow. He couldn't believe how eager he was to reply with his feet.

He left his blanket and bag behind. Dorrie, an old girl sacked out on a nearby bench and a good friend of his, shouted out to him to pick up his gear lest it get stolen but he could barely hear her. Least ways, it didn't matter. The blanket meant nothing. The few drops of rough red in his bottle meant nothing. The bag he'd carried around for years no longer existed for him. Only the silent command to follow what he now took to be an angelic apparition counted for anything.

Somewhere in his mind he remembered a preacher telling him devils were once angels. They had disobeyed God and so had lost their wings. It then occurred to him that the angel taking him somewhere didn't have wings.

She took him to the back entrance to an expensive looking hotel. They took the service elevator up to a wondrous series of rooms. He had seen such rooms on the covers of newsstand magazines but he didn't think they existed in real life. In the lounge area, there were plush black leather chairs and a black leather lounge so long it could seat a dozen people. In front of this arrangement stood a large color television set. Throughout the rooms, the various statues and paintings looked like they cost a lot of brass. The bathroom was pristine white from the bars of soap to the tiles to the various mirrors reflecting the white back on itself. Funny, but the mirrors either didn't see his angel-come-devil or chose to ignore her.

She told him to shower good and put on the suit she had laid out in the bedroom for him. Her voice electrified his mind. It was sweet but with an unexpected edge to it. He obeyed her, basking in the overall body glow he got from the heat of the water striking his body, massaging him, reviving him. The idea of death and being dead left him. Just who was this lady anyhow and what could she want from him?

He left his rags and got dressed in the suit she had provided. The clothes were Italian. The shirt was fine silk as was the black tie with the white stripes. The suit coat was expensive gray wool. The black shoes were the type that would last maybe ten years before they'd even show a hint of needing to be replaced. *Rags to riches*, he told himself and shook his head. It didn't make sense.

He was full of questions when he came out of the bathroom but she bade him join her on the lounge. From there her eyes took over. She kissed him on the neck. He felt flattered and at the same time helpless to resist. Then there was a mild stinging sensation followed by a lightness in the head he couldn't explain. It was as if something were being drawn away from him, something important. The sensation stopped and he could see her face. It was still beautiful but there was blood on her lips and teeth. Why was there blood?

Her fingernails were long and sharp. She used one of them to cut a line across one of her breasts then bade him drink. Without a second thought he did as he was told. *Was this the way sexy women behaved?* he wondered. He didn't have any references in his life to go by. He hadn't had much to do with the opposite sex. Deep down he knew something was wrong but part of him basked in the wrongness and cried out for more. He had been starved of any affection. He wasn't sure if he knew the meaning of the word.

After a while she had him sit up and she went back to doing something with his neck. He became drowsy and, before long, nodded off.

Three nights later he woke up. There was something different about him but he couldn't figure out what it was. He licked his teeth with his tongue and discovered that the broken ones, made so by years of poor dental hygiene, no longer felt broken. They didn't feel artificial like dentures either. It was as if he had re-grown a new set while he had been snoozing.

"I am Mia," said the woman whose hotel room he was in. She had been studying him up close. He could tell because his ears tingled under the spotlight of her gaze.

"Look, whatever you've done for me," he began as he sat up and climbed off the bed, "I appreciate it. I really do. But I'd like to know why and, well, what's going on."

"I am Mia," she repeated. "Watch."

He did so and noticed her skin begin to change. First it took on a gray tint then it became black. What's more, while this was happening she was shrinking and her arms were becoming thinner and more flexible. Before it could register, he was facing a flying bat, not a woman. Then the change reversed itself.

"Women can't do that," Carl said, perplexed at what he'd seen. "You can't do that. Either I'm dreaming, I've got the DTs, or I'm mad or…"

"Dead?" proposed Mia. "You've been there. You're no longer there. Take a seat. We have much to discuss."

Over glasses of blood, the blood having been procured from a car crash victim the night before, she told him about being undead and taught him how to change into bat form. She told him the plans she had for him and other male vagabonds. It was then he discovered she had a wicked sense of humor.

Long ago, in the mountains of Carpathia, Mia had met a wizened crone who had forbidden knowledge the Church had been attempting to suppress since the 4th Century. It had been knowledge passed down via word of mouth from mother to daughter. Since the old one had lost her only daughter in a snow slide and was dying, it went to the last living person she saw who was not clergy. Mia was fortunate enough to be that person.

She told Mia there were two reasons why she gave so much away. The first was to spite the Church that had kept her on the run all her life. The second was to keep alive old arts she felt belonged in the world. Mia didn't care. She remembered all she was taught and promised to pass it on someday. She wondered what the ancient would have thought had she known her recipient was a vampire.

Since those East European nights, Mia had used mesmerism to cover her tracks and to live the good unlife. Now, with Carl and other select men, she wanted to play with glamour. In her hotel rooms, she had created a handful of innocent looking necklaces she had dipped into a special brew while calling upon forces of light and darkness to aid her. Held up to a reading lamp, they gleamed with supernatural power. Sure, she could have made the necessary spells without the trinkets but she was after a more permanent solution to the question of appearance. The necklaces would hold the glamour in place for much longer than mere words and gestures. Examining the jewelry she knew that she was ready to push her plans forward and to enjoy her in-joke on a society so enraptured by mere packaging, by mere image.

After making sure he understood all he needed to know about vampirism and mesmerism, Mia gave him the necklace made for him. The central black stone reminded Carl of her eyes and the effect they had had on him. It gleamed sinister in his hands as if anxious for mischief.

"Before you put it on," Mia warned, "you must think of yourself as a handsome man. You must have an image in your mind of this look. Do you understand?"

"Yes," answered Carl, studying the necklace and concentrating on an image at the same time.

He put the necklace on but nothing seemed to happen. He couldn't look in a mirror to try to detect any change because mirrors no longer worked for him. He wondered why Mia bothered keeping them around. He gathered it was one of her eccentricities.

"It worked!" cried Mia, clapping her hands with delight. Before her stood a twenty-something Atlas with short blond hair, muscles, blue eyes and a puzzled look on his well put together face.

"It did?"

"Yes! We're on our way."

"I wish I could see myself."

"You will, dear, in the eyes of your victims."

The other bums Mia recruited over the coming weeks were a shabby lot. There was Billy Reed with his purple nose broken in three places and each time never properly healed; Samo Johnson who had cauliflower ears from his boxing days and a beer belly to boot; and Pat Ironmonger whose face was like a patchwork puzzle all in various shades of red, white and gray. How he got that way no one knew, not even Pat. Zombies might have had more appeal than this crowd. Mia cleaned them up, dressed them in nice suits, made them over into the undead and let the necklaces loose on them. She was having the time of her unlife.

Broken-nosed Billy took on the appearance of a young Errol Flynn; cauliflower-eared Samo looked like Frank Sinatra when he was in his late thirties, and Pat was a definite undead ringer for Sean Connery. Billy and Samo picked out Carl as a double for Chesty Bond, an advertising character once used to sell men's singlets.

It was weird seeing derelicts look like movie stars. The new clothes helped put them in the mood but it was hard not to see the genuine magic released upon the world. Mia was pleased.

"We have something here," she told them. "Stick with me and we can't go wrong."

What was required of the men was simple. Mia was starting up a male escort agency. Through the necklaces the men could act as escorts to women who would pay to be with good looking men. What did the men get out of it? They got blood from the women and a cut of the profits. They also got to unlive in nice surroundings. What did the women get for their loss of blood and their money? They got the illusion, via mesmerism and glamour, of having had a truly wonderful time.

For six months the escort business was a regular gold mine. There weren't any complaints from the ladies and, as for the Freemason vampire hunters that hung their hats somewhere in Macquarie Street, they had no idea there was a nest of vampires operating in their city.

Then, one night, Samo messed up bad. He drained one of his clients of blood and found he had a corpse on his hands. Not knowing what to do, he phoned Mia for instructions. She had the body weighted and dumped in the harbor. The following night everyone was called to a special meeting to discuss what had happened.

"Why didn't you follow orders?" Mia asked sharply of Samo. Everyone around the table stared with accusing eyes at the poor Frank Sinatra look-alike who had done the wrong thing.

"I don't know," said Samo. "It just happened. I lost control."

"We get three women a night," Billy reasoned. "Getting a little of what we need from each is plenty for the rest of us. Why be greedy? Why are you looking for trouble?"

"Corpses are trouble." Pat grimaced. "We don't want greed and trouble."

"It was a mistake," Samo pleaded. "We all make mistakes. I promise it won't happen again."

"Yes," Mia agreed. "Mistakes do happen."

She filled a glass with a clear liquid from a bottle and placed it on the table in front of Samo. He looked at it and then at her.

"Drink up, Samo," she said. "Drink up and we'll say no more to you about this unfortunate business."

"But I thought we only drank blood," Samo said in a confused voice.

"This is an exception," Mia said. "Drink up and we'll say no more to you about your little error in judgment."

Samo upended the liquid into his throat and regretted having done so. His eyes bulged and his mouth steamed. He shook as if being torn apart from within. He tried to scream but he couldn't. The glass dropped, shattering on the floor as the unlife seeped out of him. In mere moments, he was reduced to nothing more than a hollow, lifeless shell.

"What was in that?" Carl cried, pointing to the broken glass.

"What he drank?" asked Mia, all innocence. "Why, holy water. I wouldn't recommend it, just as I wouldn't recommend any more mistakes from anyone."

Samo's necklace was taken from him, reducing him once more to the appearance of a bum, this time a very dead bum. His body was dumped near some rubbish bins. The bite marks on his neck had healed and, as for what he died of, it would look to most coroners as a case of bad booze or maybe battery acid. Since drunks desperate enough would drink anything, his second "death" was likely to be recorded as misadventure. Problem solved.

Mia and her remaining men lay low for a week then they got back to business. Carl, after seeing the nasty side of Mia, was extra careful with his clients as were the rest. Still, about a month later, a body was fished out of the harbor and an investigation begun.

It seemed the woman Samo had killed was a visiting business woman from the USA with connections to a dozen local politicians. It was bad enough when she was reported missing. Now that she was officially dead, and the papers had made headlines out of it, her last days were bound to be gone over in minute detail and that would spell trouble for a lot of people including a certain escort agency.

As head of the escort agency, Mia was interviewed by the police and stated that she had never seen the deceased woman. Perhaps the poor dear had meant to call in for an escort but had met with foul play before she could do so. The officer seemed satisfied with this account but it was difficult to tell. Some instinct told her to be on guard. It told her to start thinking about cutting her losses.

It was unusual for Carl to be called upon to perform escort duty for two pretty, blonde twenty-something women, but he was happy to oblige. Anything to get his mind off what had happened to Samo and the danger they could well be in because of the destroyed vampire's stupidity.

Why do they need an escort? he wondered. *Surely they could have their pick of men without bothering with an agency.*

They were in his lounge room chatting to him when he began to weave a spell with his eyes. Enchanting two women at the same time wasn't easy. Knowing you've succeeded on both was as difficult. One on one was preferable, but it was hard to resist such new blood walking into your unlife even if it was only for part of one night.

Carl thought he had them both under and was about to put the bite on one when he felt a burning sensation on his face. He moved back only to realize the burning sensation had come from a small silver cross pressed against his skin. Then he discovered another silver cross aimed at him. One of the women took a little wooden stake out of her purse and held it like she wasn't new to the staking game. The other had a clove of garlic. The smell was sickening. In response, Carl threw a sofa pillow, knocking a cross out of one of the hands. He followed through by bolting for the door but, upon opening it, he found himself facing a large man with a handgun.

It didn't matter that normal bullets don't kill vampires. They could hurt like hell and wounding, for the moment, would have been bad news. If there were enough wounds, he would be helpless. He didn't want to be helpless amongst people who didn't have his best interests at heart. But the undead can be fast. Before the man could pull his trigger, Carl knocked him aside and was in the corridor and down the stairs while the fellow was busy catching his breath. When he got to the third floor, he transformed into a bat and flew the rest of the way out of the building.

He flew from the building complex where his apartment was situated, and where he entertained the ladies, to Mia's abode. It wasn't much of a distance away but, if his heart could have thumped, it would have been thumping long and loud all the way. He took on the shape of a man once more to take the elevator to her rooms. He was surprised when he found the rooms deserted. Her clothes were gone and so were the rings and other adornments she kept on her bedroom table. Mia had cleared out but, before she did so, she removed all the money from the safe including that owed to her men.

"Dammit!" he cried in fear and frustration.

Carl hung around for a while trying to figure out what to do next. He then decided that he had better get out of Sydney fast. The hunters were on his trail and they would not be slow cornering him if he stuck to his usual haunts. Common sense said to go quickly.

On the way to Central station, he met up with Dorrie. She was begging for some loose change and it looked as if she hadn't eaten properly in some time. Her skin was in a bad way and her hands trembled even though it was, according to the behavior of the passersby, quite a warm evening. He could see she didn't have long to live. Life on the street was rough on everyone and the older you got the rougher it got. He figured her to be five, maybe ten years older than he was. Now it was evident her time was drawing to a close.

"It's all right, love," he told her. "I have the solution to all your pain and problems."

"You do?" she murmured in a faint voice.

"I do," he said. "I have a gift for you. An all time gift for a good girl."

What he did next he thought he did for her but maybe it was for himself, to justify his own existence. She didn't struggle much when he took her over into vampire-hood. She didn't have the strength.

He knew it was dangerous but he spent three nights with her in an old abandoned warehouse near the Quay waiting for her to awaken. When she did, he explained what had happened and that they needed to get out of Sydney in a hurry. She took some convincing but she did come around. Man into bat and back again was hard to argue with. Even harder to argue with, via the necklace, was one minute handsome guy, and with it off, the Carl she was used to seeing.

They smuggled themselves aboard a train headed for the Blue Mountains. He spent the next few weeks teaching her all he knew about her present existence before they went their separate ways. They could have stayed together longer but both were anxious to be on their own for a while. They were wanderers with no one holding them back and had been for many years. They preferred what they called friendship to be loose knit and always would. Even though the time he had spent with Mia had been very rewarding, he had missed the open road and now he was once more back on it. A sense of adventure filled his lungs and brain.

"No ties," Dorrie said as she left him. "I'll see you around."

"No ties," Carl echoed. "We'll meet again."

Sydney, NSW, Australia, summer, 2009

The wharf area east of the bridge of bridges had been given an impressive make-over since last Carl was in the neighborhood. Gone were the dilapidated storage facilities and the weather worn warehouses. They had been replaced by modern restaurants and office buildings. The human flotsam that on occasion made their home there had long since gone elsewhere.

Carl was walking past a fashionable restaurant when he spotted Mia. It seemed that she too had returned to her old haunts. She was not alone. She was with two women. One looked like Julia Roberts and the other looked like Teri Hatcher. He knew they were fakes by the necklaces they wore but the effect on the male senses was still remarkable. All three were draped in matching black dresses that had a certain slinky quality reminiscent of the movie stars of the 1940s. They were beautiful. He suspected that one of the necklaces was the one once worn by the long gone Samo.

"Hello, Mia," he called. Even to him, it sounded like a lame greeting but his mind was in a state of confusion. He felt she had acted wrongly in the now distant past yet she had also been the one who had introduced him to a better existence and had given him the rare opportunity of seeing how the other half lived.

Mia turned around at the sound of her own name and locked eyes on Carl. There was fleeting menace in her dark gaze, for she did not like to be surprised in this fashion, but it passed.

"So, Carl, did anyone else escape the Freemason trap?" she asked.

"They were Freemasons?" inquired Carl. "I thought Freemasons had to be men. Two of them were women."

"Freemasons, yes," Mia agreed, "but not necessarily their agents."

"Fair enough, I suppose. To answer your question, I know you got out in plenty of time; I got out in the nick of time. That's all I know."

"Pity. If not for that idiot Samo…"

"You didn't rat on us before you left?"

"Rat on you?" Mia cried in a startled voice. "By killing an important client from overseas Samo had set us all up. Why, all the authorities and the Freemasons among the cops had to do was look at the necks of the latest batch of women to be entertained by our services and our cover was blown. Otherwise we might have gone on for another year or more without anyone being the wiser."

"That...makes sense. Who are your companions?"

The Teri Hatcher look-alike stepped forward and said in a cheeky voice: "You don't recognize me, Carl? Not even after all we've been through together? I'm hurt."

"That voice!" cried Carl. "I know that voice!"

"So you should!" The Teri Hatcher doppelganger laughed. "I'm Dorrie!"

"Dorrie?"

"Ha! I got to shock you right back!"

"So you have. And you're with Mia now? She treating you right?"

"Can't complain. I only met her the other night but, what she had to say, sold me. I get to look like a big shot and turn heads, don't I?"

"Yes, there is that. Who's your other friend?"

"Her name's Sasha," Mia said in a serious voice, taking over from Dorrie. "I'm afraid her English isn't very good but she's bright so she'll learn. I met her in Pakistan. Some "gentleman" had thrown acid in her face. I gave her the choice of wearing a veil to hide her ugliness for the rest of her life, or letting me make her over, first as a vampire, and then as one of my lovelies."

"Your lovelies?" Carl smiled. "So you're starting up the old escort business again but with females this time?"

"That's right. But not here. Sydney is just a stopover. It would be too much like asking for trouble to do it here. I'm looking at Melbourne. By the way, I believe I have some money to give you. And don't you dare ask for interest. For a former panhandler I believe you have done well."

"At times I have."

"You could join my lovelies. I could use one male escort. I see you still wear the necklace I gave you."

"Yes," Dorrie implored. "Do join us. It should be fun!"

"I'll take the money." Carl smiled, not willing to be so easily drawn back in.

"The night's young and my hotel rooms are near Central," Mia said. "Care for a walk? On the way we can discuss the past and our possible future and you can pick up the money."

They went from the Quay area to Central which is quite a journey by foot. He knew they could have covered the distance in half the time in bat form but perhaps Sasha wasn't up to that trick yet. At a park near Central they snacked on three bums, making sure not to take all their blood. They reminded him of the bad old days when he was fully human and, even in summer, not all that happy with his state of being. A lot had changed since then, but the memories of being half-starved remained.

When he first left Sydney as a vampire, he spent some time in the Blue Mountains, near the Three Sisters, tutoring Dorrie. Then he headed south to Melbourne, stayed a month and headed west to Adelaide. By the end of his first decade as a member of the undead, he had visited every major Australian city. In each of them he got into strife and came to be sought after by vampire hunters. The necklace helped. If they were searching for a handsome vampire, he'd take it off for a while. If they were after a worn out looking vampire, he'd put it on again. All up, the necklace must have saved him dozens of times.

He spent a decade in the highlands of New Guinea where he was regarded as a white ghost ancestor. In Japan, after months of travel in that country, he came very close to being beheaded by one of the Rising Sun Group of modern day Samurai and Ninja.

He was in Kuta, Bali during the infamous terrorist bombing and had just missed out on being in the wrong bar at the right time. This made him want to get those responsible. He made his way to Jakarta where he attacked a terrorist cell bent on harming Westerners. They weren't the fiends responsible for what had happened in Bali but they had been planning something big against the Australian and the American embassies. All up, it felt great crushing heads with his superhuman strength and turning them into corpses no one who saw them could forget in a hurry. The local police were not thrilled by this. Someone called in the Rising Sun Group and he found he had Japanese vampire destroyers once more on his trail. He lost them when he went back to Bali and, from there, he took a ship to Darwin, Australia. From Darwin he made a slow and leisurely trip across the country which landed him in Sydney. He told Mia all this and included some of his more exciting adventures with the Aboriginal tribes he met in the Alice.

Apart from the fact she'd been to Pakistan, Mia didn't tell him much about what she'd been up to. Perhaps it was a case of not being able to get a word in because Dorrie was more than happy to fill in the blanks of what she had been doing since last they met. For her, the years had involved visits to most parts of Australia and New Zealand.

"Did you know," Dorrie said, "that there's a beach in Kiwi-land where you only have to dig in the sand to get a nice hot bath? Think how that would have felt when we were bumming it. Of course being undead meant the warmth couldn't get to me but the fact that the water was very warm with rising steam to prove it was something."

"Yes, I can imagine," Carl lied. He wondered if this beach could possibly exist.

"Also they call milk bars over there dairies. Very strange but kind of cute in a way. And the people are so nice and friendly they even got me into the habit of being friendly."

"That I can believe," said Carl.

"Oh, you!" Dorrie chided. "I'm not friendly to everyone here, you big lug! This city can be cold, even to a vampire. You're warm, even if you are unliving."

Carl collected the money. He wondered, as he pocketed it, why Mia was giving it to him. She could have refused or, with the help of Sasha and Dorrie, had him eliminated. He knew, given the right reasons, she could turn on her own. Then it dawned on him that she expected him to some night change his mind about getting back with her. Seen this way, the cash was an investment in the future. They had once worked well together and she figured they would do so again. She could be cruel, sure; he'd seen that with Samo. But she saw promise in him he couldn't see in himself. And she had Dorrie.

"You treat Dorrie well," he told Mia before leaving her company, "Or there'll be hell to pay."

"There always is," Mia quipped. "Rest assured Dorrie is safe with me. I'll take care of her."

"This little Teri Hatcher clone won't go wrong," Dorrie said.

"See that you don't," Carl replied. "And Mia, tell her about Samo so she doesn't make his mistake."

"Will do."

He left wishing them well in Melbourne. He knew they were watching him from their window as he faded into what was left of the night. He wondered what would happen when they met again and what fortune had in mind for him in the intervening months and years. If nothing else, unlife could be very long but, for him, never dull.

The Life, Death and Unlife of Sue Ling

It happened during the Boxer Rebellion in China. Foreigners were being blamed, and quite rightly too, for the opium trade that was ruining people's lives. Churches were burnt and anyone not of Chinese origin and not protected by fire-power was attacked by the peasant Boxers who were wild for their own brand of justice. The dowager empress, a cunning old bird, had seemingly nothing to do with the rebels but it was clear she wanted the foreigners out. It was also clear, even for those of Chinese blood, that the best place to be at night was home behind closed doors.

Even so, there was a polite knock on the entrance way of a humble family residence in the heart of Shanghai. It was dark out and all but one soul had retired to bed. A young Chinese woman, who had been practicing her reading of Confucius and had lost track of time, opened the door. She opened the door because a mesmerizing supernatural voice compelled her to do so. It was a voice unlike any she had heard before. It was a voice tempered by centuries of practice in the black arts. She tried to resist but found it impossible. Born on some dark wind, it penetrated the barrier between them and demanded she remove the barrier. What confronted her when she did was a strange sight.

The young Chinese was in her early twenties and considered by many to be quite pretty. He, the strange sight, was a foreigner. He might have been British. He could have been, and most probably was, American. All she knew was that he had a big nose, a white face and glistening blue eyes as cold as mountain ice. He asked for asylum from the mob supposedly after him. She told him he could come in and wait but only for a few minutes. She hadn't seen this mob but his eyes convinced her of its existence. His voice reinforced this belief to the point where it was a certainty. Of course there was a mob. Of course this mob was after him. Of course she had to come to his aide. Reason had deserted her.

Normally, like any sensible Chinese woman, she would have been frightened of him. His black coat that wrapped itself around him like a living thing should have given her pause. Normally, like any Chinese woman with Kung Fu training, she would have fended off his advances until help arrived. But she wasn't frightened and she didn't put her Kung Fu to the test. His voice wouldn't let her. Instead she let him into the home she shared with her parents and brothers. She allowed this solid ghost being to sample her life nectar and, during this sampling, she must have been made to sample him. In any case, she fell into a deep black pit of what should have been eternity, her existence changing forever.

The next morning, her parents and her brothers found her dead mere meters from the now closed door. She had been made as white as her assailant and there were twin puncture marks on her neck. There was much wailing over her body and, though the local magistrate examined her with the assistance of two qualified physicians, the cause of death had to be recorded as unknown. There were two other bodies in similar condition. One belonged to a married female neighbor in her early thirties who resided but three houses down. The other was that of an eighteen year old servant girl who lived four streets away in a big house.

All three corpses were laid out on the cold clay floor inside the nearest Buddhist temple. Prayers were said over them. A night later one, and only one, went missing. There had been a break in and she was gone. Talk of foreigners spiriting her away began to circulate. A drunk had seen a tall, white-faced man shrouded in night carrying a woman down the street away from the holy place. The local authorities launched an investigation but nothing could be proven. Besides, what would foreigners want with a corpse? They were always well fed. More than likely, her father surmised in a state of misery, someone destitute and starving had taken her. Vagabonds were rounded up but nothing was found on any of them to point the way to the culprit. In the end, the matter had to be dropped and her parents and brothers had to accept the double loss.

When Sue Ling, the absent corpse, awoke she found herself at sea inside the hold of a steam ship. There the foreigner that had drained her of life was quenching her terrible thirst with blood he poured into her mouth from a cup. Where he had obtained the blood, she didn't know nor did she care. It probably came from the crew. It seemed to be tainted with something. Was that something opium? After drinking her fill she drifted off to sleep. This occurred at least a dozen times over a dozen nights. What he wanted with her she didn't know nor could she guess.

He did insist that she wear a bag filled with dirt from her country around her neck but said this was for her health and that to not have native soil near her or on her when she slept could make her very ill.

"I have not taken you on board just to see you perish a second time," he told her in her own tongue.

One night, instead of awakening to the motion of the water underneath her and the sensation she was too far from the land for her own safety, she awoke to the feeling of being on something solid and permanent. Where there had been the strong scent of salt in the air, there was now the odor of rice wine and canned lychees (a Chinese delicacy). There were other odors such as wet cat's fur and fresh apricots in a barrel. She had been moved from her native land and from the ship that had taken her hence but she didn't have a clue how far until she opened the warehouse door and looked out. What greeted her was one of the busiest cities on the face of the planet – not that Shanghai itself hadn't been described that way.

At first she thought it must be some part of China. Perhaps even Shanghai. Maybe the ship had gone around in a great circle coming back to where it had started from. Chinese men and women, dodging the heavy rain as best they could, were going about their business in the crowded thoroughfare. Some spoke a dialect she was familiar with that wasn't her own, others spoke either Peking Mandarin or the white devil's tongue, but at least they were Chinese. The sight of them gave her the impression that, at worst, she was only a few hundred miles from home.

As she moved further away from the warehouse and away from Chinatown, the buildings changed and so did the people. More and more white faces appeared with their freakish ways and mannerisms. One even tipped his hat in her direction. For the first time she saw an automobile. It coughed black smoke and made a terrible noise which frightened a nearby horse. Looking through a stained glass window, she watched a man with red hair and a well-oiled handle-bar moustache play a piano in a bar for small change. He seemed to be having a jolly time.

The rain eased and then stopped. It was replaced by a fog rolling in off the harbor. With it came an awful thirst. Her first victim was a white devil prostitute in a tattered white dress and grubby red shawl who thought it amusing to be propositioned by a Chinese not even familiar with the white devil's language. A coin plus a few hand gestures did the trick. By the time the prostitute realized that her newly acquired money was also Chinese, and therefore not able to be spent in San Francisco, it was too late. The attack was savage and the blood tasted oh so good. She didn't think blood could taste that wonderful.

A month passed and the white person who had sired Sue Ling the vampire and had moved her to America had not returned to her to offer a clue as to why he had done the things that he had done. The notion that he may have been killed a second time by vampire hunters thus preventing his return had not entered into her head. She felt she'd been abandoned by who ever had put her on her present path and she had a great desire to get back to her native land where things made more sense.

She recalled that her name was Sue Ling and, up to her death, she was the daughter of Han Ling, a silversmith. Being the youngest of three and a girl, she might have been sold by her father to keep the rest of the family together. It was a common enough practice and, even before the rebellion, times had been tough. Still, Han had been determined to keep all his children, up to marriageable age, close to him. Besides, he loved his only daughter as he often reminded her and he wanted what was best for her and his sons. She knew he would not have approved of her becoming a vampire and living the undead life so far from home. What's more, despite Chinese stories pointing the way, he would not have believed that at night a corpse could stalk the living. He would not, unless he saw her sucking the life from someone, believe her to be undead. Unless her mother, the gentle Tai Ling, had seen her murder an innocent, she would not have believed her only daughter capable of such barbarity.

It didn't take Sue Ling long to realize that she'd need money, and lots of it, to get back to Shanghai. At first she had a great deal of trouble getting any money at all. Too many of her early victims were poor. Then she found the banking sector of the city and her fortunes changed. Here there were fat white people with fat purses and even fatter wallets. Relieving her new found victims of their blood and money, however, was not without risk. It took her out of obscurity. A few dead winos or prostitutes or even street urchins didn't count for much. One dead banker and his wife began a manhunt for the killer which made things hot. Experts were brought in to examine the bodies and to hunt down the killer. Some of the experts brought in other experts.

It was Ted Hollows, a short, muscular Pinkerton agent out of Chicago, who told the mayor what was going on. "There's a vampire on the loose," he said. This got him a laugh followed by the mayor's secretary showing him the door. A week later, which amounted to another dead banker and his wife, the mayor was willing to believe almost anything. And so Hollows was given free rein to explore his rather unconventional theories and ideas. He did so by combing the city morgues looking for unusual corpses. He ended up in Chinatown where he found the oldest of the type he was interested in.

Hollows came upon Sue Ling one night on the edge of the Banking District. He followed her back to Chinatown where he caught sight of her feeding off a young homeless white girl who had wandered into the area in search of food. He pulled out his colt 45 and fired a warning shot. The noise frightened her and so she let the half- supped-upon youngster go. He fired again, catching her arm, making her scream in pain. Before he could fire a third time, the staggering youngster got in his way. Sue Ling took advantage of the moment by going on the offensive. She broke his left shoulder bone with a flying kick she'd learned from her father and her newly acquired vampire strength. He tried to punch her back but, for his effort, only ended up amongst a pile of rotting newspapers. Still, before she was able to grab him so that she could taste of him, he blew a whistle which made two nearby policemen, whom he was working with, come running.

They saw the blood on her face and opened up with their artillery. Six slugs from a colt struck her chest and five more from a Wembley hit her on the arms and legs. One shot missed her. She cried out with each strike but did not fall. Before they could reload and try again she was gone. Despite what should have been horrific injuries, she was able to stagger then walk and, in a matter of seconds, run away. Her recovery was amazing.

Hollows, once he was dismissed from the hospital, sent a wire to the Rising Sun Group stationed in New Mexico. He cabled them that there was a fresh outbreak of vampirism in the Bay and that the Pinkertons would cut them in on a share of the reward if they were to help capture the lead vampire. They cabled back with a curt: "Thank You. Be there soon."

The following night there were a dozen Pinkertons on patrol in the Banking District armed with crossbows supplied by the Rising Sun Group. They had crosses and small jade Buddha images on necklaces. Two of them chanced to wander into the greater Shopping District where Sue Ling was trying to get nourishment. The crosses and Buddhas sickened her, but they alerted her to their presence. She was thus able to avoid two wooden arrows and break two jaws with two flying leaps.

She made her way onto Fisherman's Wharf only to be forced to dive into the water to avoid a dozen wooden star knives propelled from the shadows in her direction. Some people think that ordinary water, if it is moving, can kill a vampire or at least harm such a creature. This is not true. Moving water, by its purity, only affects those in such a way suffering from lycanthropy. What it did for Sue Ling was make her wet and depressed. Also, she was hungry.

Feeding was becoming a real problem. Being chased, night after night, from one end of San Francisco to the other meant fewer times in which she would be able to pick a victim unless it was one of her pursuers. The unfortunate thing about picking a pursuer, of course, was that they had some idea of how to hurt her and probably had a few good ideas on how to destroy her. If they kept at it, they were going to find her day time hiding place and, if they were to expose her to direct sunlight, it would really be the end.

Being Chinese did not help matters. Away from Chinatown Sue Ling stood out like a brunette in a blonde convention. Even when she dressed in female white devil clothes so she could continue to hunt in the richer areas of the city she was easily spotted. The ridiculous garments of the female white devils did not suit her. They made rapid progress very difficult. The first time she tried to increase speed in a frock, she tripped over the length of fabric and collided with a street lamp. That time she barely got away from the two men chasing her. In the end, she decided to stick to Chinatown. At least there she could wear sensible clothes and blend in with her surroundings.

Three months after her first encounter with Ted Hollows, Sue Ling caught sight of Maggie O'Flinn, a young, buxom occidental vampire reduced to ash by an oriental man in black wielding twin wooden butterfly swords. It took place in an alley outside an Irish pub on the street dividing Chinatown from the rest of the city. The action was swift. Maggie had been distracted by a young Japanese woman dressed as a ninja and carrying a set of wooden star knives. She dodged the thrown knives with ease but that only set her up for the twin sword strokes that destroyed her. She didn't see them coming.

"One down," said the man with the swords.

"And one to go," said the woman with the star knives.

They then turned on Sue Ling.

She did the sensible thing and ran as fast as her legs, unencumbered as they were by a skirt (she wore long silk pants), could carry her. If she could have sprouted leathery wings she would have. If she could have turned into a puff of smoke and blended in with the surrounding fog, she would have done that as well. As it stood, her legs almost carried her into a net laced with garlic. If not for her Kung Fu ability to leap high, which had been enhanced by her vampire strength, she would have been caught and no doubt executed.

Who are these people? she wondered as she made her way back, via a circuitous route, to her sleeping quarters. She kept her eyes and other senses on the alert but no one had tailed her.

The following night a tall, spindly female ninja in her thirties, with claws made out of wood, sprang at Sue Ling from behind some trash cans. In the process of doing so this ninja frightened away a middle aged Chinese fellow Sue Ling was intent on dining upon and two occidental street kids going through the trash looking for something to eat. The attack took place outside a music theatre and it took all of Sue's strength to prevent herself from being badly scratched. Once on the offensive, she managed to high kick the ninja hard against a wall forcing her to lose consciousness. Unfortunately, before she could follow up by draining her attacker of blood, a spear with an oak tip thrown from the opposite end of the street nearly skewered her heart. Instead it embedded itself deep into the lower half of her left shoulder. It hurt like hell going in and wrenching it out was even more painful. She was lucky not to have passed out. By the time she got back to claiming the unconscious ninja, the ninja was gone, spirited away no doubt by a nearby ninja colleague.

Sue Ling laid low for a week, living off the blood of rats. The taste was not to her liking, but she dared not venture forth for what was appealing. Instead, she drank vermin, cursed her enemies and listened to street gossip.

It was around this time she realized there was no point in going back to Shanghai where she still had parents and brothers. They would not understand her new un-life and there might come a time when her thirst was so great she'd even do away with her own in order to quench it. Her father and mother wanted her to marry and have children. That was now out of the question. It was better for her parents and brothers to remember her the way she had been rather than to discover what she had become. They were good. She was now evil. It was that simple.

One thing was certain; she was coming to grips with basic English and with Peking Mandarin. She was able to learn from passersby that the ninjas pestering her were from the Rising Sun Group and that the Pinkerton detectives, the men with the crossbows, were their backup. Something was said by a shopkeeper about the bankers and their wives being killed and that was what the great hullabaloo about vampires was all about. If they had just disappeared and their corpses never located, neither the Rising Sun Group nor the Pinkertons would be on her case. It would just be four missing people, the sort of thing regular cops were expected to handle. She filed that away in her mind for future reference. Next time she feasted on an important looking person, she'd be sure to dump the body where it wouldn't be found.

Sue Ling counted the money she had taken off her victims and decided she had enough to make her escape to New York. And so, two weeks after almost being speared to death, her makeshift coffin with her inside it was placed aboard ship and sent to the Big Apple.

When she arrived, New York was in a period of reconstruction. Long ago it had been established as a major port. With a lack of space to build upon, the buildings were becoming taller and taller. They were beginning to scrape the sky. Some were still in the skeleton stage but looked impressive anyway.

Sue Ling found the white devils here a dynamic mix. There were first and second generation Jews from Russia, Poland and Germany. There were first and second generation Italian and Irish Catholics. The majority, of course, were of English descent. The Chinese Americans she met seemed more settled into the American way of life than in San Francisco and the same could be said for the few Japanese she came across.

There was crime and plenty of it. On her first night two street thugs tried to mug her. Boy! Did they get a surprise! But they tasted just fine. One thing she learned was that much of the crime went unsolved because of pay offs to the local authorities from the humble cop on the beat to the city's mayor. She knew that once she figured out how to bribe and how best to dump bodies unlife would become easier. And so it did. If she needed to, she could rely on certain members of the living to come to her aid and, if and when her pursuers made their next move against her, she knew she could count on them for a fair amount of warning. It was all a matter of whose palm you pressed with cash, when you pressed it, and how often.

Two decades or more passed in which Sue Ling feasted well upon the New Yorkers. Then came the Great Depression. People lost their savings, people were put out of work and had to hit the road to try to make a living. New Yorkers were naturally greedy, or at least the ones she was happy to do business with. Now they were even more so and it scared her. Cash was no longer easy to come by. Most of her victims, even those sporting new suits, had little in their pockets. So she pulled up stakes and made her way by rail out of New York and across the USA. She was able to hire a young woman to protect her coffin during the day and paid her off at night with what human food and coinage she had managed to get that night. It was a good arrangement which ended outside a small town near San Francisco where there were no victims on hand and so she had to sup on her day time protector.

Being back in the city by the bay meant little to Sue Ling except that it had a Chinatown where she could hide from possible pursuers. So much time had passed; however, that she didn't think anyone was after her. As it turned out, Ted Hollows had to retire from the Pinkertons due to old age but his son, Sam, had made it up the ranks and was waiting for her return. He'd been sharpening his skills on desperados of all kinds, both human and vampiric. The Rising Sun Group had people stationed on a permanent basis around the bay. Some had come in from Japan to stay. Others were of Chinese or white devil American extraction. In any event, they were all ninja and all keen on slaying the undead.

Her first night back was uneventful. On her second night she came upon two Pinkertons with guns loaded with hollow points stuffed with sawdust. She found out about the sawdust when one of them hit her leg. It stung real bad but what made it worse was when the wound it made developed an infection. If not for a surgeon who could be paid off, she might have lost a limb. If it had hit her heart instead she would have died – again but for good.

Then it came to her. Why not follow one of her stalkers, check out the layout of their headquarters, and then devise a plan to get rid of them? She now had experience under her belt. So the next night she did locate one of the Pinkertons and followed him to a lonely looking cabin on the outskirts of the city. There two problems presented themselves. Firstly, the grounds surrounding the structure were protected by garlic plants, crucifixes, and statues of Buddha. Secondly, she could not tarry as the sun was beginning to pink the sky and she had to get back to her own hideout before sunrise reduced her to dust. It was then that tackling them where they planned their attacks upon her and her kind turned out to be a bust.

Despite the dangers, San Francisco had its charms. There was the rising and falling land that made her think of ferrous wheels and a fish market not unlike the big one in Shanghai she used to frequent with her mother when she was young. There were ways of keeping out of plain sight and moving without ruffling the feathers of the law she hadn't come across in her original visit. For example, from the 1860s there had been and still were opium dens. There were also houses of ill repute where women of many nationalities and racial types plied a somewhat risky though profitable trade.

Sue Ling, in avoiding the Rising Sun Group fanatics and the Pinkerton agents, discovered that the opium eaters, whether they smoked it or ingested it in laudanum form, were good for a quick, no fuss snack. Draining one made her feel a little dizzy because of the muck in their veins but it was better than rat. For a small fee, the den operators were happy to dispose of the bodies for her.

When it came to the brothels, it was a different story. The owner of a dozen of them, Madam Lang (of Welsh descent, not Chinese), wanted her first as an exotic dancer and then as a prostitute with special talents. For a while the arrangements worked out fine. All she had to do was to remember not to drain the men and women who came to her too much and she could have as many as she needed plus cash. They'd go away pasty-faced, thinking they'd experienced the best sex they'd ever had and everybody was happy. Some even paid her a repeat visit unaware that copulation was never on the menu because the spirit-being they fancied was no longer interested in that sort of play.

Things went along swimmingly until one of her opium eater victims drifted loose from his mooring under the golden gate and was reported floating on the harbor by a weekend angler. The cops were quick to transfer the information to the Pinkertons who, in turn, informed the Rising Sun Group. A week after this occurrence a Pinkerton bumped into one of her brothel near-victims and began to put it all together. There were raids on known opium dens and brothels. Sue found herself once more on the run.

One night a flaming arrow came close to setting her ablaze. She ran after the archer responsible which led her to the outskirts of Fisherman's Warf. There she came upon two men in black with twin butterfly swords made of oak. They were Chinese and she knew they were from Shanghai. How she knew didn't at first register then one of them, in a voice choked with emotion, called out her name.

"Brother," she whispered back and the wind took her whisper to him.

"I joined the Rising Sun to avenge you," he told her. "Now I must kill you in order to save your soul."

"My soul?" she said. "It has long gone, Fong. I am now of the living dead. Go away. You cannot save me."

"Then I must kill you to save others," he said with uncertainty in his voice.

"You must try," she agreed. "How are Mother and Father?"

"Mother died of a broken heart, Father of old age. Our brother, Lee, is also hunting vampires elsewhere in this city."

"Yes, it has been some time since last we met. Even so, dear brother, blood of my blood, could you really harm your only sister?"

"I...must try!"

Her brother and the other swordsman began to close in on her. Four swords danced their swift dance before her eyes. Could she leap past them? No. Even with her enhanced capabilities, the maneuver she had in mind wouldn't have worked. An empty trash can came to hand and she hurled it at the other swordsman, felling him. She followed through with a savage kick to his jaw, rendering him unconscious. Now she only had her sibling to contend with.

She picked up the fallen warrior's butterfly swords. They felt good in her hands like reuniting with old friends.

"Father trained me also," she reminded her brother.

Fong nodded and sweated. She could smell his perspiration even from a hundred yards away. If it had been someone else, it would have tasted lovely on the breeze. Sure, it mingled with the salt from the bay but her senses were so acute she could tell the human from the marine. She could also tell one human from another and often took great satisfaction in doing so.

He charged and it was then she realized that she was only a few feet from the end of the dock. Killing him, she knew, would be simple. He would not be able to compete against vampire strength and speed. Going up against another vampire, he might have surprised them with his moves but there would be no such surprise between brother and sister. Even after all this time, she knew him too well.

The distance between them melted quickly. She was poised to strike and strike hard, decapitating him. Then something happened. Perhaps it was a remembrance of two children sharing a game of dominos or of a brother getting a ripe plum out of the top most branch of a tree for his sister. Perhaps it was dinner around a table with family or her mother's smile when Sue Ling helped her brother in a fight with some local bullies. Whatever it was, it compelled her to drop her swords, about face and dive into the water.

What happened after that shocked her. There was a terrible burning, a boiling and a sizzling. Intense pain shot through her as she struggled to get out of what should have been regular, harmless water. It ate into her and through her like sulfuric acid and all her brother could do was look on horrified by what he was seeing. Mercifully, in a matter of minutes, she was reduced to a bobbing skeleton.

By this time a female ninja with star knives had joined her brother.

"Do you think she knew?" asked the female ninja.

"Knew what?"

"That the blessing of the fleet had taken place earlier today and that the tide is just going out?"

"I didn't know so I doubt she did. But she was the smart one. Perhaps she did know."

"There must have been ten thousand people, plus the priests and the archbishop, blessing both water and ships. There were even two Buddhist monks."

"And this blessing caused this?"

"Well, even if only two thousand of the ten truly believe and are faithful, it would still have turned the bay into one large container of holy water. Only for one day, mind you and only until the tide goes fully out. Just think of it, all that holy water, made holy by so many prayers, the Buddhist monks no doubt helping a lot. No wonder she didn't have a chance."

"Yes. No wonder…"

"Do you think she did what she did for you?"

"I don't know. But I would choose to believe so. I doubt I could have destroyed her and it would be best to imagine she felt the same way about me."

"Yes, Fong, if vampires are capable of such feelings."

"Yes, if my sister as a vampire was so capable."

After a while the skeleton weakened, collapsed and bobbed no more. It was gone and with it the unlife of one Sue Ling.

A Candle to Light the Way

Gull's Haven, Cornwall, England, winter, 1827

The White Owl Inn was on the road to Falmouth and not far from where they lit the fires to warn ships away from the treacherous rocks. It was on a cliff overlooking the channel and on good mornings the beginnings of France could be seen in the distance. Every evening a light would be put in the window facing the road so as to welcome weary travelers and on certain nights, when fine wines and cognac were being moved ashore in long boat, there was a candle in the window facing the crashing waves.

One night a tall, white-haired man paid the Inn a visit. He arrived too late for a hot meal but the innkeeper's wife offered to make sandwiches. He thanked her but refused. He wouldn't even take a tankard of ale. All he said he wanted was to warm himself by the fire and then find a comfortable place to rest. To incur no argument on the matter, he tossed the innkeeper a shiny new shilling. The innkeeper thanked him and looked to the comfort of other guests. *No sense bothering with a man who doesn't want to be bothered with*, he thought, *especially a generous gent an' all who doesn't want the bother.*

The innkeeper's wife was suspicious but said nothing. She suspected the law had caught up with them at last and the new man a spy for the local revenue agent. For all his plain clothes and plain speech, this man with no appetite was different in body language from any man she had ever met before. There was something worldly about him that put her on guard. Smuggling and dealing in stolen merchandise were serious offences. Penalties could range right up to public hanging in the town square. The innkeeper's wife shivered at the thought and touched her neck as if it were in danger.

"Gawd! Why now?" she muttered to herself, shaking her head as she wiped down a table with a damp cloth. "Just as things are starting to go our way too."

Come the morning, all who stayed the night, including the innkeeper and his wife, were dead. All, that is, except for the tall, white-haired stranger. He had gone. There were ten corpses. They were milky white with weird expressions on their faces. Some looked delighted about something while others had the appearance of supreme terror. The local physician didn't know what to make of them though he did come up with the theory that the one responsible must have had accomplices. Though why such deeds should be done was beyond him. The only clue to how they died was the small puncture marks on their necks. A farmer reported seeing a flight of bats the night the killings had taken place but it seemed highly unlikely there could be a connection.

The locals insisted that the dead should be buried as soon as possible. The physician, fearing a possible epidemic of unknown origin, insisted on sending blood and skin samples to a London expert on unusual disease before allowing that step to be taken. It was no good, he argued, putting evidence in the ground that might, in the future, save lives. Three nights later, several of the bodies went missing. Included on the absentee list were the innkeeper and his wife. After that, expert from London be damned, the villagers put the remaining bodies into the ground, said prayers with the priest over them, and the physician who couldn't stop them hoped that they had all done the right thing.

"It's up to God now," the priest told him and his parishioners. "Come what may, it's out of our hands."

After a time, the Inn came into new hands and the name of the place was changed. Still, stories of what had happened and of where the missing corpses had gone persisted. The legend of the tall, white-haired man roamed far and wide.

London, England, summer, 1857

London was built on trade. Ships sailed in and out providing a livelihood for many. While in port, sailors wanted a lively time. Pubs provided some of this liveliness and then there were the brothels.

It would be fair to say that different kinds of brothels were everywhere. Some were for the wealthy, some were for the middle classes and yet others were for the working man. They catered to all tastes and interests. Love was never on the table but there were those willing to fake it. For a price you could have your heart's desire, or a close facsimile, no matter how wicked or kindly that heart might be.

Among the places of ill repute in Whitechapel, there was a two-story house that seemed to cater for everything. It had an evil reputation since some men who had reportedly gone in had never, ever come out. There was a butcher shop across the road specializing in pork pies. Gossip had it that the pork really wasn't pork at all but portions of the missing men. Regardless of what people said, the butcher did a thriving business.

The place that catered for everything was distinguished by a burning candle in the window. It was said to be a welcoming sign. Though old-fashioned, it was a pleasant sight in a world of dreary and often heartless commerce. It had, however, a dark secret.

Over the years the constabulary had been called in to investigate the brothel that could possibly be connected to certain disappearances. Bobbies would go in with their batons raised for trouble and find nothing out of the ordinary. There wasn't much they were expected to do about people sitting around a table in regular clothes playing cards. That, at any rate, constituted the final official report on the place.

"There's more excitement back at the station," one young officer had remarked. His companion, who could not find a reason for disagreement, thought it prudent to leave. Neither was aware they had been bitten or blood had been drawn. They felt a weakness in their limbs the next day but, since they quickly got their strength back, they thought nothing of it. Their wives did come across and note the strange incisions they had on their necks.

A month after this visit by the law, someone smashed the brothel's lower ground floor window with a rock then hurled a lit kerosene lamp in after it. The place was soon ablaze. The fire was put out but not before much of the building had been gutted.

Just before the flames reached the top floor, observers thought they saw several large bats fly out of the top story window and take to the night. It may have been a trick of the billowing smoke upon already stretched nerves.

No one was brought to justice for starting the fire. Some people said it was a woman out to avenge her missing spouse whom she regarded as dead, a victim of those in the house. As for the house's occupants, they were never seen again or, at least, not in Whitechapel.

Cambridge, England, autumn, 1927

Kathy Mills was beside herself with worry. She was late and she was lost. She was new to the area and all the narrow streets and lane ways meant for horse and cart happened to look alike. She had been to Mabel and Jeffrey's home once before and was sure she knew the way. Now she wasn't sure of anything. What's more, there was this damnable bird or bat or something that had been following her.

"Shoo!" she cried out loud, waving her hand in its direction while keeping her balance on her bicycle. Either ignorant of the meaning of her action or disdainful of it, her winged follower continued to keep pace with her.

She knew she looked like a bright young woman on a pleasant ride. Her suit was tweed and quite stylish. She spoke French as well as English. She could even sing in French. She was introduced to cigarettes and, though they made her cough like the dickens to the amusement of others, she thought the act of smoking made her look sophisticated. She was all of twenty-one and going for a degree in science. Why then, with all that behind her, did she feel so stupid asking people for directions?

Night was coming on and she was almost in a panic. Good girls, even sophisticated ones, did not travel alone after dark in strange, bewildering neighborhoods. Well, she certainly was doing it! What's worse, she was jumpy. The movement of a tree branch gave her goose bumps. And that damnable thing, whatever it was, had stopped tailing her and was hovering around her position. She had come to a halt without realizing she had done so. *Must push on*, she told herself and discovered just how weary her legs were becoming. She had to find a friendly place and ask directions like she should have when there was still plenty of light.

A cloud hung overhead, hiding the stars and the moon. What were once friendly, somewhat quaint homes with dainty well kept gardens out front took on more sinister roles in the night drama unfolding. Like one of her cave dwelling ancestors, Kathy found she needed the light to dispel the darkness.

Mustn't panic! She told herself sternly. *Nothing to be gained by panicking!* Why then was she chewing on her upper lip?

Then, as if to cut away her fears and make her feel foolish, there was light. It came from a house only a few hundred yards away. She could tell by the flickering that it was a candle burning in a window. She didn't know why there would be a candle when most people had electricity but it was a very welcome sight. She pedaled toward it.

As she got closer, she heard the sound of soft jazz from a saxophone. It was a sweet tease that drew her on. She loved the various innovations in music coming from the USA. Rag Time was her favorite. Jazz came in a close second. Then, as she was about to ring the doorbell, the music stopped. She heard a scuffle from upstairs and a man came crashing through one of the upstairs windows to land in a heap in a flower bed not far from where she was standing. From the way his neck was twisted, she took him to be dead.

A scream started in Kathy's throat but was killed by her sense of self-preservation. It would not do to let the people inside know they had a witness to their villainy. Self-preservation said to get the hell away from the place as fast as her legs and her bicycle would take her. Back the way she had come seemed good enough. Anywhere seemed good enough from a murder scene where she was likely to become the next victim. *How did I get myself into this mess?* she asked herself as she rode away. *Mustn't panic! Mustn't panic! Just peddle! Peddle for all you're ruddy well worth!*

An evening with friends and new acquaintances was all she wanted. Crimes were supposed to happen in slum areas not close to major colleges and universities.

Twenty minutes later the streets around her lit up like Christmas trees and she heard radios playing in various houses. A young constable on a push bike approached her. Once the gloom dissipated he seemed to suddenly appear. He could see she was upset and so gave her assurances that the blackout that had affected housing and street lamps in the general area was over and that everything was back to normal.

"Normal?!" she shrieked. "I'm lost. I saw a dead body. You call that normal?!"

"Easy, miss," said the constable in a soothing voice. "Start from the beginning."

"I'm Kathy Mills. I'm very late for an afternoon get-together."

"I know. Your friends are very worried. They suspected you might have taken a wrong turn in the gloom and phoned the station. We've been looking for you. But what's this about a body?"

"A dead body. Up the road. I'll show you!"

"Yes, miss."

Weary though she was she felt it her duty to take the constable to where the dead man lay. She didn't expect the corpse to still be there. Certainly, in the movies, bodies had a knack of not being where they were supposed to be. The criminals had had plenty of time to have moved it but they might have left some vital clue. She had been an avid reader of *The Adventures of Sherlock Holmes* and so she thought she had some idea of how the criminal mind operated.

To her surprise, and that of the constable, the body was where it had fallen. There had been no attempt at a cover-up. Everything became official after that. More police were called in and the house thoroughly searched. It seemed the place had been vacant for some time. Apart from a gramophone, a jazz record, and two modern looking chairs, the furniture inside was old and the fireplace had been boarded up. They did find the candle Kathy had alluded to in her statement but they couldn't make head or tail of what it was doing there.

The body lay in the morgue awaiting a coroner's hearing scheduled to take place at the end of the week. Before the hearing, the body vanished. It happened three nights after it had been put on the slab for examination. The police were dumbfounded. Search parties were sent out to retrieve it but it was not to be found. Its disappearance was a mystery that would linger on for decades and haunt Kathy and the constable for the rest of their lives.

Wick, Scotland, winter, 1957

There was a small but friendly Inn called The Bonny Lass that made all welcome but mainly catered to the local fishermen. It wasn't far from treacherous rocks and a lighthouse that had saved many an otherwise doomed soul. Things changed overnight, when eight strangers appeared wanting lodging but no food or spirits.

A dram each of scotch was offered to them for nothing to warm their bones from the cold night air but they'd have none of it. This the innkeeper found odd. They were English so maybe that, in part, was that. The English, to be sure, were known for their eccentricities, the eating of cold pork pies being one of them. But a dram or two of whisky to kill the chill in miserable weather was surely for every man and woman, even the pitiful English with their fancy ways and notions. Surely whisky against the fierceness of a fierce winter had to be a universal truth.

The eight settled around the fire while two of the Bonny Lass' regulars had a game of darts. There was uneasiness in the atmosphere as if a prelude to something about to happen. Then there was the crack of thunder followed by the lights going out. One of the dart players joked about the landlord not paying his electricity bill but nobody laughed. The barman and barmaid lit candles and put them in every corner of the room to scare away the devil. Everyone except old Jamie looked around to see how effective the candles were. Jamie sat next to the strangers and stared ahead into the fire's flames.

"Another ale?" asked the barman, patting Jamie on the shoulder. In response, Jamie keeled over and off his seat, revealing the fact that he was dead. There were puncture wounds on his neck.

"No!" cried one of the dart throwers.

"God no!" cried the barman who had disturbed Jamie.

As if in response, the door burst open and in stepped three big highlanders wearing the kilts of the clan MacLean and carrying primed crossbows. Before the door could be closed, the wind blew the candles out and dimmed the fire in the fireplace making everything dark and shadowy. There was the sound of three arrows being launched followed by the cries of three so-called men. Then someone dropped their crossbow and there was the butchering sound of a claymore slicing through bone followed by the gruesome sight of a head rolling along the floor near the hot coals of the fire. Someone shouted: "Let's go!" And there was a flurry of leathery wings beating their way to the wilderness beyond the door.

One of the MacLean clan closed the door against the howling night and another helped the barman to relight the candles. The third was busy wiping blood off his ancient clansman sword with a table cloth borrowed from the bar.

The innkeeper looked with uncertainty at his new guests. The God almighty sword and the crossbows were a worry, but he was glad that the English had gone. They were a peculiar lot with their weird mannerisms and ways. There were three piles of ash and a skeleton with its head still rolling under a table to mark their passing. They couldn't have left like normal folk, could they? No, they had to put on a show. There had to be something outlandish about their departure.

"They were bloodsuckers," said one of the MacLean men in way of explanation. "And we're clan MacLean Freemasons."

No one challenged him. No one asked: "How did you know they were bloodsuckers?" The crossbows and the claymore continued to be a worry.

Putting down notes and coin on the bar, one of the clan MacLean ordered a bottle of scotch and some shot glasses. At this the innkeeper, the barman, and the barmaid gave collective sighs of relief. Murderers or no, madmen or no, at least they were Scots and no mistake. At least they had some understanding for custom on a fierce winter night in the fiercest of winters any of them could remember. There was nothing like a few drams of the good stuff to warm the heart and sooth the soul provided, of course, you had heart and soul to warm. *It would be a wonder,* the innkeeper thought, *if those English had either. And, without a heart and a soul, what business did they have being in Scotland?*

None he could think of. Surely they were much better off staying south of the border where their peculiarities, such as using maggots for bait when they go fishing, were not only considered normal but even civilized.

"Each to their own," the innkeeper said to the barmaid in deep contemplation as he gathered up the notes and coins and watched the MacLean men warm themselves inside and out. "Each to their own, I say. And let the devil take the rest including the English."

Gull's Haven, Cornwall, England, summer, 2009

Peter and Susan Vance were having a restless day. They were tossing and turning in their separate but equal coffins, going over in their minds their shared past.

They had been married way back in the early half of the 19th Century. Peter had inherited an Inn from his father and was expected to run it until he died. He married Susan who was the local baker's daughter. He remembered saying, on their wedding day, "'til death us do part." Who was to know at the time just how irrelevant that section of the wedding vows they uttered so reverently to each other before a minister would become?

You see, they died at the hands of a vampire and they remained together. They went off to be vampires in the big city. People tried to destroy them, but they stayed with each other. Not only were they together but it was now the 21st Century. For a very long time they had been dead or, as some are want to say, undead and they had experienced it all, the bad as well as the good, together.

Peter and Susan winced at the memory of having the life taken from them and being made to taste the unlife. In this they were not alone. There had been five others on the same journey. There was Bill Franklin, the blacksmith's son. He was a muscular fellow, pleasant enough but rather slow witted. Sam Watts was a carpenter who worried too much when he drank and worried too little when he didn't. Morey Coates and his son William were fishermen and great gamblers. They would gamble on anything and would usually lose. Bob Turner was another fisherman but he drank very little and was frugal with his money. Some said he was saving up for a home and a wife. Perhaps that's exactly what he had been doing until the very nature of existence changed for the lot of them.

Late into the night, the guest who did not eat or drink like normal folk do must have let the others in. All Peter remembered was waking with a start when he heard noises in his room and yelling to a man grabbing his wife, "Leave her be and get out," before being overcome by a woman he had never met. She grabbed him with strong hands and went straight for his jugular vein. He had no time then to think of Susan and her struggle. He had a struggle of his own going on which he was losing. "No!" he heard Susan cry out. He wanted desperately to save her but it was no use. He couldn't even save himself. Both sank down into the abyss to the sounds of contented laughter. Both felt their precious lives desert them.

When they came to they were in the company of the guest who did not eat plus other strangers. With them were regulars to the Inn such as Bill, Sam, Morey, William and Bob. They were no longer in their Inn but a smuggler's cave.

Peter and Susan remembered the man who did not eat saying: "Like my companions, you are now beyond the living. You can no longer exist the way you used to. We will show you how to cope. Then we will leave."

For a week Peter, Susan and the rest of the newly undead were tutored by the ones who had changed them. Then they were left to their own devices. The thought of returning to normal haunted them but normality even as an abstract concept was no longer for them.

After they had been made over, Peter and Susan discovered there was no way they could go back to their business. They were officially deceased and without issue. In other words, they no longer owned their Inn. Even if they had still owned it, they couldn't operate during the day because daylight was bad for them. There were the killings to consider, including their own, which were really bad for their trade. No one wanted to stay at a place where lots of people had recently died and the criminals responsible were yet to be caught.

Of course Peter and Susan were not the only ones at loose ends. The others had lost everything they knew and understood. Bill Franklin tried to visit his father to tell him what had happened and was driven off by the old man furiously waving a crucifix at him. Morey Coates and his son William had a similar experience with Tilley, Morey's wife and William's mother. One of Watts' drinking mates tried to drive a pitchfork into him and one of the ladies Bob Turner was fond of fainted when he turned up at her door. Once you were deceased, relations with loved ones changed and not for the better. Thinking it paramount to stick together, all seven decided to leave their village for the outside world.

They didn't know what to expect, but they knew they could no longer stay where they had once belonged. They knew enough about unlife, however, to collect bags of native soil before they left.

Peter and Susan grumbled in unison in their sleep at the thought of what it was like to continually find new places to stay during the day. The hunt at night came to mean a lot to them. It wasn't just about blood. They remembered with a peculiar fondness Susan getting jealous over some of the women Peter sank his teeth into. He didn't always care for her choice in male victims either, but, as the old saw goes, needs must when the devil rides. It seemed that, of the others, Bob found the best accommodation for them and Morey turned out to be the best hunter.

When they got to London, there were more changes. The city was not what they expected it to be, though none of them could put into words what they had expected. It was the filthiest most overcrowded place they had ever seen. The Thames stank with human refuse. There were days in summer in which parliament could not sit because the stench from the river was so bad. Peter and Susan wrinkled up their noses at the memory. Since those days, of course, London had changed. It was still overcrowded but The Thames, even on hot days, was no longer a great moving cesspool.

Getting a place of their own in London seemed impossible until Peter decided to use the art of mesmerism. It was an art taught to him and his group by those who had turned them into the undead way back in Gulls' Haven in 1827. He had used what he had learnt to get into the head of a brothel madam and get her to do what he wanted her to do. It took concentration but in the end he succeeded.

"Sign over the building to me," he had told the tough looking woman and she complied. He then took some of her rough as old guts blood and told her to be on her way and to never return. Without so much as blinking she obeyed. He suspected, and quite rightly, this power wouldn't work quite so well on everybody. Still, he had amazed himself and the others. They all tried it out on the prostitutes with varying degrees of success. It was Susan who arranged via mesmerism to have the local butcher chop up their leftovers and use them in stews and meat pies. She wondered if the locals who bought the food suspected what they were purchasing. Would they have cared less if they had known so long as it was cheap and nourishing?

From then on the vampires from Cornwall had a place of ill repute to call their own and, before long; they had worked out ways to make it pay off. In a twisted sense, it was like being back in the Inn business. You had customers who would stay with you for a while and you were expected to make them comfortable so they would make return visits. Since no one expected anyone who worked in a brothel to sleep during the night, it didn't raise any local eyebrows when they slept during the day.

Everything was going fine until there was one too many deaths and a crazy woman set fire to their establishment. Even now, in their sleep, Peter and Susan could see the flames leaping up to get them. They and the others barely got out in time. If the smoke had been thicker and had confused them, they might have been goners.

Even so they got out of England altogether. One night they took a boat and left. It was the first time any of them had been abroad and, if only one of them had known French like some of their smuggler friends had, then Paris might have worked out better. As it was, they were less than subtle about gaining their wants and needs and soon had lots of trouble coming down on them from all directions. This trouble wasn't only in the form of gendarmes, who objected to Parisians being slaughtered, but also in the form of French Freemasons who understood the undead and how they might be destroyed.

Susan coughed in her 2009 coffin in remembrance of those metal projectiles from the late 19th Century hitting her. They not only hurt but, at first, they scared the hell out of her. No one in England had shot her and she didn't know what to expect. She didn't know it at the time that it was a technique, a way of dealing with the undead; the French had come up with.

The French Freemasons used bullets to slow down vampires so that wooden knives at close quarters could be employed. Nets reeking of garlic were thrown at Peter and the others in attempts to ensnare them. It was more by luck than good judgment they managed to get away. Still even the greatest optimist among them, who happened to be Sam Watts, soon realized such luck couldn't last for long. Within the month they fled Paris for Melum then Fontainebleau. Along the way they were picking up a little French. They knew, for example, the French word for blood was *sang*. They learned how to swear in French and how the French pray to God. None of this was of much use to their survival.

They kept heading south, staying away from big towns and cities. Sometimes they would attack livestock rather than humans in the hope of throwing any pursuers off their trail. A cow's blood is nourishing to a vampire even if it is rather foul-tasting.

Once they had crossed into Spain, Peter and Susan hoped their difficulties would end. Again language difficulties made for clumsy moves and they spent much of their time on the run. Portugal proved to be just as hazardous.

Somehow they survived in Europe up to the beginning of the Great War. From then on it was smooth sailing for a while. They never knew, when this conflict started, just how useful it would be. During this time, they fed better than before. It was so easy for them to hide their tracks. What did a half dozen or so more corpses matter when hundreds of thousands of soldiers were being slaughtered in every major offensive? Yes, between 1914 and 1918, France and Belgium treated them well. They could dine heartily and the chances of being caught by vampire hunters were slim. Peter couldn't help but lick his lips in remembrance of those days of plenty. Neither could Susan.

Germany in the early 1920s was a good place to be. Chaos reigned on the streets of the major cities and it was easy to lose oneself in the unrest. Chaos, however, couldn't last forever. By 1925 they were homesick for England and so made their way back into France.

Paris proved to be more dangerous than ever. Peter and Susan tossed and turned recalling some of the traps that were set for them. On a trip through a narrow walkway while in bat form, they barely escaped two assassins with flamethrowers. If they had been in human form and unable to quickly fly above and away from the men, they would have been toast. On another occasion, smoke bombs were used to hide the whereabouts of waiting spearmen. The vampires' heightened sense of hearing saved them from serious injury, possibly total destruction. The French could be cunning and innovative.

By early 1927 they were in Cambridge, England. With funds they managed to smuggle in from France, they were able to buy a house and set themselves up in a respectable neighborhood. For months everything was going swimmingly. All of them, including Bill and Sam, had learned how to control their lust for blood so they were emptying people but not unto death. If no one died then there would be no investigation and no investigation meant they could stay put. Staying put meant they could rest up from their wanderings. Peter and Susan sighed at the thought.

Then Susan came up with the bright idea of siring someone. She thought if their number was larger they would be more formidable next time they were attacked. Her idea made sense and Peter could not find a fault with it. Neither could the others.

"I'll do it then," she said. "If it works in our favor, we'll all have a go."

Peter, in his 2009 coffin, winced at the thought, at the memory of how, in the early 20th Century, during the jazz age, things had gone wrong. Petrov Blaine, an accountant, was to join them. He had been invited to the house and had turned up willingly, expecting a party. There was a blackout but it didn't affect them. The gramophone worked without electricity and so did their one candle. Susan had put the bite on Blaine and had gotten him to taste her blood. When she finished draining him, he fell backward, broke through an upper story window, and landed near a young woman who was ringing their doorbell. Petrov falling dead at her feet frightened her and she dashed away on her bicycle for help. In a panic, knowing their cover was blown; Peter, Susan and the others changed into bat form and hightailed it out of there. Three nights later, they collected Petrov Blaine and left Cambridge. He was reluctant to join them at first but, once he realized he couldn't go back to his old life, he settled into their company.

A local Cambridge newspaper of the day mentioned a bat or a large bird following the woman who had seen Petrov fall. Peter still wondered about that flying thing. What was it? He knew that it had nothing to do with him and his people. It made Peter wonder if there had been other undead around. Susan had come to the same conclusion. There was the possibility that the vampires who had sired Peter and the others had been in Cambridge checking up on them. Peter and Susan were still none the wiser why they had been sired by them in the first place.

Peter and Susan couldn't help but smile in their 2009 slumber at certain golden memories they had of the late 1930's and the following decade. World War Two, when it began in '39, showed the promise of being bloody like the Great War and also being a good hiding place for them. Dunkirk, France in 1940 turned out to be a vampire's paradise. Humans were so busy dodging other humans trying to kill them they didn't have time to spend wondering about the undead. Finding a safe place to sleep during the day was a problem but, otherwise, unlife was good. Besides, they had that difficulty in the Great War and had made out fine. It was a matter of looking for deep, dark holes and ways to close them against the light.

Between 1941 and 1945, Peter, Susan and the others followed the German army. They dressed in German uniforms and learned enough of the German language to get by. When some German soldiers went missing, it was blamed on either the underground movement of whatever country they were in or British infiltration. By the end of 1944, with the Americans and the British on the move in many areas that were once dominated by Germans, it was even more difficult for German higher command to keep track of their men in the field. Yes, the war was wonderful if you're a blood drinker. Peter and Susan were sad when it came to an end.

"If only Hitler and his cronies hadn't been so incompetent," Peter had said to Susan at the time. "With proper management, the Third Reich might have gone on for at least another decade."

"Perhaps in an alternate world where some lucky vampires live," Susan had replied, "that's exactly what did happen."

Still, from 1945 to well into the '50s, the European roads were full of people trying to get home. Such people were easy pickings. Homesickness, however, called them back to England. It seemed they needed to return to collect more native soil to sleep on top of but also for sentimental reasons hard to acknowledge and hard to explain.

London and Coventry were quite a surprise. Both cities sustained a lot of damage during the war. It would be at least a decade for them to return to what was normal before the war. Still the British spirit was strong and it made a vampire proud of being of that particular stock.

Peter and Susan became restless in their coffins when they recalled how policemen in the know about their kind and cunning Freemasons chased them out of England and into Scotland.

At first, Scotland was a haven. They stuck to the small towns and villages and everything was fine. Winter set in and it was a rough one. Being undead, the cold didn't bother them but it did make game scarce. By then they were way up north and getting careless. They left the bodies of men as well as animals in the snow figuring they were safe enough. Most hunters, they reasoned, were likely to be on the hunt come spring and, during the more bitter months, be at home in front of a comforting fire. Then they got to an Inn called the Bonny Lass in Wick.

Who knew there were Scottish Freemasons? Who knew some of these Freemasons were vampire hunters who knew their business and were possibly insane? Peter and Susan groaned at the memory of finding out.

In one fell swoop members of the MacLean clan took out Bill Franklin, Bob Turner, Sam Watts and their newest member, Petrov Blaine. It was well planned and they weren't expecting trouble. The action came on fast and furious and there was fear. During it, Peter found he was reacting rather than thinking straight. The follow up was equally devastating. The next night Morey and William Coates were struck down via arrows through the heart while hunting deer in the woods. They were trying to lie low by not bothering humans with their need for blood. In the end it didn't matter. Once the arrows were in them, they didn't last long. Peter was a few hundred yards away when it happened and it still made him squirm in his coffin to think how fast it did happen. One minute they were immortal and the next they were gone. They became ash and the ash was wrapped up by the falling snow. Life had extinguished unlife. Whiteness had hidden the gray.

Fear had pounced on Peter and Susan, the remaining vampires, and like a relentless enemy wouldn't let them go. They had entered the land of the clansmen eight strong. In less than two nights, six had perished. For two weeks the survivors traveled without eating. Getting out of Scotland and going anywhere else became top priority. They were determined to prevent the Scottish Freemasons from getting the rest of them.

Northern Ireland was good for a long while. A couple of missing Protestants could always be blamed on the IRA and a few missing Catholics could always be blamed on the Black and Tans. Peter and Susan smiled at the decade or so they spent milking hostilities between Catholics and Protestants. Perhaps they should have stayed longer. Southern Ireland was less hospitable than the north but better than Scotland. They stayed in the south for a mere five years before they felt the need to press on to other parts of Britain.

In the summer of 1975 they arrived in Wales. At first it seemed like fresh new territory well worth exploring. Fishguard reminded them a little of their old home in Cornwall. It was around this time that the idea of settling down somewhere gripped them. If it wasn't so close to Southern Ireland, where there was talk of a rise in Freemasonry activity, Fishguard might have been perfect. There was no point buying trouble or waiting for it to come for you. After staying for a couple of weeks, they moved on.

They found the hills of Wales honeycombed with tunnels, some man-made and some far more ancient. There were tunnels that went on for miles with lots of side junctures and byways. This made for so many perfect hideouts during the day where hunters would have great difficulty finding them. They could have stayed there forever experiencing some degree of freedom from being hunted but, England was still calling to them.

In the spring of 1995 they made it back onto English soil and, for a time, rented a flat in Birmingham. They were there a decade before English Freemasons sniffed them out and they had to once more move on.

Peter and Susan breathed a profound and deep sigh in their sleep. It was hard being in England and not being welcome. It became even harder when, in the spring of 2005, on the outskirts of Kings Lynn, Peter was almost liquidated. He winced remembering the pain and the closeness he had come to leaving this plain of existence.

Peter was feeding on a horse when he was shot twice in the back by someone with a colt .45. He reacted by going for the gunman and crushing the bones of the hand that had wielded the gun. Since he had been shot plenty of times before without dying, it was easy to understand his confidence that the bullets meant nothing. They were a painful irritation or, at least, that is what they were supposed to be. When his arms and legs began to shake, he knew something was wrong. He began to sweat and his sight blurred.

"They're special bullets," the gunman said through gritted teeth, nursing his hurt hand. "They are hollow points with slithers of wood inside. The wood will do the trick."

After that the gunman passed out. Then Susan turned up. She'd been supping on another horse some two hundred yards away and, when she heard the gun shots, came running to see if Peter needed help.

"Get me to a doctor. Hurry!" cried Peter. "Bullets must come out! They must!"

The gunman was forgotten and so survived. Susan found a doctor and she convinced him to operate. The bullets and the slithers of wood that had broken free with the impact were removed and Peter regained his health. He was fortunate. If the second bullet had been propelled a quarter of an inch closer to the heart he would have perished.

After that they headed south to London and then to Gulls Haven, Cornwall. Peter and Susan smiled as they remembered finding their old Inn up for sale. It had been renovated a number of times since they had officially owned it but it was still recognizable. It had been renamed The Candle in the Dark but that name could be changed back to White Owl. They had more than enough money, mostly in English and Irish pounds collected from their victims over the years, to pay for the place. The present owner, who admitted he couldn't make a go of the business, was happy to take cash in various denominations. For Peter and Susan, moving back in was like coming home to stay. They didn't know it until they made their comeback but they had missed The White Owl Inn, now The Candle in the Dark.

They had hired help to run the place during the day and had cleaned out part of the cellar as a place of daytime rest. This was their second day. Why then were they, for the most part, dreaming about past wrong turns and out and out disasters? It was not like either one of them to do so without some reason behind it. What was it the back portion of their minds trying to tell them?

A knock came. It was a great thud and there was this weight on Peter's chest that woke him with a start. In a similar fashion, Susan was also woken.

Hovering over Peter was one of their barmen. He had in one hand a hammer and in the other a wooden stake pressed into position over Peter's heart. Susan had one of the barmaids hovering over her in a similar manner.

"It's almost nightfall," the young barman said. "We must act quickly."

"But they look so innocent, so peaceful," the barmaid protested.

"We do this to avenge our family."

"Yes. Our family and their honor."

Peter and Susan wondered who these two were going to avenge. Over time there had been so many dead, so many nights of gorging on this human or that. How was it possible to remember them all?

"For our grandfather, Petrov Blaine," cried the barman with gusto as he hammered in the wood. Peter screamed and perished. Blood spurted high, getting in the barman's eyes. He wiped it away with a handkerchief.

"For Petrov Blaine," echoed the barmaid, hammering her stake home into Susan who also screamed and perished.

As the last of the Gulls Haven undead went the way of all things, she reflected on the irony of going to pieces over the only human she had ever sired. *Perhaps it's just as well,* she thought as blood ran from her mouth and her eyes turned to jelly, *I hadn't been big on siring.*

"It took us ages to track you down," the barman said to a skeleton becoming dust. "Of course we knew about Cambridge. Then we lost track of you. We knew you were in Birmingham at one time and then many miles away at Kings Lynn."

"But, when this Inn went up for sale and we heard the legends, we suspected this to be where it had all begun for you. We suspected this was old stomping ground…"

"And, if that was the case, you just might return."

"And we were right."

There was something about Susan's skull turning powdery that moved the barmaid. She breathed in and sighed: "Rest in peace, Susan and Peter."

"Rest in peace," the barman echoed. He hoped to never have to perform such a service ever again. He knew his sister, the barmaid, felt the same way.

The Trials and Tribulations of Kara

Black Forest, Germany, winter of 1936

It was bad enough being stuck in the middle of nowhere, with little to occupy one's mind save work, without the work becoming more and more hazardous. Gone were the carefree college days but gone also was the alarming poverty. Still the project wouldn't last forever and might, in its final stages, yield some benefits to the country.

There were moral issues he had to ignore because it was better that way. Sometimes advancements were made in less than scrupulous circumstance and, regretfully, from the bones of victims. He had to make sure he wasn't going to be one of them.

Doktor Emile Glass was thinking about the money when he took skin and fur samples from the creature. Even sedated it howled and clawed at him through the bars of its cage. There was something human about it and yet canine. It was as if some tribe had risen from the wolf pack rather than a hairless type of ape. Perhaps the evolutionary theorists were wrong.

The eminent surgeon, Doktor Klaus Heinemann, took the hard won samples from Doktor Glass and looked at them under a microscope. The fur proved to be useless for Heinemann's purposes but the skin cells had possibilities. They glowed brilliant with life.

In another cage, which was kept out of direct sunlight, there was a naked Gypsy woman. She had long, black tresses that she used to cover up her ample breasts. From what the state had implied about Gypsies, it was strange to think of her as being so modest. Her eyes and lips were soft in the semi-darkness. For the unwary she was but a helpless prisoner. For any scientist, what she was could not be explained.

"I'll get a sample from subject X," said Heinemann. "You be sure to hold the crucifix steady."

Ordinarily, the assistant would collect from the subjects but someone had to hold the religious artifact to make sure she behaved.

Heinemann hadn't been brought up in a strongly religious household. He considered his belief in God wavering at best. Glass came from a Catholic background and had, in the past, used the crucifix to good effect. There was the question of whether a non-believer or a waverer could use the crucifix at all, and Heinemann didn't want the answer at his own expense. He was getting used to the idea that there were things in this world for which science hadn't come close to forming a working hypothesis.

Subject X wanted to resist having her arm scraped with a thin metal rod and having a few strands of her hair removed. The crucifix, however, kept her from doing so. She had to look away and let Heinemann get on with it. Glass wondered how far his boss was willing to go in his experiments. Hell seemed such a real place. He wondered if he would soon be on his way there.

"Amazing." Heinemann studied the new samples under the microscope. "Compared to the lycanthrope's cells, subject X's are lethargic. Most likely they are being affected by the light coming from my viewing apparatus."

"Most likely," Glass agreed.

Heinemann proceeded to mix the skin sample of the lycanthrope with the skin sample of the Gypsy vampire. He added a few drops of blood from a beaker so that the cells from one skin sample had a liquid bridge by which to travel to the other sample. What he saw via his microscope after doing this was disappointing. The lycanthrope cells attacked the weaker vampire cells. They looked like they would triumph without much resistance.

"They won't combine," Heinemann said.

"No," said Glass who was given a chance to look through the microscope. "My advice is to leave these samples in the dark and come back later."

"What good will that do?"

"Possibly nothing. Possibly everything."

For twelve hours Heinemann left the samples in complete darkness. During that time Glass gave the vampire a live rat to drain of blood and provided a chunk of raw steak to the other prisoner. He then left the confines of the lab, acknowledged the guards on duty and walked the corridor to his room. It contained shelves full of books, an old oil lamp on a stand and a bed. He suspected the oil lamp, given to him by Heinemann, came from a time when the place was a wood-cutter's cottage. Back then life was less complicated and the concrete monstrosity that had replaced such simple trappings, and which he was residing in, spoke of a more frightening, even more complicated future.

Glass packed his pipe with tobacco, lit it via the lamp and settled down for a peaceful smoke. He was one of many scientists who had come to the realization that smoking was not good for one's health. Still it relaxed the nerves. Besides, most things were becoming a health hazard. Simply saying what is on your mind, in the wrong place in the new order where someone in authority, or who wants to be in authority, might overhear, was far more life threatening than a few puffs of burning dried leaf.

Outside his window the trees and stars beckoned to him. They reminded him of his earlier interest in nature which prompted him, as a young man, to take science seriously. He started out with an interest in biology which changed to chemistry when that became more likely to put food on the table. What he was doing now was neither true biology nor true chemistry but it paid well. Heinemann, who came from a wealthy aristocratic family, and the government were taking care of the bills for the project and both wanted results. What results they would get was as yet unknown. Glass prayed they would get something useful and that he'd live long enough to see a brighter, better day. Somehow he had his doubts either prayer would be answered for they were stepping into either God's territory or the Devil's with little understanding of what they were doing.

Glass and his country had been through some lean times. First there was a year of starvation after the armistice of 1918 which lead to fighting in the streets of many cities. This was followed by a period of grace which came to an end with high inflation and more starvation. With the crash on Wall Street in America came a period where money was scarce throughout the Western World and jobs were even harder to come by. Germany was hit hardest by this depression and it looked as if the people would never regain the pride they once had in themselves. Then the Nazi Party rose to prominence and there was new hope. Glass suspected it was false hope but it was at least something the ordinary people could cling to for a while. He couldn't see what was now ahead but he knew that it couldn't be good. The world was changing too fast and not for the better.

Once his pipe was out, Glass settled down to sleep. The oil lamp stayed on. He didn't really think its light would scare away evil but its fully functioning presence was a comfort and that's what counted. The crucifix was under his pillow.

Glass was awakened by a knock on the door. One of the guards told him that he was required in the lab. Slowly he got up, combed his hair and put on a clean shirt. He washed his face in the basin of cold water provided by his minder and thanked him for such consideration.

"Your work is important," replied the guard and took him back to the lab.

Heinemann was overjoyed by what had happened in a mere twelve hours. He congratulated Glass for his insightfulness.

"At last we're making progress," said Heinemann. "The cells have come together. In a month's time we can begin the next phase."

"Why not now?" asked Glass, anxious to get his association with Heinemann over and done with as soon as possible. It was hard to believe this fanatic he was faced with was a married man. It was hard at times to believe he was anything but a crazed scientist all too willing to play with strange, never before played with fire, the blaze of creation and possibly unprecedented destruction. It was like being a brand new Prometheus bringing something to Man that the gods, or perhaps the one true God, would ban as far too dangerous for humans to possess.

"That's why." Heinemann pointed toward subject Y. "We need him at full strength."

Subject Y, the lycanthrope, had gone from being a hairy brute with superhuman power to a sallow youth covering up his nakedness before the Gypsy vampire in the next cage. Glass almost felt sorry for him. Pity, however, was a luxury in the new order few could afford. Like many of the softer emotions such as sympathy and love it didn't belong and never would.

"What now?" Glass asked with a sigh. He could see his time living on the edge of the border between life and a horrible death stretching to infinity.

"Relax," Heinemann said in a light hearted voice. "I have acquired ancient texts on alchemy and the occult that may give us new insights into what we are dealing with. In the meantime there is a bottle of schnapps around here I have been saving for a special occasion. We will toast our minor success."

In the weeks that followed, Glass became engrossed in the ancient texts Heinemann brought him to study. Much of the writing was in Latin and had come from various provinces of Europe. For the most part, there was little mention of either lycanthropy or vampirism. Where they were mentioned, there were warnings against venturing blind into the realm of evil. Terrible things had happened to those who had tinkered with manifestations of the dark side of the supernatural. It was best to leave well enough alone. This wasn't a scientific attitude but then Glass didn't consider the texts to have been put together by people he could refer to as scientists. This did not mean that they couldn't be right in their findings and in their beliefs.

One scribe from 12th Century Madrid had it that vampires are dead creatures radiating death. Their only claim to the universe of the living was their ability to absorb energy from those who are alive. Conversely, werewolves or lycanthropes, as they continue to be referred to in pseudo scientific circles, are superconductors of living matter. Being two creatures in one, they had energy that, at given times, reached out beyond our earthly plane of existence to some other place in time and space. Thus vampires and lycanthropes could be considered complete opposites. Both were also a dire threat to mankind.

The day before the next full moon, Heinemann met Glass in the conference room where he usually met important military men, noteworthy politicians, and visiting scientists. He bade him to relate what he had learned from the dusty tomes.

Glass cleared his throat, took a sip of coffee from a mug and began: "The more pertinent data had been gathered in the Middle East during the many ages of Man and translated into Latin in Southern Spain between the 11th and 14th Centuries. Translations come with problems, though. Sometimes the languages do not permit the translator to be as accurate as he might wish to be. Then there's the translation from Latin to German I do in my head."

"Yes, yes, understood. But what did you find out?" prompted Heinemann who then took a sip of his own coffee.

"Apparently, in Egypt soon after the city of Alexandria was built, two alchemists tried to create a formula for controlling lycanthropes when they are in their manic, hairy state. The idea was to put together an army the like of which had never been seen before."

"A laudable aim."

"Ya, well…The end result was the deaths of the two alchemists at the hands of the lycanthrope they thought they had tamed."

"A pity. Go on."

"In 2nd Century AD Palestine a female vampire tried to seduce a priest but was put off from doing so by the symbol of the Star of David. In the 5th Century AD, in the same part of the world, a female vampire, possibly the same one, was put off from putting the bite on a follower of Mohammed by the Holy Scriptures he was carrying at the time."

"Interesting. Go on."

Glass drank more of his coffee and looked at his colleague. "All the texts that do touch upon lycanthropy and vampirism agree on one point. What we are doing is foolish and likely to end badly."

"The talk of old men who are frightened by their own shadow," laughed Heinemann in good humor. "Anything else?"

"All religious symbols can affect the vampire. It is becoming clearer, however, that the user of the symbol must be a believer. Faith is the real defense."

"Just as I thought. Anything on lycanthropy we can use?"

"Only that most of these writers agree that we are dealing with great forces."

"Ya. Great forces…But when are scientists not dealing with great forces?"

Glass looked at Heinemann wondering what difficulties this man's cavalier attitude was likely to get them into. He liked to think that the man who invented dynamite had misgivings about giving mankind the ability to blow things up in such an efficient manner and that the man who developed mustard gas hoped his great find might never be used. Even if Heinemann didn't have any misgivings for what was going to happen in the name of scientific progress, Glass had plenty for both of them. That night he sat up in bed, smoked and worried about the future. Cancer seemed like small potatoes compared with what might happen to him in the morning.

At nine the guard knocked on Glass' door awakening him from a fitful slumber. He walked with trepidation to the lab where the subjects had already been secured to work benches. They had been fed sleep gas to make them more amenable. The lycanthrope looked as if he could easily tear away his leather straps. The vampire was weak from only being supplied live rodents. If Heinemann hadn't known to provide her cage with native earth she would probably be in no shape for the coming experiment.

"Further testing of the samples," revealed Heinemann, "suggests that, in both the case of the vampire and our werewolf, a steady current of electricity might well stimulate cell growth. Place the electrodes on subject Y and I will place the electrodes on subject X."

"Very good, Herr Doktor," Glass mumbled, even more unsure that they should continue.

"Stout heart, Glass," cried Heinemann. "That is what is called for in this day and age."

The electrodes went under the ears and on the palms of the subjects. They were attached via insulated wire to a large control box and a small dynamo. Heinemann flipped a switch and a mild humming sound invaded the chamber. A cold, blue glow enveloped X and Y. Slowly they stirred out of their drug induced stupor. The lycanthrope growled from a place deep in his soul. The vampire hissed, showing her teeth.

Subject X looked angrily at Heinemann as he pushed a needle into her arm. With fear in his eyes – fear he suspected the lycanthrope could smell – Glass did the same to subject Y. Due to a small pump, blood began to flow, via tubes attached to the needles, from the beast to the fanged maiden. Heinemann turned up the electricity. The blue glow increased and subject Y howled his displeasure.

"I'm feeding her intravenously rather than orally," lectured Heinemann as if addressing an eager student, "because I don't want any interference from her digestive system. I don't want her to filter out, or in any other way, reject the power and the abilities he has to offer."

"Ya, Herr Doktor," said Glass.

This was all very well but there was something fundamentally wrong in giving even more power to a type of being that had, for centuries, been designated an evil on earth. Add to this the nervousness of the guards, the struggling of the brute to be free and a seer would not be needed to see trouble on the gallop. Glass swallowed hard.

Still seeing subject X as wan and lackluster, Heinemann yet again increased the electrical current. The beast screamed and managed to snap one of his restraints. In response, a guard opened up. For ten seconds, machine gun bullets struck the lycanthrope moving him about as if he was a rag doll. They were coated in silver and therefore deadly to him. In his final moments he reverted to human form and became little more than a bullet riddled boy. "Why?" he asked Glass before he died, but didn't receive an answer. What was there to say?

Subject X slipped into a coma. There was lycanthrope blood everywhere including on Heinemann and Glass. There was blood on the guards. It was all Glass could do not to throw up. He couldn't help shaking and was surprised that Heinemann looked so very still. One of the guards tried to speak but the words would not come. Glass washed his face in a basin of water and tried calming himself with brandy from a bottle that was kept on a top shelf but it didn't help.

The guard who had fired was dismissed from his post but the damage had already been done. Heinemann was devastated. His only hope of any useful outcome was now to somehow revive the vampire. When he was able to speak, he arranged for her to be fed intravenously with various human blood types in order to stimulate her mind and bring her back to him.

"If we knew her name," Glass ventured. "If we called her by name it might help."

"Kara," said Heinemann with a faint smile. "She told me her name the night we captured her."

"Yet you have insisted on calling her subject X."

"Ya. For professional reasons. It does not pay to became too attached to one of your subjects. Do you understand?"

"Ya, Herr Doktor."

A week later subject X did revive. She snapped her bonds and, before her guards could respond, she snapped their necks. She then proceeded to hunt down Glass and Heinemann. She caught up with them in a small library near the lab. They tried to lock her out but she was too strong. The bolt across the door shattered. Glass used his crucifix but she didn't seem at all concerned by it. He wondered if it was because he was losing his belief in a just and merciful God or whether it had something to do with the blood transfusion. She threw Heinemann hard against a book case breaking his spine. An old encyclopedia fell on his head further injuring him.

"Why?" screamed subject X at Glass who was cowering in a corner. She shook him until he answered.

"He did it for science!" cried Glass, at last, pointing a nervous finger at Heinemann.

"And you?"

"The money. God help me, I didn't want to be poor ever again! I didn't want to starve ever again!"

"Rest assured, little man, you won't."

Subject X opened her mouth to reveal her fangs. Her breath was fetid but he expected that. Her teeth glinted at him. They sank into his neck, and a warmth he didn't know he had began to leave him. He was dying and rather quickly. She was beautiful in her own way. Quite stunning. The slightly darker-than-his-own skin of her cheek touching his cheek as she fed was somewhat erotic. Her breasts moving against his chest was provocative but it meant nothing. How could it mean something when he was fading away? And he was a fool. *Just as well*, he thought as the last ebb of life left him.

Sated on Glass' blood, subject X left the library and then the compound. She became Kara once more, glorying in the hunt, Kara the Gypsy who could sing and dance and play and Kara the vampire whose lust for freedom was matched only by her lust for unlife.

From the spring of 1937 to the winter of 1945, there was a section of the Black Forest neither Russian nor American soldiers dared cross. Stories of strange, cannibalistic rituals performed by some demented occult tribe circulated far and wide. Gnawed bones were found at the beginning of certain trails and bloodless corpses were discovered on the outskirts of nearby towns and villages. No one suspected that it was Kara on the loose.

There's a file in a German archive vault in Berlin dealing with a set of incidents that occurred on the first and second nights of the spring of 1942. A young officer named Fritz Lieberman was taking his patrol deep into the forest when they came upon a wolf-like beast bending over the corpse of a half eaten doe. It was bright enough to see because the moon was full, shedding a silvery eeriness on the gruesome scene.

The beast, covered in blood and gore, growled when it came to realize Fritz and his men were there, staring at it. It sprang at one of his men, taking him away with it into thick bush. What followed were wild, bestial sounds matched by all too human screams and cries for mercy. By the time Fritz and the rest of his men got there, it was over and the beast had moved on. Not much was left of the soldier; his clothes in their entirety were missing.

Fritz decided they would retreat rather than advance and, on the following night, they came upon a young, attractive woman of dark complexion. She was wearing the bloodied shirt and pants of the butchered German soldier. *I must be dreaming or going mad*, Fritz had thought at the time but there she was and his men saw her too. He demanded to know who she was and why she was dressed in dead man's clothes and how she had come by them. All she said was: "I am Gypsy. I am the wind. Catch me if you can."

She ran off and Fritz sent one of his men after her thinking she would be caught and made to give a better account of herself. When his man failed to return with the girl he went after them with the rest of his patrol. The girl was not found but they did locate the soldier. He was stark white, dead and with, strangely enough, a smile on his lips.

After the war, the American government took a more active role in dispelling old superstitions. Too many soldiers came into Kara's area of forest and it became obvious to her that, sooner or later, they would discover her day time refuge. So one night she gathered up some native soil in a sugar sack and left.

From 1945 to well into the 1950s, there were a lot of displaced persons wandering the roads of Europe. Some, after fleeing their homes during the war, were trying to get back to where they belonged. Others, who had had their homes destroyed, were trying to find a place, any place, which would accept them and allow them to live like normal human beings. Many were without identification papers since, before the war; many of them had never strayed more than a mile from their village. Where everyone knew you, there seemed little need for papers stating who you were and where you came from. British, Swiss and Russian authorities, just to name a few, were given the unenviable task of looking after these people and helping them to get to where they could belong. Stragglers along the various roads became easy pickings for the likes of Kara. They would disappear, and there would be no one to bear witness that they had ever existed.

Among Kara's many victims for those years only one would stay in her memory. It was the winter of 1946 and her name was Anna. They met on the road going from Poland into Germany. It was a desolate area offering nothing in the way of shelter or warmth. No one else was around and even if there had been others few would have cared about either one of them.

Anna, who was dressed in rags, had been in some dark place and was now free but freedom had come too late. The poor woman, who Kara knew was Romany by certain inflections in her speech, had been in a state of starvation and near starvation for far too long. She was weak and she was dying. What's more, she knew it. Her eyes were failing and her feet were blistered from the walking she had already done. She was going to collapse and become food for the local vermin.

When Kara came to her, she said in a shallow voice made so by aching lungs: "Are you an angel?"

Taken aback by this, Kara asked: "Are you expecting one?"

Anna gave her name and said: "Yes, I am expecting the angel of death."

"I am here," breathed Kara who wished to be of service. She knew that this woman's blood would not be much good because of the recent life she had led but she took it anyway. It seemed the kindest thing to do even if vampires weren't supposed to be kind. Perhaps it was the only good thing she'd ever done as a member of the undead and it was likely, she knew, to be the only good thing she'd ever do.

Liverpool, England, winter, 1966

Kara was not bothered in the least by the frigid wind that so bothered others. Under her straw hat and gray raincoat she was naked, awaiting the change. It was something she did not look forward to but it was something she did her best to plan for before it came upon her.

She was in Strawberry Fields, a small park that allowed slum kids to know what grass was like and have a glimpse of how their world would have been if not for the industrial revolution. She was about to lose her mind and there was nothing she could do about it.

In the park were three men affected by freezing temperatures but not in a hurry to escape the cold. They were advancing toward her with some determination, the breeze playing with their brown great coats. Two were muscle types with black truncheons and pug-ugly faces. The third was a silver haired man past middle age. His face was craggy and there was an old scar that ran from his forehead to just a fraction of an inch above his left eye. He was confined to a wheel chair, a tartan shawl covering his damaged, useless legs.

"Do you recognize me?" called out the seated man. "I have not forgotten you." The wind whipped around his words eventually carrying them to her. She studied him for a moment. Then who he was dawned on her. She had suffered both mentally and physically at his hands and continued to suffer.

"Heinemann!" she cried, her eyes blazing. If her heart could have raced it would have with her desire to destroy her tormentor – the man she thought had been long since removed from this world.

"Yes, subject X," Heinemann confirmed with a sour half smile. "I have been searching for you for a very long time."

"But you're dead."

"Crippled, not dead. After you left me the way you did, I was rescued by two soldiers whom you had not destroyed in your rampage. They took me to a nearby hospital knowing I would amply reward them for their loyalty."

"And you went on to torture more lycanthropes and vampires?"

"No. I accepted my lack of success as stoically as I could and went on to work with liquid rocket fuel. When the war was coming to its inevitable conclusion, I made sure to be captured by the British and not the Russians. I have been working in England ever since. When word came to me that a mysterious woman dressed like a Gypsy had booked passage on an ocean liner bound from Liverpool to New York, I was hoping it was you. I came down from London to see. Obviously, despite it being based on very little, my assumption was correct."

"Now?" asked one of Heinemann's thugs, a man who didn't care to listen to a lot of talk.

"Ya," answered Heinemann. "She is a failed experiment from long ago. Eradicate her!"

They moved on Kara with drawn clubs just as the moon, hidden behind a cloud, came out in all its richness and fullness. There was no way to push it back or to get it to call upon the earth some other time.

The transformation was upon her but it wasn't the gentle and elegant ballet of humanoid into bat she rather enjoyed. It was ugly and quite brutal. Her joints cracked as bones elongated then reformed. Her nose sprouted into a wet snout. Hair and muscles grew, ripping apart the raincoat and hat. Her fingernails became claws and her teeth became flashing blades. And her mind ran for cover into the gathering darkness and a more primitive, bestial intelligence emerged. It emerged and looked upon the earth anew as if this was the moment of its birth.

Heinemann's men got in a few solid whacks with their clubs while the process of becoming was being completed. The beast howled in pain as its own blood dripped down from the center of its head into its eyes. Then there was the slashing of claws and a guttural growl that must have originated from the very seat of Hell. In response, the men with the clubs begged for their lives but what they were addressing was far from human and not at all concerned with their pleas for mercy. Both got the chance to see their internal organs dripping in the creature's hands before they perished. It was all they could have expected from the monster, especially after hurting it, and it was all they got.

The beast sniffed the air and, realizing there was still one human to contend with, turned in Heinemann's direction. It was at this moment Heinemann whipped away the shawl, grabbing the two primed crossbows he had been hiding. They were twelve inch by six inch miniatures each with a three inch bolt made of hazel wood. He fired them simultaneously. One bolt went into the beast's shoulder and the other pierced its heart.

"Die!" Heinemann cried as the beast staggered. But it wouldn't die. With a whimper, it withdrew the wooden shafts from its flesh and hurled them into the bushes. It then turned on the man Kara hated most of all who happened to also be the man the beast had learned to hate.

"If only I'd foreseen," Heinemann muttered as death descended. "If only they had been tipped with silver…"

Heinemann was given the time to scream long and loud. He availed himself of this opportunity with great vigor before passing on to the next world. The beast feasted knowing that its wounds would heal with one good day's sleep. The meat and blood would help its recovery. Kara slumbered within the creature unaware of the activities going on around her, unaware that her revenge upon Heinemann was complete.

New York, USA, autumn, 1967

The sleet and the rain gave the city a face lift, making it appear shiny and new. But it was the home for all sorts of vermin including the two legged variety. There were streets said to be more dangerous than lion country in Africa. There were streets where death came at the point of a gun and true justice was hard to find.

Dressed in fashionable attire, Kara walked down the most unsavory of streets hoping to meet the most unsavory of people. She figured, and quite rightly, that muggers, purse snatchers and beggars would not be missed. Still the disappearance of too many vermin did lead to questions being asked and experts brought in to look into the developing situation.

Kara was about to put the bite on her twelfth New York victim when he spun around and shoved a crucifix in her face. It burned slightly but, no doubt because of her unique metabolism, didn't affect her as much as it might another vampire. She knocked it aside and went for his throat. It was then she heard footsteps and found herself surrounded by pseudo-tramps with stakes, more crucifixes, and spears. Why hadn't she been aware of their approach? Why hadn't she scented them before now? The answer was the rubbish around her that was interfering with the better workings of her nose. Moving rags and papers had also affected her hearing making the trap close to perfect. She tossed what should have been her meal at those in front of her and, in the ensuing confusion, changed into a bat. Spears were flung at her but she dodged them as she made her escape.

It was fortunate that none of her pursuers could fly. It was fortunate for them. She was tempted to circle back and attack but decided not to. From the top of a nearby building she sat silently and watched the men gather up their equipment and leave.

Who are they? she wondered. The following day a fellow vampire told her they were Pinkerton agents hot on her trail. There was a time when the Big Apple had been a safe haven for the undead but that was fifty years ago. It was now a place in which to keep a very low profile and to get out of as quickly as possible. The fellow vampire was planning to follow her own advice and ship out on the next ocean liner that would take her. Kara decided to stick around for a few nights and catch a freight train south. There was something about these Pinkertons that rattled her. Perhaps it was the fact that they were devious. Perhaps it was the fact that they had caught her with her guard down.

New Orleans, USA, summer, 1976

The French Quarter had a charm to it that reminded Kara of her Gypsy heritage. There was street theatre and bands of young artists.

There were hippies and people who had looked like hippies even before the term was first coined. Getting accommodation in a cellar that had been transformed into an artist's studio hadn't been a problem. Rent was cheap and she had accumulated some money from her wanderings.

Color hadn't played much of a role in her life at least not when it came to her prey. She thought an African American's blood might be different from a Caucasian American's but, when she sampled an African American she couldn't discover any difference at all. A negative was A negative whatever color you might happen to be. She thought this would be the case but hoped for a new taste sensation.

The only thing she didn't like about her new locale was the heat. The air was stifling, not that she really needed it. The locals found comfort in their frosty beers and in food so heavily spiced it could knock a stranger's socks off then curl his toes. Of course Jazz helped. It was the heart and soul of the place. It wasn't by chance that her first African American victim had been a talented sax player.

There were fortune tellers and curio shops open for business at all hours and doing a bustling trade. Tourists wanted to see examples of voodoo and zombie magic. Most were satisfied with the purchasing of a fake shrunken head to take home and show the folks while others took a more serious view. Likewise there were shops that best catered for the novelty seekers and there were shops that only those keen on the truth sought out.

On her second night Kara walked into a rather old and decrepit curio shop hoping to buy something that reminded her of her youth. Back in the 1950s, she had read in a German newspaper how in the 1940s German soldiers rounded up free range Gypsies and herded them into death camps. Part of her had always hoped that her parents, as well as the rest of her kin, had somehow been spared. Over the years, she had not learned the fate of her own Romany. If they were alive and living in the USA, what better place for them to live than in New Orleans?

The shop was run by an old and decrepit man with a French accent who had, unfortunately, never come across her particular Romany. He could show her scarves and trinkets he'd bought in his travels from Italian, French and Bulgarian Romany but such items were of no interest to her. Still he was trying to be helpful and so, when he brought out his collection of Tarot cards, she was patient and understanding. Some of his sets dated back to the 18th Century and may even have been used by Marie Antoinette. They no doubt would have fetched him a small fortune if the right buyer were to come along. He had wolf's bane, the smell of which made her feel ill, and dozens of lucky charms. He sold her a wolf's paw necklace he claimed would protect her from evil. In wearing it, she hoped to prevent the beast from rising within her come the next full moon.

It was fortunate she didn't put the necklace on when she was in the shop because, when she did so, where the wolf's paw met her skin it gave a nasty burn and she had to take it off. *So much for instant remedies*, she told herself, wishing she could tell someone about her monthly ordeal and get proper advice. If she could have been more honest with the curio shop owner he might have been more helpful but there was too much danger in doing so. For all she knew there were Pinkerton agents already closing in on her.

Weeks passed and she was feeling as if she was settling in nicely to her new home when the change came upon her. She chained herself to some hot water pipes hoping they would stop the beast from roaming. Then she sighed and waited for the full horror to assail her. She didn't have to wait long. The first major sign was her eyes. They became very large and deeply brown, almost black. Next her nose enlarged as did her molars. As she was adjusting, her nails became long instruments of death and hair sprouted everywhere. The creature, once formed, cried out at being bound. It cried out and she went down into that place she always went when it came into existence. With one mighty tug from savage limbs, the chain gave way and it was off to cause havoc. The front door to her artist's cellar was locked but that wasn't much of a barrier. With a few good lunges, the wood broke and the monster was free.

Artists scattered in its wake. Even so, it managed to slash and disembowel a young man who was so involved in making a painting of an old coffee shop sign he didn't realize the danger he was in until it was too late. After snacking on the young artist, it turned its sights to the nearest pub where it scoffed down a gallon of beer and tore the head off a waitress. Blood fountained and people screamed. There was much pushing and shoving to get away and, for a moment, it stood there, by the headless waitress, confused. Then it picked up an interesting scent and moved on.

The police were summoned and the beast was cornered in a little alcove adjacent to an old fashioned barber's shop. It roared as bullets went flying into it. All but one merely made it angry. The one that did more, the one made of silver, was fired by the man who had sold Kara the wolf's paw necklace. Knocking the creature for a loop and smashing its collar bone, the offending bullet left its body and hit a wall. Fortunately for Kara and her alter ego, it was the only silver bullet the old man had. Even so, the wound made getting away difficult. Only one claw could lash out and it's canine like leaps were out of kilter. Still it did escape and it did manage to get back into Kara's home without being seen doing so.

The following week, the Gypsy vampire left New Orleans. It was doubtful if the place was still safe for her. Some fortune teller or seer might have already worked out who she was and what might be done about her. It was certain that it was far too dangerous for her werewolf half to remain. Perhaps the person who had fired silver at it was already making more such bullets. She could be subtle in how and where she took her meals but it could do no such thing and so they, the vampire and the werewolf in one, had worn out their welcome.

San Francisco, USA, spring, 1986

A city made up of hills and valleys took some getting used to. The first week Kara in bat form had trouble with the sudden dips, curves and climbs. One night she almost ploughed into a fast moving street car on its downward run. On another she barely cleared out of the way of a motorcycle on her climb to the top of a street built like a roller coaster ride. There were nights when she alighted atop one of the giant cables of the Golden Gate Bridge to study the landscape and to take a break from what she was beginning to think of as some architect's idea of municipal madness.

She was getting comfortable with the idea of houses and office buildings sloping down one minute and sloping up the next when she ran into real trouble. An arrow thundered past her sensitive ears, missing her by inches. In response, she banked and swooped in the direction of her attacker. She turned to avoid a second arrow, which whizzed past her left wing, then resumed course. She gathered speed, smashing through a half opened window to confront the bowman. Unfortunately, he was not alone.

The room was empty save for five figures in black and one centrally located light bulb. With great panache, Kara transformed back into a human female while the bowman notched another arrow. The others moved with appropriate caution. There was a swordsman with an antique Samurai blade, two with wooden star knives in hand and a giant with a spiked wooden club.

"Who are you?" asked Kara, her eyes searching for whoever would make the next move.

"The Rising Sun," said the swordsman bowing. "San Francisco chapter."

Before Kara could make further enquiries, the bowman loosed his arrow. She ducked out of the way, the shaft almost sailing into the giant. Charging forward, she grabbed the bowman by the shoulders and hurled him at the light. With a crash and a tinkle of shattered glass it went out plunging the room into darkness. In the dark, with her heightened senses, she thought she'd have the advantage. She thought she'd end the battle and be on her way. She was wrong.

All was still until Kara decided to go for the giant. A dozen star knives whizzed in her direction and she had to twist her body into positions impossible for most humans to avoid them. Even so, one nicked her left cheek and another cut across the knuckles of her right hand. She tasted her own blood wondering as she did so who the Rising Sun were and why they were after her. It was becoming obvious they were another group of vampire hunters.

Kara moved again and the swordsman came at her, his sword whirling about in his hands making a sound only a vampire or a bat could hear. She moved back, out of the way and into the path of the giant's club. The club scrapped her arm but, before the giant could take another swing, she had hold of his hand and was swinging him about the room. She used the giant to send the swordsman crashing into a wall and the star knife throwers into opposite corners of the room. Finally, she let loose of the giant propelling him into one of the occupied corners. Then and there she considered the fight over and herself the victor.

She was about to sink her fangs into the unconscious swordsman when half a dozen star knives whizzing in her direction changed her mind. Of the half dozen, two missed, three struck her right boot and one clipped her right ear. In response, Kara threw herself at the door, opened it and began to run down a flight of stairs. She had had enough of being a target. She had had enough of the Rising Sun.

On the twelfth step of the flight of stairs, she tripped a wire and there was a great explosion followed by a great deal of pain in her legs. A shotgun aimed at the steps and triggered by the wire had gone off, crippling her. Through the red veil of agony, she summoned enough strength to become a bat so that wings could carry her where injured legs no longer could. She flew down to the open door leading to the street. She was outside the building when two arrows flew down the stairs, pinning her wings to the door. With incredible will power, she managed to tear her wings free of the shafts imprisoning them and fly off.

She didn't know how she could maneuver the half a mile distance between the ambush site and her cellar hideaway. All she knew was that she had to do it or perish. With every movement the rips in her wings grew and the red dripping from her legs made her more and more lethargic. As the sun was pinking the sky, she swooped into the cellar and collapsed. She was too weak to change form so she slept the day away as a bat. The next night her legs were much better and the same could be said for her wings. She changed back to a human and examined herself. She could move her legs and arms but there was stiffness and an ache in her joints only a good dose of blood and perhaps meat would cure. That night, being a full moon, her beast would rise and for once she didn't give a damn how many humans it slaughtered. She didn't even mind going into hibernation somewhere in its head while it roamed.

Once freed, the creature inside her sought greenery and, once finding it in a park near one of the greatest suspension bridges ever built, went wild. Three dogs and their owners were torn inside out and feasted upon. Limbs were scattered over a wide area. The press and the police put it all down to a pack of wolves that had to be rounded up and destroyed. Where a pack of such animals could have come from no one knew. Frightened by the Rising Sun, Kara stowed away on the first transport leaving port. San Francisco was not for her.

Miami, USA, autumn, 1996

It was restful but not very exciting by the sea. The constant warmth was enough to lull many residents of the various motels, caravan parks, villas, bungalows and apartments into what was for some a false sense of security. Young people came to Miami to break free of college or university for a while and indulge their passions. They were easily manipulated. Old people came to Miami to eke out the last of their years baking in the sun. If one or two college or university students turned up face down in the surf, it was assumed that, while on a binge, they ventured too close to the water. If one or two of the old folk keeled over and died, it was seen as the passage of time catching up with them. If Kara nudged that passage, who would know? Besides, she had been disciplining herself. It was better to take a little of life from a few people of a night and leave them dazed but alive rather than leave a single corpse likely to someday arouse the authorities.

For a year Kara had been in her apartment overlooking the beach. The only real threat to her tranquility had been the change that came over her every full moon. The only answer she had come up with, to keep it as quiet as possible, was to get as far away from humanity as she dared, without roving too far from her address, when she began to feel the effects of Luna. She simply ran, with the thought of getting back in time to escape the sun, and hoped for the best. So far there had been a dozen dogs and cats ripped apart and one old drunk terrified out of his wits. In other cities and towns the tally had been much higher. Perhaps the beast understood that its rampages could be a danger to both of them. Still it needed flesh as well as blood and that would not change.

Kara went out onto her balcony to breath in the salt off the not-so-distant waves. She preferred the black hills of Dakota with their equally rugged trees but, last time she was there, she was almost captured by FBI agents with rifles, stun guns, gas grenades, crucifixes, lariats and nets soaked in garlic juice. The only reason she got away was the moon came out in its entire splendor and the beast couldn't have cared less about the smell of garlic. The men who had roped her were torn apart and she made it into dense forest before the gas grenades could be employed. It was one of the few times the creature had proven it could be an asset. Usually it was a problem she had to unlive with.

Sometimes she wondered at the naivety of Heinemann and Glass. Did they really believe they could create and control an army of half vampire/half werewolf beings for the greater glory of the Third Reich? Were they even aware that by combining vampire and werewolf together that neither would be whole? Since the experiment, Kara had not been able to turn humans into her kind. The ability had somehow been lost in the transfusion process she had undergone and, on some nights, she felt the loss. Siring was the nearest thing the undead had to procreation and, without it, she felt, every now and then, incomplete. If she could have wept for her lost children, she would have.

There were times when she wondered at her own naivety. She was once a Gypsy princess. Her folks were genuine Romany. This meant their ancestors had come from Romania. For centuries they had wandered the byways of Europe making a living the best way they knew how. Her grandfather had started a trading route between mother Russia and the German fatherland. It had kept them well and happy for a long time. Then there was a major European war that made Germany and Russia enemies. It began in 1914 and came to an end for the Russians in 1917. For the Germans it dragged on till 1918 and concluded in loss of face and general fear for the future. There followed a time of uncertainty for Russia and Germany. Then a creeping insanity came over the Russians and the Germans making trade with both difficult though not impossible.

Growing up Romany meant Kara was supposed to marry into Gypsy royalty. In order to do this, she was taught from an early age the skills she would need to fulfill such a destiny. She had to be as good with a needle and thread as the men and women around her. She had to throw a knife with accuracy and dance with gusto the dances of the Romany. To her father's delight, she took to the flute as if she were born to play. Her mother taught her what she knew about fortune telling and one of her aunts taught her how to cook. By the time she was nineteen, she was considered fit to marry and word went out to other wandering Romany for a suitable groom.

In the summer of her nineteenth birthday, a small stream of visitors began to arrive at her camp site. It might have been a river if not for the dangers of travel. There were tensions between Russia and Germany. A treaty between them the Germans would eventually break was yet to be signed. What's more, Russians and Germans were looking to purify their race. Even mild contact between Russians and others and Germans and others was frowned upon. There had been violence against Romany as well as Jews. No one was safe. Still much of that was kept from Kara. Her parents wanted her to have a carefree life so they did the worrying for her.

"Just be happy," her father had once told her. "Your mother and I will gather the frown lines and be all serious for you."

Standing on a balcony in Miami in the late 20th Century, she could not help but smile at the memory of the girl she once was fussing over the niceties of Romany etiquette with her suitors as if it were the only thing in the world a person could be concerned about. Most of them were around her age and just as nervous at the prospect of wedding a stranger. One, however, was different. He was in his mid-forties and showed his wealth by the gold rings he wore on his fingers. He only came to her at night and insisted on kissing her neck. He was tall, white-haired, and very thin. He said his clan was in Transylvania and that he had journeyed many a mile to meet her. She considered this. There was something about his eyes that drew her to him and bade her listen to his words.

"If you become mine," he said, "you will learn the mysteries of life."

"What do you mean?" she asked. "What are the mysteries?"

"I kiss you the Transylvanian way," he told her. "Then you will know."

"Then I will know," she murmured under his spell.

He pinched her neck with something sharp and she felt a slight dizziness. His eyes told her that everything was all right, that everything was fine.

Kara recalled that her mother didn't like the stranger. There was something unnatural about him, or so she said. By the time the older woman had explored this idea through a family seer, it was too late. Four nights of the special kiss had passed together with the one special reply kiss. Her daughter was dead and the tall one gone.

Miraculously, Kara's story didn't end there. She remembered waking up all alone in a tent. Three nights had passed since her death but she wasn't, at the time, aware of this. She was decked out in funeral attire. *What am I doing dressed like this?* she wondered. She went out to ask her parents what was going on and received strange looks from her people.

A great thirst came over her and she wanted to kiss one of her remaining suitors in the special way of the tall one. She made her intentions known to a young man in his early twenties who fled from her in terror. Then she was driven from the camp by the throwing of flaming torches and stones. There was a lot of shouting and gesturing. Her parents were in tears but they didn't prevent her being removed from their sight. She found this the most disturbing thing of all.

"What's happening?" she cried out. "Why am I being cast out? Why are you doing this to me? Father! Mother! Help me! Please!"

The only answer she got was more flaming torches and stones. Fleeing into the forest, she came across the tall one who told her what she had become and what he expected of her.

"You will become one of my brides," he told her. "Now come with me. The day is almost upon us."

She remembered spending a restless twelve hours in a cave with the tall one and a dozen women of varying age. The following night she made her first kill. It was a deer drinking by a cool mountain stream. She had never before been able to get so close to such a swift animal let alone taking its life with nothing more than her nails and teeth. It was frightening and exhilarating. She could see herself changing, becoming less human or perhaps more than human.

The tall one expected her to stay with him but she only stayed for a week. She did not want to be owned by anyone least of all someone who had turned her away from her family. Upon reflection, she felt she should have stayed longer. There was a lot she could have learned and she could have run away any time.

Was the tall one Vlad Dracul? she wondered, looking out over the waters of Miami. It may have made a difference back then if he had been and if she'd known but not now. She was far from those early nights of blood drenched fang and, thanks to two German scientists; she would soon have to be on the move again.

With a sigh she left her balcony, closed the drapes and settled down for another day of sleep. The beast was forcing her to move on. *Where shall I go next?* she wondered. There was still plenty of America to cover. Some of it was said to be green and beautiful. *Upon reflection,* she told herself, *I could do with more greenness and beauty in my unlife.*

Los Angeles, USA, summer, 2007

Kara looked around. She was in a dank attic of an old toy factory. There were broken dolls and model airplanes about. She had managed to make a straw bed for herself and, underneath it, was the sack of native soil from her homeland. As a safeguard, she had a few grains of her native soil hidden in three of the rings she wore. In the past, the beast had not managed to snap the ring bands perhaps because they were made of silver. She hoped it would never be able to snap them. Rats and cockroaches did not dare make a visit. Not even spiders were game enough to spin their webs anywhere near her. A depressed vampire was not only a danger to herself but anything and everything around her and Kara was feeling depressed.

The city was in the grip of a heat wave and, though she couldn't sweat, her victims did so in abundance. Some used cheap deodorant to cover it up which only made their smell worse. Only on the beach or at a public pool did her senses receive relief. Otherwise it was like having salt from strangers forced into her nose and mouth. It made her thirsty and irritable. She wanted to continue to take a little from a number of people nightly and not leave corpses everywhere. Staying in her attic all day and most of the night helped but she still had to feed and discipline herself not to go too far with her feeding. It wasn't easy.

Her last victim was a Texan visiting the city of angels for the first time. He had a habit of chewing tobacco. He reeked of the stuff and a number of his dark brown teeth were rotten because of it. She tried to sink her fangs into his neck but the odor was too much so, in frustration, she crushed his skull with her hands instead. She left him in an alley where the police would make what they would of his body.

She was walking along a street near a Taco Bell one night when a car pulled up ahead of her. A young man in a cream colored suit beckoned from the front passenger's seat for her to join him and his companions. The car was a white Rolls Royce with a white interior and the young man, Brick Grange, an up and coming movie star.

Kara couldn't believe her luck but, then again, she sometimes forgot what an attractive woman she was. She climbed into the back seat and looked at the three other passengers. They were also young men in cream colored suits. The brightness and light in the car was dazzling. The driver, who was in his thirties, offered visual relief with the dark uniform he wore. Suddenly she had five good looking men to herself in a superbly air-conditioned mode of transport. Things were looking up.

"Where are we going?" she asked Brick.

"To the studio where I made my last picture. It's a schlock horror flick based on some hambone piece of '70s trash. My agent told me it would have comedy appeal. Some African American dude becomes a vampire, terrorizes Harlem and it's up to me to stop him."

"How nice for you."

"Yeah. Nice. Offer the lady a drink, Vance."

The man next to her pressed a stud on the back of the front seat and a tiny bar with shot glasses and bottles opened up. The upholstery of the bar was black so it was a relief to Kara's eyes.

"What would you like?" asked Vance.

"I don't drink."

"Sure you do. How about a bloody Mary? At least that's what we'll call her. B negative fine with you?"

"Yes. You know about me?"

"Relax. It's fresh."

"Are you…?"

"Undead? Nah. We're here to see to your comfort."

"Why?"

"You'll find out when we get to the studio."

Kara lifted a glass of delicious smelling blood to her lips then thought better of it. She had better not drink. There weren't many ways in which to poison a vampire but there were a few. She decided not to take the risk. For all she knew they could be Pinkertons or agents of the Rising Sun.

Years ago, she had met a group of men and women in their early twenties who wanted to party with her. It was in Beverly Hills, California and they were the children of wealthy bankers and wine growers. They wanted to party with her because they had caught sight of her feeding on a panhandler one night and they had a rather romantic notion of vampirism. They wanted her to turn them into vampires. This she couldn't do but they did provide her with some choice midnight snacks. Were the men in the car with her of the same ilk? Were they after perpetual youth at any price and whatever else their fertile imaginations told them they'd get if they became undead? Before she could discuss the possibilities with them, the Rolls eased to a halt in front of the gates to Wilmont Productions.

The night guards looked at the driver, nodded, and let them through. The car pulled up outside the second building on the lot and

Kara was escorted inside. There she saw in one corner, via her night vision, a fake 19th Century British lounge room equipped with over-stuffed furniture and in another a fake dungeon with harmless 'torture' devices. In the center was open space. When the lights were switched on it took a moment for her eyes to adjust. When they did, she became aware of at least another, unknown presence in the building. In the lounge room area a commanding voice rang out: "Greetings. Thank you for coming. I do hope my associates have been perfect gentlemen."

"They're alive, aren't they?" answered Kara. "Now tell me what this is all about."

"Now boys."

In response to the command, her companions drew crucifixes out of their stylish coats and pointed them at her, forcing her to look in the direction of the 19th Century set.

"A trap!" hissed Kara, showing her fangs.

From behind a large lounge chair stepped a tall, well built man with blond hair. He was dressed in a gray pin-striped suit that gave the impression he was used to dealing in big money.

"I am Victor Heinemann," he said, smiling. "I am the great grandson of Doktor Heinemann."

"And you've spent years tracking me down so that you may take your revenge?"

"Yes and no. It is true I have spent some time locating you via my contacts in local law enforcement, the FBI, the Rising Sun and other groups and societies. But I never even met my great grandfather so revenge isn't my motive. To me you are subject X, a useful commodity."

"A commodity?"

She felt outrage and curiosity all at the same time.

"Yes. I have buyers interested in both my ancestor's notes on the supernatural and in you. As a package deal, I'm looking to make at least a cool five million, possibly fifteen. Not bad for two night's work plus the research. We'll be meeting the prospective buyers in San Diego."

"Never!" Kara cried, brushing aside the men nearest her. They had relaxed their guard enough so that the crosses they had were not pointing directly at her and they were not thinking the kind of thoughts that would make the crosses at all useful. *Are all Heinemanns so arrogant?* she wondered. *Is it in their genes?*

"Now, boys!" Victor ordered. Miniature gas masks came out of coats and were donned. Glass pellets filled with tear gas were taken from pockets and smashed on the floorboards. White vapor drifted upward.

Throat burning and eyes watering from the rising fumes, Kara managed to knock three of her assailants out before she was handcuffed and roped. Then she was given an injection to further settle her. A lump of wood landing on the back of her head made her lose consciousness.

The following night, she woke up to find herself in a Lear jet taxing a runway. Her five guards had their crucifixes handy and one had a large bottle of holy water.

"You don't want to do this," she told them as the plane took off.

"Yes we do," Victor said from beside the pilot. "Five to fifteen million dollars, remember?"

"No. You don't understand," she told him. "Surely you've read your ancestor's notes. Surely you must know. You're...No! Too late! It's too late!"

"What do you mean?" Victor asked. "What is wrong with you? Why are you grimacing that way?"

Kara's dress began to rip. Then, as if made of light plastic, the handcuffs holding her snapped. The ropes burned with the pressure of her growing mass and then flew from her.

"I tried to warn you!" she screamed and, in the next instant, lost the power of human speech. Her face was elongating making room for lots of big, sharp teeth.

"It's the full moon," Victor shouted. "I didn't know about this success. My great-grandfather never alluded to it. I thought, well, a crude blood transfusion and simple electric stimuli. They had no idea about DNA...everybody! Cover up the windows!"

Victor's minions obeyed but it was no use. Once the change had begun it could not be so easily stopped. Thick hair grew all over Kara's body. Claws replaced fingers. The beast lived once more and it wanted out of the container it found itself in but first it wanted to eat.

With a roar, the lycanthrope attacked the five men around it. Flesh was rendered from bone. Neither crucifixes nor holy water meant anything as it went on its killing spree. Victor pulled out a gun but, since the bullets it contained did not have silver, it was useless. The bullets fired stung the beast, angering it into tearing Victor and the pilot to shreds. By this time, the plane was hopelessly off course and now there was no one alive capable of making the flight corrections.

After feasting on Victor and his men, the creature made its bid for freedom. The lycanthrope slammed itself against one of the cabin exit doors until the hinges gave way and everything that wasn't nailed down was sucked into space.

Free falling was a new and frightening experience for the beast. It tried to grab hold of something, anything but there was nothing to grab hold of. It howled to the stars and the bloated moon but they did nothing to help. Then time passed and it saw a forest coming up fast from below. Before long it could spot individual trees.

Tree branches exploded on impact with its body. This slowed it down though not enough to save its life. Then there was a net a handful of scientists had rigged up so they could catch wild birds for study. This net tore upon contact with the hurtling creature but the net plus soft, compost like undergrowth to land on added up to survival. This does not mean that the landing was not brutal or that bones were not broken.

Limping into a cave with a smashed wrist and a fractured ankle, the beast growled at both its luck and its misfortune. It had a full stomach which meant it would heal quickly. It had shelter from the rising sun and could smell new growth around it. Before long, it would be content.

The following night, Kara rose from the cave floor with a slight limp and a tender wrist. She was glad to be in a place where the land was green. She had vague memories of how this had come about. Apart from the silver rings she wore, she was naked. *When next I see humans*, she told herself, *I will take some clothes off their dead bodies.*

She suspected the only humans she might see in the immediate future were the ones who had set the bird trap. It didn't matter. Clothes were clothes. There was no sense in pretending to be a fashion plate in the middle of nowhere.

Perhaps, for a time, she could stay in the wilderness. Even if she had to subsist on animal rather than human blood, it would be worth it. Perhaps if she laid low long enough people would believe her existence had ended when the Lear jet crashed. Surely, with everyone sucked out, it had to have come down with an almighty explosion. Maybe that would put a stop to various vampire hunters hunting her. If not, then a forest was good country upon which to create and launch plans against any and all pursuers. It was easy to stay hidden and easy to strike out at enemies that had less developed senses. Plus it was where the lycanthrope could feel at home and cause her less strife. It was cooler here than it had been in Los Angeles. The smells were fresher and cleaner.

"This place reminds me of the Black Forest in Germany," she said to the wind. "I think I will like it here."

A Treasure beyond Price

Cleveland, USA, summer, 1948

Professor Billings was a tall, balding man in his early fifties who required rather thick glasses in order to see. On the plus side, he was in early retirement from Columbia University, had a fully equipped lab, two able-bodied assistants and an incredible goal in mind. He wanted to discover his own version of the fountain of youth. He wanted to reverse the aging process then, at some convenient stage, stop it.

"Hormone replacement is the answer," the Professor said to Doctor Carver, a Columbia graduate, and to Doctor Manse, a Swiss chemist from Zurich. They were his assistants and they'd heard it all before or so they thought.

Doctor Carver adjusted her glasses and looked at the Professor's eyes. "It's been tried," she said. "It provides some benefits but it can hardly be referred to as reversal of aging."

"Ya." Doctor Manse stroked his gray beard reflectively. "Animal hormones go so far. Human hormones extracted, treated to bursts of infrared radiation and then reapplied go even further. But they do not reverse aging."

"The complete answer," the Professor told them, "requires a leap of faith."

"A leap of faith isn't science," Doctor Carver argued, wondering at the same time what Billings could mean.

"It is okay for medicine men," said Doctor Manse in good humor, "but not for men of medicine or science."

"Then perhaps we need to become medicine men," the Professor said with a strange half smile on his face. "Come, I have something to show you in the lab."

The lab was next door to the lounge area where they had been relaxing after a day of experimentation with little progress. As they walked the short distance, both doctors thought of what had been done and, as far as they knew, what could be done about aging. They could treat the skin of a subject to combat much of the damage caused by the years, even the decades, of living but this was cosmetic. It did not address the issue of bones and vital organs becoming worn and, with continued wear, useless. The body broke down after a while and there was nothing to be done about it.

Asexual creatures didn't have this problem of aging but they were simple one or two celled life forms. It seemed the complexity of being a sexual animal meant that someday you would die of old age if some other mishap didn't get you first. Being human meant you had the intellect to know what was going to happen to you. Of course, being a scientist made you want to question the whole business and come up with a solution that would at least allow you to live longer. It made you want to do what others said could not be done. But wishing for something didn't always make it so nor did the hours of hard work they'd already put into the project.

Once in the lab, Professor Billings handed Doctor Manse a slide and told him to look at it under the most powerful microscope they had. The Doctor did so and then Professor Billings instructed Doctor Carver to do likewise.

"This is a blood sample?" asked Doctor Manse with a touch of emotion in his voice.

"Yes." Professor Billings took his thick glasses off and wiped his face with his handkerchief. Without his glasses on he looked more human.

"What animal?" Doctor Manse stroked his beard in thought.

"You tell me," replied the Professor. He cleaned his glasses with his handkerchief then put them back on.

Doctor Manse and Doctor Carver put more effort into studying the slide's content. They were familiar with animal and human blood types. This was something new. Could this really be that near impossible breakthrough they were after? And what was meant by a leap of faith and becoming medicine men?

"It is almost human," Doctor Manse said at last.

"Are you certain it isn't human?" ventured the Professor.

"I am certain." Doctor Manse shook his head and smiled wryly through his beard. "I am certain...of nothing. Where did you get this?"

"What is your opinion, Cynthia?" asked Professor Billings.

"Well, Bob," she said, brushing a stray blond hair out of her eyes, "I agree with Fritz. It is something new to us. It appears to be human but I cannot assign a blood type. It is reminiscent of the blood of certain bats found in South America that feed on the blood of other creatures but it is only reminiscent. Like I said, it appears human. What is it?"

"Something we never believed could exist," spoke Professor Billings. "It is out of mythology. It is out of modern romantic fiction and horror. Yet I have proof of its existence. Not just this blood sample. Not just this small tease for the intellect but much more. You want to know what I have been doing downstairs for weeks? Come with me. I will show you."

He took them across the corridor and down a flight of steps to a large concrete area that once housed machines for making blocks of ice for iceboxes. Of course, once refrigerators came along, the machines were sold off for scrap, the area closed, and the building sold to whoever wanted the space and the offices. A decade later, it was Professor Billings who wanted these things.

Under Billings, the area now housed cages and work benches of varying sizes with lots of scientific paraphernalia. Doctor Carver would be the last person to admit it, but the place gave her the creeps.

In one of the small cages there was a rat. It was as stiff as a board with its front paws curled up into fists. Its eyes were closed and its fur unmoving. Here the Professor stopped and so did the others.

"What is your diagnosis?" asked Professor Billings.

"A dead rat," said Doctor Manse, rubbing his hands as if to clean them. He hated rats, even dead ones. They brought disease and he hated disease even more.

"I agree," Doctor Carver said sourly. "Is this what you have dragged us down here to see?"

The Professor consulted his watch and said: "Patience, Doctors! For now please make certain for me that this is an ordinary rat and that it has truly departed this veil of tears. There's a stethoscope on that bench over there. You may pick up the beast and shake it if you wish or, if you are feeling squeamish, there are glass rods you may poke it with. If you wish, you may attach electrodes to it and give it jolts of electricity. Do what you will. You have fifteen minutes. After that time the rat must be secure in its cage."

"I don't understand," Doctor Carver said. "You brought us down here to examine this thing?"

"Please humor me," Professor Billings said in a patient voice. Once more he looked at his watch. "I need reliable witnesses."

"Witnesses to what?" Doctor Manse asked.

"For now," Professor Billings said in his gentle voice, "do as I say, please."

The doctors tested the rat and came to the conclusion they had reached when they first saw the animal. They tested it some more and the conclusion they reached remained the same. They told the Professor so and called upon him to tell them what this was all about. Why all this mystery over a deceased rodent?

"Patience." Professor Billings consulted his watch for the final time. "Watch the rat. Any minute now…any minute now…There! Did you see that?"

"See what?" asked Doctor Carver.

"I think the animal twitched," Doctor Manse answered.

"That's impossible," Doctor Carver said. "The animal is dead."

"Put your hand in the cage then," the Professor said. "After all, what can a dead animal do?"

Slowly, Doctor Carver did put her fingers through the bars of the cage. She felt foolish doing so. What was the Professor up to?

Suddenly, a nose that shouldn't move, moved, red eyes blazed to life and there was a streak of blackish-brown fur.

"Ow!" Doctor Carver pulled her fingers away from the cage. "It bit me! See?! It drew blood. It's alive! It must be! How is it possible?"

"In a sense it's alive," Professor Billings replied in his lecturing voice. "In another sense it is dead. Look at your watches. The sun has gone down. When the sun rises again it will be dead again."

"But that's nonsense!" Doctor Manse reasoned.

"Nonsense or not, it is true."

"Is this what you meant by out of mythology?" asked Doctor Carver, wrapping her handkerchief around her injured finger.

"Not precisely though rats do enter the picture," the Professor replied. "Mythology would best suit my other more human specimen."

Professor Billings led the doctors past cages containing dogs, cats, rabbits and chimpanzees. All the animals were agitated as if they sensed something unpleasant, even hazardous was about to happen. Doctor Carver could almost cut the primal fear in the air with a knife it was so damnably thick. She sensed Doctor Manse pretending not to notice. Scientists, after all, were not supposed to be moved by such things. She suspected Professor Billings was so caught up in his work he was oblivious to the warning signs that something might very well be very wrong.

They came to a large cage containing a table, a chair and a bed with soil on top. It was when Professor Billings looked in and discovered it was devoid of a subject that he put his left hand to his throat and fished a crucifix out of his top lab coat pocket.

"Gone!" he cried in astonishment and growing panic. "But how? The lock has not been disturbed. The bars are so close together not even the smallest bat could escape. Yet she's gone. Gone!"

"What's gone?" asked Doctor Carver, thinking in terms of some kind of female animal.

"Who's gone?" Doctor Manse jumped in. "What's this all about?"

"Shall I tell them Professor?" a voice came from the shadows. It was feminine and rich with promise and menace. Professor Billings seemed to shrink at the sound of it.

"Stand behind me!" the Professor cried to the two doctors. "We must leave here at once and lock this place up."

"Won't you introduce me to your friends?" came the voice once more. A lofty, angular woman dressed in a tattered lab coat she had taken from one of the benches stepped out of the semi-darkness. She had long black hair and piercing aquamarine eyes. There was unmistakable mischief in her gaze and in her languid, almost liquid smile. Whatever she intended to do she was in no hurry to do it. She was enjoying the waves of fear, even panic ebbing and flowing around her. It was as if she were basking in them.

"Back, Penelope!" commanded the Professor waving the crucifix.

The two doctors looked at him and then the rather impressive if strange woman in surprise and growing apprehension.

"I see you have shown your visitors the rat you forced me to sire," Penelope said with a hint of humor in her tone. "I do hope the girl, or should I say doctor, wasn't badly hurt by him. Whatever you do to them, they will always lack the essentials of good table manners."

"Back!" the Professor snarled to Penelope, aware now that the doctors were behind him. When in doubt, they were willing to be cautious and they had their doubts about the sanity of everything going on around them. In an even tone he addressed the doctors: "Move slowly to the steps and we'll be out of here. Don't look into her eyes. Just slowly back."

"Don't you want to know how I got out?" the lofty Penelope asked petulantly but also in sugary sweetness. "Or perhaps your friends would like to know why I was captured in the first place."

"She's a vampire," said the Professor, aware that Doctor Carver's left foot had made contact with the first step of the stairs. "I captured her with a net soaked in garlic and wolfsbane juice. Her hormones, I believe, are the answer to defeating the aging process."

"And for this theory you have kept me cooped up in here, feeding me on live rats, for how many weeks now?" Penelope cooed, showing her glistening fangs.

"Four," the Professor said with as cool a voice as he could manage. "How did you get out?"

"It took me ever so long," Penelope sighed, "but I figured out how to change into mist and float out between the narrow bars. It is a latent ability in some vampires. I wasn't sure if it was latent in me but what did I have to lose? It's not as if you left me any magazines to read to pass the time. So I concentrated ever so hard, and now I am free."

"Don't come any closer." The Professor waved his crucifix about with even more energy. Doctor Carver was now on the second step of the stairs and Doctor Manse was on the first step. They were convinced of nothing save the growing tension between Penelope and the Professor. This tension was frightening enough.

"Really?" Penelope lunged forward and slapped the crucifix out of the Professor's hand. "That only works against me if you are a believer. You are not a believer, are you? Except maybe in your science. You should have stuck to garlic, wolfsbane, and mild doses of UV lighting to control me. Trying to go religious all at once will not help you."

"I am a Christian." Doctor Manse left the step and bent down to pick up the discarded symbol of Christ. Whether he believed in the Professor's claim that the woman was a vampire or not, he did appreciate the power certain superstitions had over the sick mind. Penelope kicked it out of his way and once more turned to the Professor.

"Let me taste your blood," the sultry creature of the night said to the Professor. "It has been so long since I've had a man. Rats are not very appetizing."

"No!" cried the Professor, his eyes wide with horror as she grabbed his lab coat lapels and drew him to her.

"It wasn't a request," she breathed.

To the distress of the doctors, they witnessed fangs that shouldn't be part of a woman sink into human flesh. For some moments they were caught up in the drama but then they came to their senses and bolted up the stairs. By the time Penelope had finished with Professor Billings, the doctors had long gone. She didn't mind. Before they left, they locked the door into the area that once held ice-makers and now held Penelope. Since they had not applied any safeguards to the door such as garlic, wolfsbane or a crucifix, the lock presented no problem at all. She shattered the door with her fists. She couldn't have done that on a diet of rat's blood, but the human variety she had just ingested rejuvenated her back to full strength. Before she left she freed all the animals from their cages. Some, like the rat that bit Doctor Carver, she sired so that, in three nights' time, they would be responsible for much terror, confusion and death not only among other animals of their kind but humans as well. It made her feel good, if good is indeed the appropriate word to think of the havoc they would cause.

For decades to come, certain parts of Cleveland would hold a reputation for weird events. Little wonder then that, during the late '60s and going well into the mid '70s, bizarre writers, artists and movie makers would find a ready home there. Also there would be home grown writers, artists and movie makers of the bizarre who could not feel at home anywhere else.

Two weeks after killing Professor Billings, Penelope headed north into Canada. Around that time the lab was boarded up and the doctors went their separate ways. Neither wished to continue the work or even to acknowledge that there was more to the world than their science. For decades Professor Billings was not discussed in academic circles nor his experiments investigated. What he did at Columbia University before coming to Cleveland was forgotten. It was as if a chapter in scientific research had been closed forever.

Cleveland, USA, summer, 2008

Professor William Oats spread out on his office table the contents of a very old satchel. It had been given to his mother, Sarah Oats whose maiden name was Sarah Billings, and now at last it had been passed on to him. He was tall like Professor Billings had been but didn't require glasses. He was in his late forties and had already published a number of papers on DNA and its relationship to aging. In the satchel there had been a battered diary stained with chemicals, a first edition in poor condition of Dracula by Bram Stoker, a pile of barely legible handwritten notes, a Columbia University tie, a crucifix and a yellowing copy of the King James Bible.

It was an odd collection and, in monetary terms, not worth much. Yet up till now it had been hidden from him. His mother would not even acknowledge the satchel's existence or talk about her great uncle, who originally owned the material, until he had completed his education. It was all strange. Why keep this from him for so long? What had Professor Billings been up to that frightened people so? Was his mother frightened of the man or of what he might have discovered?

Together with the satchel he had been given the deed to the building where Professor Billings had died. Various attempts over the years had been made to sell it but there weren't any buyers. No one wanted the offices, the lounge room, the lab and the basement area. No one wanted the land everything stood on. It was as if the place were cursed.

The neighborhood had changed over the decades. Heavy industry connected with the steel works had moved out and it had become quite residential. Still that didn't make any difference to the building or the land. There were rumors of weird glowing lights at night coming from the small and barred basement windows. They were said to be like tiny red eyes sparkling with menace in the dark. There were banshee-like wailing and the upper story lights, for no apparent reason, would switch themselves on and off.

It was easy for Professor Oats, in his role as a scientist, to dismiss stories about the haunting of the building he'd inherited as nothing more than local color. His main concern was the state of disrepair. He wanted the place up and functioning again as proper offices with tables, chairs and computers, a lounge room, a proper lab with excellent equipment and a basement good for, if nothing else, storage. Equipment that was too old had to be replaced along with faulty wiring and plumbing. A building inspector had looked it over and had found areas of dry rot that had to be addressed before it could be brought up to code. Finding people to do the necessary work was at first hard but money talks. Everyone thought the new owner was fixing everything up to get it sold. Some local residents breathed a sigh of relief when they saw the old cages broken up and removed. If only they had known what he was really up to.

The notes left by Professor Billings could not be deciphered in places. The diary was just as bad. Still Professor Oats was able to piece together the hormone experiments and the belief his predecessor had had concerning the use of the undead to make a breakthrough. It was all so fantastic that, despite illegible passages, it made fascinating reading. Still, was it science? If not for something bizarre that happened one night, Professor Oats might have dismissed Professor Billings as nothing more than either a fool or a fantasist.

It happened before ten pm when Professor Oats was in the basement area looking at the instruments on one of the tables, deciding what could be cleaned and reused and what needed to be thrown out. He saw, in the dim light that had always been subdued, a rabbit attack and kill a cat. The rabbit then proceeded to suck dry the cat. *So,* thought the Professor, *vampires can and do exist in the animal world outside vampire bats found in South America. If this is so, then there is a reason to believe that human vampires exist and that Professor Billings had had dealings with one.*

Professor Oats, like his predecessor, had a powerful interest in doing something about the aging process. Unlike his predecessor, he felt that even hormones from a creature that could defy time would not, in the end, prove to be a permanent solution to creating perpetual youth in ordinary humans. Vampire hormones might well slow the aging process down longer than either animal or human hormones but there was no reason he could find for the belief they could be used to reverse the pattern. There was no reason he could find for the belief that they could, not only stabilize it for good, but in other ways control it. What then was the answer to the vampires' longevity? Could it be discovered, broken down and then controlled? Such questions Professor Oats found intriguing. Like his predecessor, but in his own way, he would seek the answers and nothing this side of Hell, would stop him.

For months Professor Oats studied what books he could find on vampirism. He bought online from Europe. For direction, he read the novel left to him by Professor Billings. Nothing seemed to shed enough light. Then it came to him. While he was reading up about South American vampire bats and how their saliva and blood produced an enzyme capable of breaking down all types of blood, it struck him that human vampires would require something similar. And it also struck him that this enzyme would have to be unique to vampirism. If it was then so unique, perhaps it was why the undead are able to defy the aging process. It was quite an idea but how was he to test it? Where was the human vampire enzyme to come from? *I need a human vampire,* he said to himself, *but where can I get one?*

Just how do you get in touch with a vampire? he wondered. *Do you put an ad in the paper or on the internet, run up some posters and put them on every telephone pole or ask around?* The answer he came up with had the merit of never having been tried by anyone before.

He set about trapping the vampire rabbit that chose to inhabit his basement. He tried conventional nets but the rabbit chewed its way out of them. Then he decided to treat the rabbit like a vampire he wished to capture. With that in mind, in order to lure the creature out of hiding, he set down a bowl of fresh rabbit's blood he got from the local butcher (he told the fellow he was making black pudding) and had in hand a net soaked in wolfsbane and garlic juice. Once he did get the net over the rabbit, it took him some time to subdue the beast and put it in a cage he had bought from a pet store. It had taken him most of that particular night. Still, it was worth it. At last he was making progress.

The following night he put a living rabbit in with the undead rabbit and watched the undead one get to work on the living. Just as the ordinary rabbit was showing signs of grogginess, Professor Oats grabbed one of the front paws of the undead animal, cut it with a knife, and then had the dying rabbit taste the undead one's blood. Then he allowed the undead rabbit to finish off his companion. Three nights later, Professor Oats had two unliving rabbits. He continued this process until he had ten.

With ten undead rabbits he felt he could move on to the next phase of his plan. He bought himself a really big cage for the basement plus three cots with mattresses, pillows and a couple of plastic chairs. He also bought lots of garlic and wolfsbane. Then he put an ad in the paper for an assistant to take dictation and to do general secretary work.

The first person to answer his ad was a young smartly dressed twenty-something brunette named Jackie Fan. She was half Korean and half English but what sold him on her was the fact that she was from San Francisco and didn't have any close friends or relatives living in Cleveland. She hadn't heard anything about the house, not even a hint of the horror stories the neighbors perpetually told.

Professor Oats told Jackie she had the job and offered her a cup of coffee. She drank it and, before long, slipped into dreamland. The drug he had added to her drink was tasteless and fast acting. While she slept, he moved her down to his basement where he tied her to a cot in his big cage. He felt guilty about doing so but only a little. It was, after all, for the advancement of science and she wasn't likely to be missed in a hurry.

By the time sunset came, Jackie was wide awake and in a panic. Apart from bra and panties, she was naked. She was not alone. There were ten hungry rabbits with her. Garlic bulbs and wolfsbane branches around the cage prevented them from escaping and they found the smell of the human with them intoxicating. Professor Oats watched outside the cage as the feast began. They were quite fast at getting to the prime areas where blood flows rich and nourishing. Jackie screamed a few times but her mouth was soon blocked by fur. Her eyes pleaded with the Professor to stop the madness but, having come this far, he wasn't listening. He wondered what the rabbits thought of this sort of meal.

"Cheer up," he told the girl. "You wanted to help me in my work and here you are being a great help."

Just as Jackie started to nod off with blood loss, Professor Oats rushed into the cage, took the rabbit feasting on her neck away, cut one of its paws with a knife then allowed the blood from the injured paw to drip down Jackie's throat. After that he put the rabbit back where he had been and watched as the poor girl was killed in a most unusual fashion. Only in parts of Cleveland, he realized, were rabbits not vegetarians. *Monty Python would be so proud of me and my family,* he thought in good humor. He remembered seeing the British comedy *Monty Python and the Holy Grail* way back in his student days and what has always made him laugh about the film was the scene in which a fluffy bunny leapt out and attacked one of the knights. *Yes, British comedy was weird,* he said to himself in contemplation. Sometimes he felt his current mode of research just as weird.

Three nights later, Professor Oats had his first human vampire. She hissed and clawed at him but the garlic and wolfsbane prevented her from getting too close to the bars of her cage. "Why?" she screamed. "Why have you done this to me?"

"I have some blood for you," the Professor said, ignoring her question. "Its cow's blood from the butcher but it's the best I can do for now. I told him I wanted to make more black pudding. He told me I must be kidding. Then I told him I had an aunt from England visiting me who loves the stuff and wants it fresh and it was all right after that."

"Who are you and why am I here?" cried Jackie.

"Drink up," he said in way of reply.

Professor Oats slipped the dish of blood into the cage and Jackie took it. She sniffed it, or at least her new demonic half did, and then drank greedily.

"Not very sweet," she said after licking the last of it off her lips and fangs. "You smell sweeter."

"I dare say I do," the Professor commented, "but I'll get you someone who smells even sweeter."

It isn't as if Professor Oats hadn't thought of allowing Jackie to sire him into vampirism. It would be one way of beating aging but not very scientific. Besides, could he be certain she would sire him rather than just out and out murder him? She was sexy enough for that to be a lure and had somehow become even sexier since her contact with the rabbits but he had a strong mind. He could not be swayed either by beauty or, he hoped, the vampire's ability to mesmerize.

A day later, Professor Oats came across two homeless women in their late teens begging for small change in the park not far from his estate. The redhead's name was Pam and the other, which had long black hair, went by the handle of Angela. They were in ragged clothes and, by the looks of their bony arms and legs, more than half starved. He offered to take them home and give them a good meal and a place to stay for a few days. After some convincing that he didn't want to do anything else, they gave in and agreed to go with him. They were desperate and they did want to believe in good Samaritans. They were also people not likely to be missed in a hurry.

The Professor was true to his word about the meal. They were given lamb chops in mint sauce with mashed potato and pumpkin on the side and, for desert, apple pie with ice cream. There was orange juice and mint chocolates. After they had eaten, they were treated to coffee with knock out drops. The knock out drops worked.

They woke up on chairs outside a large cage containing a woman in her underwear lying asleep on a cot. They were surprised that they too were not so casually dressed. They were not surprised, however, to find that their arms were tied behind their backs and the man they had trusted was leaning over them.

"Ah! You're awake," said the Professor.

"You can't do this," murmured Pam.

"It's done," said the Professor. "Since you spoke first, you can go first."

Professor Oats lifted Pam out of her chair, opened the cage door and hurled her in before closing it. Pam's grunts at being thus manhandled woke Jackie who was scheduled to wake up soon anyway.

"What have we here?' Jackie asked. "Who are you, little girl?"

"I'm nineteen," said the trapped redhead. "My name's Pam and I don't know what I'm doing here."

"Pam? That's a precious name, a sweet name. How nice for you. See my fangs?"

"Yes."

"All the better to eat you with my dear."

Jackie couldn't believe what she had just said. She couldn't believe what she was about to do but the girl was there and her veins were throbbing as if to tease, as if to entice. The rest was that demon part of her which was so young and yet so knowledgeable. She wondered how much of her true self was left and whether it did matter.

"Don't!" Pam cried but it was no use. The new demonic side of Jackie had to have its way. Pam squealed as the fangs entered her neck and began to withdraw her life essence. Jackie found herself reveling in the red nectar. It was so much better than cow. It was probably better than the taste of that moldy old professor. Unlife could be good. If you just forget your humanity it could even be divine. Jackie could feel her hold on her own humanity going and wondered why she should want to even try to hang onto it.

Just as Pam's struggle for life was ebbing, Professor Oats pushed a cattle prod through the bars and shocked Jackie with it. The new vampire yelped and jumped back, away from her victim.

"Why?" she screamed. "I'm doing what you want, aren't I? I'm doing it!"

"Cut your left palm with a fingernail from your right hand," the Professor ordered. "Do it or I will shock you again."

Jackie, with new found hatred in her eyes for the Professor, did as she was told. She had always disliked the thought of being controlled and her demon half was against it too.

"Now let Pam taste your blood," said the Professor, cattle prod at the ready in case she disobeyed. It was a device he couldn't have used on a human without causing severe nerve damage because of its power but it was just right for vampires since they were supposed to be stronger than humans.

Pam tasted of Jackie's blood, and then the Professor allowed Jackie to finish her off. The redhead was left slumped on one of the cots.

While Jackie was attacking Pam, Angela tried to get away. Seeing her chance while the others were occupied with her traveling companion, she left her chair and crept toward the stairs. Just as she reached the second step, Professor Oats caught up with her and threw her over his shoulder. He then took her to the cage, opened it, threw her in and locked it behind her.

"Do what you did with the first one," said the Professor to Jackie. "But remember to have her taste your blood or I will give you another nasty shock."

Jackie did as she was told. The blood was lovely but the whole experience was marred by the fact she was following someone's orders. Despite the fact that he wouldn't taste as good, it was a pity she couldn't sink her teeth into the Professor's neck as well and take to the night. She suspected she could fly and longed to find out. She also suspected that the night had more to offer than she had seen so far.

The ten undead rabbits made their escape. They burrowed under the floor boards their cage rested on, and had then tunneled underground for four hundred yards or so, until the smells above them changed. When the smells registered as a garden with flowering plants, they tunneled upward and out. From the garden it was a simple dash through a fence neither meant to keep rabbits in or out to freedom. They were gone half the night before Professor Oats knew they were missing. He was more angry than anything. On the loose they might jeopardize what he was trying to achieve. Still they were gone and there was no way, without first informing the authorities, to get them back. This he was loathe to do.

When it came to the rabbits, he didn't want tall tales and innuendoes about his estate and what went on there to turn into fact. He realized they would eventually, of course, if he persisted with his activities but he was determined to stave off that time for as long as possible. *Most people wouldn't understand what I'm doing,* he told himself. *Most people wouldn't even have the intelligence to try to understand even if everything was laid out before them.* He felt alone but not wrong in what he wished to achieve.

With the threatened use of the cattle prod, Professor Oats was able to get blood samples and saliva samples from his female vampires. They would use the needles he gave them to draw samples. They would use the tongue depressors and tiny sample bottles for the collection of their saliva.

"Why are you doing this?" Angela asked.

"Yes," Jackie added. "What is this all about?"

"I will assume that you all have some basic medical knowledge," Professor Oats said in a patronizing voice. He watched them place the samples on a tray. He then slipped the tray out of the cage. "Do you have any understanding of why people age?"

"God's will, some would say," said Pam.

"We're sexual beings," Angela put in. "It's part of our nature, our design."

"It's part of our programmed nature," the Professor told them. "What if I told you I could change your programming, alter your design?"

"That's not possible," Jackie said. "I know enough high school science to tell you that DNA cannot be altered. You're stuck with what you've got."

"Impossible or not," the Professor beamed, "yours has changed. The same goes for your friends in there and, of course, those rabbits."

"You're mad!" Pam cried.

"Maybe so, but you, my dear, will never age. As a scientist I wish to understand why."

"By keeping us in here?" Jackie asked. "I tell you what, I'll give you the magic bite, we'll all leave here, and you'll know what it's like to be one of us. How does that sound?"

"Tempting," the Professor said. "But I wish for the benefits of vampirism without any of the difficulties. I wish not to be trapped in the blood drinking cycle and I wish to still be able to live in the daylight. I believe an enzyme you carry is responsible for your longevity. If I am right and I can isolate it, then we are on the verge of a medical cure for age related death."

"But we're not supposed to live forever." Pam frowned. She could just imagine an overcrowded world caused by people living past their time. It would be a nightmare.

"Aren't we?" the Professor challenged her. "We shall see, my dear."

Finding the enzyme was not easy. Professor Oats had to run a dozen samples over as many days before coming close to finding it. When he did, that night his undead ladies were given live cats and dogs to feast on instead of cow's blood in way of celebration.

"There," he said as they gorged themselves on the terrified animals, "I can be generous."

"Human blood!" cried Jackie. "We want human blood and our freedom."

"We'll see," the Professor answered in a bemused tone. "We'll see."

Once he isolated the enzyme, the next step was to examine its properties and then find a way to put them to use. A month later, he had what he felt was a liquid capable of bearing the desired results. It was his elixir. It sparkled in the beaker like champagne but its potential was far more incredible. The question was what to do with it? He needed a human subject. Perhaps more than one since he had to take into account variables in the existing human condition. But there was one person, against all scientific reason, crying out to be the only one used in this manner. It was his inner self who had been opposed to the aging and dying process for so long it couldn't wait for others to go first. It was madness but it was his madness. It wasn't difficult to talk himself into abandoning proper science for self interest and then figure out a way to later justify such a decision.

He would keep a diary on his computer of the elixir's effects. He would go down in history as both scientist supreme and as subject. He would live like no man has ever lived. *Never to age*, he told himself, *never to be burdened with the rigors of aging. How marvelous!*

151

Not completely without common sense, he put two drops from an eye-dropper only of his elixir into a glass he then filled with mineral water. With measured sips he drank the contents of the glass. The taste was bland and he felt no immediate effect. Was it a failure? He was tempted to take more of the elixir but staved off. *I can't afford to be too impatient,* he told himself.

The next morning, as he was brushing his teeth, he noticed some minor changes in his appearance. Lines he knew had been on his face for years were no longer there. His remaining hair seemed darker and not so gray. He made notes.

Next he tripled the dose. *I shouldn't be doing this,* he told himself, but he did it anyway. This meant the taste was not very pleasant but he didn't care. Twelve hours later hair on his head he thought he'd lost forever was back. What's more, his hair had gone from dark gray to original mahogany. He was thrilled, but was it all only skin deep? He went to his doctor to find out. To his delight, his internal organs were in tip-top shape and his muscles were better toned than they had been in years. He made more notes.

Jackie, Pam and Angela were getting restless but the cattle prod kept them in line. Still, in order to make his discovery marketable, he had to either synthesize the enzymes or find a workable substitute for them. There was also the consideration that he could not keep his captives captive forever. If they got loose, he knew he'd be the first human on their menu. He didn't want to follow too closely in Professor Billings' shoes.

By the fifth dose of the elixir, he was up to ten drops. He was still mixing it with mineral water but he knew that what he was doing was increasingly dangerous. The scar he had on his knee from the time he fell off his bike as a child had gone. He could hold his breath like a twenty year old and he was jogging of a morning again like he did first year at university. He did, however, note certain bothersome little side effects. He now liked his steak rare where once it had to be well done. The noon day sun bothered his eyes and the neighborhood dogs cowered as he passed them. Did these animals know something he didn't?

By the sixth dose he could hear better than he ever could and his eyesight topped what optometrists call 20/20. At night he could see colors he was sure no human was meant to see which he found frightening and wondrous. Blood had many more shades than variants on red. With practice, he was sure he would be able to tell the difference between blood types via the use of his naked eyes. Also there was something strange about his ears. Were they becoming more curved?

For two days he left the elixir alone. In those two days he sweated and grew anxious. One night he had a peculiar dream in which there were three middle-aged women at a bus stop. They were doing nothing more than waiting for a bus when some man ran at them with a sharp knife and, in one movement of his wrist, slit all their throats. They bled a river and this man sopped it all up in his shirt then squeezed the liquid into his mouth. It was all so glorious and horrific at the same time. How could he think in terms of glory? Who was this other man and was he coming for him? *Is he me?* wondered the Professor as he snapped awake.

A nightmare was usually the brain playing games with itself. Why the brain wants to do this on certain occasions has baffled scientists for generations. Since it wasn't within Professor Oats' field of expertise, he left his own bad dreams alone. They happened and that was that. This one could not be ignored because it had tipped over into reality. His pajama shirt was beside him and it contained the remnants of a blood meal. His steak knife, tainted red, lay on his dresser table. He went to his bathroom and saw how his mouth was stained in shades of wondrous red from A plus to B negative. What did it all mean apart from the bloody, bleeding obvious?

"What's happening to me?" he asked himself.

He took more of the elixir figuring it would prevent whatever had occurred from occurring again. At any other time he would have seen this for false logic. He knew, however, about withdrawal symptoms and, though he hated to admit it, he was hooked on his bubbly solution. He also knew it was taking him to the brink of some abyss few had ever been taken to and even fewer had ever returned from.

After the tenth dose he could barely stand the light of the morning and part of him longed for the coming of night. His ears were now pointed and his skin was becoming gray.

"God help me!" he cried when he saw his eyes in the mirror. The color fluctuated between various shades of blue and brown. The fluctuating stopped at hard black marble and there was coldness about them, staring out at him from the glass.

While all this was happening, the female vampires grew more and more restless. It had been days since the Professor had renewed the garlic or the wolfsbane around the cage. The old weeds were withering and thus becoming more useless. He was growing careless and they knew it. It had been a night since his lovelies were fed. This was another serious mistake. When he did return to take more samples from them so he could make more elixir, they were in less than cooperative moods.

153

Professor Oats brought out the cattle prod to quell the rebellion but this time it didn't work. Sure, the shocks Pam and Jackie endured were painful, but they did not falter in keeping him occupied while Angela smashed open the cell door with her cot and her fists. Jackie then snapped the cattle prod in half with her teeth and, still groaning from the last shot of agony from the thing, joined Pam and Angela in subduing the Professor.

Revenge should have been quick but sweet. The Professor shouldn't have stood a chance. They were amazed then when he was able to knock Pam and Angela aside. Jackie slashed at him with her claws cutting deep into his chest. He responded with a roundhouse punch. Pam and Angela were about to charge at him but thought better of it. They charged for the stairs instead while the bloody-nosed Jackie slashed some more at him.

Professor Oats fell back against the cage. Jackie went for his eyes and he responded by head-butting her in the stomach. He followed up by cracking her neck with his hands. She gargled for a moment then collapsed. To finish her off, he broke a leg off one of the old benches and drove it deep into her heart. She gargled again and died her second death.

"One down!" he snarled. "Now for the others."

In a fury, Professor Oats broke two more legs off the now collapsing bench and went for the remaining undead. They were halfway up the stairs and thought they'd be out the basement door and away before he could even get close. They were wrong. A few leaps and he was on top of them, driving the stakes home.

"Die!" he screamed as their blood splattered his face. "Die! Die! Die!"

After the heat he felt from his killings passed, he realized the extent of what he had done and what it would mean to him. He had destroyed his only source of human vampire enzymes for his elixir. He could gather samples from the recently dead and the dying but that would be it. Once deterioration of the vampire set in, there would be no more enzymes or elixir.

"Why?" he sobbed to himself, looking at what was left of his undead. "Why did I do it?"

In a panic, he made a new batch of the precious elixir but it didn't seem to have any effect on him. It did not reduce his anxiety to have it as it had in the past. He needed a bigger hit and one such hit was not to be had. He felt desperate for more but there was no more. He had seen to that.

Sweat poured down his face. He made coffee and waited for the sun to rise. Then he put on his track suit and went for a run. It was a long run which took him past the park where he had picked up Pam and Angela. It also took him past the pet shop owner that had sold him the innocent rabbits and past the police station where investigations had begun on three very distinct bus stop murders. He kept going until well past morning. He kept going until he was literally smoking. He burst into flame and his semi-life/semi-unlife came to an abrupt but blazing end.

The police did not apprehend the killer of the three women whose only crime was waiting for a bus. As unpaid electricity and water bills mounted in Professor Oats' building and the Professor's safety came into question, police broke into it in search of him. What they found in the basement was astonishing. There were three dead women with stakes protruding from them and, among the second time dead, three rabbits were lapping up the blood.

"Rabbits," said a sergeant new to the area who was taken aback by what he was seeing. "I've had rabbits as pets. They don't act this way. What happened here?"

"You grew up in Connecticut, right?" asked a plainclothes detective who was examining one of the dead and, at the same time, shooing away one of the rabbits.

"That's right," the sergeant replied.

"So you're used to cute, cuddly Connecticut rabbits?"

"I suppose…"

"Well these are Cleveland rabbits, my friend. Cleveland Rabbits. Get used to them."

Professor Oats' computer was bagged for evidence but eventually sent to his mother. In the computer were his notes. Once more the building was abandoned. The locals' hope was that it would sit derelict forever but that was wishful thinking. To this day, like a great cat or a vampire rabbit, it waits in the gloom of the supernatural events surrounding it to once more pounce on humanity. Like a gateway to Hell it is looking forward to the next professor. God help the next genius that crosses its sinister threshold.

The Inquisitor

The Vatican, autumn, 2002

Brother Augustine stood before Monsignor Rafferty eager to begin his mission. The brother had been born in Austria and was tall, lean and blond. The Monsignor was of Irish descent and though just as lean was far shorter, silver haired and two decades older. Both knew the dangers of every mission. Both knew that their existence in the Vatican or anywhere else in the world was a closely guarded secret.

Monsignor Rafferty had other operatives aside from Brother Augustine but Brother Augustine had proven himself to be the best in the most difficult of circumstances. This mission was going to be difficult. It was most likely going to be the most difficult mission their little group had ever undertaken. Even so, it offered a chance to prove that the new inquisition, unlike the old, was for the people and not against them. Unlike the old, people were going to be saved not condemned.

"You have the tickets," the monsignor said. "You fly to Boston. It has been arranged that customs will not interfere with you and your equipment. Outside of this we may be of small help to you. Do not trust any members of the cloth you might meet. We do not know who has been tainted. You will have to use your best judgment. You will carry the Pope's seal. Use it wisely and God bless you."

The Monsignor handed Brother Augustine a scroll with a large wax stamp on it. Brother Augustine took it in all humility praying that he was worthy of the honor of receiving it.

"I have packing to do if I'm to catch my first flight," the Brother said. "I thank you for the seal and for the blessing."

In his cell, Brother Augustine looked over what he planned on taking with him. There was his Kevlar vest capable of stopping small rounds fire, several bottles of holy water he could keep on his specially designed belt with five sharpened stakes, a miniature crossbow with twelve pine bolts, two daggers made of oak, a .22 caliber hand gun with two spare clips, a Saint Christopher medallion on a necklace, a mini-medical kit, and a crucifix once owned by Saint Augustine himself. He removed his cassock and put on a gray business suit. He was to go out into the world as a civilian. The only link to the Church, other than the Pope's seal, would be the fact that the Vatican was paying his expenses but even that, via computer science, could be kept hidden.

The journey to Boston was uneventful. It gave Augustine a chance to read up on the latest details concerning the evil he would soon be facing and the newspaper accounts of the incidents that had drawn his monsignor's attention. *I must once again prove worthy of his trust*, Augustine thought, *and also the trust of his Holiness the Pope.*

It seemed that in America pedophilia amongst priests had so weakened some places of worship that the faithful no longer gathered, opening the way for yet further evil. What's more, there had been cover-ups by high ranking church fathers resulting in mistrust and anger by the laity. Added to this were the disappearance of two nuns and the discovery of three priests dead and drained of blood. There was talk of prostitutes being forcefully taken from the streets.

The police had put the disappearances and the murders down to ritual sacrifice either by dishonorable priests or by members of the public so disillusioned by the Church that anger had turned to hate and hate to action. Augustine knew better and also knew that the disappearances and murders would continue until those arcane powers responsible were dealt with. He was an Inquisitor, one of a new breed, and now much needed in a world seething with sin and corruption. *I pray I may be of service*, he told himself. *I pray I may be an instrument of God's good grace on earth.*

He got off the plane at Boston Logan Airport in East Boston, breezed through customs as he had on the other stopovers, and was heading out the glass doors with his luggage, when he was accosted by four armed men. They marshaled him into a waiting black sedan which, once his luggage was aboard, drove off. It was all done with military precision as if it had been done countless times before in similar situations. *Kidnap 101*, Augustine thought as he looked around at his abductors. One was still pressing a gun to his ribs. Another had frisked him and found his knives and the Pope's seal. He was glad his gun was stowed in one of his bags where they were not likely to get to it in a hurry. That meant he couldn't get to it in a hurry, either.

"Who are you?" Augustine demanded in his best indignant voice. "What is the meaning of this?"

The leader, a thin-lipped, balding man in his early forties, moved from his position in the front seat next to the driver to look at his captive. There was a touch of malice in his gray eyes. "Shut up," he breathed coolly, "or we will shut you up."

After traveling straight for twenty miles, the car made a number of twists and turns before pulling up outside an old bottle factory. Augustine was dragged from the sedan and escorted at gun point inside the structure. Past the entrance doors, there wasn't much to see – just some old crates and broken windows. One of the crates was in the center, the other crates in a circle around it. Augustine was put in the center and the others sat around him. They looked like ordinary working class men with not only a grudge but an agenda. Then the interrogation began.

He was called upon to answer every question they could think of concerning Catholicism and the role of the Church. Someone waved a crucifix in front of his face and then he was made to drink a glass of water which turned out to be holy water imported from France. The local holy water, apparently, was not to be trusted. They told him so. The same could be said for holy wafers or anything else of religious significance coming from a Catholic church in Boston. "Until the priests who have sinned against their flock and not repented are exposed and removed," the leader told him, "this will remain the general rule."

Augustine knew that a priest who had sinned grievously but had not repented, and goes on sinning cannot commune with God to the extent of being the instrument upon which God can make, or keep things holy. You cannot serve good soup in an unclean bowl and expect the soup to remain good. It was little wonder then that forces of darkness were starting to look upon Boston as a new home. The Protestant Church groups and the Synagogue rabbis had tried to take up some of the religious slack, but there was little they could do for Catholics who wanted decent, honorable, God-fearing Catholic priests to guide them. Not all Boston Catholic priests were bad, but it was the not knowing who was good and who was not that created the most upset.

As a final test, Augustine was told to recite a prayer both in Latin and in English. He chose the Lord's Prayer. It was something he knew Catholics and many Protestants understood and had a fondness for. As he said the words, harsh faces softened and guns were returned to holsters.

"No vamp could stomach anything that holy nor could someone under their control," voiced one of his captors.

"You understand," the leader said in way of explanation, "we had to be sure you weren't a set-up. We had to be sure you were the Inquisitor sent from Rome and not a human stooge of the vamps."

"Yeah," added a red-headed fellow in his early thirties. "We got word from a vamp we'd caught and injected with truth serum that there was a drive-by shooting planned for you. Lucky we got to you in time. They weren't expecting us to just whisk you away. We think there's a leak in the Vatican, possibly the monk or priest who arranged your transportation. We know your Monsignor is clean."

Thank God for that! thought Augustine, though he couldn't imagine Rafferty as anything but a hard working agent of the true faith. "Tell me," he said wryly, "is there anyone in Boston who doesn't know about my mission?"

"Two weeks ago," put in a square jawed man with beady eyes, "two Pinkertons were getting off a train at Haymarket Station when human vamp agents opened up with machine gun fire. Two people were killed outright, including one of the Pinkertons, and several people were injured. The other

Pinkerton managed to escape without a scratch. Since it happened before sundown, it was considered by the police to be street crime, even though it is rare, up till now, to have drive-bys here.

"Last week the lone Pinkerton ran down one of the missing nuns near an old cemetery. She had been 'turned' and so, with fangs and claws, she attacked him. She ripped open his jugular with her nails but, to his credit, he stabbed her through the heart with his stake before he died. They must make Pinkertons tough."

"The point is," spoke the leader, "the vamps are using human agents more and more during the daylight hours when they can't be on the move. They're not just using them as guards anymore but also as assassins."

"They use a form of powerful hypnosis," the red-headed man said. "Their stooges are innocents made over into killers. They don't know what they're doing when they're under. They say with hypnosis you can't be made to do what you wouldn't do otherwise or be tempted to do. We believe the ill feeling going around right now is making the difference. It's turning ordinary men under hypnosis into murderers."

"Can you now tell me who you are?" asked Augustine. At this stage he wanted to believe he had found allies. It was better than contemplating an eventual bullet in the head. It was better than attempting to do what was looking more and more like a mammoth job on his own.

"Freemasons," the leader said. "First names only here for safety's sake. I'm Jack from Australia, never mind exactly where. The bloke with the red mop, that's Todd. Him and his big mate with the squint, Ian, come from some place in Scotland. The other three, Phil, Brian, and Tom, are locals. Oh, and if you're wondering, we're all Catholics. We just happen to have separated ourselves somewhat from orthodoxy and so belong to a very special lodge as well."

Very special indeed. Augustine had to wonder just how special. "What now?" he asked, feeling a little more comfortable though he didn't know much about Freemasons or Freemasonry. "It'll be getting dark soon. We're not staying here for the night, are we?"

"You're not," Jack said. "I wouldn't do that to a dog. We're not taking you to your hotel either. You wouldn't be safe. We have a place where you can sleep off your jet lag and figure out what you're gonna do next."

"And if I choose to go to my hotel?"

"We'll take you there," Jack sighed. "It will be your funeral and no mistake. Better act smart. We don't want to write you off when you just got here."

"Not when we went to all this trouble making sure you are who we thought you were," Todd added.

"Very well," Augustine said. "It would be a pity to have traveled so far without at least giving one's self the chance to accomplish one's mission."

"That's the spirit, Brother," Jack said.

Augustine was taken to an old but well preserved brownstone where he was shown a bedroom, a bathroom and a kitchen. Once alone in the bedroom, it didn't take long for him to drop off to sleep. He did so while keeping firm hold of his ancient crucifix and praying that he had trusted the right people.

The next day he rose an hour after sunrise to find Todd scrambling eggs in a frying pan over the stove in the kitchen and Ian setting the table.

"Eggs fine with you, Brother?" asked Todd as he saw Augustine enter the room.

"Yes." Augustine soaked up the wonderful though somewhat greasy smell of the food. "Eggs will be fine."

"Can't fight vamps on an empty stomach my mum used to say," Todd quipped.

"Your mum fought vampires?"

"Listen to the man," Todd said to Ian. "He's got no sense of humor. He must be an Inquisitor."

After breakfast, Augustine was told he'd better suit up with his vampire fighting gear. When he had done so, and the others had done something similar, he was driven in an old gray Beetle to a terrace flat where Jack was looking over some maps of Boston.

"It's a process of elimination," he told Augustine. "We suspect the human stooges wouldn't travel too far from their charges during the day so we've been looking at the hit sites and the surrounding neighborhoods."

"We've checked the underground maintenance areas of the train station where the Pinkerton man bought it." Todd leaned over one of the maps and pointed. "No coffins or boxes large enough for consideration found. We went through a derelict clothing factory and today I think we should concentrate on a nearby series of office buildings."

"Right," Jack said. "That's the plan. While we are about that mission, Phil, Brian, and Tom are going over to the airport for possible leads."

"And if we run into human stooges using lethal force," reasoned Todd, "we will have to reciprocate. Agreed?"

"Aye," Ian nodded.

"No choice in the matter," Jack said. "I am not losing people over indecision in this. They shoot at us, we have to shoot back."

"Agreed." Augustine spoke with a catch in his voice. Even though he was opposed to harming innocents, logic was on Todd and Jack's side.

"So you're coming with us then, Brother?" Jack asked.

"I will go with you," Augustine told them. *So long as my mission is also yours it is the only sensible thing to do. Only a fool chooses to fight the good fight alone if there's a better alternative.*

The first building, a law firm, was a fairly new high-rise and had just been completed. It was, in fact, a bit too new. As a rule, vampires preferred something more dark, earthy and crumbly. Creeping decay, Augustine knew from his studies and personal experiences, made them feel comfy.

The next three buildings drew blanks. They belonged to advertising companies and were far too busy during the day. It would be hard to sleep with a lot of noise and movement going on all the time.

The fifth on the list was owned by a large horticulture business. It didn't look promising at first because of all the mini-vans parked in the car park but, when a bullet parted Todd's red fringe, it became obvious they were near a spot where the vampires didn't want them to venture.

"Get down and fan out," Jack said. "Let's not give them easy targets."

For a man of his bulk Ian moved fast. Within minutes, he was where the shot had originated, his gun drawn. Augustine saw movement a few feet to his left and watched warily for a face or a gun to appear above the bodies of the mini-vans that made the area a metallic maze. He had never shot a man before let alone an innocent. He was hoping he wouldn't have to now. He was even selfish enough to hope that someone would do it for him. Now that was something he would have to tell an honest priest in the confessional. Instead of seeing a face or a gun, he saw the back of a man's head bob up from behind a mini-van's boot. He moved in and clubbed the fellow. He clubbed him rather viciously three or more times until the man fell to the cement, unconscious.

"Nice pistol whipping, Padre," breathed Jack from a short distance away. "I didn't know you had it in you."

It took twenty minutes of low level activity to confirm that there had only been one shooter stationed among the mini-vans. While Augustine was busy patching up the gunman with his mini-medical kit, the others were breaking into the three large storage rooms belonging to the residents of the building. Two gave up their secrets without much fuss, their locks shattered via the use of a four by two block of wood, found propped up against one of the mini-vans, and Ian's elbow grease. The third was more stubborn and required a couple of sticks of dynamite brought along just in case.

"Fire in the hole!" Jack cried as he lit the fuse and ran for cover.

There was an explosion and the steel plated, well locked door gave way with a satisfying crunch but something unexpected happened. There was a long scream from inside that could have curdled fresh milk. It was the sound of someone being burned quite badly. Jack, Ian and Todd kicked what remained of the door in and rushed inside to see what they could do. After a few more heartbeats, the scream stopped. Jack rushed out to summon Augustine.

"In here quick!" he yelled. "This you got to see!"

Augustine left his patient and ran to where the others were. He didn't know what to expect but what he did come across would haunt him for a long time. There were a dozen boxes with a spattering of soil in each one. Only one was occupied and the occupant was not having a good day. In the explosion a shard of metal smashed one of the small, blacked out windows above the boxes, allowing sunshine into the room. The closed lid of the occupant's box had been damaged enough for his face to come into contact with the sunlight. The result was as gruesome to behold as it was awesome.

The vampire was a writhing figure of shock and pain. His flesh was being stripped away and, even if they wanted to save him, there was nothing they could do to stop the sun from reducing him to ash. With shaking hands,

Augustine pointed his gun at the deteriorating fiend and, with two pulls of the trigger, pumped two slugs into the unhappy creature's head.

"Why'd you do that?" Todd asked in surprise.

"I couldn't watch him suffer," Augustine said, his hand now steady. He felt like he was about to vomit. *Not in front of the guys*, he told himself sternly.

"As long as you being soft don't get one of us killed," Jack grimaced. "I thought you'd tackled 'em before."

"I have," Augustine said. "I've staked three and it was quick, not slow like this. The Inquisition doesn't practice torture any more. I am not a torturer."

"An Inquisitor with a heart," quipped Todd. "Don't that beat all."

"This one was old," Jack said contemplatively. "And he was important. But he wasn't the head vamp. The head vamp would have a proper coffin and more than one day time protector."

"What do you think this place was for?" Todd asked.

"I can't be sure," Jack answered. "I'd say they're geared up to transport vamps interstate, maybe even overseas. The boxes for transportation are here and I'll bet that there are more boxes in the vans."

"I'll sprinkle holy water inside all the boxes I can find," said Augustine, "that way they won't be able to use them."

"You just do that," Todd told him. "If anything jumps out at you let me know."

Augustine was thankful that all the boxes he located and gave the holy water treatment to were empty. He wasn't looking forward to scalding a monster on the face with the stuff though he knew that sooner or later he would have to do so. Five years ago he'd wrestled a man who was about to stab a nun with a kitchen knife to the ground and had taken the knife off him. People told him back then he was brave. This, however, was different. People who didn't deserve to get hurt were most probably going to be hurt and the best he could do was to minimize the damage. He prayed he was up to the tasks ahead and that he would not let anyone down.

They looked at three more buildings before calling it a day. By that time the sun was an hour away from setting and they couldn't see any point in pushing their luck. Taking on a creature with superhuman strength at night isn't recommended.

They had dinner at a local pub and, on the way out, a car screeched around a corner followed by a hail of bullets. If not for the screeching sound, they all would have died. As it was, Todd got lead in the shoulder, Jack got his ear nicked and Ian threw Augustine to the ground in time to save both their lives.

"Now we're even," the big man said to Augustine in so many grunts.

"What do you mean?" asked Augustine, taken aback.

"He means you stopped the stooge in the underground car park from wasting him," Todd said.

"He had a bead on Ian and was about to fire when you conked him on the noggin," Jack added.

"I didn't know," Augustine confessed. "I couldn't see who he was aiming at or even if he was aiming at anyone. The vans were in the way."

"Let's get Todd to a doctor," Jack said.

"Do you think they'll be back?" asked Augustine.

"Not likely," Jack replied, "but we better get moving just in case."

A doctor at the local public hospital took two slugs out of Todd. A report had to be made on how the wounds had come about, but that was fine. Jack knew only those in the know about the undead would ever read it. Those in the know and in authority in the hospital would make sure it would only ever be read by those who respected the need for security against the undead. Jack was aware that the chief hospital administrator was a Freemason and he knew him to be a Freemason in good standing as well as a careful administrator. Todd was to remain in the hospital overnight for observation. Outside his room stood two of the hospital's chief administrator's top aides, who also happened to be Freemasons, standing guard.

From the hospital the rest of them journeyed back to the Brownstone where Ian and Augustine were dropped off.

"Take it easy Brother," Jack said as the car sped away.

Though his bed in the Brownstone was comfortable enough, Augustine didn't get much sleep that night. When he did drift off, he dreamed about dancing around sudden sprays of lead and of how that old vamp looked before he was put out of his misery. Bacon and eggs the next morning, served up by Ian with hot coffee to follow, helped ease him into the new day. Jack came over with news about Phil, Brian and Tom.

"The lads were ambushed in one of the loading bays," said Jack. "They had to kill four stooges and wound three. No vamps though. Someone must have figured out what we're about and tried to reduce our numbers."

"Anyone hurt?" asked Augustine.

"Nah. We were lucky. We won't be if there's a next time. Vamps are capable of learning from their mistakes. They'll send in more stooges. Either that or find a way to get to us at night."

It was Sunday so they spent time at prayer in one of the churches they felt worthy of the name. Todd, with his arm in a sling, joined them. So did Phil, Brian and Tom. They looked a little scruffy but none the worse for their recent experience. No one spoke during the service. All were aware of the gravity of the situation. They were not only the hunters but very much the hunted.

In the afternoon they checked out an old, abandoned distillery. It was only a mile from Haymarket Station and it was structurally sound. Most of the outside windows had been broken years ago by kids and drunks. A lot of the timber flooring had rotted away but the steel supports were good and would no doubt remain so for quite a few more years to come. What interested them most was a basement where crates were once stored. It would make for a nice little concrete hole to hide in if you were undead.

Down the winding stairs, which led to the basement, they went until a scurrying sound gave them pause. Augustine sighed with relief when he saw a rat dash past him. He was not so relieved, however, when a bullet sped upward from down below and smashed into the rat's chest. There wasn't much left of the rat after that.

Jack signaled the others for silence. He took a stick of dynamite, lit it and tossed it down. There was shooting as it made noise striking steps on its way to the bottom, followed by an almighty roar. Flames shot up. There was screaming, yelling and the sound of a lot of running.

"That's from one stick?" asked Tom.

"That and there must have still been some hooch on the premises," Todd told him.

"Shall we go down and see what we've done?" ventured Phil, keen for some action.

"Not just yet." Jack took a handful of marbles out of his pocket. He looked at them, smiled and rattled them around in his hand.

"So we're going to play kid's games?" quipped Phil.

"Watch!" Jack commanded them. "And be very quiet."

He rolled the marbles down the stairs. At first they didn't do much apart from go on their merry way. Then, when they were more than half way down, two shots rang out.

"Someone's still kicking," Jack said.

"What now?" Todd asked.

"We can't stay here forever," Augustine said. "I'm going. The rest of you can follow."

"Easy Padre," Jack said. "We need you alive and Kevlar won't protect you from a head shot."

"But the Lord will."

Augustine winced at the words he had just uttered. Tempting the Lord to act in your favor was not a good Christian thing to do. It was, in fact, basic Christianity not to have done so. He said a silent prayer for forgiveness for his arrogance as he made his way further down the stairs. He almost tripped on some broken bricks and fell. The hand railing saved him. It was wobbly, however, and not to be trusted. When he was within a foot of the bottom, a bullet struck the wall an inch from his left ear. He froze in fright for a moment then checked his gun. Yes, it was loaded and he had on him his crucifix and his Saint Christopher. If he were to die, he had at least a pretty good chance of going in the right direction. Slowly he continued.

A bullet hit him in the chest, winding him. Kevlar had done its thing but that didn't mean he couldn't be hurt. He wondered if he should go on but it seemed too late to turn back. One thing he feared more than anything else was a bullet in the back – the sure sign of a coward. After getting his breath back, he went on.

The walls of the basement were scorched. There were pieces of the drum that must have contained the alcohol strewn everywhere. In one corner a coffin was burning. Augustine knew it was a coffin because of the brass handles. He also knew, by the smell of roasting meat coming from it, that it contained a vampire. There were three stooges. They were all dead. Two died in the explosion. Their bodies were too messed up for it to have been otherwise. The third, which wasn't as messed up, must have lived long enough to create the problems he and the others encountered on the stairs.

Augustine called the others to come join him. Even so, they descended with some show of caution. When Jack saw the remains of the coffin he came to the conclusion that the creature had been of more importance to the undead hierarchy than the one they had previously destroyed.

"When other vamps warrant only a box," Jack said, "this vamp would have to be pretty high up to rate a fancier rig."

Augustine agreed. They might not have gotten to the head vampire but they were now more than an irritation to the fiend. The head vampire would have to consider them a real threat and take appropriate action.

"They'll be out for revenge," Jack said. "We'll have to move everyone to a new safe house right away. Tom, we'll need new wheels again and in a hurry."

The new car was an old Ford Falcon station wagon in original blue. It was a '65 model with some grunt behind it and new tires that hugged the road. Augustine was tempted to ask where it had come from but refrained from doing so. The new safe house turned out to be a terrace home about ten blocks from where Augustine had been staying. It was in a good neighborhood less than a block away from a private hospital and a very old cemetery. Two blocks further on there was a new mall and four blocks distant a country club that had been around since before the American Civil War.

Augustine was given a room where the one window faced in the direction of the cemetery. It was a small window that could be partly opened in winter to let in fresh air but not too much of the cold. After a meal of steak and potatoes washed down with beer, he played cards with Ian, Tom and Phil in the lounge room for a while before retiring.

He was sleepy from lack of shut-eye from the previous night and from the activities of the day. Yet he was having trouble getting to sleep. What was preventing him from nodding off was the bruise on his chest from the bullet that had hit him (Kevlar can only do so much) and thoughts of seeing burning corpses in his dreams.

As a way of drifting into sleep, Augustine looked out the window at the full moon and at the bushes in the nearby garden. Counting leaves seemed to him to be as promising a solution as counting sheep might have been if they were in a more rural setting. He thought, by using nature, he might be able to fool himself, for just a little while, into believing that the supernatural was less than he knew it to be. He would, after all, need to be alert during the following day.

The trick of imagining the world to be a safer, saner place might have worked but for the bats that flew across his view of Luna. One raised alarm bells in his mind. It was bigger than the others. He called his companions to his

165

room to see the bats and to make their own appraisals. By the time they had arrived, the large bat had already gone.

"Relax," Jack laughed. "Not all bats are vampires you know."

"Boston does have bats that are just bats," Todd added.

"Some are attracted to the fruit trees they have in that ancient bone factory," Jack said. "We went over all the cemeteries before you arrived looking for signs of vamp activity. It got us nowhere. Besides, that place is crowded with real dead. Not much room there for the undead unless they like the idea of sharing."

"What about the hospital?" Augustine asked. "Wouldn't that be a perfect front for them? Maybe the smaller bats were interested in those trees you're talking about but the bigger one I saw earlier might have come from the hospital and be on its way back there."

"It's a possibility," Jack agreed. "We'll check it out tomorrow afternoon. We still have a few more sites near the train station in the morning. In the meantime we'd all better get some kip."

The sites Jack wanted to explore were buildings under construction. They had car parks and basements but not much else. One was being put up for an insurance group and the other a tea import company.

They got to the first site a little after nine in the morning. The car park was clear and the basement an open invitation. The door wasn't locked and, beyond the door, there seemed to be nothing but loose bricks, sand bags and concrete mix. Phil walked in and, by doing so, tripped a thin cord. The result was a massive C4 style explosion which killed Phil and mortally wounded Tom.

"Damn!" Jack cried. "From now on we've got to be more careful!"

"Not...your fault," Tom gasped through wheezing lungs as he lay dying. "Booby trap!"

"Damn!" Jack cried a second time.

Augustine had trouble looking at Tom. There was an arm missing and part of a face, and also blood everywhere. The blood, he suspected, hid the worst of it.

"Is there anything we can do for him?" Todd asked anxiously.

"Yeah." Jack's voice wavered. "If you will, Padre, give him the last rites."

It wasn't until noon that they arrived at the second site. Even though they didn't find anything, they were so cautious that it took them till three in the afternoon to be satisfied the place was not a vampire stronghold. They arrived at the hospital a little before four. They were making anything but good time.

The hospital was almost as old as Boston itself. Part of the building dated back to colonial times and the extensions were mostly from the post American Civil War period. Since then there had been some repair work but every effort had been made to keep the structure true to the architects and builders of the past. It was white and flowing, surrounded by beautiful gardens, and a few apple trees whose ancestors might have been planted by Johnny Appleseed. The entrance with its large windows and airy space had been designed to give an impression of openness and friendliness. It didn't seem the sort of place a vampire would care for but, then that would make it an excellent place to hide.

There wasn't anything worthy of note on the ground floor. What Augustine did discover was that, apart from being a vampire hunter, Brian was part of local law enforcement. He was a plainclothes cop with badge to prove it. It wasn't something he mentioned when he was after the undead, but here he had to use his badge to get hospital personnel cooperation and to assure patients that they had a right to be there. He didn't have a search warrant but he knew how to bluff. No one seemed interested in stopping them.

Next they checked the basement. It was clean, perhaps a little too clean as if what had been there had been moved to a new location. There were deep scratch marks on the concrete where something heavy had been taken away.

"This place gives me the creeps," Brian said. "My instincts tell me to keep looking."

"Agreed," Jack spoke grimly. "There's something here all right. We just haven't found it yet."

On the first floor the orderlies were more formidable than the ones on the ground floor. They were not impressed by the badge. They gave way, however, when they saw the weapons. They were especially moved by Brian's shotgun. One of them said they were going to phone the police. "That's okay with me," answered Brian, suspecting as he said it the orderly was going to do no such thing. Here the patients were much more docile and very pale. In all three wards they had patches on their necks. He suspected the patches were hiding vampire bites.

"I think we're getting somewhere," Jack said as he examined the eyes of a young twenty-something female so white and so lethargic she could barely move.

The second floor was much like the first. Guns kept the hospital staff at bay and the people in bed had so little energy it was a wonder they remained among the living.

"Wait till the authorities get a load of what's been happening here," grumbled Brian.

"Let's just get on with it," Jack said. "Maybe we can save some of these poor people."

"I dearly hope so," Augustine agreed, crossing himself.

On the third floor they were confronted by a dozen orderlies with clubs and open straightjackets.

"Come along quietly," one of them ordered.

"Not bloody likely." Jack savagely hit the man with his gun.

Augustine shot to wound, hitting two of the advancing orderlies in the shoulder and striking a third with his fist. The third he had to belt a second time before he went down. Ian gave a man trying to get a straightjacket on him a deciding punch and Brian blew someone's right knee cap off. After that, with the intense screaming and blood forming a grim lesson, the other orderlies had second thoughts about charging them.

"Let's get out of here," Brian cried. "We'll take the stairs. I have the feeling what we're looking for is on the fourth floor."

With some trepidation, and knowing that they were running out of daylight, Brian led the way upstairs. Where the stairs ended, they found their way blocked by a steel plated door with a large lock. Since it was getting late and he didn't have any more sticks of dynamite, Jack was about to call it a day when the door burst open. A hand reached out and grabbed Brian, drawing him in, making him disappear inside.

All but Augustine was stunned by this change in events. In grim determination, he took out his small crossbow, loaded it with a bolt and went after Brian. The others, upon seeing him go into action, checked their firearms and followed.

Past the door, there were a dozen small storage rooms. The first they came across was empty. The second contained one coffin and two stooges. Todd gave the two stooges gut wounds. He then kicked the coffin open and Augustine threw in his Saint Christopher. There was a great cry of agony as a disgruntled vampire left his resting place to seek retribution for a nasty burn on his right arm. What he got instead was a bolt through the heart. He hissed, moved forward a few feet to accost his attackers and collapsed, dead for the second and last time.

"He was a real soldier," Todd said.

"Let's move," Jack cried. "We have a lot of territory left to cover and there's got to be more vamps and stooges."

The third room contained two coffins and a load of bottled blood. Jack and Ian shattered the bottles with bullets from their guns while Todd and Augustine kicked open the coffins. This time the vampires left their places of sleep without being urged to do so and one of them forced Todd up against a wall. With his bum arm he was not up to pitting his strength against the supernatural. He was struggling to stay conscious. He began to get the better of the fiend, however, when Augustine managed to put a bolt into its heart through its back. Jack was slowing down the other one with bullet after bullet. He was hurting it but there was no chance for a kill. It gave Ian the opportunity to take a stake from his belt and plunge it into the miscreant's chest. Both vampires howled, tried to remove the wood doing them in and perished.

"Reload now," Jack said as he followed his own advice. "Then move on."

"What about Brian?" asked Todd.

"Do as you're told," Jack said. "We'll be useless to him and ourselves if we don't go into the next situation fully armed and ready for trouble."

"Agreed." Augustine broke off some long splinters from the shattered coffins to use as bolts for when his more professionally manufactured bolts ran out. He thought of sprinkling the coffins with holy water but changed his mind. He could not afford to waste any on the resting places of the destroyed.

The fourth and final room held four coffins, two male and two female vampires spoiling for a fight, and five stooges. It also held what remained of Brian. There were bite marks all over his now naked body indicating that every vampire in the room had had a go at him. All Augustine could do was to fire a bolt into their fellow vampire fighter's heart to make sure he didn't come back as one of the enemy. He was about to reload and fire a bolt into the tall vampire woman when a stooge fired a bullet which only just missed his right hand. Ian killed the offending stooge with two shots, one to the chest and the other to the stomach. Another stooge tried to get a bead on Ian but was stopped by a bullet to the head delivered by Todd. Jack got busy with an African American vampire, dressed in long white shirt and long brown trousers reminiscent of colonial days, who had him by the throat. Augustine made the dark fiend let go with a bolt that went straight to his heart. Jack slumped to the floor, rolled and came up ready to resume combat.

Two stooges with rifles were taking aim at Augustine. Todd saw this and took them out with two shots to the head. One managed to get a shot off but, instead of hitting Augustine as intended, it struck the last remaining stooge in his left leg.

The second male vampire, a big Mexican fellow dressed like he belonged on some Western set, picked up Todd and threw him onto one of the coffins. He was about to follow through this attack by ripping out the smaller human's throat with his reaching fingers when Ian opened up with Brian's shotgun. He had found it next to a wall. The blast made the Mexican blood sucker howl and forget about doing in Todd. Ian's blood on his hands was now preferable. By this time, Augustine had reloaded his crossbow and was sending a bolt toward the last of the male vampires. It hit home, into the heart and though the vampire struggled on for a few minutes, he became removed from unlife.

Meanwhile, amid vampires deteriorating in their second death throes, the last of the stooges came at Augustine. He had a knife drawn and the wound to his leg only slowed him down a little. Jack shot the stooge in the throat but, despite this more serious wound, the man was able to stab the cleric in the chest. The Inquisitor fell, but he managed to retain consciousness. He looked over at Todd who was out cold and in no position to defend himself.

The second nun, now one of the female vampires, descended upon Todd and was putting the bite on him when she received a nasty surprise. Augustine had gotten up on his knees and, grunting in pain, hurled the Pope's seal in Todd's direction. It landed in the nun's lap and set her on fire. She ran toward the last vampire for help and was brought down by a shotgun blast from Ian. She crumpled up and continued to burn.

Jack and Ian then turned to the final vampire. She had to be the queen bee. Lofty and regal, she stood like someone used to being in command. Her black hair was long and luxuriant. Like her silk dress, also black, it fell in the right places to inspire lust in men and envy in women. She seemed to be ageless. Her golden eyes were something. They pulled Jack and Ian right in. Were it not

169

for the pain in his chest, Augustine was sure he too would have found her irresistible.

"Many centuries ago, in the days of the sailing ships, I was Spanish royalty," the golden-eyed one said, speaking in a velvety voice. "I am also admired among the undead. You may kiss my hand. You may worship at my feet. It seems I am in need of new champions. I need new blood – your blood!"

Jack and Ian showed signs of resistance. There was tension in their faces and, for a few moments, they did not move. Then they obeyed. First the kissing of the hand and then bowing low like slaves.

"What about you, little Padre?" she teased. "Why don't you join your friends?"

Augustine struggled with his injury to load his crossbow and aim it at her. She watched him with a look of disappointment on her beautiful face.

"You think you can destroy me with that toy?" she cooed. "Surely you jest. Don't be a fool. I have no wish to destroy you."

The bolt left the crossbow but did not encounter flesh. It was one of his makeshift bolts and did not fly true. Even so, in the half second it had taken to miss its target, she had become mist. Thus, even if it had flown the way it should have, it wouldn't have done any good.

"You cannot win," she told Augustine in no uncertain terms while still in her mist form. "Why don't you surrender yourself? I know I attract you. I know we can please each other. I could do with a priest. Perhaps I will have the Pope one day. Wouldn't that be lovely?"

"Never!" Augustine cried in defiance.

In a fit of anger and desperation, he picked up a fistful of sawdust produced by the damage the coffins had sustained and hurled it at the talkative mist. It was at this very moment she returned to human form. The sawdust, which was wood in a different form to the traditional stake, mixed in with her essence. It caused what can be best described as a short-circuit of her system. She found herself stuck as mist with partially formed hands and face. Try as she might, she could neither become wholly mist or wholly human. In her confused state of being, she could no longer control either Jack or Ian. Both came to their senses and backed away from her.

"What's going on?" Jack cried, looking understandably bewildered.

"Quick!" Augustine yelled, the effort making him wince. "Throw sawdust at her! Ian! Make more sawdust with the shotgun."

Jack grabbed some sawdust. Ian lumbered with the shotgun over to a coffin.

"What good does this do?" Jack asked, throwing a fistful of dust into the air. "It won't get rid of her."

"No it won't," Augustine agreed," but it will stop her for now."

There was a small explosion as Ian reduced part of a coffin to so much powdery wood.

"How's that?" asked Ian.

"That's fine," Augustine told him. "Now, Ian, what we need are portable, battery powered UV lamps. Six should do the trick. Phone the police, mention Brian's name, and get them onto it. Also phone any mates you have who might be able to lay hands on them. You should find phones, maybe mobiles, either on the hospital staff or at reception on the ground floor. Jack and I will keep her occupied for as long as we can, but you must hurry."

"UV lamps?" Jack questioned him.

"Just…do it." Augustine sighed wearily. *May God give Ian wings, and may God give the rest of us strength.*

It took an hour for the UV lamps to arrive. First Ian had to search for a phone. Then finding the contraptions became a problem. Finally he had to convince those who had them to part with them. In this last difficulty the police were of immense help. By then Todd had recovered his senses and, even though his back and his shoulder hurt like crazy, he was doing what he could with the sawdust.

The lamps were placed in a circle around the semi-mist and turned on. At first the semi-mist remained stable and Augustine felt caught in the net of failure. Then it wavered. The emerging face cried out for help but the eyes did not have the power they once had. Pleading did no good, nor were threats effective. Within twenty minutes the UV rays did their thing. All that remained were three flimsy pieces of flesh on the floor, melting in the heat. One piece came from her face and the others from her hands. The great vampire went out with a whimper followed by the crackle of dissolving skin. It was very much an anti-climax, in Augustine's view, to all that had gone before.

"How did you know about the UV lamps?" Jack asked Augustine. "I didn't think you were mechanically minded."

"I used to love science," the Inquisitor confessed. "I got the idea from the time I was bruised during an assignment. After it was over, I was told to go to a sanitarium to recuperate. They had the UV lamps there. I couldn't imagine one lamp doing any good against our misty head vampire. I thought five; maybe even six would be required to produce enough heat. As it turned out, I was right."

The next day, after doctors informed him that the knife had missed all his vital organs, Augustine left for Rome. Jack, Ian and Todd told him they'd stick around for another two weeks to make sure all the vampires were gone. No vampires, of course, meant no stooges. It meant the local church people would have an excellent chance to work out their other problems and hopefully come to the right solutions. As things turned out, Jack, Ian, and Todd would remain in Boston for the next three years as word of the city being open to vampire activity continued to spread even when it was no longer true.

In the Vatican, a week later, Monsignor Rafferty met with Augustine in his office to get his verbal and his written report. He was pleased the younger man was healing well and would in a few more weeks be fit for active duty. To loosen the younger man's tongue, he plied him with a few nips of Black Douglas whisky. Augustine didn't object.

"So these Freemasons were helpful?" the Monsignor inquired.

"I couldn't have succeeded without them," Augustine said in all modesty. "May I speak frankly?"

"Yes, my son, always."

"Monsignor, if we are to continue to be of use to anyone, we must be open to change. We must be receptive to others who can be of immense assistance. On certain occasions, we must even improvise. I can see a time when humanity will again need those Freemasons. I can see a time when we will need their help."

"Yes. You are right. I'm sure his Holiness will be in agreement. The Church can accommodate some change. It has done so in the past and will do so in times to come. So raise your glass to your Freemason friends...living and dead...and to the future."

"To the Freemasons...To the future!"

"God bless them...and may God have mercy on us all!"

"May God have mercy."

The Thirsty Blade

Nagoya, Japan, spring, 2006

Black as the night they came. Neko danced along the rooftops like her namesake until she closed in on the warehouse and the men unloading boxes of pens and plastic rulers from the back of a truck. Ordinarily such unloading would happen without much interest from anyone. It wasn't as if there isn't a big world market for quality Japanese pens and other plastic items and the warehouse was near the docks. What was unusual was the fact that this delivery was taking place at eleven o'clock at night during festival time.

Following closely after Neko, the feline was Tetsu, the Samurai, with his blade drawn and Sakusha, the marksman, with his high powered rifle. At ground level, Sekitan, the conjuror, was in the shadows of the work men, awaiting his opportunity to strike.

The men doing the unloading were armed with guns, grenades and rifles. One even had a hand-held rocket launcher. This seemed like overkill when it came to the guarding of stationery. The goggles Neko and Tetsu wore informed them via built in infrared and spectral analysis gadgetry that three of the nine unloaders happened to be unliving. The three did not have heat signatures that could register on the goggles like the heat signatures of the living. Instead of being composed of various colors they came up as corpse blue instead.

Tetsu gave the attack signal by waving his blade in the air. Neko was the first to jump into action, her wooden claws moving in her hands. She landed from the warehouse roof onto one of the boxes being carried, kicked in the head the struggling man holding the box then, after startling him with her wooden claws, karate chopped a man raising a pistol to shoot her with in the neck. Sakusha shot at the fellow carrying the rocket launcher, getting him between the eyes with the first bullet and through the heart with the second. He then fired at the driver of the truck who was trying to drive off. He hit him in the back of the head. Sekitan, who was large, loomed up in front of two men with rifles, knocking their skulls together with his massive hands before they could even think of using their weapons. He threw down a smoke bomb and disappeared into its rising blackness. When he emerged from the darkness, he had two men by the throat and was throttling them into unconsciousness. That left one of the enemy standing.

Tetsu jumped down from his perch landing in front of his adversary. With one swift motion, he removed the man's hand, the one carrying the gun, from his wrist. Both gun and hand fell to the ground, the gun clattering. Tetsu was about to follow through with a decapitation when his foe became incorporeal. Despite the blood loss and the pain, this being was able to marshal enough self-control to become mist in order to drift away and escape. Tetsu slashed at the mist but it did no good. The once man who was an Old One was moving away and could no longer be harmed by sword.

"Damn!" Tetsu cried. "I almost had him!"

"Never mind," Neko said. "Sakusha got the other two. Those hollow points filled with slivers of wood soaked in holy water do come in handy. We'll stake them to be extra sure."

"Cheer up, mate," Sakusha said to Tetsu. "You can have the next one."

Sekitan remained silent. He did that often reminding Neko of a mountain that could explode into a volcano.

They searched the boxes and came up with nothing worthy of their time or their effort. The pens were just pens and the rulers were only rulers. Apart from cardboard and plastic wrap, there was nothing else.

"I think we've been had," Sakusha said.

"I think, my Australian friend, you are right," Neko agreed. "But why risk three vamps including an Old One?"

"It's the best way to move something of value," Sakusha replied, "when you don't want the opposition getting in your way. While we've been busy here, I guarantee you things have been happening elsewhere."

"A sad but apt conclusion," Tetsu said. "We must inform the master."

"Two vamps are gone for good," Sekitan grumbled. "He can't be too mad at us for that."

"No, my friend," Neko said. "He can't be too mad."

Less than an hour later they were in Rising Sun headquarters and in the home of wise old Master Otosan. It was a place reminiscent of ancient Japan. Originally build in the 17th Century; it was once the town house of a well-to-do lord, and a place where ninjitsu was taught. There were at least a dozen secret passages in and out. Master Otosan loved tradition and he could see the need for quick and efficient escape routes. A lot of things had changed since the 17th Century; a lot had remained the same.

In the main chamber there was a wall covered with the rudiments of ninja weaponry. There was the grappling hook, a length of fine cord, the long knife, several star knives, the scarf, the sword, and a pouch full of black gunpowder. Otosan, in his teaching, was forever telling his students that, from these simple items he had on display, and with sleight of hand, the ancient ninja could create wonders capable of winning battles.

On the opposite wall there was a collection of more modern weaponry including a tazer, various guns and rifles, a grenade, goggles and glasses, and several electronic forms of listening device. The lesson here, created by the two walls and their paraphernalia, was simple. Don't forget the past but be aware of the present. If ninjas only kept to the old ways, they would become irrelevant to the modern world. The old skills and disciplines were good but combining the old with the new was much better. In this way and only in this way, according to Otosan, can the art of ninja truly live on.

Otosan, when he was encircled once more by his pupils, sitting on their cushions and being attentive, felt comforted in being able to first look at the wall containing reminders of a bygone age and then, in the next moment, at the modern tools of their trade. As a teacher he continued to strive to fully understand both. This morning he was not very happy but, lucky for his followers, he prided himself on his fairness.

"It is not your fault," he said to those around him, adjusting the cushion he was sitting on. "My intelligence was faulty. My contact lied or was lied to. The fault is mine."

"If we had cleared out that rat's nest quicker...," Neko began, also adjusting her cushion but Otosan dismissed her argument with a gentle wave of his hand.

"You could not have done more," Otosan said, "except perhaps Tetsu. Wounding an Old One means nothing. By the end of this week he will have his hand back. They regenerate quickly and have long memories. Next time, and there will be a next time, you must kill him – give him the second death – or he will surely kill you."

"Yes Master." Tetsu bowed apologetically.

"We will need you," Otosan said. "I know what was stolen in the night and I know what they intend to do with it. Only you, my right arm of the Rising Sun, have a chance of stopping them. You, Tetsu, are the key but you must be a strong key. If you break, all may be lost."

"I will not fail," breathed Tetsu, bowing once more.

"What was stolen, Master?" Neko asked, her short cropped blond hair revealing her Anglo-Saxon heritage while pushing her Japanese heritage into the ninja blackness.

"A demon's skull," Otosan said. "It once belonged to the last of its kind. Since then it and its ilk have receded into our common nightmares, the reality of their once existence now merely legend."

"Where was this skull taken from?" Neko asked.

"It was removed from our local museum. Up until now it had been hidden, you might say, in plain sight," Otosan told her. "Over time the skull became like stone. Our local museum had mistaken it for decades as a good example of late 16th Century stone art. Only we have known the truth and believed the museum guards insurance enough against theft. Up until now our enemy has not known of its true nature and power. I don't know how they found out; but they have, and now it is gone."

"What's the big deal about some old skull?" Sakusha asked.

"You are still an outsider and do not know about symbols of ancient power," Otosan replied. "With this skull a handful of Old Ones might unite the world of the undead."

"I thought they didn't like getting together in large groups," Neko said.

"This may change their nature. They are afraid of the day. Legend has it this demon was as relaxed in the light as he was in the darkness."

"So we make a raid on whoever has the skull," Sakusha said.

"The skull is on its way to America," Otosan said. "The Old One you took on is American and logic dictates he will create the kingdom of the undead there where he feels at home. He is a New Yorker and New York is where you will find Wall Street. They will need to finance their revolution. New York and, in particular, Wall Street are perfect for what he and his leader have in mind."

Otosan stood up and paced for a few moments and then turned to the still seated Tetsu. "Do you know about your sword?" he asked.

"Yes," Tetsu said, thinking the question odd. "It has been in my family for generations. It has been handed down from father to son with much honor."

"And?"

176

"It is said that in the cooling process of forging it was cooled in the blood of a great demon."

"And?"

"It was later used to lop this demon's head from its shoulders. Apparently the blood for the sword making had been gathered from a wound in the side of this nether world creature. The decapitation ended the demon's life. It has been said that in the killing the sword drank deep a second time of the demon's blood and so became either twice blessed or twice cursed."

"I believe the skull we must destroy belonged to the demon your ancestor slew, the one whose blood makes your sword something special."

New York, USA, summer 2006

There were plenty of vampires around after dark but none of them were talking. Not even the fear of being exposed to the sun's merciless rays could convince them. Not even being made to kiss the holy cross or eat a holy wafer would do the trick. Not even being raked on the face or hands by Neko's wooden claws or threatened by Tetsu's sword would move them. Something was scaring them worse than they could be scared by the Rising Sun group. That, in itself, was scary.

It was organized evil on a massive scale and there was a lot of power behind it, including money. The money made for enough non-vampires getting into the game to make things awkward. No vampire hunter wanted to kill deluded, even out and out criminal humans if he could help it. The trouble was, sometimes it couldn't be helped.

"We've been here three weeks," Tetsu told the others, "and we're getting nowhere. I've scoured the Wall Street area without any luck."

"I'm satisfied nothing's happening in the Battery Park area," rumbled Sekitan, looking about the lounge room.

"Queens has its vampires," Neko said, "but I think the meeting place with the skull is elsewhere."

"The ones coming into the city meet at Central Park," Sakusha informed her. "They're sent from there to the skull but we don't know where that is."

"What about infiltration?" Neko asked.

"It would be marvelous if we could pretend to be vamps and get away with it," Sakusha said. "Sure, we could get false fangs but the trouble is we don't smell right to them. We smell like food not friend. Also some of the vamps, especially the Old Ones, have hearing so acute they can pick up your heartbeat. Vamps don't have heartbeats. They have no need for them. Just the sounds your body makes all the time to keep you alive could give you away."

"Then we need a vampire to go to Central Park for us," Otosan proposed, "and find out for us where the big meetings with the skull are held."

"How are we going to get a vamp to help us?" Sakusha asked.

"I will tell you," Otosan said. "But first obtain for me an out of town vampire. I suggest the train station. I suggest such a creature hailing from as far away from New York as, say, Boston would be ideal."

The following night Archie Strong got off a train near Central Park and found himself surrounded by people waving crosses and other religious symbols at him. He shrank away from the holy glare and the next thing he knew he was in handcuffs and being blindfolded. They escorted him with haste to an unknown destination. He tried to speak to them, to reason with them to let him go but they weren't interested.

Generally speaking, handcuffs are not a problem for the vampire. They can be easily broken. The pair Archie wore, however, was special. They had Christian symbols on them, such as the sign of the fish, the cross and the face of the Virgin Mary, thus weakening the vampire enough so that, even for an Old One, they would be difficult to remove without a key. The blindfold took into account the creature's extraordinary eyesight by being triple thick. Every so often Neko would spray perfume at him so that Archie would have trouble using his sense of smell to work out where he was and where he was going. They didn't do anything about his hearing. They hoped that attacking his other senses would be enough to disorient him. They wanted him as confused and frightened as they could get him.

They took him back to the rooms they shared with Otosan. The blindfold was removed and the vampire found himself face to face with the master of the ninjas. Apart from his eyes the old man did not look dangerous but, after what the timid vampire had just been through, the eyes were enough.

Archie was asked his name and he gave it freely. He was asked when he was sired and he said fifty years ago in Nebraska. He moved to Boston when he had heard it was wide open for his kind. He was in New York because he was invited and because there were a bunch of Invisible Compass Freemasons cleaning up Boston. He knew if he stayed in Boston he'd be finished. Now it was his misfortune to run into hunters just as he steps off the train in New York.

"Some nights you can't win," Archie complained.

"Cheer up," Otosan said. "You may yet survive your time in New York if you are smart and careful."

"You're not going to kill me?" Archie asked, hope in his voice.

"If we wanted to do that, we could have done it at the station," Otosan said. "You are not a talented vampire."

"Ain't that the truth!" quipped Archie. "What do you want from me?"

"While you were blindfolded, I planted a tracking device on your left wrist. Do not attempt to remove it. Once activated, and it has been activated, it must be turned off before removal. Otherwise there will be an explosion."

"How big an explosion?"

"It will take out your arm, most of your rib cage and at least one of your lungs. Possibly there will be something of your face left."

"Get it off! Switch it off and get it off. Please!"

"There is a reason why it is on your wrist."

"Reason?"

"You will join your fellows in Central Park. They will take you to their secret meeting place. We will track you. Then you will report back to us. When you have completed your mission, you will be set free."

"What if I don't believe you?"

"What if you were to die now and we sought the aid of another?"

The idea of dying a second time scares the hell out of most vampires. There were worse things, and the developing vampire cartel was aware of them, but this vampire was so green to New York that he didn't know about any of that. He was perfect.

The following night Sakusha kept an eye on his computer screen as Archie went into action. Sakusha noted that Archie was kept in the Central Park area, with the other vampires new to New York, for about an hour; then he was moved to the Bronx. From the Bronx he went down to Battery Park and from Battery Park he was taken to a ship in the harbor. It was an old passenger liner capable of holding a thousand or more vampires. There the meeting took place. It ran for a little over an hour giving the vampire guests time to find shelter elsewhere for the coming day. It gave Archie the opportunity to report back to the Rising Sun who told him to meet them at a small café just outside Central Park.

Archie spilled what he had learned. He was anxious to get the tracker off his arm. Otosan listened intently, asking the occasional question. Yes, the liner was the place. Yes, the skull was on display like a prized trophy or an object of worship. Yes, it was the rallying point for vampires coming into New York from everywhere. Yes, there was one ruler over all and five Capos who were Old Ones. They talked of plans to rule the world, and maybe one day, find a way to live in the sunshine.

The big mover and shaker was Lord Anton Vascari, a vampire sired by a Gypsy mistress in Venice sometime in the 18th Century. He had amassed a fortune on the London and New York stock markets. He was heavily invested in the Japanese stock market and was expecting good returns. No one doubted his word on any of this. The New York Capo, the one Tetsu had fought, said the lord was a champion swordsman and an excellent shot – two qualities undead of any stripe should respect in a leader.

Vascari tended to dress like an 18th Century dandy but that was to fool his rougher spoken opponents into taking him less seriously. For too many, not taking him seriously had proven fatal. His immediate night time protectors were Japanese vampires of the Samurai class and his day time guards, apart from the Capos who slept in separate coffins near him, were New York street thugs he'd trained into a formidable fighting force. All this made him hard to get at. The skull was inaccessible too; Vascari kept within a hundred feet of it.

"I don't know what you think you're going to do," Archie said, finishing up, "but I want out."

Otosan removed the tracker after looking at his watch and said: "Go! You have half an hour before the sun comes up."

"Oh Gawd!"

"God will not help you. Go!"

Archie bolted out of the café door and ran for his unlife.

"He was a sap," Sakusha said rather unkindly.

"Yes," Otosan agreed. "But useful. I almost hope he does make it."

For a week the Rising Sun did little save keep an eye on the comings and goings of the undead. Neko and Sakusha managed to save a few people from them, but that was it. The others rested up for what they knew would be a great battle.

Otosan held meetings over coffee in various cafés and restaurants with the New York heads of the Pinkerton agency, the local chapter of the Invisible Compass Freemasons and the FBI. Each organization had twenty men they could spare for a day time raid on the vampire ship. The FBI could get four limpid mines packed with C4 explosive they'd be willing to give to the Rising Sun effort, provided the explosions took place out to sea and not in New York harbor.

"Understand we're going against policy here," an FBI top man told Otosan, "but it's getting hard to know who to trust even in one's own set-up. They're trying to close us down from within. There are FBI, Freemasons, and God knows who else among the enemy and they're getting stronger and stronger."

"I understand," Otosan said. "That is why it is important to act soon."

Two weeks and a day after Archie had told them of the ship, was designated as the time in which to strike. Neko, Sakusha and Sekitan were anxious to get going. The waiting grated on their nerves. Otosan and Tetsu wanted as much time as they could muster to bring in the other organizations and discuss strategies with them to make sure that all would go well.

"The FBI will spearhead the operation," Otosan told Tetsu the night before the day of supreme effort. "I know you are against this, I know you believe they are far too reckless but it is their country."

"We still strike first?"

"Yes, my son. You will see what you can do to minimize their casualties and succeed in the mission."

At noon on the day designated, Neko and Sekitan slipped into the waters of the harbor. On their belts they were carrying two mines each. The mines were circular and weighed no more than two pounds apiece. They had star knives, smoke bombs, and grappling hooks with nylon lines. On their backs were oxygen cylinders they could slip off with but the gentle push of a button. The goggles and breathing apparatus attached to the cylinders could also be shucked. Everything they wore and everything they carried, including the oxygen cylinders, was black. Going into the darkness of the water, as dark as the deep water was, even at noon, they would be invisible. They would be ninja on a mission.

There was no knowing how many undead would be asleep aboard the ship. Otosan thought there might be as many as five hundred – half the number expected to attend a night meeting. Keeping watch over the five hundred sleepers, there was not likely to be less than two hundred well armed, well paid human mercenaries. That added up to a grand total of seven hundred or more souls to deal with quickly.

Neko and Sekitan swam out to the ship keeping deep under the glassy top waters to avoid detection. They surfaced for a moment three hundred yards from their goal to take their bearings then dived down deeper than they had yet gone.

The limpid mine was designed to magnetically adhere to any metal. Placing them once you had the depth was no problem. They had to be placed in strategic areas on the outer hull to cause enough damage to sink the ship, rather than have it limp back to port suffering only minor leakage. After poring over the liner's design specs, Neko and Sekitan knew the best spots to place their limpids. They knew to set the timers for one hour.

As they surfaced after planting their little forget-me-nots, Neko and Sekitan were pleased to note that things were on the move aboard ship and in the sky overhead. Two FBI gun ship helicopters had begun strafing the walkways leeward side forcing the enemy to take cover. While this was happening, fifteen FBI frogmen in dark blue scuba gear were climbing aboard the sternward side of the ship with grappling hooks and lines. They carried machine pistols wrapped in plastic to protect them from salt damage, bowie knives and plenty of hand grenades in their belts.

Four of the FBI frogmen were gunned down with high powered rifle shots before they could finish the climb. One of them went up when a bullet hit one of the grenades he was carrying. Another three were shot by mercenaries with revolvers as they were getting their machine pistols out of the plastic and their oxygen cylinders off their backs. The rest managed to either mow down or blow up twenty of the opposition.

Two fishing trawlers, loaded with the Invisible Compass lads and the Pinkertons all in their James Bond like suits, plus the rest of the Rising Sun in basic black, were sitting not far off the liner's port bow. They were waiting for the FBI 'copters to finish up and move off.

As planned, twenty minutes into the assault, the helicopters turned tail and headed back toward shore. Perhaps three maybe four of the enemy had paid the ultimate price at their hands. Confusion was their true gift to the operation and those surviving mercenaries who had missed out on being strafed to death were truly confused.

Someone had to get to the anchor and get to the ship's controls. The ship had to be out to sea before she exploded. With this in mind, Neko headed for the anchor chain and Sekitan for the controls. Both were at opposite ends of the ship.

Neko tossed her grappling hook and scampered up the side of the vessel as fast as she could. Even so, a marksman from a crow's nest position had spotted her and almost nailed her with the first shot. She responded by tossing a black smoke bomb in his direction while she continued with her scampering. She swayed as she went up so as not to present an easy target. Once on board, she pulled the appropriate lever to weigh anchor and headed for cover. The marksman had two more goes at her before she spotted the glare from his rifle and took him down and out with two well thrown star knives. His grunt on being hit and the sound he made upon impact with the deck she found satisfying.

Sekitan wasted no time in getting from the water to the deck. Before tossing his grappling hook, he threw two smoke bombs. Instead of climbing or scrambling, he used his line to leap frog up thus making a big man more difficult to hit. Once on deck he listened for sounds of movement then cut down two men emerging from the smoke with two of his star knives. They got it in the part of the neck where vampires preferred to sup.

The control room cabin was guarded by a stocky individual with long greasy hair and an Uzi. The Uzi was the problem. The guard knew Sekitan was coming because of the smoke and so he sprayed bullets in the vampire hunter's direction, breaking the glass of the cabin and hitting the rubber heel of the hunter's left boot. Another spray and it was all the member of the Rising Sun could do to get out of the way without doing himself an injury in the process. A third spray broke some of the controls and caused a minor fire. Seeing his chance while his foe was distracted by the flames, Sekitan went for the fire extinguisher and only just got to safety with it behind a crate when the forth spray occurred. Then he waited for the fifth spray and, when that was over, threw the fire extinguisher with all his might at the would-be killer. The man was knocked off his feet and was made unconscious by a swift karate blow to the back of the neck. The dented but still useful fire extinguisher was then employed to put out the fire.

Sekitan managed to set the ship forward at full speed. Then he locked the wheel so the course could not be altered. With any luck it would be past the heads before the first limpid detonated. With further good fortune, he might even be off the vessel before the last of the limpids went up.

Half an hour into the assault, the fishing trawlers docked against the side of the ship. Forty two grappling hooks with lines were put into service. Forty two men made their way into danger. Forty two hearts beat the faster no doubt awakening Old Ones who were still asleep.

The remaining FBI agents were moving from the deck to the first series of holiday maker cabins. They employed grenades whenever they could to clear out the cabins and thus avoid costly firefights. God only knew how many men they killed in doing so. Opposition was sporadic. One FBI man was taken out with a spear that got him in the throat. Another was felled by a thrown fishing knife that nailed him in the chest. The thrower received a dozen bullets to his upper body for his trouble and perished with a look of surprise on his face.

Sakusha, Tetsu, Neko and Sekitan met up with each other and, with the Invisible Compass men and the Pinkertons, followed in the wake of the FBI. It might have been possible to get ahead of the American federal agents but common sense dictated it wasn't a good idea. Being bumped off by friendly fire from G Men would be the probable outcome.

From the second series of cabins down to the storage hold vampires were stirring from their coffins. When the FBI reached the first cabin of the second series, two lithe females with fangs grabbed two of them and, before a shot could be fired, had crushed their skulls with their hands. A grenade was used to get them and it blew them apart but nothing could be done for the men they had caused to die of brain hemorrhage.

According to one theory, since wood wasn't used in the explosions, the vampires this harmed could put themselves back together. This was not likely to happen in the immediate future and the FBI in action that day were all concerned with the immediate future.

The last of the grenades was used on the second series of cabins leaving nothing for the hold except machine pistols, knives and grit. Still they pushed on. They had twenty five minutes left to get their part done and to get out. It wasn't a whole lot of time so they were anxious to make every second count.

Pistols blazing, the FBI entered the hold. Ten vampires walked up to them and, in spite of the pounding bullets striking their flesh, grabbed them by their throats, for some two vampires on one man, and squeezed the life out of them. It was over in less than five minutes. None of the ten unliving attackers were even Old Ones. Men who had, up until recently, scoffed at the idea of the walking dead were deceased because of them.

At seventeen minutes before the first limpid was scheduled to do its thing, the Rising Sun, the Pinkertons and the Invisible Compass entered the hold. Straight away Sakusha destroyed four vampires with rapid fire from his rife. The bullets he used were the hollow points with slithers of wood that had been dampened by holy water. When such slugs entered the undead heart, it was over quickly. The Twenty Pinkertons raised their crossbows to fire. Fifteen of them succeeded in destroying their targets while five were too slow and had their throats slashed by sharp fingernails instead. Blood spouted and noses sensitive to such smells became excited. Two Invisible Compass men managed to smash bottles of holy water against the heads of several menaces to humankind just getting out of their coffins, thus sending them smoking to Hell. The other Compass men were busy keeping eighteen angry vampires at bay with their hand guns and holy crosses. The Pinkertons gave a hand to the Invisible Compass with this eighteen with their crossbows and bolts.

A dozen men with hand guns tried to protect their toothy masters by laying down a blanket of fire from behind some now empty coffins. The noise they made was horrific. Six Pinkertons died outright and a further two were wounded. One of the Invisible Compass men had brought along a hand held rocket launcher with one rocket he had loaded. He used it to clear out that despicable dozen.

Three male vampires, including two of the Old Ones who were Capos, went for Tetsu, their red eyes ablaze, their fingernails long and sharp. Three flashes of his sword later and three vampire heads were on a roll. Three seconds later and the bodies, heads and all, had turned to dust.

An army of rats, commanded to do so by an Old One, attacked and destroyed two Invisible Compass men. They then went after Neko. She responded by leaping away from them, grabbing a living supporter of the vampire and throwing him into their path. She took out the Old One, who happened to be the undead that had escaped Tetsu in Nagoya, with two well thrown star knives and a long knife with a wooden tip. The star knives, which hit him in the throat and in the stomach, distracted him while she went for the killing stab into his heart with the long knife. He didn't last long after that but quickly went to powder. The rats, no longer under anyone's control, scurried off.

Five Pinkertons managed to put three bolts through the hearts of the last remaining Capo Old Ones. At this time, there were two Capo Old Ones left standing to receive the bolts but one of the Old Ones got two of the bolts through the heart. The five Pinkertons were then shot at by a lone gunman before an Invisible Compass man shot the gunman dead.

Sakusha was the first of the Rising Sun to notice the demon skull on a podium in the center of all the coffins and all the fighting. Beside the skull was the lord of the vampires. At the same time Sakusha became aware of the vampires guarding it and their lord. They appeared to be a fierce, well disciplined group. They were four Japanese warriors and they looked as if they knew all about war. Lord Vascari was relaxed as if the minor disturbance to his day he was experiencing would soon be over and he could get back to sleep. Such confidence said something about this lord and the high regard he had for those closest to him.

The skull was fearsome in its own right. It was larger than human but could have passed as such if not for the three horns atop its brow ridges. Also the color was wrong. It was too dark, as if, at some time, it had been blackened in a fire. It also looked like something that should be gotten at with a sledgehammer and not a sword. He knew his bullets wouldn't do the job.

With infinite patience, Sakusha took aim and shot two of the Japanese vampires with his special hollow points before being winged by a nearby human guard. There were now two Japanese vampires left making Lord Vascari not so confident any more but Sakusha's firing arm was useless. He had to take serious cover behind well built coffins and pray someone else would be able to finish up what he had started. The human guard fired a few more times showing persistence in trying to kill him.

Three Pinkertons with crossbows at the ready advanced on the last of the Japanese undead drilling wooden bolts through their hearts. Before these vampires perished, however, they managed to break the necks of the men who had destroyed them. In less than ten seconds all three Pinkertons were gone.

Sekitan was keeping busy. He used his smoke bombs to appear larger than life in one corner of the hold and take out two armed mercenaries with his long knife. He then disappeared into smoke and reappeared in another corner to take out two more armed mercenaries.

Two dozen vampires changed into bats to dive bomb and tear at the faces of their enemy. Pinkertons and Invisible Compass delighted in this move and reached for their bottles of holy water. The result was two dozen undead on leathery wings smoking and screeching their way to a fiery end. Some of them, in their final agony, bumped into fellow vampires that had not become bats thus setting them ablaze.

A lone Invisible Compass man, seeing his chance, picked up the machine pistol of a fallen FBI agent and sprayed the human trying to kill Sakusha. In less than three seconds, the offending human was a bloody corpse.

Two male vampires with four by two blocks of wood were advancing on Tetsu. They should have known better. His sword sang its blood drinking song twice and there were two bodies missing their heads.

By this time, there were about two dozen vampires left but only ten minutes until the first limpid went off. The skull had to be destroyed. It wasn't enough for it to be lost at sea with the ship. If it were merely lost, it might someday be found and once more become a symbol for vampires to unite. An explosive charge might do the trick but Tetsu felt that the only sure way was with his own sword. It was, after all, forged in the monster's own blood. With this in mind, he dodged past three advancing vampires allowing them to be confronted by three Pinkertons with crossbows. Even as he moved on Lord Anton Vascari, he could hear that the Pinkertons in question had won.

"You have ruined everything," Vascari said to Tetsu, flashing his sword as a challenge. It was an antique saber no doubt from the 18th Century.

"On garde," said Tetsu, flashing his blade. Sweat was pouring and adrenalin pumping.

"On garde, Mon Ami. You will die," intoned Vascari with re-newed confidence. "I am as good with the French language, you will find, as I am with the finer points of swordsmanship. And I am very good, mon Capitan, with the finer points of swordsmanship."

French was one of the many languages Vascari had mastered over the centuries. It was considered by some to be the language of the fencer, the European style dualist. Tetsu understood the reference as he saw Vascari thrust, slash and parry European style. Tetsu fought in his own way. His was not a European weapon; therefore European ways did not apply. For him bushido was the spirit of his understanding and, if he was firm of purpose enough for the spirit to take hold, then he would win. His confidence against that of his undead opponent he knew would be tested.

Vascari was as first-rate as his reputation plus he had reflexes no living human could match. In less than two seconds Tetsu was nicked on both shoulders. Two seconds more and he had a deep gash in his side. He tried again for the chest area of his foe but it was no good. Vascari was too fast, too experienced. Via body language, he could read Tetsu's next move even before Tetsu was aware of it. He could, no doubt, smell Tetsu's fear.

When a stray bullet hit a beam near the vampire lord's head, thus distracting him for a milli-second, Tetsu saw his chance, dropped his sword and picked up a coffin lid. It was big enough and long enough to be used as a battering ram against a very surprised and stumbling Vascari.

"Don't be ridiculous!" cried the head vampire in annoyance as the coffin lid made contact with his chest. "What will that do?"

With the lid, Tetsu pushed the less than sure footed Vascari against a wall some twenty feet away. He then snatched up his sword and made his way to the skull.

"No!" Vascari screamed when he saw what was happening. He had been played for a fool and knew it.

Tetsu brought his blade down upon the demon remains, shat-tering it into a thousand pieces. The sound of blade upon skull he found to be much to his liking and tired muscles drew strength from the deed.

"Well played," Vascari admitted, swallowing his anger. "But now, no more play, mon Capitan, now you die."

In one stroke from Vascari's saber Tetsu's sword left his hand and clattered against a bulkhead. *I'm finished*, the Samurai thought. *It is over.*

"Beg and I will make it quick," snarled Vascari.

"No," Tetsu whispered, for his throat had gone dry. He stood still waiting for the fatal blow.

A shot rang out. It was fired by Sakusha. Somehow he'd managed to use his other hand and to fire true with it. To Tetsu's astonishment, Vascari fell. The look of being robbed was on the old vampire's face as he died that fatal second time. Showing his age, he went swiftly to ash. Tetsu picked up his sword.

"Right through the heart," Tetsu remarked, looking at the ashes, his words complimentary.

"No mucking about," Sakusha agreed.

Around them the mopping up was going on. Vampires were trying to get away and being brought down the sooner. Then, right on schedule, there was a massive explosion that shook the whole ship.

"We have to get out now!" Neko cried, leaping to the nearest exit.

The Invisible Compass and the Pinkertons picked up their wounded and followed. Tetsu helped Sakusha onto his feet. He then turned at the right time to avoid slashing claws, his sword acting almost without him, the cutting edge once more drinking its fill of a creature of darkness. Sekitan picked up a crossbow dropped by a dead Pinkerton, the bolt still in place, and fired it at a vampire about to attack one of the Invisible Compass. After that, the few remaining vampires hid, unwilling to take on the humans and, unaware their vessel was doomed.

The surviving vampire hunters were on deck when the second limpid blew causing the ship to rock. It then started to tilt.

"We have to be onboard the trawlers and well away from here before the forth one goes," Sakusha said urgently. "Otherwise the trawlers will be caught in the back wash of the liner sinking and they'll go under too and us with them."

Just as the third limpid blew, everyone among the living managed to get onboard the waiting vessels. They pulled away, engines on full, from the disaster yet to come.

A horrific explosion signaled the fate of the forth limpid and the liner. After that it was fast going under and nothing short of a miracle was going to stop it. The trawlers were struggling but they were going to make it. Everyone could see that and feel grateful to be alive and safe.

"What do you think will happen to the remaining vampires on the ship?" Neko asked of anyone who would offer an answer.

"If they make it to the surface before dark, they'll fry," Sakusha said. "Other than that I don't know."

"We've done well," Tetsu assured, who was aching from his arms to his chest. "It's time to rest."

In the weeks that followed, the out of town vampires left New York. The cartel was no more and, to them, New York was just another place with all the hazards of a big city. Word got out of the destruction of the demon skull and of the forces responsible. It would be some time before so many undead would try to unite and that in itself was a triumph.

The Rising Sun Group stayed in New York for about six months before heading back to Nagoya. They stayed to further help out the Pinkertons and the Invisible Compass. They stayed to explain to the FBI what had happened to their agents aboard the liner and to offer advice for future dealings with the unliving.

They thought that, while they were in the USA, they might look for new recruits to their team. It was felt that two more team members with the right skills and nerve would come in handy. Otosan felt that the idea of new blood into the ranks sound. It was just a matter of finding the right people. As it turned out, the right people would be two Japanese from Tokyo who happened to be studying in the Big Apple at the time.

Warriors of the Rising Sun

A flap of leathery wings overhead sent a thrill up Neko's spine. Was it them? A dozen bats flew past her position in the direction of the city. Would they come back for her? They were big and ugly. There was one capable of carrying off a cat or a small dog. If they changed, they would be capable of anything.

For a few seconds her concentration on her entire surroundings was absolute. It needed to be if she was to survive. No amateurish attack of nerves just concentration and a super-normal awareness that came out of it. She could hear dust falling on a leaf two hundred meters away or the rustle of cloth at a similar distance. She'd been trained to have this enhanced knowledge of place and time. It was an ancient knowledge going back over four hundred years. Gaining it hadn't come easy. Still, somebody had to do what she did. It was her calling, perhaps one of the oldest callings. Her garb made that notion rather comical – rather comical indeed if she cared to voice it.

"Relax," word came from Tetsu over the listening device in her ear. "They are Seibutsu, living creatures. My goggles register their heat signatures."

Neko relaxed a little but not too much. Bats were sometimes the eyes and ears of the enemy as were rats and cockroaches. They might have been figuring her out for their masters. One false move on her part, and a week of careful preparation would go down the tube. Worse since the enemy would then know someone was after them.

An orange cat meowed and brushed itself against Neko's legs before going on its way. Neko appreciated the touch of furry warmth but said nothing. She crossed her arms and continued to wait.

She did not look up into the branches of the trees around her or toward the nearby bushes. The leafy pathway out of the park which dodged and darted around century old oaks caught her eye and kept it. Then her gaze drifted toward the garbage bins and the deserted benches.

A scrap of paper lifting itself into the air on a cool current and moving in her direction startled her. She admonished herself for thus being taken in. Tetsu the mighty and the others were probably laughing at her foolishness. She was tempted to search for them with her eyes but knew that it was not in the mission's best interests for her to do so.

It was her turn to play Sato (sugar) for the fiends they hoped would come. No one in her pack had ever been taken doing what she was doing but there could always be a first. Right now slipping into a daze brought on by boredom was extremely dangerous and easily done.

She was a compact blond woman in her early twenties. Being half-Japanese and half-Caucasian American, she was of mixed heritage. Her father had been a carpenter with connections to the Rosy Cross. He had been killed for making wooden stakes. Her mother was something much more clandestine. Inevitably she had followed in her mother's footsteps. She was called Neko because her eyes were big and green and she liked milk. She didn't purr like her namesake but she did have claws. They were made out of hard wood and were kept razor sharp at the points. Unfortunately, she didn't have them on her.

At the request of her teammates, she put on red lippy instead of her usual black to give herself a come hither look. Despite the night having turned chilly, she was in a silky blue blouse that was open at the neck and screamed metaphorically "take me". The impractical pair of black high heels she was talked into wearing added to her discomfort. She felt like a hooker or maybe a turkey the day before Thanksgiving. She was a skinny bird and much tougher than they were likely to suspect.

She missed the little St. Christopher she usually wore on a tiny gold chain around her neck, but to wear it would have given the wrong signal. She had to look stupid and vulnerable – just a dumb blond street walker so green she's in a place no street walker in her right mind would venture into alone.

"Damn, it's cold," Neko whispered, rubbing her arms.

"Steady," Tetsu whispered back. She wondered what tree he was hiding in.

"Easy for you to say. You're not freezing your tail off."

"You do have a tail then?"

"I'm not saying and you'll never know. But if I had one it would be frozen."

"Cut it!" hissed Sakusha, his tongue sometimes as sharp as his notoriously keen eye. "If they see you talking to yourself, it's over."

"An hour till dawn," Neko sighed. "I'd say it's over right now."

"Shhh! Someone's coming."

It was a man with dark glasses walking his dog. His brown coat was crumpled as if he'd been sleeping in it and he wore a hat and scarf. At first sight the dog was a German shepherd. Then Neko got the impression it was a wolf as lean and mean as you pleased. It loped along at the man's feet but seemed to have a mind of its own. It wasn't on a leash. She stepped away from the trees to be better seen by them. She couldn't have been in a better position for a snatch and she knew it. Perhaps it was too perfect and being too perfect it was a dead giveaway. Still, the creeps they were after didn't have a rep for being subtle or smart. Others of their ilk elsewhere did but not this lot.

"How much?" asked the man. The wolf growled.

"More than you can afford," Neko said coolly.

"Let me take you to some place warm where we can discuss this," he said. "I'll even buy you coffee."

"Sure." Neko shrugged her shoulders. If it turned out to be a regular John she'd ditch him. If it was something more interesting she'd spring into action. There was little point in staying in the park any longer.

He took her down a well lit path toward a prominent coffee bean joint. The place was full of people coming off night shift. From even a distance of six hundred meters she could hear them. This was New York, the city that never sleeps and hot Java in plentiful portions kept it going. She was half-dreaming, which was a big no-no, of her favorite Brazilian blend, which had plenty of whipped cream, when something happened. She was a few meters from the café when he shoved her hard into an alley and then spirited her into a small warehouse. The wolf seemed to fly rather than leap after them.

She took the place to be a shoe warehouse because there were lots of cardboard shoeboxes about. There were stacks on pallets five boxes high and ten boxes wide. She took where she was to also be a trap because he threw her into the center of the docking area and she was surrounded by people with decidedly pointy molars. They seemed more comfortable than she was in the semi-darkness, the only light coming from the slightly open entrance doors. She landed on her backside and made a little bit of an effort to get up. They pushed her down and grinned toothily. The wolf growled in her face, its fetid breath wilting her button-like nose.

"Here's the best I can come up with," said the man who had abducted her.

"What you got for us?" asked a gaunt blond woman with greasy hair who was wearing a thick tweed coat Neko wanted badly. "Not another needle jockey I hope."

"Not much, Jill," the man said. "There's not much out there. With luck this one's blood won't be tainted like some of the others. The last thing we need is a habit. This will have to keep us going."

"Barely," groused a gaunt man with equally greasy hair to the woman's.

The whole dozen nodded in grim agreement. In the dozen Neko included the wolf who was nodding too. In a show of panic she took her shoes off and waved one at them. They let her because they found it amusing. It was, however, only a show. She felt the rush of adrenalin that came when things were about to pop. In the corner of her eye she caught movement in the lacework of overhead metal rafters keeping the roof from collapsing. *Friend or foe?* she wondered.

The guy with the hat who had compelled her into this situation leaned close to her, his breath as foul as the wolf's had been, adding to the tension she felt. He said in a light tone: "You don't really think that shoe will do you any good against us, do you?"

"I don't know," she replied, twisting the heel off. "One can but try."

Before he could say another word, she blew a fine powder into his face and that of the wolf. At first he was prepared to gloat and so, in its own fashion, was the wolf. His lungs and those of his canine companion were dead like the rest of him. He didn't take in oxygen to breathe because he had no need for it. Breathing was just a pattern he retained from the days when it did matter. Why then were he and his friend choking? Why was he sputtering and wheezing and the wolf hacking? The others took a step back.

"Fine sawdust," Neko said, answering the unasked question she knew was on their minds. "It won't kill but it is a damned nuisance, isn't it?" She kicked the man aside then threw the now empty shoe at the wolf. It hacked and yelped, shrinking back from her as much as it could without loping off for cover.

"Get her!" the gaunt woman cried, moving back to Neko. The ring of fangs had been taken aback for all of three seconds. Now they wanted blood – literally. It was enough time, however, for Neko to remove the heel of her other shoe and to press a small stud on the inside.

"Look out!" the greasy haired man hollered. "She's up to something."

A spectacular light display which lasted five seconds erupted from the former footwear. Neko closed her eyes in time to avoid being blinded. Her adversaries were not so lucky. They shrieked with pain and thrashed about knocking over shoes and sending them everywhere. For them the light was far more damaging than it would have been to a human caught in such a blast. For them it not only bedazzled with instant day but also burned. By the time their eyes cleared and they were able to see again, Neko was gone and so was the coat she was coveting.

"Look for her!" the gaunt woman screamed, menace in her voice. Her eyes were streaming tears and becoming redder than a well-done lobster. The victims of wood particles in the lungs continued to cough, splutter and, yes, hack.

The gloom became a worry to the toothy ones. They could detect movement but, because of the assault of the light, their senses were not functioning well.

"Run!" cried the man in the hat but failed to take his own advice. He didn't move a centimeter. Something bulky was blocking the entrance way and he wasn't sure if it was a good idea to try to escape in that direction. A simple meal had gone terribly wrong. Humans weren't supposed to be this tricky or dangerous. It was like a cat finding out for the first time he might be beaten by a bunch of mice.

From above an apparition all in black descended. It was shaped like a man and was waving a great big samurai sword.

"Tetsu, master of the blade," Neko's voice came from seemingly everywhere and nowhere. "The weapon is very old. It was forged in the 16th Century in demon's blood. It has ancient symbols of purity cut into the grip, the hilt and the guard."

The blade moved swiftly in the hands of the man in black. It kissed what light there was as it entered and exited bone. Cut in two, the greasy haired fellow couldn't make up his mind which direction to run in so he went in both. Shoe boxes were sprayed in his blood. The sight of this fifty-fifty split, in broad daylight, would have been ghastly. As it was, the movements of this second-time-dying corpse were enough to rattle his companions into fleeing anywhere and everywhere. The result was two of his mates bumping heads and then having them split open by the sword and chopped clean from their necks. One head rolled away into the darkness.

Then the wolf, after bolting for a dark corner only to find five of his compadres shivering there, decided it was time to make a stand. Fear had turned to hate. It had little of the sawdust left in its lungs and was wanting revenge on anyone and everyone responsible for its recent discomfort. It charged the back of the large swordsman thinking to rip the fellow's throat out before he knew what was happening. Too late it saw Tetsu turn to meet the attack and cut a slither of night in twain with the silvery edge of what was as much a part of him as his right arm. The wolf saw its body go one way as its head went another. The head landed in Tetsu's hands and began to morph into something human. It was male, balding and gray. The body, also morphing, landed naked, blood gushing everywhere, against three fellow vamps who squealed in fright.

They didn't squeal for long. Two humans came from behind a loaded pallet to confront them. One was tall, feminine and lithe. The other was squat and masculine. Both were in black like Tetsu.

"Odori the dancer," came Neko's voice, "and her companion, Shimo. Don't be shy; show them what you can do."

Odori somersaulted away from the vamps and then toward them. Shimo barreled straight ahead and, in the last instant, snagged an overhead beam with a cable shot from a wrist device. As the gruesome three grabbed for him, he pressed a stud on his wrist device retracting the cable and, at the same time, threw hundreds of flakes of white into their faces, temporarily blinding them.

"Ice and snow," Neko said to the confused vamps clawing the flakes from their eyes. "Followed, no doubt, by chest pains."

Odori's gymnastics ended with her sinking two thin wooden knives that popped out of her wrists into two of the undead. The third, in an effort to get away, smashed into a stack of pallets and, in doing so, impaled himself on the broken material.

Five undead decided to try for the back exit, a single narrow door marked for emergency use only. In doing so, they tripped a wire sending a net covered in garlic balls down on them. They cried out in anger and frustration as the garlic played havoc with their already traumatized senses. The feeling of vertigo they must have been experiencing was no doubt debilitating. Ordinarily, they would have had little trouble tearing apart the ropes fettering them and they knew it.

The gaunt woman, who looked even scrawnier without her coat, eyed her adversaries with growing loathing. She was only wearing a thin gray top and men's trousers but showed no signs of being affected by the cold. Seeing her chance, she sprang at Odori, grabbing her by the throat and arm. "I'm getting out of here or I'm snapping her neck," she said to Tetsu whose sword was at the ready.

"You're arm's smoking," he said matter-of-factly.

She looked down and screamed in fright, swiftly letting go of her captive. A nasty burn mark was developing on her upper limb the size of an American one dollar coin and in the shape of the Taoist symbol for Yin and Yang. It had come from contact with the acrobat's Taoist medallion she kept on a silver chain around her neck. Released, Odori span around and stabbed her captor in the chest. The gaunt woman's

195

eyes bugged out as she fell, her hand clutching at the place where the wooden knife had gone in and out.

The man in the hat sprinted for the doors, hoping to steamroll out of the way the big human guarding them. There was a sudden puff of black smoke and, when it cleared; the human was gone, replaced by a board on a stand sporting deadly-looking spikes all over it. Unable to stop in time, the hat man slammed into the sharpened wood, driving two of the spikes into his heart. Before he expired in a wash of his own blood, he heard Neko say, from everywhere and nowhere at the same time: "For a big fellow, Sekitan is full of surprises, isn't he?"

With Tetsu's help, Neko, who had come out of hiding, removed the net from the remaining five undead. They were wide-eyed and shaking. Gone was any notion of superiority until one of them, out of sheer panic, picked up a nearby pallet, emptied it of boxes, and threw it at Odori and Shimo. Despite the speed of delivery, the duo ducked out of the way in time. When it hit the back wall, it exploded and a chunk of wood slammed into the back of Tetsu's head, knocking him out.

Seeing the swordsman down, the vamps charged Odori and Shimo. Before they got far, a man in a navy blue suit, who could have come from some executive board meeting only he was packing a gun, stepped forward out of the shadows. Like most of the others, he had, no doubt, come from above. What he thought he could do with even a modified police special sporting a silencer the vamps weren't sure and they didn't want to find out. They'd had enough surprises. They changed direction and headed back toward the entrance way.

Two sounds similar to escaping air from a diving rig caught everyone's attention. They were followed by the sound of two bodies hitting the floor. Two more vamps went the same way. Rich red oozed out of mid-section wounds into factory dust and groans were replaced by death rattles. The fifth vamp, who had looked back and stopped his flight after his companions went down, gulped in horror. His companions, for what they were worth, were gone forever.

"Stay put," the gunman ordered. "I won't end your existence if you do what you're told. Understand?"

"Yes!" the last vamp cried. "I understand…but how did you? How did you…to them!"

"Oh that. The name's Sakusha. And this is your lucky day. You see, mate, we want some questions answered. As for the ammunition I use, each hollow point has a slither of wood dipped in holy water inside to give it extra punch. Vamp stopping power you might say. Works a beauty, don't it?"

"Tell us where the one who made you can be found," Neko said, hugging the coat she'd stolen about her shoulders. Her legs felt frozen but she wasn't in the mood to complain.

"Dracula?" the vamp asked. "You want me to tell you where he can be found?"

"Let's waste him," growled Sekitan who appeared out of a puff of black smoke next to Neko. "Let's waste him for wasting our time."

"No! Don't. I really do know. Honest!"

"Sure you do," Neko said. "I bet your secondhand shoes with the holes in the toes, your torn-up checkered shirt, and your stained baggy pants you know."

"Ever hear of Bram Stoker?" Sakusha asked.

"Bram who?"

"Stoker."

"Never heard of him," the vamp said, looking about for sympathy.

"Never mind," Neko grimaced. "Just tell us what you do know."

"Don't bother," called out an old man as he entered the warehouse. He skirted the bodies of dead vamps and scattered shoes as he made his way to the group. He was wearing a heavy brown coat and had a matching scarf around his neck. Under one arm he carried a large box covered over with a heavy black cloth.

"Otosan!" Sakusha cried in good humor, motioning the old man to come closer. "We were just getting some information out of this cur."

"Don't bother. Let him go."

"Let him go?"

The old man known as Otosan turned to the vamp and said in a crisp, clear voice: "We don't need you. You are free to go. No one here will stop you."

"No one? You mean I can walk out through those doors?"

"Please do," said Otosan, bowing his head.

The vamp bolted for the doors only to stop halfway. He turned and said to Sakusha: "You're going to shoot me in the back, aren't you?"

"No," Sakusha replied, feeling offended by the accusation. He holstered his gun and crossed his arms. "If honorable Otosan says it's okay to let you go, we let you go."

"There's a trick. There has to be. There's a booby trap waiting for me out there, isn't there? You, the big man, rigged it, isn't that right?"

Sekitan shook his head.

"Go!" snapped Otosan, "Or I will have you slain here and now."

In a panic the vamp bolted the rest of the way, opened the doors and left. There followed a terrible scream and, seconds later, the unhappy return of the undead. He staggered back into the warehouse, his burnt hand putting out the fire in his hair. His skin was pealing from third-degree burns and his eyes were boiled goose eggs. Every bit of exposed flesh was red and smoldering. Apart from all that he smelled awful.

"The time!" he clacked at the old man with a tongue swollen to twice its normal size. "You knew!"

"Yes," Otosan said with a smile as the vamp collapsed before him, "It was dawn ten minutes ago. A lovely day is beginning outside. There's a bit of frost but it will soon clear."

"You knew!" Shimo gasped. "I shouldn't have doubted you, not even for a second."

"Let that be a lesson. Trust me in these matters. I have over fifty years experience."

"We will," agreed Odori and Shimo, bowing in humility.

The burnt vamp staggered about for a while then collapsed. After that, the odor of overcooked meat began to fade.

"What have you got in the box?" asked Neko.

"Never mind that. What happened to Tetsu, our shining blade?"

"He took a spill but he's coming around. A piece of wood hit him."

"Yes," Sakusha agreed. "It only hit his head."

"Fine talk," Tetsu groaned, getting to his feet. "Now, Otosan, can you please tell us what you have there?"

"Here?" the old man inquired. He lifted the cover with a flurry to reveal a cat in a cage. The cage was made of wood and it had garlic balls dangling from the bars. "It's Neko's feline friend, the one who rubbed up against her. I also have the scrap of paper she wasn't much interested in. Want to read it?"

Otosan pulled the paper out of his pocket, straightened it and handed it to Tetsu.

"What's it say?" Neko demanded, alive with curiosity.

"It reads," Tetsu began, "*The experiment in turning vagabonds, street urchins and bums into competent disciples has failed. They are completely useless. Only one has managed the rudiments of morphing. Do what you like with them.*

"You wouldn't believe the signature."

"The signature?" Odori echoed.

"Yes, the signature."

"Okay, okay," Neko implored, "I'll bite. Who's it signed by?"

"None other than Count Dracula," Tetsu grinned.

"No!" Neko snatched the note off him. "But you're right. It does say Dracula. How about that?"

"Dracula," Shimo said. "You look like you're about to burst into laughter. Why?"

"Do you mean you don't know?" asked Neko.

"Yes," a voice, which was as much a harsh meow as it was human talk, came from the cage. "Why do you act so? I am…Dracula!"

"You're Dracula?" Neko looked at the cat with undisguised humor. It was a big ginger with beady green eyes.

"Yes," hissed the feline. "I am Count Dracula, the prince of darkness."

"And I am the Pope," Sakusha said, an amused grin stretching his lips. Neko, no longer able to contain herself, burst into laughter.

"Stop it!" the cat grated. "I really am he. You will keep me alive, yes? I know many secrets, yes?"

"Maybe we should keep him alive," Neko said, tears in her eyes. "Maybe we should let him take his act on the road."

"He does know how to spin a yarn, doesn't he?" offered Sakusha.

"It isn't that my people don't want to believe you," Otosan said contemplatively to the agitated orange fur-ball, "It is just we know for a fact Count Dracula is fiction."

"Fiction?!" vexed the cat. "Fiction!"

"He was based on two historic personages. One was Count Vlad Dracul, a terror to the Turks and to his own people. He was made undead by a corrupt nun, roamed the Transylvanian countryside for centuries, and then in the 19th Century, fell afoul of a band of Freemason hunters. His ashes reside in a silver box covered by crucifixes and hidden in the deepest vault of the Mitchell Library in Sydney, Australia. There, members of a local order of Freemasonry have been tasked with keeping the occasional eye on his remains."

"Who's the other person?" Odori asked.

"Countess Elizabeth Bathory who, when she was alive, did unspeakable things to young girls in her charge. She was made into a vampire by a maidservant and, for a time, terrorized the whole of Hungary. When she moved to Bavaria, she was caught and brought to rest by members of an order of German Crusader Knight. Her ashes are in a silver chalice surrounded by crucifixes and held by a brave order of alchemists that are part of the famed Knights of Malta. I believe her remains are now in Spain."

"So this can't be Count Dracula?" asked Shimo.

"Not unless fictional characters come to life," Neko said, "Or should I say fictional characters come to unlife?"

"Who is he then?" Odori asked.

"Well," the feline spat, "even if I am not Dracula, I'm still a very powerful vampire. I have followers and I did manage to transform myself into a cat. It takes skill to pick a form pleasant to a human's eye."

Neko poked her finger in the cage to touch the talking animal's fur to see how real it was. One nasty cat scratch later, she withdrew it and stuck it in her mouth.

"Oh, the indignity!" The feline bristled its coat to show how taken aback it was at being prodded. "I am not an illusion, dear girl. I'm not! Your cut digit can now attest to that fact. I am what I am. Let me out, and things will be different. Mark me, things will be different!"

"Your name is Franz Hopper," Otosan said, looking at the unhappy ginger in further contemplation. "Before you were made over, you served beer to customers at an Inn in a small village in Bavaria."

"So?" the cat meowed angrily. "That was a long time ago. Anyway, how do you know that?"

"Undead you sired and abandoned have told us."

"Abandoned? Me? Never!"

"Oh Franz," Otosan began with a touch of sympathy, "you tried to recruit followers. But they either left you because they were too smart for you or you said they were too dumb and you left them. You were no leader, not like Vlad. You may be old but – how do the Americans say it? – ah, yes, you are small fry."

"Small fry!" the furry-one whined, further bristling. "Small fry?"

"Yes. See how easily I caught you. Just a little stealth and you were in my cage."

"Then why go to all this bother?"

"We are the Warriors of the Rising Sun," Sakusha said proudly. "Ridding the world of demons, especially vampires, is what we do and what our order has been doing since the 17th Century. You are a vampire, ego we bother."

"All vampires have the potential for great evil," Otosan said. "Even you might become a real menace."

"Besides," Tetsu added, "Odori and Shimo are new to our ranks. Otosan thought we'd take them on a milk run involving run-of-the-mill vamps and a second rate Old One just to take them through their paces and see how they work in with the rest of us."

"We were once an order of Japanese Christian vampire slayers," Otosan said. "Now we recruit from around the globe and give our members Japanese names. Odori and Shimo are Taoists from Japan. I am a Catholic from Japan; Neko is also a Catholic but of mixed heritage. Sakusha is an Australian marksman, again a Catholic. Sekitan, as the name implies, is an African American and of the Protestant faith. Tetsu is a Zen Buddhist."

"We're quite a mixed bag," Sakusha smiled.

"We are the Warriors of the Rising Sun," Otosan repeated. "We are united by our desire to rid the world of monsters and by our faith in the one true God. It keeps us safe and allows us to win. Also, we are all ninja, and have been for hundreds of years."

"If I am not important, why tell me all this?" asked Franz.

"I am reminding our newcomers," Otosan said. "As a good father, it is my duty and pleasure to do so. As for you, let me put it this way: neither Odori nor Shimo have ever seen what happens when an Old One dies for the second time. They have seen new vampires fall and bleed but never an Old One expire."

"Expire?" Franz gulped, curling up as tight as possible within the confines of the cage.

"Sakusha, you may do the honors."

Sakusha pulled out his gun and took aim.

"It is a regular gun and you are joking, yes?" Franz pleaded. "That's right, isn't it, Sakusha? Otosan?"

A second later, the trigger was pulled and there was the sound of released air. Five seconds after that the cage leapt out of Otosan's grasp and blew apart as the metamorphosis back to man began. It took less than a minute.

"Stand back!" Otosan ordered as their mortally wounded ex-captive got to his feet and eyed his executioners. He was a balding man of medium height and weight similar in appearance to the wolf vampire. He was also naked.

"He's no prize," Neko whispered to Odori. "I much preferred the cat. At least, if we pruned the claws, it would have been cuddly."

"You die!" Franz rushed toward Sakusha, his goal the ninja's throat. The gunman took a crucifix out of his pocket and aimed it at the undead. He fished in his other pocket and threw Neko her St. Christopher. Odori and Shimo showed the vamp their Taoist symbols and Sekitan held up his miniature edition of the Bible. Caught in the light of so many holy objects radiating powerful psychic energy from their owners, Franz was forced up against a wall where the chest wound gushing blood began to have more of an effect. Ten minutes after the shooting the blood ran out. He became a mummified corpse of dried, powdery skin, and minutes later, crumbled into a pile of ashes.

"Wow!" Odori cried.

"And that, my children is how an Old One is removed from this world," Otosan said sagely.

"Quite spectacular," Odori said.

"Quite." Shimo nodded in agreement.

"Still want to be an active member of the Rising Sun?" Otosan asked Odori and Shimo.

"Yes," answered Odori and Shimo in unison.

"Good," Otosan said. "Those in ninja black get changed now."

Tetsu, Sekitan, Odori, and Shimo jumped up to the rafters and five minutes later rejoined the others. Tetsu was now in a pin-striped business suit and Sekitan in a thick black jumper and blue jeans. Odori had on a black evening dress with a fake fur stole over her shoulders. Shimo was looking dapper in a black suit with gold tie. They were all carrying small bags containing their battle gear, including weapons. While she waited, Neko put the St. Christopher around her neck.

"What about the bodies?" Odori asked as she approached Otosan. "Surely we can't leave the undead lying here?"

"Before I ventured into this warehouse, I phoned, on my mobile phone, the men we have for the clean-up. They should be here in half an hour. They will chop off the heads on the intact bodies and stuff all the mouths with garlic. Then they will load them into sanitation trucks and dispose of them safely. Though the majority of the population doesn't know the truth about what we do, the city officials here and elsewhere are aware that vampires exist and so make sure our work goes unhindered. They too have been notified."

"Where to now, Otosan?" asked Tetsu as he rejoined the others. He threw Neko a pair of track pants which she donned.

"Let's get some coffee. I believe there's a coffee shop not far from here. Isn't that right, Neko?"

"Yes. Not far…Not far at all."

Cold Comfort

Sydney, NSW, Australia, summer, 2005

Of late, Greg Reese had been through enough changes to confuse anyone. He was putting on his whites to go try out for the NSW team in the hopes of someday playing for Australia like his all time hero, the Don, when it happened.

A tall woman with flaming red hair who looked somewhat like Nicole Kidman, the Australian actress walked into the change room. He put the flame effect down to the silvery tinsel she wore to hold back the locks from her face. He could not, however, put down the effect she was having on his heart. Her presence was taking his breath away.

He should have told her to leave. He should have said please, please come back later when I'm not trying out, but he didn't. Then they were in each other's arms and that was more than just pleasant, though she could have done with a Mintie or two. Her breath was rancid like bacon left out of the fridge two days running. He saw fangs glint in the subdued light, heard a soft, feminine hiss, felt a stabbing in his neck and, for a long while, knew no more.

Waking up on a slab in a place reserved for the dead and those who take care of them was pretty creepy. The redhead was there but her hair was no longer flaming. As evidence of change, he was more interested in her neck than any other part of her. He thought her neck lovely. He thought her neck adorable and, for some strange reason, he thought her neck tasty.

He was naked. His whites were gone. She was holding out to him new clothes. He wasn't cold and he no longer cared about respectability but he put them on anyway. They were a symbol of change. Black shirt, black pants, black tie, black coat. Black everything.

Her name was Night Sky and, despite the redness of her hair or perhaps because of it, she wore black too. Maybe it was the official color of the dead even if his old art teacher had always insisted that black wasn't really a color at all. Since he was alive but not really alive that fitted in nicely with the odd way he felt.

She explained to him what he had become and, over the next few nights, gave him lessons on vampirism. He picked up the blood drinking bit and the things he needed to avoid, but he was still having problems with the humanoid into bat trick when she decided she had spent enough time with him. He could manage the ears and the leathery wings but that was it. Without a complete transformation he not only looked and felt ridiculous; he did not have the power of flight.

Why she had sired him in the first place he didn't know. He suspected she wanted an extra vamp or two around as she made her escape from Sydney. He, being a newbie, was expected to be caught and destroyed by the Macquarie Street Freemasons, who call themselves the Invisible Compass, while she got away. The more distractions she could create for the hunter while she fled the city the better.

She had told him about the Invisible Compass; but if she had been fair dinkum about his safety she would have made sure he knew all he needed to know about survival before cutting him loose. As things stood, he felt at a loss but determined not to play the fool if he could help it.

Two weeks later, it was Night Sky who was staked and Greg Reese who had managed to smuggle himself aboard ship. The reason why things had worked out this way was simple. While Night Sky continued to dine on humans, Greg decided rats and the occasional cat would do until he understood the dangers of his new existence a little better. In this way, it was Night Sky who stood out like a red flag to the Invisible Compass. Greg did not appear on their radar.

Greg sighed at the thought of never being able to wear the floppy green cap the Don, Ponting and other notaries had been proud to wear. Australia would have to keep The Ashes from England without him. As he sailed away in the direction of the USA, it came as a real blow. He had trained so long to first represent his state and then his country. Now he wouldn't even get the chance to represent his state. Life had passed him by and his unlife beckoned. *New York here I come*, he thought as the Sydney Harbor Bridge and the Opera House faded away into the distance to be replaced by lots of ocean. He patted the small bag of native soil he had in his pocket. It would help him stay healthy. "New York will be good to me," he said aloud and hoped that would turn out to be true.

Once he got there he would spend months in the Big Apple having a great time dodging the local police, the Pinkertons and the FBI. He would be subtle with his killing when need be, taking from animals as well as people, and outrageous at other times, thumbing his nose up at the law. He would give them a merry chase and then lose them before he needed to retire for the day. In his heart, however, he still had the urge to play for Australia. One Pinkerton detective in the Battery Park area would almost get him with a wooden dagger. Luckily at the time he would be wearing an oversized coat he could slip off and throw over his pursuer. "There! That looks better on you than me!" he would cry out as he ran off.

New York, USA, summer, 2006

Greg followed a small Japanese woman with short blond hair into the fresh food section of a supermarket chain warehouse. It was dark inside but his eyesight was vampire excellent. He thought she'd panicked and gone in there to hide. He was now beginning to wonder if he was wrong.

There were at least four armed hunters poised to spring out at somebody and he had the distinct impression it wasn't the girl they were after. He could smell them before he could see them and they smelled young and fresh.

A great black land mass of a man materialized from black smoke ten feet in front of him. He picked up an orange from a box and threw it over arm at the intruder. It rocketed at the fellow, hitting him with the power of a loosed canon ball. With a groan the man mountain collapsed. He would have a nasty ball shaped chest bruise for a few days and his lungs would ache every time he breathed but at least he would live. The thrown orange was now history.

"How's that?!" Greg cried, feeling for the first time as a vampire to be in his own element. A second later he answered his own question by saying: "All right! Out for a duck!" He knew they wouldn't understand but what did he care?

"How's what? Out for a duck? What duck? What is this?" asked Neko of Odori as she changed out of her street clothes and into something loose and black.

"Doesn't matter," said Odori, her smile widening. "Tetsu will sort him out."

Greg picked up another orange and waited for the man with the sword to come out into the open. He knew there was a sword because he could hear it being unsheathed. Sure enough, Tetsu did come out, sword swinging. Since the business end was moving so wildly, Greg felt his orange wouldn't stand a chance. With a sigh, he cheated. This time he bowled short, the orange kissing the concrete floor a few feet from the warrior in such a way as not to go splat. As it spun up, it belted the swordsman under the chin, hard, sending him into unconsciousness. Greg said, shaking his head: "Sorry about that. Bodyline. Tisk! Definitely against the rules and the spirit of the game. But definitely out for a duck."

"What rules? What game? This duck again?" whispered Neko to Odori.

"Who cares? Just get him!" cried Odori.

Star knives went flying from Neko and Odori toward Greg. In response, he snapped off a plank of wood from the box and used it as a bat. It was thus that six well thrown star knives were collected onto the wood and Greg cried: "No run!"

"Does he think he's playing baseball?" Neko asked in disbelief.

"I don't know," Odori replied.

Shimo tossed a light ball in Greg's direction and Greg hit it for a six. Instead of exploding in front of the vampire, blinding him and possibly taking his second life via its concentration of UV rays, it detonated above Odori and Shimo temporarily taking away their eyesight. Neko just missed out on the full effect. She was about to throw more star knives when an apple bowled over arm with a lot of spin came hurtling toward her. She dipped out of the way in time and it ricocheted off the back wall striking Sakusha, the man who was hiding with his rifle in the rafters. Sakusha, apple throbbing in hand, fell to the floor, his fall broken by packing straw, his rifle ending up in a box full of mangoes.

"This can't be happening!" Neko cried.

"I still have it!" Greg shouted in triumph. "They haven't taken it away from me after all."

Greg was now facing Neko, the woman who had lured him into the trap. She was the only one standing capable of offering resistance and he knew it. He also didn't feel much like sinking his fangs into her since she and her fellows had put him into such a good mood.

"Look, love," he said. "It's been a great test match, cold comfort really for what I've missed out on, but I've got to go. Maybe we can have a rematch again real soon."

He walked up to her and then past her on the way to the exit. When his back was turned she threw a star knife. He heard it coming and moved out of the way. She put on her wooden claws and went after him. She was about to pounce when he opened the door, ducked outside and closed the door in her face. By the time she got the door open again he was nowhere to be seen.

"Damn!" Neko cried.

206

"I take it he got away," said Odori whose eyes were beginning to recover from the light ball explosion.

"I don't understand." Neko returned to the others. "What was he talking about? Was it baseball? Was it softball?"

"No," Sakusha shook his head. "Didn't you recognize the accent?"

"He's Australian?" asked Neko.

"I'd stake my life on it," groaned Sakusha, feeling his sore left hand come up in one all mighty semi-circular bruise from the pounding of that supersonic apple delivery.

"Then you can tell me what he was on about?"

"Cricket," Sakusha grunted. "We were beaten by a demon fast bowler and a fair batsman."

"The Rising Sun Group, vampire hunters' supreme, beaten by cricket?" questioned Neko.

"The game of empire," Sakusha quipped before again reviewing his pulsing hand.

New Jersey, USA, autumn, 2006

It had taken him months but Greg was now able to take the form of a bat and to sustain it for as long as he liked. It was thus as a bat he was spotted entering the top floor of a sporting goods warehouse. There had been vampire activity of late ten blocks from the location. When police sent word to the Pinkertons of a possible nest of the undead hanging out there they were quick to respond.

Equipped with crosses, crossbows, hammers and stakes, ten Pinkerton vampire hunters entered the warehouse at nine in the morning. They went upstairs and found, amid sports equipment of all sorts, a man lying as if dead in a large crate. With the lid on top of him he might have gone unnoticed for quite some time, the lid being marked "Sporting goods Australia," if the Pinkertons hadn't known what to look for. They had been informed that an Australian vampire was on the loose and that the Rising Sun Group was keen to catch up with him. Could this be the vampire? He was laying there, a bag of native soil near him, with a wooden bat in one hand and a hard ball in the other. It was a curious sight.

"Die!" one of the Pinkertons cried as he pounded a stake into Greg's heart. Blood shot up horribly.

Greg gasped awake and screamed: "This is not…This is not…!"

"Not what?" asked the blood splattered Pinkerton with the hammer.

"Not cricket!" Greg finished, rolling his eyes. They probably wouldn't understand, but did he care? It had to be said anyway.

"Tough," said the Pinkerton wearing lots of damp red. He proceeded to hammer some more.

Greg passed away a second time with thoughts about how it wasn't fair and of how these well dressed men hadn't given him a sporting chance. It was all he could do to bleed over as many of them as possible before the end. Spoiling nice suits wasn't his idea of a bold last stand but at least it was something. *Maybe if the laundry bill is high enough they'll think twice about tackling another vampire*, he thought to himself. The pain increased. A trembling and then, finally, a still body and he was no longer on the plain of the living.

"We'll let the Battery Park Pinkerton agent who almost got him know and also the FBI," one of the Pinkertons said, "that we got their runaway."

"He's not turning to dust," another added. "He's not even turning into a skeleton. He must be young. He must be fresh undead."

"God knows why that Pinkerton and those Rising Sun people were having trouble with this one," put in yet another.

"They were probably having an off night," the first said. "It happens to the best of us."

"Yeah," agreed one of the others. "It happens."

Killing the Jocks

Sydney, New Year's Eve, 1975

Peter Key woke with a start. He touched his arms and legs to see if he was solid, to see if he was real.

Three nights ago he'd died or, at least, that's what he thought had happened. Now he wasn't so sure. It had all been a blur. For some reason, he had always pictured death as slow and methodical. Well his, if it had happened, could be regarded as the latter but definitely not the former. There was this perfume and a swirl of fangs in the moonlight. He may have closed his eyes in fright. He remembered the scent of his own blood and the taste of something warm and metallic slipping like cough syrup down his throat. Did he imagine it or did a woman, at this junction, purr and say nice things about the future?

Peter was lying on something cold like concrete in winter. He was still dressed in that dumb safari suit a pretty sales assistant had talked him into buying. It was a damnable rag that had gotten him nothing but ridicule at his local disco. Since he paid for it, he was stuck with it but surely not even his mother would have him buried in it. And, yes, he was lying on a slab and the single light in the room, which was really a chamber, gave the impression it was clean and tidy if somewhat empty. He suspected that there were train depots with more character and bottles of scotch less sterile.

Slowly he got to his feet. His legs were rubbery at first like those of a toddler. The wobbliness subsided after a few steps and then he noticed an old rickety bamboo chair with a 007 suit straight out of *You Only Live Twice* draped over it complete with stylish black socks and shoes.

Cautiously, he bent forward and touched the lapels and buttons. He felt the smoothness of the white silk shirt and wondered, despite the feel of it, if it were truly there.

"Go ahead," a female voice came from the shadows. "I know you want to. Take off that ridiculous garb you're wearing and put it on – put on something sexy. Start your new life right, here and now, with some class."

Peter looked to where the voice came from and, out of the gloom, stepped a small, mousy blonde with glasses.

"Who are you?" he asked, picking up a tie and examining it.

"Glorianna," she said, giving him an inviting smile. "Glory to you. Best you shake a leg if you're going to change. The night won't last forever and we have to feed before daybreak."

"You mean to say I'm a....You're a..."

"Undead, yes. Time's ticking. Are you hungry?"

Actually, Peter was famished. He could smell food of a sort outside the building. Somehow he knew a rat, being chased by a cat, was scurrying past some empty garbage cans. What was coursing through the frightened rodent's veins stood out as sour but potentially nourishing. He suspected human blood to register as much more appetizing.

After changing, he threw the worse-than-useless garment on the floor and adjusted his new tie before going out. Glory led the way.

"Back to the disco?" he asked.

"Where else?" came her reply.

She took him not to the disco he was familiar with but to a larger place, with much the same noise, lighting effects and obnoxious citizenry. As the young men and women danced to sickly sweet and stupid lyrics, he could smell every drop of their sweat as if it were an intimate thing. More important, he could smell the rich red liquid moving under their skin. It reminded him of tomato soup warming in a pan on the family stove, only richer than and as gently textured to his nose as a kiss from an angel would be to the lips.

"I think I'm going to enjoy this new existence," he told his companion as he surveyed the jumping and gyrating crowd.

Glory cut in on a tall, weedy-looking blonde who was gyrating away with a big football player type. The big football player only blinked once as she dragged him off to a dark corner. The tall, weedy-looking blonde followed and, for some reason, remained still as the smaller undead woman fed on her former dance partner. She then allowed herself to be drained as well.

Seeing one of the women who had been rude to him a few months ago, Peter zeroed in on her at a table where she was entertaining some punk muscle-brained type. She was a redhead with deep green eyes;

a lovely hour-glass figure poured into a white tank top and a black mini-skirt, and long black boots going almost all the way up.

"Care to dance?" he asked her and she looked at him dumb-founded.

"Can't you see I'm with someone?" she said. "Twerps like you I can live without."

"Beat it, shrimp," said muscle-brain. "I'd hate to have to mess up such nice threads."

It was then he made real contact with the redhead's eyes and, in doing so, made contact with the silly, ugly thing in her chest she owned she tentatively thought of as her soul. He recalled some of the Hammer horror films he'd seen over the last few years and knew, to some extent, what he could and should do.

"No, that's quite right," he told her in a confiding voice. "You don't care to dance with me. In fact you hate dancing. What you want to do is come with me. You want to be alone with me. You'd like that, wouldn't you?"

"Yes," she said as if in a dream. Slowly, she got to her feet and put out her hand for him to take.

"What is this?" muscle-brain growled, readying for battle.

Peter suspected he could dispatch the brute with a single blow. He would have relished the idea, but he was stopped from doing so by his hunger. Instead, he looked into the savage's eyes and told him to sit down and go to sleep. This the fellow did and, before a dozen heartbeats from the redhead could pass, Peter had her in a dark place near the ladies toilets.

The redhead cried softly as his fangs penetrated her neck. Her neck was the most sensual, sexy part of her. Later, he would discover that sex the human way was no longer either possible or desirable. It had been replaced for all time by the bloodlust and its fulfillment. Still, his victims would be bimbos, disco bitches, and cheerleader types. He would have his revenge upon them and the generations of them to come and, in doing so; savor nothing but the best in ripe, delectable crimson.

Too soon the redhead was a washed out corpse in his arms, her tank top now matching the color of her skin.

"That's the way," said Glory as she took the redhead from him and put the body down on a nearby seat next to a table. "There. Now if anyone sees her, they'll think she had one too many and collapsed. By the time someone gets around to examining her and discovering she's dead, we'll be long gone."

"Will she come back?" Peter asked with some concern in his voice.

"Like you? Is that what you mean?"

"Yes."

"Would you want her to?"

"Hell no!"

"Then, rest assured, she's not coming back. You didn't sire her the way I did you."

"I didn't?"

"You don't know how. Someday I'll let you in on that secret. In the meantime, enjoy yourself. I have the male blockheads, beasts and sport freaks. You have the females."

"Sounds good."

"It does, doesn't it? Now you know why I chose you, why I sired you."

"Yes. I think I do. You wanted to give the power to someone who needed it and who would appreciate it."

Glory gave him a friendly peck on the cheek then led him out into what remained of the night. They made it back to her crypt, the basement in a condemned building, with almost an hour to spare before dawn. She settled into her coffin and bade him settle into the one next to hers. He did so and, feeling comfy and content with the life force of the redhead coursing through him, went to sleep. Unlife was good. It promised to get even better.

Sydney, New Year's Eve, 2001

Peter was back in Australia. He'd flown in on a false passport. He'd planned the trip, as he planned all trips, by way of avoiding the direct rays of the sun. He'd come from Hawaii where he snacked on three surfer chicks and a bimbo waitress. Prior to that, he'd been in California, mostly traipsing around Berkley. The college girls there were most accommodating. He'd made a dozen converts and did away with a couple of dozen of the airiest of airheads.

A little earlier, it had been the Iraq/Iran part of the world where no one was asking many questions when the occasional corpse showed up. In the '80s, he was in Pakistan. There he could cover up his nocturnal feeds by making his victims look as if they'd died from ritual murder. It was a grisly business but they were not alive to feel any pain. Inflicting pain outside the incisions to draw out the vital fluid was not something he enjoyed. Maybe there was a tiny piece of the human spirit left in him after all. Besides, if he was ever caught, he figured the authorities would go easier on him if they thought he wasn't a sadist. In his travels, he'd come to realize he was not invincible and that there were people around wanting to, if not needing to exploit his inherent vampire weaknesses.

Going off to where there were crazy cults, lots of religious nut jobs running about with sharp objects, or savage wars out of control was an excellent way of not being found out by the hunters. The hunters tended to do their hunting in civilized, peaceful places where catching their prey was more likely to occur. Their numbers were small but they were effective. Still, he couldn't help but like the taste of stupid women bred in violence-free settings. Their blood was less watery than the other sort and smelled of lives led where three squares a day was expected rather than fervently prayed for.

In San Francisco, Peter came close to being captured and destroyed by a pack of Spanish speaking monks. They had thrown a net laced with garlic over him and were about to use their wooden knives when a band of men he'd mesmerized the night before to do his bidding, and protect him during the daylight, came to his rescue. They created enough confusion for him to find a weak link in the net and get away.

Some months ago in Boston, he'd been cornered in a narrow alleyway near a church, by seven members of The Invisible Compass, an elite order of Freemasonry skilled in the art of dispatching vampires. But they were using faulty equipment. They had obtained their crucifixes and holy water from a place of worship where, as it turned out, all the priests were child molesters. Since the priests, in the eyes of God, were evil and unrepentant sinners, neither the crucifixes nor the water had any effect on Peter. He snapped the necks of three of The Invisible Compass making his dash for freedom. As he did so, he narrowly avoided a spear with a hazel tip to the heart and a thrown axe made out of cedar. He would have stayed in a city where the clergy were being found out to be corrupt but he knew the remaining members of The Invisible Compass were not likely to make the same mistakes a second time. They were likely to bring in reinforcements to track him during the daylight hours when he had less of an ability to defend himself.

Now he was back in his native land watching the revelers bring in yet another new year. Glory, whom he hadn't seen in some time, was beside him. He felt at ease. He neither loved nor hated her. He did feel beholden to her and that was enough.

They were at Circular Quay near the water. A soft breeze stirred her hair. It was warm or, at least, it would have been to a human and made even more so by alcohol. Everyone except the vampires were drinking and admiring the wine color – a rich Burgundy – produced by the city lights on the gently rippling harbor.

There was a time when Peter would have admired the view along with the others. Back then the placid touch of a woman's hand on his would have sent a thrill through him with the possibilities it evoked in him. All that, plus the heartache of being fobbed off, and the dressing down if he didn't get the idea soon enough, were long gone. Now, he took what he needed and left the husk.

"You're looking very Goth," said Glory to Peter. "I don't think I like it very much. The all black look, I mean."

"It suits me. Besides, you can't be James Bond forever."

"Why not? You don't age, you know."

"You simply can't, that's all. The tie began to feel like a noose around my neck. None of my victims care what I wear unless I tell them to, and so I please myself."

"I care."

"Yes, I suppose you do."

Glory was in a black widow dress that did nothing for her eyes, her hair or her glasses. Still, she wore an attractive pink band around her neck and a woman's neck was her most adorable asset. He hadn't realized it before, but she did have a gorgeous neckline. He complimented her on it and they got to talking about their mission. Neither of them knew the exact number of jocks (for her) and jockettes (for him) they'd taken out of circulation since they'd last met. He wanted to believe that they alone were responsible for the death of disco and for inspiring the bloody nerd revolts at American high schools in recent times. But he knew that was wishful thinking. Besides, he wasn't sure if he agreed with the sexual politics of some of those nerds.

"Have you recruited many?" asked Glory.

"About a hundred," Peter told her. "I'm very particular."

"And so you should be."

Both could picture at least two hundred avengers of their own collective making, terrorizing the humans they still saw as the killers of dreams, the killers of innocence, the despoilers of all that discos could have been but weren't. If they were more human they would have felt pride in what they had so far accomplished. As things stood, they wanted to make it four hundred then eight. Before the year two thousand and ten, they imagined it being well over a thousand sired into the cause by them and also those they had previously sired. Neither had the delusion of disposing of all the jocks and jockettes, but the thought of making the coming of darkness a time of fear for the survivors warmed the part of them where the soul had once resided.

That night, both of them got tipsy on the revelers they bit into. Peter's buxom brunette was at least sixty percent gin and tonic. Glory's lifesaver reject was even more gone. He was about seventy five percent Guinness spent, with some Scotch chasing around his gut to catch up with the Irish suds in him.

The next day, Peter and Glory slept together in the same crypt, the basement they'd shared years before, and then they went their separate ways. They were supposed to meet up at the Opera House to party on patrons coming out of the various theatres but Glory never showed. A week later, he saw her neck band in the window of a second-hand clothing store. He knew it was hers because, even through the glass, with his enhanced sense of smell, he could pick up her scent on it. He came to the conclusion that some less than scrupulous hunter had claimed her. If he had been more of this world he would have been very upset by such a revelation. As things stood, he sighed and shrugged his shoulders. He would go on even if she wouldn't. Such was unlife.

He remembered her telling him, a fistful of nights after his being sired, that she had become one of the undead in the mid-fifties. It had taken place outside a country dance hall in a small country town in northern New South Wales. She had been lured outside the hall by a European gent she'd never met before and summarily pounced on. It was Frederick of Austria who had done the pouncing. He was out to create a harem of vampire lovelies. Why he had picked on her to join the rest she'd never know. She didn't think herself to be attractive. Even so, once the deed was done there was no going back. When Frederick was destroyed by the Ash Wednesday bush fire (yes, they were in Victoria in the early '60s), Glory left the harem. Upon seeing the possibilities of the hippy age corroded by ill-mannered and thoughtless brutes of both sexes, she decided to do something about it. Thus the campaign against the jocks was begun. Now it was up to Peter, if he so wished, to carry on with the work. He wondered if he would do so. It never occurred to him to seek out Glory's killer and exact revenge. He was taken with the big picture. Also, he lacked a discernable soul or so he told himself.

Sydney, New Year's Eve, 2006

After Glory's demise, Peter had spent a fistful of years in Queensland where he dined on surfer chicks. At Surfer's Paradise one night, he took out a meter maid dressed in a bikini and another night took out a middle aged woman who was reminiscing, in a bar over crème something-or-other, about her days as a cheerleader for her high school rugby league club.

The closest he came to regretting his actions as a vampire was when he was in a small country town with few delectable targets to prey upon. There he sapped the life from a jillaroo. Being nothing more than a woman good with horses, she didn't deserve to die. He would have made her over into one of his own if he weren't so hungry. He hadn't supped in a week and needed every drop that she had. He couldn't even spare the few drops from himself to turn her. Sure, a vampire can live his unlife three weeks or more without feasting but even a week can cause stress and bring out the animal within in all its stark simplicity. He couldn't think past his hunger at the time.

Peter was thinking of the jillaroo and how he would have liked to have spared her total destruction when a small, dark-haired woman approached him. He was at the spot near the quay where he last saw Glory. He wasn't reminiscing but it did feel right being there.

The dark-haired woman was of Euro-Asian appearance. He suspected she must have been picked on a fair bit in high school. Racist names such as chink and chow came to mind. She had a beauty much superior to that of Glory and a superb neck-line. He was wearing the flash 007 suit similar to the one worn in *Tomorrow Never Dies*.

"I'm Cat," said the mystery woman. She was half in pink and half in black. She carried a dainty black handbag she rested neatly against the black in her outfit. The John Lennon glasses she wore, which had pink glass, suited her. He wondered if she needed them to see with or whether they were just worn to enhance and further beautify her hazel eyes. He suspected the latter and would not have been in the least disappointed if he'd been proven right. He thought women should dress up from time to time. He also thought he should too even if it wasn't appreciated.

They chatted for a while about the latest trends in music, art and writing. The more she talked, the more he liked her. He hadn't sired anyone in a long while and he felt the time was right to sire another. It would make up for the loss of Glory on the anniversary of when she was lost to him.

Cat suggested they make their way past the crowds in the street to a little pub in the heart of the Rocks. It was a pub which hadn't changed much since the '70s and wasn't likely to change. The clientele liked it the way it was. Small bands singing old Beatles and Rolling Stones songs rocked in every weekend and on New Year's Eve. There were always at least a dozen of them going on one after the other. It was hard finding an empty space in a corner but, after grabbing schooners of Guinness from one of the barmaids, they managed to do just that.

"Cheers," shouted Cat above the noise of the other revelers and took a mighty sip of her frothy, creamy black drink. Peter watched her do so knowing that he'd taste the Guinness in her blood later on. She took several more sips, which were really gulps, to finish it. He set his own aside where it was bumped into and spilled by an apologetic couple. He told them to think nothing of it.

"I'll get you another," Cat offered. She began rummaging in her little black handbag for the money turning over combs, brushes, handkerchiefs and what looked to Peter to be something that might contain face powder to take the shine off her nose though he never understood what was so wrong with having a shiny nose.

Peter shook his head and said: "No thanks. What if I told you that you could live forever as a better, more powerful person?"

"I'm not buying any pills, or having goat hormones injected into me, thank you very much," she said with a touch of amusement in her voice.

"Nothing like that," came back Peter's reply. "But, just tell me, would you like to be a better, more powerful person and live forever?"

"Sure, who wouldn't?"

"Then look into my eyes."

"Wait! I'll powder my nose."

She reached into her dainty little black handbag and took out the compact. He didn't realize that women still bothered with such things. It snapped open from very little pressure and then she blew him a kiss. Suddenly, he was choking hard and gasping for air. That smell! What was it? He remembered it from Woodwork when he was still in high school. It was sawdust!

He ran for the exit, pushing people aside as he went. One bloke he hurled through an open window. *Fresh air!* He wanted to scream as he wheezed like an asthmatic in need of an inhaler.

Outside, a big black man who could have been a gridiron player slammed him against the wall and pushed a sharp stake into his heart. Ordinarily, he would have dispatched the black man with his superior speed and vampire strength but the sawdust had tipped the scales against him. The sawdust wouldn't have been enough to kill him but it did prove to be an uncomfortable distraction leading to his demise.

Cat joined him and his silent assailant. She put the compact away and looked down at his already withering form. So! She was a hunter! The color in her glasses was probably there to add a barrier against her being hypnotized by him. How clever! What he hated was not the fact that she had betrayed his trust but that she was with a jock. He hated the notion she'd choose a jock over immortality and the chance to do harm to a despicable part of humanity. And to think he was going to give her everything and not just take her life.

"If it makes you feel any better," said Cat as Peter's eyes began to grow dim, "Coal and I are just good friends."

"She tags 'em and I bag 'em," rumbled the man known as Coal.

"We're members of The Rising Sun," said Cat as one of Peter's ears left him. "We're ninja."

Ninja? thought Peter and wondered what that meant under these circumstances. He didn't have long to do so, for his hair was falling out and blackness was taking him. He speculated that he hadn't been undead long enough to fade to dust but that he'd make a fine, if not handsome, skeleton in his fake British spy outfit. In this respect, he was absolutely right.

Saving the Night

Sydney, NSW, Australia, 2006

Jenny Book had a temper which had seen her serve time in prison for assault. Breaking a man's arm in three places outside a nightclub was no laughing matter. Doing it just because he got fresh with her was stupid. Boasting about it made her the poster child for dumb bimbos with muscle. Getting caught was the outcome. It would take years to live it down. Meanwhile the man whose arm she'd broken was probably still getting fresh with women and maybe doing worse things besides.

There were new gangs out on the streets. In areas such as Darlinghurst, Kings Cross, Redfern and Bankstown, women after dark weren't safe past their own front doors. There had been protests along George and Elizabeth streets with women waving signs calling for a fair go. There had been interviews with the protesting women, the police, and certain male gang members some of whom were Muslim extremists.

One Lebanese Australian nut-job who thought of himself as Muslim though any respectable Lebanese Australian Muslim - and there were and are plenty around - would disagree with this assertion, thought he was safe from the media. When cornered outside the town hall at Bankstown, he was asked by a small blond female reporter, who looked and even sounded quite harmless, if there should be a curfew for women. There were hundreds of men and women of different ethnic backgrounds there wondering what his reply was going to be. There were Lebanese Australian men and women there who had a good idea of what he was going to say and they did not look happy. The last thing they needed was a bad apple nut-job supposedly speaking out for them and, in twisting their beliefs, making them look as crazy as he was.

"Damn straight there should be a curfew," said the nut-job, basking in the attention and not at all concerned that much of it was hostile. "What business has a respectable woman got being out late anyway?"

"So women who travel at night on public transport deserve to be harassed?"

"You bet, harassed and worse."

"What if you are hurt and have to go to hospital? Would you allow a woman nurse or doctor to treat you?"

"A nurse, yeah. Why not? A doctor? I dunno."

"What if there was only a female doctor available and you would die without treatment? Would you allow her to treat you?"

"Yeah. I suppose…"

"What if you were in the hospital late at night and you needed surgery to save you? Would you allow the woman doctor to treat you?"

"Yeah. I suppose…"

"Well, I'm sorry. She cannot treat you. She is the only doctor who could have been there in time to save your life but, because of miserable types such as yourself, she's going to be very late and, when she arrives, she'll be in no fit state to help you or anyone else. You see, she works at night and she travels to work by public transport. She has been so severely punished for doing so she won't be helping anyone for months, maybe years. Now how does that make you feel? You are dying, and someone could have saved you but she wasn't allowed out at night. Now how does that make you feel?"

There was profound silence then the nut-job collected himself and cried out: "No matter how you twist things, lady, women have no business traveling at night, being out late. Got that?"

"Sure," said the reporter. "Thank you very much for your time."

Jenny watched all this from her lounge room on her television set and shook her fist. The way the reporter ran rings around the nut-job and how most of the crowd, including the men, enjoyed it was lost on her but not the meanness of the nut-job.

Something real had to be done but what?

Jenny had been born into a less than ideal family. Her parents were abusive and uncaring. They were alcoholics and too often there wasn't enough food on the table to feed a sparrow. As soon as she could walk she learned how to beg for what she needed from the neighbors. At an early age she was molested by her father. Two years later, when he tried it again, she broke his jaw with her fist and left home. Since then her belief in the goodness of men and in relationships had not gained any discernable ground.

Once on her own, her desire to stick up for herself and other women against the male oppressor turned manic. She got fit at the gym and kept fit. Fellow workers, both male and female, became afraid of her.

Jobs slipped through her fingers because no one wanted to be around her when she blew. After it did happen, and she did her stretch, she could recognize the fear in the collective eyes of the people she wanted to befriend. This fear frightened her more than the men she wished to take down. It was a strange world when people feared her more than they did the evil men out to control everything.

One night she was getting a beer in a pub in Darlinghurst when a tall, white haired man sat down on the stool beside her. He was dressed in black. She couldn't work out his age but it didn't matter. She didn't want anything to do with him.

"Get lost!" she told him. "I buy my own drinks and I don't want the company."

"You're the Book woman, aren't you?" he said politely. "You're the woman the papers were all aflutter over a few years ago."

"That's right! And I've already told you, get lost."

She took a swing at him and he moved away to avoid being struck. No one saw him move but he did it anyway. Her punch hit nothing but empty air, the momentum sending her off her stool and onto the floor. He helped her to her feet and, in a standing position, she took another swing. This time he had her fist meet his open palm. Neither was hurt by the impact but she was stunned by his speed and agility.

"Shall we take it outside?" he suggested.

"Yeah, right," she grumbled in response.

She followed him out looking for the best moment to jump him and teach him a lesson. It never came. He just turned and stared into her eyes and she was lost. He told her to follow him and she followed. He took her to an apartment three blocks away where he sat her down on a couch and sampled her blood. He allowed her to sample his then he drained her. As the light around her faded, she knew she was going to die. *Good* was her last thought. It hadn't been much of a life anyway.

Three nights later, she opened her eyes to discover that she wasn't in Heaven or Hell but that damned apartment where she had passed away. On a small coffee table there was a note explaining what had happened to her and what her new existence was going to be like. She had a feeling he was never going to return and, as per usual, she was on her own. The difference was that she was more powerful than she had been in her life and so could do amazing things in her crusade against men. Why a male being sired her, she didn't know. If not for her obsession she might have spared a moment to think about it and what she should be doing with her unlife. As things stood, she was thirsty and only male blood would do. *Now let's see them try and stop me,* she thought.

221

There was a bar nearby. It was a wine bar and it was frequented by business types. Japanese visiting Sydney would stop by for the unique pleasure of sampling Australian wine. It was the sort of place that did not attract a lot of trouble. It was most unusual then when the nearest male customer to the door was reefed outside and dragged down the street. There followed a terrible cry of alarm. The barman and several customers phoned the police on their mobiles. The fellow's girlfriend rushed outside to help but there was nothing she could do. By then he and his assailant were gone. One week later he turned up in a dumpster six blocks away with broken ribs, severe bruising and zero blood in his veins. No one could understand why he was killed in such a fashion or at all. No one could conceive of him having an enemy in the world.

"He was a nice guy," the barman told the police as if being such a person should be a shield against the insanity that can be found in others.

Jenny made her real impact on her neighborhood when she took out for good three members of the biker gang, The Desperadoes. She did it the week after she had been sired and in their clubhouse. A tattooed giant with an amiable air had asked her at the door who had invited her and whether she'd like a V.B. beer. In response she said no thank you to the beer and snapped his neck. His tattooed girlfriend rushed at Jenny with a heavy plumber's spanner and was brushed aside. A tall, skinny dude in dark glasses smoking a joint pulled a revolver out of a leather pouch on a nearby table. He shot her several times in the chest and all she did was smile. It must have hurt even if it couldn't kill her but she wasn't giving anything away. When she charged he tried to make himself scarce. It didn't do him any good. She caught up with him real fast and ripped his heart right out of him. The others scattered but she did manage to grab one more. This one was somewhat rotund with graying beard. She supped on him, throwing him aside when she was done.

The cops were summoned and notes were taken by the plain-clothes detectives. One of them sent the information on to a special section of the Mitchell Library in Macquarie Street. Then assignments were given out and specialists called.

Another week passed in which any male out after dark around Darlinghurst, Kings Cross, Redfern and Bankstown were anything but safe. Jenny didn't discriminate. It didn't matter whether you were a white Australian, an Aborigine, a Lebanese Australian, a Turkish Australian or a tourist from anywhere, if you were a bloke you were fair game. Blood didn't flow. Jenny became too thirsty for that to happen. But there were bodies. Everyone in the area was frightened. Over night the little chapel in Redfern did great business and a number of the ladies of the night decided not to walk the streets for a while. The cops became edgy.

One evening Jenny was tossing around street punks who had shown her their knives when she was confronted by six black leather clad warriors carrying unusual hardware. Two of the men had guns and the third a wooden butterfly sword. The ones with the guns were of Anglo-Saxon origin and the fellow with the sword looked to be Chinese. The three women were Japanese and they were small, lithe and had star knives at the ready. *Who are these people?* thought Jenny. *Why are these women with these men? Can't they see they're no good?*

"You women should get out of here," Jenny advised. "I don't want to hurt you. I only want to hurt the men. Those street punks are a menace. Your men are also a menace. I am here to save the night for you, for all women, so please let me get on with it."

"There we have a problem," said one of the Japanese women.

"I'm afraid so," answered another. "We're not that fussed about what you do to those punks but…"

"We simply adore our men," said the third, winking at one of the gunmen.

"Die then!" screeched Jenny, her eyes blazing, the fury peaking within her. She rushed at the gunman who had been winked at and she was shot in the stomach. Usually this wouldn't mean much but something was wrong. She doubled over with much more pain than she had experienced before from a gun wound. *Who are these people?* she wondered. *And what was that?*

"The bullets are hollow points," the gunman offered. "They have slithers of wood inside. Not good for your digestion, I believe."

So that was it! Damned crafty men making damned crafty weapons.

With tears in her eyes, Jenny grabbed the offending gunman by the neck and threw him against a wall. He bounced off it and collapsed with a groan. Then she was shot in the chest by the other two gunmen. It wasn't pleasant for her but somehow they managed to miss her heart. The women then threw their star knives, hitting her on the arms and legs, making her howl. With blood frothing from her mouth, she turned to the swordsman who leapt into the air and came down on her neck with his blade. She turned her head to see where he had landed and felt an uncomfortable sliding sensation. Then her head fell from her shoulders and one of the women caught it before it could land. To her great horror, she found her mouth stuffed with garlic. It smelled awful and made her feel sick despite the fact that she didn't have a direct connection between mouth, nose and stomach.

223

"You had best put a few more bullets into her," advised the swordsman. "We must make sure we deal with the heart as well as the head."

Jenny watched, her eyes beginning to glaze over, as more bullets were pumped into her already bullet-riddled body. Then she saw her body quiver and stop. She looked one last time at her executioners, especially the women, before her eyes too were finished. She couldn't help but listen to the dialogue between the men and the women as the last of her neurons sparked out.

"I'm glad you were able to help us on this one," a gunman told the women and the swordsman.

"The Rising Sun is always happy to lend a hand," said the swordsman.

"Especially when it comes to helping such handsome Invisible Compass members," one of the women teased.

"I think you Compass guys could have handled her on your own," the swordsman said. "But we did need the exercise. Will your friend be all right?"

"He's getting to his feet as we speak," the second gunman told him. "Want to check out that wine bar we saw earlier?"

"Sure," the swordsman replied, "kill a vampire and sample the local produce. And on such a lovely night."

"A true romantic," quipped one of the women as they all headed away from a creature whose existence had just come to a complete end.

Jenny didn't turn into a skeleton or go to dust because she hadn't been a vampire long enough. Instead her corpse, decapitated head and all, was bound to make some police officer in the morning wonder what new maniac was on the loose. Unless, of course, the Freemason clean-up crew got to it in time.

Thanks to the Invisible Compass Freemasons and visiting Rising Sun, parts of Sydney that weren't safe were now relatively safe. As for the gangs, they'd mostly laid low because of Jenny. Some might even be in the process of mending their ways. The ones who wanted to go back to business as usual, and this included poor conduct toward women, were going to get sorted out, not only by the police but, for as long as they were permitted to stay in Sydney, by the Rising Sun. The difference between the Rising Sun and Jenny, however, was that the Rising Sun would slap down malcontents not destroy them. The streets were going to be fine for all good citizens. Friday and Saturday nights were once more going to be times in which the free spirited rather than the criminally insane would be permitted to unwind from the working week.

The Goodbye Demon

Penny tried to remember. Here was a sweet smelling morsel she'd cornered in an alley. Yet she hesitated. Claws out, eyes sparkling like red hot coals and she wasn't making her move. She was just standing there staring into her past, the non-violent aspect of her being having taken the reigns.

It had been five years since the dark half had staked its claim upon her so she should have known better. Humans without pointy objects, guns or crosses equaled food. And in Sydney, not far from Macquarie Street with its vampire hunters, it didn't pay to play with your food. People got wise and then the chaps with the pointy objects, guns and crosses appeared. It was better to be quick and discreet. It was even better to pick a different part of town. But here she was and here was food. So why was she being so hesitant?

"Who are you?" asked the blue plate special. She could see the gorgeous vein in his neck throb provocatively making her mouth water.

Penny still hesitated. Back when she was among the living, meals didn't ask questions. They were usually quiet. Fish and chips wrapped in paper didn't want to know you. It didn't even want to know itself.

"Penny," she told the blue plate. Her eyes had gone from red hot coals back to warm hazel and there was color in her cheeks. Was she blushing?

"Not Penny Keyford?" he enquired, sounding relieved. "I'm Tom Banks. Remember? We were in high school together. Then we were tellers at the bank at Revesby and then…"

"I disappeared."

"What happened? Where did you go? Did you lose your memory? Are your parents still looking for you? Did you just drop out or what?"

Penny tried to think past her demonic urge to plunge her fangs into his neck, empty him of his blood and move on. Vague associations of a time before she was sired by a tall man with bad breath came to her. They were like fragments of a dream belonging to someone else.

She saw a fresh faced teen typing away on a computer board, sending her a comment about one of the more stuck up basketball players. She saw him being scolded by the P. E. teacher for tardiness and, in the next instance, kissing some pig-tailed, freckle-faced girl on the cheek. The girl went red and wondered why she did so. The girl was Penny and she was looking in the mirror to see what a kiss looked like. Then there was the prom where the football players and their female supporters shinned and, after that, banking.

It was all such a whirl of places, times and people. None of it seemed real. Yet there was Tom, the blue plate special, in the present. Was there love between them once or was it friendship? And was the difference between love and friendship merely a question of intensity?

She remembered those bank days. She remembered thinking she was making a future for herself and that life had plenty of untapped promise. She remembered being attracted to the smell of new money and thinking it a good omen.

The bank was dull but at least it was hassle free. The thickest of the thick jocks could not find employment in such places. You got on with your work, had lunch, and then you got on with your work some more before you went home. You did that five days out of seven. The last two were your own. It was a steady, no-nonsense form of existence and it meant being able to get a secondhand car and your own apartment.

"So what did happen to you?" pressed Tom, bringing her back to the present and her burning thirst.

"I cannot say," she replied through clenched teeth, fighting the growing urge to jump upon him and take his life. "I must go!"

"Wait! What will I tell your parents?"

"Tell them nothing."

She couldn't remember her parents. Her demon half wouldn't let her and maybe that was just as well. If she remembered, then she might someday bite them and part of her didn't want to do that.

"You were going to attack me weren't you? Until you realized who I was, that's what you were going to do, right?"

Penny's eyes went from hazel to crimson and her cheeks turned milk white. She grabbed him by the collar and drew him closer to her fetid breath. He tried to pull away but she was too strong. She licked his throat like it was candy and was about to go further when more echoes of a time she could no longer truly connect with came to her.

She recalled the time she saw Tom being bullied by two class-mates who were into surfing and mindless violence. One was the son of a famous football player and the other was the son of an industrialist. The son of the industrialist had, unfortunately, not inherited any of his father's intelligence or good will. Both hated Tom for the way he got around computers and his understanding of the dynamics of commerce. She was the one who had saved him a few bruises in the playground by getting a teacher to sort out those idiots. Tom was anything but grateful. This incident, however, prompted him to learn judo and discover ways of taking care of himself. He then talked her into taking it up.

"Come with me," Tom of the present told her. "We're old friends. We've been through a lot together. Let me help you."

"Go!" she rasped, tossing him aside and bolting down the alley. He landed hard against a trashcan.

"Wait!" he called out. "If you're on drugs, there are clinics…"

"No!" she screamed as her arms took on a leathery appearance. He saw the transformation and was aghast by it. No, this was not something he could handle. This was not even something he could understand.

She vanished into the alley's shadows and, after flying over a building, moved down one of the main streets. In her hurry to put some distance between herself and her former companion, she didn't know which street nor could she have cared less. *Did he see the change? He must have*, she told herself. *At least now he'll know I'm not on drugs.*

In her bat persona she flew in the direction of Town Hall and then out toward Kings Cross thus making a wide zigzag pattern across Sydney.

The Cross was a place of vice and corruption. It had lost its innocence sometime during the 2nd World War and was not likely to get it back. She was not likely to get hers back either. That savage part of her pressing for blood could not be dislodged. Even now it called to her to find a victim and to feast before morning and her daytime nap. At the Cross there were prostitutes, drug dealers, sex shops plus the occasional street mugging. It was not a good place to eat because of what the locals tended to put into their bodies. It was, however, a good place to hang out and think about who or what she was and where she was going.

She perched on top of a rundown structure built as a hotel palace sometime in the 1890s and watched humanity down below act vile, contemptible and foolish. She imagined herself superior but knew that was far from the truth. She was just another predator out for the night. As a member of the undead she delved into the weaknesses of others and exploited them for her own gain. So why didn't she do so when it came to Tom Banks? Why, when it came to him and his life, did she draw back?

Two sheets from a newspaper drifted her way and she snatched them out of the air with the speed and dexterity no ordinary daughter of Adam and Eve could match. The headline and lead story of the first sheet was about the opening of a new methadone center aimed at treating heroin addicts. It was being run by some protestant church group with the reluctant blessing of the local council. The other sheet featured an article on Australian soldiers in Cambodia removing and destroying land mines left over from the late 1960s and early 1970s.

Both sheets were signs of humanity trying to repair itself. Could she likewise make repairs? Could she someday reclaim her soul from the evil within? Surely not killing Tom was a start. But survival demanded blood and she had to survive.

"This has nothing to do with me!" she cried to the wind, tossing the printed matter aside. So what if humanity could do good? So what if humanity could renew its goodness in the face of its own folly? It could mean nothing to her. What did ordinary humans helping their own mean to a vampire? What could one human in particular, even one she had once known so well, mean to a hellish creature such as herself?

Finding only confusion of the heart in the Cross, Penny transformed back into a bat and took off in the direction of Centennial Park. On the way she met up with a colony of fruit bats on the wing. They were somewhat smaller than she was but, nevertheless; joining the group gave cover against vampire hunters.

At the old park, which still retained that look of something British, she spotted a teenage couple out for an evening stroll. The moonlight had obviously drawn them out. It promised to be the death of them. She swooped, changing form as she landed. With one blow she knocked out the girl and, in the next instant, she was on the boy, her fangs sinking deep. She almost depleted him before moving on to the female. Suddenly she was driven back by the sight of the crucifix on a chain around her second victim's neck and by the smell of garlic. The girl had a clove or two of the sickening weed somewhere on her person. Why would this be? Examining the boy she found a bottle of holy water and a stake.

"Amateurs!" she hissed, tossing the bottle and stake aside. She was tempted to rip their throats out but refrained. They were no doubt out to avenge some wrong done to them by the undead. Perhaps a mother or father had died from a vampire's actions. Nevertheless, they were no real threat and perhaps if she let them live they might desist from future foolishness. Besides, her hunger was sated and that was enough. She had no passion for cruelty and no desire to destroy if she didn't have to.

She rose into the sky once more and made her way to her Redfern apartment where she would sleep the day away. There she would dream of Tom Banks, an old friend from a distant time and of her new existence which had cut her off from all that she had once known. There, in a half dreaming, half awake state, she vowed never to talk to Tom or any other mortal ever again. There was little sense in looking back, wondering how things might have been. Tom's life continued, she would not take it, and her unlife continued. That was all.

The following night she roamed a different part of Sydney, the memories of the previous night haunting her. Yes, unlife would go on and the demon within would require its fill of blood. She would suppress what little remained of her humanity or at least try to do so. It wasn't as if she would ever be human again. Sadness came over her which was dispelled when she went into hunt mode. Ah, the smell of rich, ripe humanity on the hoof! The lust for a sweet trouble-free, conscience-free kill was on her and all else was mercifully forgotten.

About the Contributors

Rod Marsden:

Rod Marsden was born in Sydney but did most of his growing up while on holidays in the northern NSW fishing village of Iluka where his mom, May, and dad, Chic (short for Charles), taught him how to fish. It was on these fishing trips he discovered through his mom, he actually did like to read and wanted, one day, to be a writer.

Way back in the '70s, Rod visited the USA but never got to meet his heroes Ray Bradbury, Robert Silverberg, Leonard Nimoy, Jimmy Doohan, George Takei and, last but definitely not least, the lovely Nichelle Nichols. He also never got to meet his all time favorite members of the Marvel Comics bullpen Stan Lee, Jack Kirby and Gene Colan. It can be said that USA artist Gene Colan's renderings of the sexy, slinky Black Widow made him wonder about becoming an artist.

Rod was first attracted to vampires (femme fatales of course) by the British Hammer series of horror movies, which included *Vampire Lovers* and *To Love a Vampire*, and by certain early Universal films such as the original Bela Lugosi version of *Dracula*.

Academically, Rod has a BA in Liberal Studies, a Graduate Diploma in Education and a Master of Arts in Professional Writing.

Rod's short stories have been published in Australia (*Small Suburban Crimes* anthology), New Zealand (*Australian Animals are Smarter than Jack 2* anthology), England (*Voyage* magazine), Russia (*Fellow Traveler* magazine) and the USA (*Cats Do it Better than People* anthology, *Night to Dawn* magazine, *Detective Mystery Stories* magazine). He lives on the south coast of NSW, Australia.

Marge Simon:

Marge Ballif Simon free lances as a writer-poet-illustrator for genre and mainstream publications such as *Strange Horizons, Flashquake, Sniplits, Vestal Review, Flash Me Magazine, The Pedestal Magazine, Dreams & Nightmares, Tales of the Unanticipated, The Magazine of Speculative Poetry,* and the anthologies, *High Fantastic and Nebula Anthology 32.* She edits a column for the HWA Newsletter, "Blood & Spades: Poets of the Dark Side. She is the editor of *Star*Line,* Digest of the SF Poetry Association.

Her illustrated poetry collections include *Eonian Variations,* Dark Regions Press, 1995; *Night Smoke,* with Bruce Boston, *Miniature Sun Press,* 2002 and *Artist of Antithesis,* Miniature Sun Press, 2003. Publications in 2008: *Legends of the Fallen Sky,* with Malcolm Deeley, Sam's Dot Publishing; *Dragon Soup,* with Mary Turzillo, Van Zeno Press, and *Christina's World,* Sam's Dot. Her dark poetry collection, *Vectors: A Week in the Death of a Planet,* with Charlee Jacob, Dark Regions Press, won a Bram Stoker award in 2008.

Along with her solo work, Marge collaborates with her husband, writer-poet Bruce Boston. Their poems and stories have appeared or are forthcoming in *Strange Horizons, Dark Regions, Dreams & Nightmares, Star*Line,* and *Fantasy Commentator.* Website: www.margesimon.com